THREAT BIAS

BEN PORTER SERIES – BOOK TWO

CHRISTOPHER ROSOW

THREAT BIAS

For information about this title or to order other books and/
or electronic media, contact the publisher:
Quadrant Publishing, LLC
354 Pequot Avenue, Southport CT 06890
QuadrantPublishing@gmail.com

Library of Congress Control Number: 2020906499

ISBN: 978-1-7347147-2-2 (print)
978-1-7347147-3-9 (eBook)

Printed in the United States of America

Cover and Interior design: 1106 Design, LLC

AUTHOR'S NOTE

WHILE THIS STORY IS constructed in the real world, including but not limited to referencing actual companies, places, news outlets and articles, events, and things, it is a novel, and it is a work of fiction.

However, it's not entirely far-fetched.

PROLOGUE
AUGUST 2019

SATURDAY, AUGUST 3, 2019 — 9:15 PM — BURLINGTON, VERMONT

THE 12TH ANNUAL "Festival of Fools" had gotten off to a roaring, raucous start under sunny August skies the day before at noon, and the Festival had continued all day Saturday with a friendly and fun-loving crowd growing through the day. Now, with the sun set, the temperature was perfect as revelers crowded the Church Street Marketplace, a four-block long, pedestrian-only, brick-paved street at the core of Burlington. A hip and sophisticated city overlooking Lake Champlain, Burlington could be considered as the center of the arts in Vermont, but it was also the home of Ben & Jerry's Ice Cream, countless bistros, cafes, shops, and galleries, three colleges, and forty-two thousand people.

On four "pitches" on Church Street, buskers, or street performers, amazed the cheering crowds with their daring acts of acrobatics coupled with an eclectic and unpredictable mix of archery, ladder free-climbing, corny joke-telling, and juggling—not just with colored balls, but also with fiery torches and knives. The buskers' shows comingled with the music of two live bands and the din of outdoor diners enjoying a meal and more than a few drinks under a canopy of twinkling lights in the trees that dotted Church Street.

Two blocks away from the hullabaloo of the partying crowd and the antics of the entertainers, Suzanne Cahal snapped the turn-signal stalk upward in her Tesla Model X to signal a right turn, growing more and more frustrated by the minute as she carefully guided the spotless, white car from Battery Street to Cherry Street, scanning the sides of the road for that impossible-to-find prize at the Festival of Fools: a parking space.

Suzanne had circled for a solid twenty minutes, hoping to nab a spot and to meet her friends for the live band that had been scheduled to start playing their first set at nine o'clock, outside of a pub just off Church Street. Given the dearth of parking in Burlington, and with over a thousand people massed for the Festival, she was out of luck.

Approaching the intersection of Cherry and Church Streets, she slowed, now focusing on the bodies that ambled back and fro, crossing Cherry on a wide, brick-paved crosswalk. Unlike, say, the flatlander New Yorkers in the melee of their city, Vermonters don't hurry, enjoying the magic and the energy of their laid-back home state.

A Vermont-born artist who had recently sold out a show in New York, she was rightfully proud of both her new notoriety and of her new eco-friendly, hi-tech electric SUV. She gazed at the car's exquisite interior, the dashboard dominated by a large, vertically-oriented touchscreen that controlled every aspect of the car's features. In front of the steering wheel, even the display in the binnacle was digital; no old-fashioned analog dials to be found. The car was so new to her that she had not figured out how to use all of its features yet, especially the nifty Autopilot feature that would enable the car to almost drive itself. There was an app for her phone that she needed to learn how to use, and there were all sorts of clever ways to access her car. There would be time to dig into that later.

In the meantime, she was happy to enjoy this wondrous vehicle. Suzanne brought her Tesla to a gentle stop and waited, somewhat impatiently, as festival-goers slowly ambled their ways across the brick-paved crosswalk. Glancing at her silvery Swatch on her right wrist, forgetting, as usual, to scan for the time display on the giant screen in her Telsa, she drummed her fingers on the unworn leather on the steering wheel. She didn't fault her fellow Vermonters, taking their time and enjoying the festival, but she wanted to be part of it, too; to find that elusive parking spot and to seek out her posse of friends. "The drinks will be on me tonight," she thought, grinning at the prospect of being able to treat her group without worrying about every nickel.

Darting her eyeballs left and right, she tensed imperceptibly, realizing that there was going to be a break in the stream of pedestrians. She smiled, willing herself into patience for just a moment longer, and she inhaled deeply, holding her breath for a second more than necessary to better absorb the lingering new-car smell.

Suddenly, in the blink of an eye, the Tesla shot forward, its dual electric motors spinning all four wheels as the tires chirped on the brick pavers. The steering wheel spun rapidly, yanking itself from the light pressure that Suzanne had been applying and torquing the car right, onto the pedestrian-only Church Street.

The five-thousand-pound white projectile slammed into person after person, bodies tumbling off the shell of the car. Swerving around larger obstacles, the Model X twisted and turned, the windshield eventually spider-cracking as the long, angled hood lifted three men at once off the ground and launched them into the glass.

As she wrestled with the unresponsive, leather-wrapped steering wheel, Suzanne's screams of terror and abject panic were drowned out by the horrifying crunches of metal and rubber on bone as the SUV pounded over legs and arms. With the air suspension now at its maximum height, the car crashed through table after table at an outdoor restaurant.

The artist took her eyes from the carnage outside the windshield and looked down, dumbfounded, making sure that her right leg was not mashing the wrong pedal—but no, her foot was instinctively planted firmly on the brake pedal; the muscles in her calf straining as she tried to push even harder as, against all logic, the big car rocked and bobbled over the brick pavers.

The Tesla nicked the side of a food cart set up to serve sliders, toppling the cart and pouring hot grease onto its unlucky staffers. A child stood stock-still, frozen in the glare of the bright LED headlights of the white monster as it bore down on her and her two sliders carefully placed in a small, red-checked paper tray. Her mother stiff-armed the child out of the way, but not soon enough, and the little girl was caught by the front right bumper, her tiny body lifted by the dented and battered hood of the car, launching her over the vehicle as her two little sliders smacked into the mess of the windshield, ketchup blending with blood.

Suzanne's blood-curdling scream, inside the luxuriously-appointed SUV, may have matched the scream of the child's mother outside as the little girl's body disappeared behind the car's rear flanks.

For the briefest moment, the car slowed, but as the rolling weapon neared the next intersection at Bank Street, it rocketed back to speed, the torque-heavy electric motor allowing the car to reach sixty miles per hour in under three seconds as it aimed dead-center at the parked fire truck that had been positioned on the crosswalk to block off the street. With an astonishingly loud crash of metal-on-metal, the front of the bloodied-red-and-white Tesla collided into the side of the red ladder truck.

The Telsa's momentum pushed the massive mash-up sideways fifteen feet as the front half of the Tesla's roof sheared off under the raised bulk of the fire engine.

For a beat, there was silence, punctuated only by the creaking and popping of the twisted metal, and by the weak moans and cries of injured.

Then, controlled chaos, as first responders and Samaritans alike sprang forward to help the fallen, the shock of the moment dulled by the visceral need to react. Sirens and shouts created a cacophony of noise as the triage began.

Inside the topless remains of the Tesla, Suzanne Cahal's fingers still grazed the unworn leather of the steering wheel, but her decapitated head lay on the backseat, sightless eyes remaining open. Eyes that had processed sixteen seconds and three-hundred-and-eighty feet of horror.

Eyes that would see nothing more.

PART ONE
NOVEMBER AND DECEMBER 2018

CHAPTER

1

FRIDAY, NOVEMBER 9, 2018 —
FBI BOSTON FIELD OFFICE, CHELSEA, MASSACHUSETTS

MY NAME IS BEN PORTER. I'm twenty-eight years old.

I'm a Special Agent with the Federal Bureau of Investigation. Cool, huh?

Yes!

If we've met before, you're wondering, wait, what? An *Agent?* This is new. And you'd be correct. I was sworn in as a Special Agent last week.

For those of you who I haven't met, let me give you the backstory.

The citizens of New York and Chicago still, to this day, have no idea how close they had been to a nuclear attack in their cities in July of 2017. And, can you imagine the fallout of a nuclear bomb detonating in the heart of two major American cities? Not only the weaponized kinds—the direct destruction from the devices exploding and then the indirect radiation hazard—but also the emotional fallout. The panic, the inevitable economic crash, and the uncertainty. Will there be more attacks elsewhere? Who's next? The ultimate damage, had the attack been successful, would not be reserved for the two target cities; it would be felt nationally, if not globally.

In short, the United States got lucky. Because there was every reason that the terrorists should have succeeded, except one.

Me.

Well, that's maybe a little bit cocky. Obviously, it wasn't *just* me. But it was me who believed the tale told by a sailor named Miles Lockwood, who played a critical role in stopping that nuclear attack. Initially, no one believed him until I got the chance to talk to him. That interview kicked off the investigation that would eventually become known as Operation E.T.

Huh? you ask, rightfully. As you might know, the FBI assigns a code name to each major case under investigation, because generally, it is easier and faster to refer to the name than to a file number. Some code names are randomly generated; some have a vague relevance to the investigation at hand. Originally, the terror threat case was proposed to be called "Operation Flying Lady," referring to the name of Miles Lockwood's boat, *Flying Lady*.

Apparently, someone in DC took exception to the code name, and upon further investigation (something we do very well, of course), it was discovered that the name of the boat was an indirect nod to the hood ornament on a Rolls-Royce.

This is where it gets a little weird, because, despite the staid attitude and stiff upper lip that one generally thinks of with Rolls-Royce, the flying lady hood ornament, officially called the "Spirit of Ecstasy," had been developed in the early 1900s by an English sculptor, who had scandalously (well, for the time) used his mistress as his model. And her name was Eleanor Thornton.

Betcha you didn't know that—that every Rolls rolling through Beverly Hills or Palm Beach is adorned with someone's mistress. Scandalous, indeed. Harrumph!

Few at the FBI knew that either, so when the Operation Eleanor Thornton code name was assigned by the wonk in Washington who did that research, we all, too, scratched our heads in wonderment that it was approved.

Nevertheless, the Washington wonk had selected a code name that was so *out there* that it was immediately recognizable, easily remembered, and, per FBI tradition, instantly acronymized, which is how, Bureau-wide, my terror threat case became known as Operation E.T.

The judgment call on my part to believe Miles Lockwood's story made me into an unlikely hero. When it all started, I was working for the FBI in our Boston Field Office as an Information Management Specialist—which means I was basically a data-entry guy, toiling in a cube and doing electronic case file management and intra-agency coordination work. On the morning of July 12, 2017, my direct boss, Senior Supervisory Special Agent Bradford Macallister, assigned me to interview Miles Lockwood.

By September of 2017, the active portion of Operation E.T. had been resolved. We had the mastermind of the plot in custody. A (then) sixty-five-year-old wealthy and powerful Russian immigrant named Anatoly Petrikov had been sequestered to a clandestine facility for questioning. We had discovered that his life in crime had not been limited to this case; he had been successfully eluding law enforcement since the early 1960s. With a rap sheet that grew by the week as our investigation continued, Petrikov was held as an unlawful enemy combatant, and his whereabouts were a closely-guarded secret.

Petrikov's primary accomplice, to our shock, was an Intelligence Analyst working in the Bureau's Boston office. Anastasia Volkov, a stunningly smart and good-looking computer and technology wiz, had been working side-by-side with me during the investigation. She had been assigned to the case by none other than my boss, Macallister. Of course, back then, he had no idea she was a mole working in cahoots with the mastermind.

Not only was Volkov currently in custody for treason, for her attempt to undermine the investigation and for collusion with an unlawful enemy combatant, she had also been charged with one count of murder. Volkov had been implicated in the death of Vanessa Raiden, a junior Intelligence Analyst who had also worked on the case, and who had exposed Volkov's role.

And, the accusations against Volkov didn't stop there. She was also charged with the attempted murder of Bradford Macallister and me.

Fortunately for both Macallister and me, and despite totaling my Ford Taurus after being chased through the streets near our office in Chelsea by Anastasia Volkov driving a souped-up Dodge Charger, I had shot Volkov before she had a chance to shoot me. Volkov had been taken into custody and sent to the Massachusetts General Hospital for treatment of my gunshots, which had come close to killing her. She was then transported to a secure medical facility outside of Washington, DC, and we have been waiting since for her to recover enough to stand trial as a coconspirator in the terror plot, as a traitor to the United States, and for the murder of Vanessa Raiden.

In the meantime, my trajectory from invisibility to prominence had attracted a lot of attention, most notably from the Special Agent in Charge (SAC) of the Boston Field Office, Jennifer Appleton, a cool, collected, sophisticated woman who was as feared for her unwavering attention to detail and procedure as she was admired for her poise, for her impeccable dress code, and for her conservatively styled, shoulder-length auburn hair that never stranded out of place. After we successfully apprehended Petrikov and Volkov, and we had resolved what was considered to be an ongoing threat, the SAC had congratulated me for my role in the investigation and then, in her usual chill manner, promised me a promotion.

And that promotion, dare I say, would be well-deserved. After all, I'd saved the world, or something like that. I was hoping for a nice raise, my own office, an expense account, and a company car.

Unfortunately, what I was offered was not nearly as comfortable.

CHAPTER
2

IN EARLY 2018, WITH NO thanks to the "promotion" from SAC Appleton, I found myself crawling through the partially-frozen dirt at the FBI Training Academy in Quantico, Virginia, enrolled in the Basic Field Training Course (BFTC).

It wasn't all about snorting dirt, of course; the BFTC is an extensive curriculum in law enforcement, and I spent over seven months learning how to become an actual FBI agent.

Seven months for training was a long time, and yes, it took me longer than the usual New Agent Training (NAT) progression, which typically takes approximately five months. Part of the extended time in training was my fault: I went into it a bit overweight and out of shape, so the physical part was tough for me. And I confess, despite the workouts, I'm still no superspy with chiseled abs; I don't rock a six-pack at my waist, though I am skilled at carrying one in a paper bag, in preparation for doing some twelve-ounce curls.

It also didn't help that my fitness regime (really, can I even call it that?) and my NAT schedule were interrupted on several occasions by obligations to work on the file for Operation E.T. Given my sort-of exalted status for being the sort-of hero of that case, the trainers at Quantico humored my superiors by allowing me to come and go as directed from the academy, but to my face, they cut me no privileges.

The NAT program is comprehensive: it covers everything from legal training to firearms proficiency, to the Tactical and Emergency Vehicle Operation Course (TEVOC). Ironically, had I taken the TEVOC before Anastasia Volkov chased me through the streets of Chelsea, I might have evaded her, and I might not have had the chance to shoot her, and then the case might still be open. Funny, right? Not in the funny, ha-ha way, but in the funny way the world works.

The training at Quantico was intense. I was initially part of a class of fifty wanna-be agents. You get assigned everything, from what you wear (polo shirt, standard issue), to where you sleep (dormitory, comfortable enough), and how you are labeled (my class was 18-4, which meant it was the fourth class to commence in 2018).

It's almost equal parts classroom work and hands-on field training, but it's all parts exhausting. Yet, at the same time, it's incredibly rewarding.

My first roommate, Abdullatif al-Hamid, was also from Boston. Turned out, I vaguely knew of him; he had graduated from our shared alma mater, Boston University, in 2009, three years before me.

We two NATs from Boston bonded. I'd ridicule my weight and my struggles with the physical training sessions. He'd say, "That's nothing, Ben," and he'd launch into a long-running mockery about his own name and how it would play during a pretend bust. Laughing, he'd boom out, "FBI! Agent Abdullatif al-Hamid!" And then, playing the part of his perp, he'd snicker in a meeker voice, "Duel a tiff what? What you say?"

We agreed that he would have to shorten his moniker for use in the real world, and eventually, the swarthy, bulbous-nosed, dark Middle-Eastern skinned Abdul Hamid and the stocky and mildly overweight me became good friends.

Despite his name, Abdul was American as apple pie. He was born and raised in Massachusetts to immigrant parents who had made a fortune selling perfumes or something. Abdul was one of those carefree guys who was nice to everybody. Not flashy, but not the quiet, studious type either. When I got called back to Boston for an internal interview related to the Operation E.T. case, Abdul remained at Quantico and finished out his training in the expected amount of time. He got assigned to the Bureau's Albany, New York, field office, only about three hours by car from my home outside of Boston. I hoped we would stay in touch.

On a chilly, dank November 1st, which was Thursday, last week, I finally graduated. My parents and siblings traveled from home in Rhode Island to Virginia to attend the ceremony. I was handed a shiny gold badge and a new credentials packet. My parents beamed. I couldn't believe it.

Only days prior, I had passed the final test. The dreaded pepper spray test. I didn't think I was going to make it.

Each NAT is required to pass the test, no exceptions. And it is brutal. Outside, you are hit with a massive dose of oleoresin capsicum, which is the scientific name for pepper spray. Your eyes burn in the most unimaginable, intense pain. And then you have to open an eye, or both if you dare, or must, in order to fight, as a trainer tries to wrestle your fake orange pistol from your holster, as the involuntary tears from the searing pain in your eyes drip down your cheekbones, and your nostrils contract as you try to avoid swallowing and, therefore, find it hard to breathe.

Let's just say it's nasty. And gross. And exceptionally painful.

I'd come a long way since starting the Quantico program, and I was in the best shape that I'd been in since, well, ever, and yet the pepper spray test attacks all your senses. The spray is debilitating, even though you know it's coming. Even though you've heard the stories of the NATs who got this far and couldn't make this final hurdle—and you did not want to be that trainee.

Fortunately, I was not.

It didn't really sink in that I had made it until the day after the graduation ceremony when each newly-sworn Special Agent visits the armory to receive their very own FBI-issued weapon, a Glock Model 22 pistol.

Holding the weapon in my hands was a transcendent experience for me. Bradford Macallister had passed me *his* Glock in the Taurus on that fateful day, and I had shot his weapon at Anastasia Volkov, saving my own life as well as Macallister's. And now I held my own Glock—a lethal version of the fake, orange toy pistol that I had defended during the pepper spray test.

I remember considering the gun carefully, under the fluorescent lights in the armory. I was once a data-entry guy, head down in front of a screen in a cubicle. Now, I'm an armed agent of the Federal Bureau of Investigation.

And I wondered if I would ever pull out that weapon and aim it at another human being. Someone who had me in the sights of their own gun. Someone like Anastasia Volkov.

I was assigned, as expected, back to Boston, where I was greeted by my colleagues earlier this week with a little party and with a lot of stories. I was on top of the world.

In the mornings, I'd wake up with a new purpose, look in the mirror, and beam. I'm an FBI *Special Agent*!

That feeling lasted for what, a week and a half? Until Tuesday.

Until that one person who haunted my dreams, that one person who once hunted me, reappeared in my life.

Anastasia Volkov.

And when *that* name resurfaced, that wondrous feeling of being a newly-minted FBI agent was dulled by the sensation that, once again, *I* was the target.

3

TUESDAY, NOVEMBER 13, 2018 — WALTER REED NATIONAL MILITARY MEDICAL CENTER, BETHESDA, MARYLAND

FOR ANASTASIA VOLKOV, it had been a long year and a half since she had last tasted the freedom that most people take for granted. That was about to change.

Patience came naturally to her. She had learned long ago to suffer in silence, to wait out whatever it was that was difficult, and to persevere. That mental grit was, in her mind at least, her defining characteristic.

To others, it was not that. It was her striking looks, her olive complexion framed by her flaxen, long, straight hair. It was the hint of a Russian accent in her voice as she spoke. It was her computer sciences degree from the Massachusetts Institute of Technology. It was her aptitude for computers and for her intelligence. It was never her patience.

But it was her patience that gave her all of those things. The patience to grow into her physical looks while growing her mind, equally adept at the digital world as it was in the human world. The patience to observe and to learn. The patience to convince those who may have otherwise dismissed her as just another pretty face to realize that she was a force to behold.

And the patience to survive the past seventeen months, since Ben Porter had shot her, almost killing her.

She had pursued Ben Porter for a day and a half. First, by technology—giving him a phone that transmitted his every word and movement back to her. She could see what he saw through both the front-facing and rear-facing cameras on the device, and its sensitive microphone allowed her to hear everything he heard or said. When he looked at the screen to tap an icon, she could see his face. When he muttered to himself, she heard his thoughts.

She had given him her car to drive. A murdered-out Dodge Charger, with black wheels and black badging and black leather, customized for her with engine and suspension upgrades to go along with its menacing cosmetic enhancements.

It had been amusing to Volkov that her peers in the FBI all assumed that the Bureau had provided the car. Not exactly. She had procured it to her precise specifications, then altered the Bureau's electronic records to make it appear that it was an FBI-owned asset. If the time came to move on, she would simply change those records again. Child's play for the computer wiz.

And, on that Wednesday morning in mid-July, 2017, it had been greatly amusing to Volkov that Porter had been assigned to the case. Volkov had known, of course, that the assets of the Bureau would be stretched thin thanks to a planned visit by the President of the United States; that had turned out to be an excellent coincidence that distracted the Bureau from the plot she was working. What was even more excellent was the decision to send Porter out in the field to interview a sailor named Miles Lockwood, who had been picked up out of the Atlantic Ocean a few miles from Cape Ann, just north of Boston, and who had claimed that his boat had been hijacked off the coast of Canada and loaded with an ominous cargo.

While it was unfortunate that the sailor had escaped, it was controllable, especially with the inexperienced Porter assigned, for lack of any other options, to pursue a terror-threat investigation which had initially been considered to be a hoax.

The unfortunates began to accumulate, at odds with Volkov's initial expectations, and despite her best efforts to thwart his intuition and his investigation, he had persevered. Little by little, he put the pieces together. She had *grossly* underestimated him.

She reluctantly gave him credit for his patience, so much like her own.

She gave him no credit for his marksmanship, though. After she had chased his crappy brown Ford Taurus with her monstrous Dodge, boxing him into a turn that left the Taurus upside-down, he had surprised her one last time. Two times, to be precise. Two shots that connected with her body.

One bullet pierced her abdomen, below her heart, missing her lungs but damaging her intestines. Painful and debilitating, for certain, but treatable.

The other bullet was far more problematic. It passed partially through her neck, just barely clearing her jugular but carving a slice from her throat and airway, then burying itself scant millimeters from her spine.

Spinal injuries can be touch-and-go, and the neurosurgeons at the Massachusetts General Hospital Intensive Care Unit were hopeful that this particular patient exhibited quadriparesis, a condition shy of complete paralysis, otherwise known as quadriplegia. Volkov exhibited sacral sparing, and the reflexes in her groin, lower body, and extremities appeared to be preserved.

Immediately upon being admitted to Mass General, the surgeons performed a tracheotomy, connected her lungs to a ventilator, and inserted a feeding tube. And while the doctors at the Mass General ICU successfully patched her body where the first bullet entered, and while they were able to remove the offending second bullet in her neck, they had little choice but to merely wait for her spinal cord cells to heal themselves. In the meantime, because she couldn't move, her muscles were exercised for her, and because she couldn't speak, she was unable to answer any of the FBI's many questions.

The doctors at Mass General were puzzled at how this patient presented. Typically, after severe spinal cord injuries, reflexes disappear for weeks, even months. Yet Volkov, despite suffering from apparently profound weakness, had preserved reflexes. This observation was noted in her chart, but for privacy reasons, the chart was not shared with the FBI. Therefore, no one from the Bureau was offered the opportunity to review her file when the doctors declared that it was safe to relocate her, six months after the gunshot wounds. Volkov was transferred to a military hospital, the Walter Reed National Military Medical Center, a few miles outside of Washington, DC, in Bethesda, Maryland.

Little did the doctors know that their patient was a master at the art of deception. The patient was able to speak. She chose not to. She was able to move. But she allowed the nurses to work her joints and muscles without offering resistance. And all the while, she waited.

Anastasia Volkov would prove again that she was one step ahead of her foes. She was ready to get out, and when the doctors transported her from Mass General, away from Boston, away from Ben Porter and Bradford Macallister, she would seize the opportunity to plot her escape.

CHAPTER

4

ANASTASIA VOLKOV KNEW THAT any plan of escape would need to be simple. No technology, no computer gimmicks, no hacking. She would rely merely on subterfuge, which would take advantage of the complacency and of the false assurances that people feel when they take something for granted.

Naturally, when she was transferred to the Walter Reed National Military Medical Center, she did not know where she was or where her new recovery room was located, but over the course of several months, she was able to not only deduce her location, but also use it to her advantage. In the meantime, she continued her act as a patient, for she knew that once recovered, she would be transferred to a prison—a place that would be infinitely more difficult to escape from than a hospital.

She had admired the professionalism of the doctors and nurses at the colloquially-known Walter Reed facility; despite her status as a prisoner, they had treated her fairly and kindly. Nevertheless, she was a prisoner, and she was guarded twenty-four/seven, always by at least two men (and always men, she had noted) outside the thick door to her small room. The guards appeared to rotate on an irregular basis; Volkov had figured it was not a duty that anyone wanted to pull, but they performed their functions stoically, if not stonily. They did not attempt to converse with their prisoner—not that she would have responded.

When the doctors examined her airway, she eventually made it clear that she could breathe and eat on her own. The trach was removed, and her throat healed, but instead of speaking, she would gurgle, feigning that vocalizing was impossible, and she would lapse into silence. Initially, with her throat damaged and trached, speaking was impossible, not even an option. One would have expected that as she had healed, a conversation would become a possibility. Yet, with her infinite patience, she never said a word, realizing that silence is awkward for most. And silence creates almost a feeling of deference, and, often, confusion.

She would communicate with the doctors and nurses on a pad of paper, always ready and reachable at her bedside, or on the little table bolted to the floor next to the reading chair in the windowless room. Frequently at first, once the doctors had determined that she was probably able to speak, the interviewers from the Bureau would visit and ask question after question.

She would remain mute.

The interviewers never gave up, but they perhaps became a little less persistent with their visits. At some point, she knew she would be transferred from Walter Reed to a less comfortable prison environment, and they knew that, too, so perhaps they were also just waiting.

Like her. Waiting for her time.

Her outings for physical therapy, once she had signaled to the doctors that she had regained muscle control, were key to her observations as well. Always escorted by her two guards and whichever therapist was working with her, she began her reconnaissance with short strolls from her room to the nurses' station, assisted by a walker. Eventually, she disposed of the walker and then attempted more and more distance, finally graduating to a treadmill. She took her time. Walter Reed was preferable to prison.

She also had been taking detailed mental notes of her surroundings. She didn't dare write her observations on the pads of paper; they would have seen that through the seven cameras in her room, poorly hidden in her opinion, since she had been able to find them in short order. Perhaps there were more. It didn't matter. She knew she was being watched.

To ensure that her memory was flawless, she casually repeated her strolls, day after day, each time attempting to show a bit of progress in her physical recuperation, enough to forestall suspicion by the nursing staff, but not enough to accelerate a relocation to a prison.

She made note of room numbers and elevator signs. Her recovery room was located in a subbasement, two floors below the main level. Of course, it had no natural light, but there were digital clocks in the halls, and the ebb and flow of the staff made it obvious when it was day and when it was night. Pretending not to notice the time, and of course, forbidden a watch, she made certain to slowly alter her daily stroll to earlier and earlier in the morning. She would want the cover of the predawn dark.

As she walked, based on the layout of the halls, she determined she was in a corner of a building. The fitness center was an elevator ride up one floor. It didn't have windows, either, just televisions above the various machines, which all remained off when she was allowed to use the equipment as the sole occupant in the area.

And, critically, based on the footprints that the guards made when they changed shifts, she knew that she was not far from an entrance; when it must have rained, the soles of their boots were still slightly wet on the polished floor.

She had dressed, as usual, in the bathroom. There were no apparent cameras in the bathroom, a tiny three-piece affair with a plastic-molded shower, a toilet, and a wall-hung sink. There was no door, either, but the cased opening to the space was slightly askew of the obvious camera in the adjacent room.

Privacy was the least of her concerns. Indeed, it had been the lack of privacy that gave her the justification for her request, made months ago, that would be a cornerstone to her cunning strategy for escape.

She had seized the opportunity after one of the visits to the fitness center, as she changed from sweats into the open-backed gown they forced her to wear. As usual, the guard on duty snuck a leering glance at her figure. Volkov always noticed, but that day was different—the kindly nurse who had accompanied her back to the room had noticed too.

The nurse had grimaced, disgusted by the guard's thinly-veiled ogling.

And so, on the nurse's next visit, Volkov had grabbed her pad and scrawled, *Those scrubs look so comfy. And a lot less revealing than this gown. Any chance I could get a set?*

The nurse had nodded, shaking her head in apparent dismay at the guard's misogynistic behavior. "Absolutely. I'll set it up."

And why not? *Allow the prisoner/patient her privacy*, the nurse rationalized, as she took a few sets of scrubs from the nurses' dressing room. Volkov took to wearing the scrubs daily so that her guards and her nurses would become accustomed to the look.

It was a colossal error in judgment, in Volkov's opinion, that no one at Walter Reed commented or told her to remove the nurse-like outfit, but an error that she would use for her full advantage, as she slipped on a fresh set of the light-blue surgical scrubs in the camera-less bathroom.

On top of the scrubs, she pulled on the gray sweatpants and gray sweatshirt that she wore for her workouts. She carefully examined her cuffs and her neck; the light-blue fabric of the scrubs was completely hidden. Still in the bathroom, so that a raised cuff at her ankle wouldn't give her away if she sat on the chair, she jammed on bland blue sneakers they had given her.

The door to the room was already open; they had seen her movement into the bathroom on the camera and were ready. Because she never spoke, they had fallen into her carefully-planned habits and had begun to anticipate her. Helpful, indeed.

It was the friendly nurse waiting in the hall. In this area, Volkov had noted, they didn't wear their nametags. Occasionally a newcomer would forget, but the friendly nurse was conscientious; she would typically tuck her ID, strung from a lanyard, into the top of her scrubs. The faint outline of the plastic-encased ID card was visible through the fabric.

Volkov had mentally nicknamed her Julie.

"Julie" walked side-by-side with her patient as they wound their way to the elevator for the short trip up one floor to the fitness center, the two guards in tow behind the two women.

As the elevator doors opened, Volkov, as always, was the first to enter and, as always, she turned and casually leaned against the far wall of the cabin, so that she could face the door. Julie did the same, stand-ing slightly off to the side of her patient. The two guards entered the elevator after the two women and stood at the mouth of the elevator car, shoulder-to-shoulder, and, perhaps by some human instinct, also faced the open doors.

A critical mistake born from repetition, Volkov had thought happily as she tensed her body, ready.

The guards had taken their eyes off their prisoner.

With his back to his charge, one of the guards casually pressed the correct floor button. It lit a yellowish-white.

The double doors, wide enough to accommodate a wheelchair, began to slide shut.

With a crooked leg planted firmly on the cabin wall, and with her other leg angled at the knee, Volkov lunged forward, each of her bent arms connecting with the guards at the flat space on their backs between their shoulder blades. She rammed the men, leveraging her weight off the elevator cabin wall and driving the men clear of the elevator doors.

At the sudden, unexpected onslaught, the men pitched forward into the hall, falling face-first to the polished floor, instinctively bracing their tumble with their arms.

The guards attempted to collect themselves off the floor, their eyes wide in astonishment as their prisoner disappeared behind the stainless-steel skin of the closing elevator doors

CHAPTER

5

INSIDE THE ELEVATOR CABIN, "Julie" stood stock still, unbelieving that her patient had forcibly shoved the two armed guards out into the hall. Mouth agape, she stared, speechless, at Volkov.

Volkov knew she would have very little time before the guards would sound an alarm. Ten seconds, fifteen at the most, for them to grab a radio and to make a call, or to sprint to the nurses' station and to press the round, red emergency button. And she needed Julie out of the way.

Before the doors had finished their slide together, she spun toward the friendly nurse, and with her right arm, jabbed an uppercut sucker punch into Julie's gut. The nurse gasped and bent at the waist involuntarily, as Volkov, without a split-second of hesitation, clamped both her hands on the back of Julie's drooping cranium and pulled down even as she lifted her left knee upward. The nurse's forehead smacked Volkov's knee with a dull thud, and the hapless nurse blacked out, her body collapsing to the floor of the elevator cabin.

"I'm sorry."

The words rasped, whisper-like. Volkov had not spoken for seventeen months. It felt odd; it sounded like someone else. And, she realized, those were the exact last words she had spoken, seventeen months ago, to Ben Porter, seconds before he shot her.

She caught herself. *Stop it*, she thought. *This is no time for reminiscing. Focus!*

Volkov yanked her sweatshirt over her head and tossed it onto Julie's motionless body. With an uncanny efficiency of motion, she slipped out of the sweatpants with one hand, dancing on one foot at a time, as she reached toward the nurse's prone figure. She snagged the lanyard and yanked the ID card over Julie's neck.

As the elevator dinged and the doors started to slide open, Volkov drooped Julie's identification lanyard around her neck, scanning the name printed on the laminated card: Carolina Barrington, RN.

Sorry, Julie, Volkov thought, quickly dismissing the nurse's proper name from her mind. Figure-eighting an elastic, she gathered her hair into a messy but acceptable ponytail and stepped out of the elevator car, looking no different than any other harried nurse in the halls as she was met with a wall of sound.

BLAMMMM!

The alarm had been triggered by the guards, and in the hall outside the fitness center, nurses, doctors, and patients alike froze, processing the klaxon as an automated voice announced, "Security breach. Security breach. Lockdown. Lockdown." The klaxon sounded again, and the voice began to repeat its preprogrammed message. Volkov tuned it out and turned for the emergency stairs adjacent to the elevator bank.

Taking the wide, precast concrete steps two at a time, she trotted up a half-flight and, grappling the handrail, lightly lassoed her body around the corner of the landing to mount the next half-flight to the main level. The months of physical therapy had been effective, and she had hidden her progress skillfully. Her doctors would have been greatly impressed.

Ignoring the sound of footsteps pounding down from an upper level, she pulled open a heavy door at the top of the stairs. Her recon had been correct; she found herself on the main level—with windows. Lit from outside in the glow of the perimeter exterior lighting, her timing was spot-on as the sky beyond was colored the charcoal-blue of early dawn—a sight she had not seen for seventeen months.

She refocused her eyes on the hall, where, a mere three feet away from the stairwell door, she located the rectangular, red, wall-mounted box of a fire alarm pull station, mounted forty-two inches off the floor and in easy reach. Two fingers inserted above the "T" in the box and a quick yank, and instantly, a second alarm sound blasted in dissonance to the first klaxon.

The cacophony, Volkov guessed, would cause chaos.

With a fast quadrant search, taking in the surroundings in four staccato glances, she found what she needed: the interior building signage, which indicated the direction of the lobby. *Not that way*, she thought, as she bolted the opposite direction.

In the hall, the light-blue scrubs of nurses mixed with the white lab coats of doctors and the camouflage uniforms of servicemen and the sweats and tees of patients and the suits and ties of officers and executives as people swarmed, ears ringing with the jarring, grating sounds of the alarms . . . Volkov weaved through the turmoil, her ponytail bobbing up and down and Carolina Barrington's ID lanyard swinging to and fro officiously.

Twenty-eight seconds later, she found what she wanted, an emergency exit door with a push-bar marked "Push To Open—Alarm Will Sound." Mashing her left hip into the bar, the door clicked and swung out. Over the strident alarm bells and klaxons, Volkov couldn't tell if a new alarm had sounded, nor did she care. The fire alarm had done what had been needed: the life-safety system had overridden the building lockdown system.

Another quadrant scan and she identified her escape route: a patch of small trees, a visual buffer grove of landscaping against the building and beyond, a sidewalk and street. She put her head down and trotted, the blaring of the alarm fading as she opened distance between her and Walter Reed.

Four hundred feet and fifty seconds later, she found herself at the edge of a brightly lit parking lot.

Not good. I can't go back.

Retracing her steps was not an option. She squinted in the glare of the brilliant, metal-halide parking lot lights, unaccustomed to being outside, and, for the first time since passing through the exit door, she shivered. It was cold, and the thin scrubs were not only inappropriate for the temperature, but also bound to grab someone's attention.

She had to risk the exposed parking lot, and she steeled herself to the cold as she darted down an outside row of the lot, putting distance between herself and the building as the sounds of the klaxons faded slightly.

"Hey!"

The voice called out with authority, and Volkov barely slowed as she angled her head to face the voice.

A man. Plain-clothed. Standing by an open car door. Perhaps arriving for work.

"Freezing out here! Forgot my coat inside!" Volkov gasped, her raw, unused vocal cords rasping the sounds. "And I'm in the wrong damn row!"

The man made a move to follow her, but instead shrugged and turned back to his vehicle, slamming the door closed, watching as Volkov trotted to the opposite side of the parking area.

Move it—move it—move it! she commanded herself, putting the parking-lot man out of her thoughts.

Within seconds, she saw an automobile gatehouse, brightly lit with red stop lamps showing on all lanes. She was at the perimeter of the complex.

Wasting no time and keeping her pace steady, just short of a run, she picked a wide path away from the gatehouse, heading for a line of trees for cover. Once in the treeline, she slowed her slow jog to a brisk walk, picking her way carefully around branches and roots, paralleling the road that led from the gatehouse.

As the sky gradually lightened, she could hear sirens and see the flashing blue-and-red strobe lights of emergency vehicles. And, with a start, she saw, barely, a black chain-link fence topped with concertina wire. *That's a problem*, she grimaced.

Barely slowing her pace, she backtracked toward where she knew the gatehouse would be, to her left. It was a risk, of course, but if there was a fence, there would probably be a man-sized gate.

Sure enough, within seconds, she saw such a gate, straddling the concrete sidewalk that ran alongside the access drive. To her amazement, the gate was open.

But not for long. An armed guard was walking smartly toward the man-gate.

Ears perked and eyes narrowed, Volkov scouted her area: the man-gate, a line of cars backed into the intersection of the main road, waiting to enter through the automobile gatehouse, and a smattered blare of horns as early-morning drivers navigated around the backup. With one last look to judge distance to the gate, Volkov broke into a full sprint, legs and arms pumping, ponytail bouncing.

The incongruous sight of a figure in light-blue surgical scrubs caught the guard's eye, and, for an instant, he stopped in his tracks.

From a distance, at a run, Volkov met his eyes, but did not falter her pace.

The guard collected himself, pulling his pistol from a hip-holster, yelling "Stop!" as he attempted to chase the fleeing woman.

Her headstart was enough. She dashed through the open man-gate, stealing a glance at the "Jones Bridge Road" sign hanging about the access drive.

At a full sprint, dodging honking vehicles, the figure in the light-blue scrubs raced across five lanes of dawn traffic and disappeared into a residential neighborhood; while in the distance, the klaxons continued their blaring screams at the Walter Reed National Military Medical Center.

On the far side of Jones Bridge Road, the guard's gun dangled uselessly by his side, but he had a portable radio at his lips. Radio waves travel faster than bullets.

Nevertheless, it would be too late.

6

TUESDAY, NOVEMBER 13, 2018 —
FBI BOSTON FIELD OFFICE, CHELSEA, MASSACHUSETTS

MY NEW TITLE OF Special Agent came with a gun *and* a new desk.

In Boston, the Bureau had formed an Operation E.T. squad that reported directly to Senior Supervisory Special Agent Bradford Macallister, who, in turn, reported to Special Agent in Charge Jennifer Appleton.

The five working agents of the squad were Special Agent Don Jordon, Special Agent Brenda Connelly, Special Agent Wilson Zimmerman, Special Agent Amber Jones, and Special Agent Ben Porter.

See what I did there? Still felt good.

Until that Tuesday morning.

Normally, the squad's days were spent working the case. Over the past year and change, they had built, sometimes with epiphanies but more often with painstaking analysis, a giant file of detail upon detail: the names and the dossiers of the for-hire terrorists, their backstories, their trails, their accomplices, and their funding sources.

On my periodic trips back to Boston from Quantico, I got to know the squad somewhat, and I'd help fill in the blanks on details that I recalled. For the most part, though, I was considered "too close" to the case to be of recurring value to the team. While I had firsthand knowledge of what went down, I was not yet a trained investigator, and I was assumed to be personally biased to my own recollections. I wasn't insulted; that was a perfectly valid point. Still, I wanted to be part of the team and to see the case through, and it was more or less a foregone conclusion that when I graduated from Quantico, I'd be assigned back to Chelsea and to the Operation E.T. squad.

There were two overarching goals to the Bureau's continued investment in the Operation E.T. case, and both goals were crucial for national security.

In Boston, the squad focused on one of those goals: Anatoly Petrikov and the mechanism behind the plot I had foiled in July 2017. The squad teased out the tiny details and weaved them into a bigger picture, all while waiting impatiently for our chance to question our star witness: Anastasia Volkov.

Meanwhile, a team in Washington, DC was intent on the second goal: trying to determine how Anastasia Volkov had been hired by the FBI. That team's assignment was also to deduce if there was someone else in the Bureau, potentially linked to Petrikov, who facilitated Volkov's employment.

The story that Volkov had maintained, back when she worked side-by-side with us, was that she was adopted by an American family at a young age and that she was a Ukrainian orphan by birth. Her adoptive family was wealthy, and she wanted for nothing but had no interest in a privileged lifestyle. After graduating from the Massachusetts Institute of Technology, majoring in computer science, she joined the Bureau.

After I shot her, and after her involvement in the Operation E.T. plot became apparent, the Bureau established that her backstory was partially fabricated; there were no records of a Ukrainian orphan's adoption nor of her alleged adoptive family. She appeared "on the grid" at MIT using the name Anastasia Volkov.

Every person hired by the FBI, regardless of whether they would be an agent or a staffer, undergoes an extensive background check, and no one with that sort of gaping hole in their background would be hired by the FBI. It's not like she simply materialized at MIT one day, and then joined the Bureau and went to Quantico to train as an Intelligence Analyst.

Therefore, the Bureau surmised, someone had covered for her *within* the FBI.

Which meant, plainly, that we still had a mole at large, in our midst. And therefore, our investigation into the mechanics of the terror plot was segregated from the investigation into the potential mole who had allowed Anastasia Volkov to be hired by the FBI.

And we really wanted to talk to her. Except, she wasn't talking.

The doctors at Mass General, where Volkov had been taken after I shot her, had warned us that the nature of her injuries would make it impossible for her to speak for some time. And so, when I had been sent to Quantico, I had not been surprised to hear that she had remained mute even after being transferred to the Walter Reed medical facility outside of Washington, DC.

After I returned to Boston as a Special Agent, I had joined hours of discussion at our squad's conference table, where we theorized why Volkov had still not spoken a single word. Was it medical? Was it trauma, some sort of Posttraumatic Stress Disorder? Or was it her choice?

The FBI does not interrogate; we interview. Perhaps, in a different world, or nation, or situation, a person can be compelled to speak via torture or physical abuse. We just don't do that.

It takes an incredible fortitude of mind not to speak. There's an Indian derivative of Buddhism called Vipassana, a type of meditation, and people take part in Vipassana meditation retreats where they don't speak for ten days. I learned from the internet that the retreats are grueling, both physically and mentally. And Anastasia Volkov had clocked *seventeen months* of not saying a word.

She would have to break at some point.

Looking back on it, we were so foolish, so naïve. We knew her. We knew what she was capable of. We should have known that she would break.

She would break out.

At 10:37 AM, Special Agent in Charge Jennifer Appleton glided through the open glass door of our conference room. Her usually placid, incalculable demeanor was missing; in its place was a scowl that would have melted ice.

Without a word, Appleton selected a seat at the table next to mine and gently, carefully sat. She scanned the table, meeting our eyes deliberately, person by person. It was so quiet I could hear the second hand of her small, silver wristwatch advancing.

Tick. Tick. Tick.

Appleton exhaled softly and finally spoke. "Anastasia Volkov has again managed the impossible. She has escaped from Walter Reed. She has disappeared."

Tick. Tick. Tick.

No one said a word. Macallister's face, usually perfectly tanned to go with his perfectly framed, tailored Brooks Brothers-suited body, went ashen white. I felt my fists unconsciously clenching.

"Just after five this morning, while it was still dark, Volkov was being escorted to the physical fitness center. This was her usual time; her pattern was that she preferred to do her P.T. when the center was empty, and the security folks at Walter Reed accepted this since it made the protection detail straightforward. As usual, she was escorted by two armed guards and accompanied by a nurse.

"This was routine. And as you know, routine breeds complacency. Volkov and the nurse boarded the elevator first. The guards boarded second and turned their backs on their charge. Volkov shoved both guards out of the elevator. They sounded the lockdown alarm as the elevator rose to the next floor. Camera footage of the elevator, which by the way, was not being monitored in real-time, showed Volkov knocking out the nurse and then stealing her ID. Volkov then stripped off her sweats to reveal that she was wearing nursing scrubs. She got off the elevator, took the stairs up one flight, and pulled the fire alarm."

"She would know," Macallister muttered, interrupting the SAC.

"Know what?" I asked.

Appleton looked briefly at Macallister. "She would know that pulling the fire alarm defeats the locking mechanisms that are triggered on the emergency exit doors by the lockdown signal. She found a fire exit door and bolted.

"The perimeter of the facility was secured, as per protocol. All vehicular traffic in and out of the facility was halted. A security guard at one of the gatehouses was walking to manually lock one of the pass-through gates into the property. The guard spotted Volkov. He unholstered his weapon but did not fire it. We have Volkov on video, and the guard radioed in his observations. Volkov ran through the open gate, bolted across a road, and disappeared into a residential neighborhood.

"Obviously, our people at Walter Reed immediately notified the Bureau. Washington put a bulletin out, and local police are cooperating with the search for her."

I snorted. "But they're not going to find her, are they?"

"Doubtful," Appleton nodded. "They don't know what they are up against. I have a hard time concluding that she had help from the outside and some sort of getaway waiting. She has been strictly forbidden to use any electronic devices. But all the same, she's very resourceful. I would expect that she could easily steal a car and, by now, could be hundreds of miles away, or maybe one mile away. She's that good. She knows how we are going to look for her."

"And because she knows *exactly* what we are going to do," I added, "she's going to be one step ahead of us."

"Right," Appleton replied.

I shook my head. "Wrong."

CHAPTER
7

IN RETROSPECT, I WAS WRONG. I was still feeling the euphoria of my new title and the comforting weight of my new gun, nestled in a shoulder holster, tucked up close to my left abdomen. Excuses of new-found swagger aside, as it would turn out, I was still wrong.

But I guess it was a good lesson.

"Okay," I started in, "we know that she knows everything about our technology. Our access to cameras, credit card data, airline and train tickets—all that stuff. You can't move without triggering something, somewhere. So, what's she going to do?"

I looked around the conference table for answers. My colleagues remained silent. Appleton apprised me with a faint squint. Undeterred, I barreled on, confidently, "She's not going to do anything! She's going to find a hideout, and she's going to stay put."

Heads began to nod. Special Agent Wilson Zimmerman, a tall, lanky, afro-topped, dark-skinned native of San Diego, nodded especially strongly. I hadn't really connected with Zimmerman since I had joined the squad upon my return to Boston; perhaps it was an East Coast versus West Coast thing, or perhaps it was my background. I lapped up the affirmation as Zimmerman opined, "Right on. I read her files over and over. She can spot a camera from a mile away. She knows the coverage angles. She knows how to track, so she knows how to be tracked. She's also got nothing. No identification and no proper clothes. What was she wearing, anyway?"

"Scrubs. Your basic matching set of scrubs. Light blue in color," Appleton answered.

"December in DC—that's not exactly scrubs weather," Zimmerman concluded. "She'll find an unoccupied house, and she'll make herself comfortable."

Macallister was shaking his head back-and-forth, "I dunno. She got out at what, five or six this morning? Four-hour head start? What have our people down there been doing since then?"

Appleton leaned forward. "It's a full-on manhunt. We have the Washington agents on alert and beginning an investigation. We have an All-Points Bulletin out to not only the Bethesda police but also with the police departments in the surrounding towns. She was last seen on foot. However, there are obviously other variables. The nearest train station is five miles away. That's walkable in that amount of time, but unlikely that she would not have been spotted. And, she might have stolen a car."

Zimmerman interjected, "No wheels, no possibility of any significant movement."

Special Agent Brenda Connelly was squirming in her swivel chair, clearly waiting to get a word in. That's the problem with these group discussions; everyone wants to look engaged and to get their wisdom to the table. What we needed was action, not more discussion, but with my newbie status, I didn't dare interrupt the veteran agent. Connelly, originally from Florida, was sort of a legend within the Bureau for her undercover work in drug busts run out of the Miami field office; her average-sized frame and her plain, brown-haired, brown-eyed, tanned skin looks were unremarkable and unmemorable. But that boring veneer masked a very sharp mind. "Problem is," she said, "most cars these days are push-button start. Volkov is going to have a hard time finding something to hot wire. She'd have to break into a home and get a fob. I don't see that happening."

Appleton was reading something on the screen of the tablet she typically carried and was nodding affirmatively. "We've got twenty agents and at least as many police on the ground surrounding Walter Reed. More personnel are arriving by the minute. The search is already underway."

"They need to go door-to-door," I said confidently. "She will find a place to hide, and she'll stay there. We need to establish a perimeter around that residential area and then close it in. She won't dare come out and risk the cameras. Just have to tighten the noose!"

Standing, Appleton confirmed, "I'll pass your theory to Washington. Let's get set up in the Operations Center." She floated from the conference room as the rest of the team stood, gathering pads and laptops and phones. After months of investigative work, the action of actual fieldwork seemed to have a galvanizing effect. And I was convinced that we would find our missing traitor in no time. December was not an ideal time to traipse through a wooded area in Bethesda after being hospitalized for seventeen months.

Only Macallister remained immobile, casually leaning back in his imitation Aeron swivel chair, legs crossed as he picked an imaginary speck of lint off the sharp crease on his navy-blue suit pants. "Nope," he said. "You're all wrong. She's gone."

CHAPTER

8

SAME TIME — OUTSIDE OF WILMINGTON, DELAWARE

CRUISING AT A CONSERVATIVE sixty-two miles per hour, Anastasia Volkov realized that she was finally warm, and she decided to switch off the heated seat. Scanning the instrument cluster, she noted that the fuel gauge indicated well over a half-tank. A glance out the windshield, she confirmed that she was in the correct lane to continue northbound on Interstate 95, toward Wilmington, and away from Washington, now some ninety-odd miles behind her rearview mirror.

She felt fantastic. The morning traffic had thinned, and the German sedan had been humming smoothly. She had even sung a few words along to the music playing on the excellent sound system; the sound of her voice still startled her, but she knew she needed the practice for her vocal cords to regain their strength. There was still time for that, though.

"Textbook," she said, aloud, chuckling to herself. "Good practice. Strange to talk to myself." She looked left then right, wondering if other drivers would observe her talking to herself. "No," she said, again out loud, the sensation of speaking becoming more comfortable with every word. "They'll think I'm talking on the phone. On the Bluetooth. Keep talking."

Volkov smiled, now feeling still fantastic, but also a tiny bit foolish.

No one paid her any attention. She smiled again as she guided the black Audi north.

The Audi was the *perfect* find. And the Audi had saved her from the messy business of having to kill someone for their wheels and for their cash.

She had known that she would have very limited time before the area was crawling with cops and with FBI agents, who would be highly motivated to hunt down a traitor. Wheels were a priority, but she couldn't find any. Either the cars had been driven to work by their owners or were tucked away inside garages. In one scenario, she didn't want to waste time breaking into a home, finding and killing an occupant, and locating a set of car keys. Or, in a worse scenario, going through all that only to discover that was no car in a garage.

No, she hoped for something else as a combination of fear and adrenaline that kept her motivated against the stinging cold through the thin scrubs while she trotted through the West Chevy Chase Heights neighborhood just south of the Walter Reed compound. The search had taken almost an hour—too long, and she was considering that she was inevitably going to have to break, enter, and kill.

Then she found it. A clean, inconspicuous, somewhere in the mid-2000s vintage vehicle parked very close to a house. It was not really a difficult ask in a reasonably well-heeled neighborhood, seeking a ten-plus-year-old vehicle in an area populated by government functionaries and local professionals.

The age of the vehicle was critical. As manufacturers adopted push-button start technology, early vehicles with this feature could be started without the key fob inside the car. The manufacturers quickly solved for that shortcoming, realizing that a fob detection system would need to identify whether the fob was inside the car before allowing the electronic wizardry to engage the ignition.

But back in 2006, Audi had not figured that out yet, and the black sedan sitting scant feet away from a well-kept, two-story home had turned out to be exactly the car Volkov needed. The trusting owner had left it unlocked; she had carefully lifted the driver's door handle and felt a satisfying *click* as the latch released. Swinging the door open, she had slipped into the driver's seat, placed her right foot on the brake pedal, and held her breath as she pressed the center-console-mounted start button.

Sure enough, the key fob inside the house was close enough to the car outside in the driveway, and the sedan started instantly. Without even a second of hesitation, Volkov had shifted the vehicle into drive and accelerated onto the quiet street as she pulled the door shut.

Driving south toward Bethesda proper, away from Walter Reed, she had piloted the German car carefully, searching for her second target: a quiet parking lot.

Turning onto Wisconsin Parkway, it had taken less than ninety seconds to find a CVS with a large lot where, at the back perimeter, she found her third target.

Leaving the Audi running, of course, for she had no way to restart it if she turned off the ignition, she had grabbed a quarter and a nickel from the cupholder in the car and hopped out. Slinking around a gray Ford Explorer, she had used the coins as rude screwdrivers to remove the license plate from the back of the SUV and then repeated the process on the Audi. The plate swap would buy her miles of unobstructed travel once the owner of the Audi reported his vehicle missing, and the FBI connected the dots and realized that it was stolen shortly after she had taken her leave of Walter Reed.

Back in the heated comfort of the luxury car, she had slowed her breathing, and for perhaps the third time, she had ducked her head slightly to confirm, again, that the white E-Z-Pass toll transponder was stuck to the windshield behind the rearview mirror. While she had recognized that the FBI would certainly try to match the stolen Audi to tolling data, something she had first-hand knowledge with, she also knew that many tolls were triggered by cameras with license plate recognition technology. In those cases, the Ford Explorer plates would give her cover. But, if she came across a toll without the camera-capture tech, she could use the E-Z-Pass, for, after all, she had no money to hand to a collector at a toll booth. It was an acceptable risk that she had to take. After all, she had only about a five-hour drive; it would take a miracle of interstate cooperation for the technology to keep up with her.

Satisfied with her subtle subterfuge plans, she had plotted a course north on the Audi's in-dash navigation system, taking care to use a circuitous route around the Walter Reed campus to avoid what would certainly be a fast-growing police and FBI presence.

Now north of Wilmington and heading toward Philadelphia, Volkov examined the fuel gauge and calculated that she would have about three more hours of drive time before she would need to switch vehicles or find some way to fuel the Audi. "One thing at a time," she muttered, before remembering that she needed the voice practice. Louder, she repeated, "One thing at a time. You've got plenty of fuel. Stay invisible. Next step: get to New York."

Grinning, she lightly pressed the gas pedal and shifted into the left lane, enjoying the smooth acceleration of the aging, but still finely tuned, German-engineered Audi A6 luxury sedan.

New York City. Less than two hours of drivetime north. A place where she could not only disappear, but she could also trigger the plan that had been put into place so many years ago.

Volkov squinted. She had no way of knowing if all the pieces of that plan remained intact. Because, if not, she was on her own. And she knew that the FBI would not be far behind.

9

SAME DAY, EARLY AFTERNOON —
FBI BOSTON FIELD OFFICE, CHELSEA, MASSACHUSETTS

ONE BY ONE, THE TECHNICIANS working in the Boston operations center had linked us to the Washington headquarters office and to the local police departments. My five-person squad, plus the SAC, plus the techs, were online and on the chase that was taking place some four-hundred-and-fifty miles away.

Agents had combed the area around the Walter Reed National Military Medical Center to no avail. Anastasia Volkov had vanished, and as the hours had ticked toward the sunset in Boston, I belatedly began to realize that I had been wrong.

Every locating tactic that we had was being thrown into the search: heat-sensing cameras, infrared cameras, live searches of individual residences down to the basements, up to the attics, and into the closets, and door-to-door inquiries for security cameras that may have recorded a figure slinking by in light-blue surgical scrubs. K-9 units sent their dogs into the field, priming their sensitive nostrils with the scent found on the sweats discarded in the Walter Reed elevator.

Nothing.

Macallister remained sanguine, as usual. "You jumped to a conclusion, Porter," he growled. "She was long gone. No way we were gonna track her. We gotta get in front of her. Where's she going? Where can she find resources? Money. Access to tech. Is she coming back to Boston? Is she coming back to finish what she started?"

Shit. That had not occurred to me. Was she coming to Boston, for me?

I looked at Macallister with real concern, now not the least bit comforted by the press of the Glock against the side of my gut. "For what? Revenge?"

Shrugging, Macallister answered, "Nah. Shouldn't have mentioned it. It's possible, of course. But unlikely that her first stop after seventeen months of captivity is going to be to barge in here to take you out. She's much more calculating than that."

After my rush to judgment earlier, I appreciated Macallister's soft approach; he was reprimanding my brashness without being rude.

Agent Wilson Zimmerman was not so kind as he butted into our conversation. "Like I said earlier, she's not gonna find an unoccupied house or car and make herself comfortable. She probably split town within minutes of getting out of Walter Reed. You made a mistake by not opening the search circumference."

I grimaced. That was *not* what he had said earlier. In fact, I got the sense, then, that he had agreed with my analysis.

And, what was that bullshit about me making a mistake on the search area? I verbalized a theory, but I most definitely didn't give orders. Well, sort of . . .

It was beginning to dawn on me that I'd have to be more careful with what I said and what I theorized. *Evidence. Facts. Find them.* That had served me well before, and I needed to shrug off Zimmerman's nonsense and focus on the case.

Taking a cue from Macallister's demeanor, I found a chair and settled myself into it, leaning back and making myself comfortable, allowing my mind to rest along with my body. Across the table, I caught Macallister's little smirk. Of anyone in the room, he knew me better than the rest. Ah, *fuck it.* I trust him. He can smirk all he wants.

Looking at Macallister, I spoke evenly, emotionlessly. "You said earlier that she might make me a target. That's one theory. Probably a pretty good one too. Boston. Potential destination. But where else might she go? Let's make a list."

Agent Connelly, nodding, stood and crossed to a whiteboard. Selecting a red marker, she spelled out *Boston – Agent Porter, TARGET* on the board. I didn't care for either the color of the ink or the capitalized letters, but I kept my mouth tightly closed, preferring, now, to remain silent while the rest of the squad voiced their opinions.

Zimmerman quickly spoke as Connelly moved her body out of the way so we could see the board, "Yeah, definitely. Top of the list." He glared at me. I didn't move a muscle.

"Not necessarily Boston for targeting purposes, though. Maybe she comes home, gets supplies, cash, identification. Risky but plausible, right?" This theory was offered by Agent Amber Jones. I liked Jones. She was plain-spoken, a little heavy, but really good on tactics and legal issues; her mocha skin matching the mocha-colored, leather-wrapped folio she carried to take her copious notes, inked to the page in her careful, left-handed ALL CAPS printed letters. At the whiteboard, Connelly penned, this time in blue, *Boston – home for supplies*.

"No fuckin' way," Macallister chopped, continuing, "She'd know that we have it locked down. And she'd know we would have searched her place already. We did, obviously. Days and days. Found fuckin' nothing. Clean as a whistle. She's smarter than that. She knew not to leave evidence."

Undeterred, Jones retorted, "She had to have something local where she could work and stay in contact with whomever she was working with. Storage unit? Apartment somewhere? Single rented office someplace? Nondescript, paid with cash, that sort of thing."

Macallister capitulated a tiny bit, saying, "Maybe. But we haven't found anything like that yet. Really, I dunno. She needed a place to make calls, maybe with burner phones. Can do that from anywhere. And a laptop with WiFi at a coffee shop or bookstore or mall. She's got the tech chops to cover her tracks. Like I said, we found nothing in her condo."

Back at the whiteboard, Connelly added a question mark next to *supplies*. Naturally, that made me stare more intently at the word above. *TARGET*. In red ink.

I remained tight-lipped, though.

"Petrikov."

The normally taciturn Agent Don Jordon had spoken. One word.

Jordon, almost as a rule, didn't say much. The geeky-looking Midwesterner, with his close-cropped blond hair, wire-framed eyeglasses, pale skin, impossibly thin and tall body—he was the nerd from central casting. Since being back in Boston, that was maybe the fifth time I'd heard his nasally voice.

But I leaned in at the sound of that name. As did the rest of the squad.

"Of course!" Connelly yelped as she used a marker to spell out *PETRIKOV* in big, black, blocky capital letters, a stark contrast against the shiny white of the board.

Macallister leaned back. "She'd have to find him, first. Nope."

I turned to stare at my boss. "Surely, she, of all people, could find him. You gotta think she's set up a back door into our system. You gotta think that it's been dormant since she left. She's smart enough to hide it, and we would never find it. And somewhere, buried in our systems, is Petrikov's location."

"Yeah, I guess," Macallister replied, somewhat meekly.

"I'll make sure we notify Petrikov's handlers that there may be an elevated risk," Appleton said, from behind me. I hadn't noticed her standing there, stock-still and silent. "Any other theories?" she asked.

"Petrikov's apartment? Yacht? Any of his old haunts? We got those things covered?"

Appleton had gazed serenely at Zimmerman as he theorized, and she replied, "No. Not for some time. But that's an excellent point." She walked to the exit of the operations center, tossing her final words over her shoulder, "But as of now, we will."

I shook my head as she disappeared. "Macallister, I still don't understand why we cannot know where Petrikov is located. Especially now. Especially given *these* circumstances."

"Compartmentalization," he said, slowly, syllable-by-syllable. That was a long word for Macallister, and he took his time to get it out. Speeding up his diction, he added, "And especially now. Only a handful of people know where Petrikov is being kept. Keeping that info locked down makes it impossible for anyone to find him. Us, or even her. Get it?"

"Yeah, I guess."

"Problem is," Macallister continued, ignoring me, "is that she doesn't know that we don't know. And pretty much any way you slice it, that means only one thing. That she's gonna go to what she thinks is the source."

He paused, probably for effect, or possibly just to scare me, before concluding, "That source is you. If I had to bet, I'd bet that her target is Ben Porter."

CHAPTER

10

SAME DAY, LATE AFTERNOON — NEW YORK CITY, NEW YORK

AFTERNOON IN NEW YORK CITY was a terrible time to try and find an on-street parking space. After making good time on the highways from DC, cruising along in the inauspicious black Audi, Anastasia Volkov had arrived in the City and then circled the Seaport neighborhood, in the shadow of the Brooklyn Bridge, for well over an hour, searching for a suitable spot. A side street was ideal. Nearby luxury vehicles were a must. The black Audi had to blend in.

Finally, on the one-way, cobblestone-paved Front Street, she had sighted what she needed, and with a little fist pump, she had deftly parallel-parked the sedan between a black Mercedes SUV and a black BMW sedan. She had appreciated the little bit of humor in slotting her stolen German car between two other German-made vehicles, but she had not been distracted from her goals by that oddity. To ensure that the Audi's Maryland tags were not as conspicuous as they might seem to be, she had taken care to push the rear bumper of the Audi close to the nose of the BMW, to the future inconvenience of the BMW driver when it was time for that vehicle to attempt to exit its parking spot.

Volkov had finally turned off the Audi and swung the driver's side door open to the cold, late-day New York air. Rearranging her ponytail and smoothing the scrubs, she had stretched and then trotted the seven or eight blocks to the New York-Presbyterian Lower Manhattan Hospital. It was time to play nurse again, and with the scrubs, she'd fit right in.

With her Carolina Barrington, RN identification card, and her scrubs-and-sneakers outfit, she bore a passable resemblance to a nurse. Confidence, though, was her most important disguise. With her chin up and her gaze focused intently straight ahead, she strode purposefully into the emergency room entrance at the corner of Beekman and Gold Streets, past the chatting security guards, past the reception desk, and into the bowels of the hospital.

Once through the gauntlet at the emergency entrance and blending into a nondescript hallway, she slowed her pace and began searching for the nurses' locker room.

It took Volkov perhaps twenty minutes to locate her target, on a lower level, down yet another nondescript hallway. The clock on the wall inside the locker room showed 3:23 PM, and in the absence of a shift change, the place was deserted. She began rummaging for unlocked cubbies.

Slowly, she assembled her outfit—from one locker, a loose-fitting sweater, and from another, a pair of black joggers. With her fingers running down the painted steel doors, she found an open locker with a purse inside; she pilfered about half the cash, maybe thirty-five dollars, and one credit card. Satisfied with her take, she bolted from the ladies' lockers and moved on to seeking her next items.

In her new outfit, but with her scrubs casually laid across a shoulder, she worked her way to the main lobby off William Street, snagging an overcoat that someone had hung on a chair but had forgotten. Slipping the slightly-oversized coat over her clothes, she ducked into the gift shop and practiced, for the first time in almost a year and a half, a conversation with the stubby clerk at the counter. "Hi!" Enthusiastic and friendly, but not intimate. "Any chance you've got a plastic bag I can use? I was in such a rush. I forgot my bag." She giggled and, for emphasis, held up the wrinkled, light-blue scrubs.

"Oh, sure," the clerk responded, reaching down to a cavity below the counter with a faint smile. "Here ya go," she said.

"Thanks so much," Volkov replied lightly, as she accepted the plastic bag with the red-printed New York-Presbyterian logo. Stuffing the scrubs inside, she nodded to the clerk and sauntered out of the shop, out of the lobby, and into the bustle of New York City. Time was both her ally and her enemy. *Be quick,* she thought. *No one place for too long.*

She had spent an hour, tops, inside the hospital building. And now she had a long walk planned.

She had made it to New York. She had proper clothing and a bit of cash. And so far, she had eluded the FBI.

One more step to go. And for that, she needed a computer with an internet connection, in a place where she could be anonymous. And then, and only then, she would discover if that long-ago seeded plan would blossom—or if it was dead.

CHAPTER 11

SAME DAY, EARLY EVENING —
FBI BOSTON FIELD OFFICE, CHELSEA, MASSACHUSETTS

"WE HAVE A HIT!" screamed the unfortunately named Louis Lewis, currently the ranking Information Analyst in the Boston field office of the FBI.

Lewis, who I'd met during the July 2017 chase, was a familiar, if not slightly eccentric sight in the operations center. With his short, spiky, silvery-blond hair and purple eyeglasses, Lewis was definitely an oddity among the starched white shirts of the agents, but in the tech world, he fit right in—even to the point where his alliterative name gave him a strange sort of credibility.

His outburst got immediate attention from the squad in the operations center, and we waited for edification. "Bethesda cops. Interviewed a homeowner who is six blocks south of Walter Reed. He's missing a car."

Pausing to read his screen, Lewis added, "Cops sent the data to Washington HQ. They sent it to me. We're getting description, plates, and best of all, according to the owner, the car has an E-Z-Pass."

"How the hell are we only getting this now? Car was stolen this morning? Guy didn't fucking notice?" Macallister growled.

Examining the digital file, Lewis grunted, "It was called into the police switchboard at 9:05 AM. The homeowner called the regular number, not 9-1-1. Thoughtful citizen. He didn't think that a car theft was an emergency situation, and the call got back-burnered."

"Fuck," Macallister spat, flatly.

"You running the data? Is Washington?" Zimmerman asked.

"Coming in now. Washington put a priority on it," Lewis responded. As he watched his screens, his thumb furiously clicked at the trigger on a blue ball-point pen. *Click-click. Click-click. Click-click.*

We watched. Mesmerized by the repetitive clicking noise, no one spoke; the only sound came from the innumerable cooling fans in the computer equipment. Around the operations center, monitor after monitor flashed with information, data streams, television news broadcasts, and images. It was an overload of information, housed in an edifice to technology.

Click-click. Click-click. Then, Lewis finally spoke, "Running everything we can. Tolls. Cameras. Plate recognition."

I leaned toward Macallister and whispered, "Déjà vu. Does Appleton know?"

"Dunno. I'll call her." Macallister pulled a smartphone from a pocket and began tapping at the screen, using a single forefinger instead of two thumbs like, well, pretty much the rest of the world. During my time at Quantico, I had forgotten just how tech-adverse my boss was, especially as I watched him compose a text, not dial a phone number. Whatever; he'd get the message out to the SAC.

Triumphantly, Macallister announced, "Done!" He put his phone back in a pocket as we waited, hopefully, for more data from Lewis.

I rolled an imitation Aeron to a vacant workstation. With my new title as Special Agent, I now had clearance and login credentials to use these computers. No need anymore to ask for permission.

Pulling up a Google Earth satellite image of the area south of Walter Reed, I imagined Anastasia Volkov brushing past tree branches and rustling through underbrush in the wooded areas that bounded the tightly-packed homes. Had she planned this all out in advance, or had she simply gotten lucky, finding a car with the keys in it? Wait . . .

"Wait," I repeated, this time out loud. "Homeowner left the keys in his car? How'd she take it? What is it?"

"2006 Audi A6. Sedan. Black," Lewis reported. "Homeowner said the keys were inside. On a windowsill. He said he meant to stash them in the drawer like he usually does at night, but he forgot."

"Makes sense," Connelly added, reclining in her seat at the oversized conference table that dominated the middle of the operations center. Earlier today, she had posed that very scenario. Now she walked it back. "Older car, no interior proximity for a key fob. It must have been parked close enough to the house. How did Volkov stumble on that particular car?"

"A setup?" Don Jordon's second and third words today.

Before I had a chance to respond that I thought that was plausible, Macallister once again chopped at a theory. "No way. She had no way of communicating with the outside. She hadn't spoken. Unless there was someone at Walter Reed that she used some sort of sign language with, there's no way. She waited for an opportunity to bolt and got lucky with the car. Simple as that."

I wasn't so sure, but I kept my thoughts to myself.

An hour later, still huddled as a team around the gigantic conference table and now joined by SAC Appleton, we finally got an update from Lewis. And it was not what we were expecting. I mean, granted, I was hoping that he'd tell us that he found the burned hulk of the stolen car somewhere with Volkov's charred body inside, but I knew that would be wishful thinking.

Lewis spoke simply, "We found the Audi."

He surveyed the room; the squad stared uniformly back at those purple glasses, waiting. He added, "It's in New York City. Abandoned."

"In the City? What the fuck? Where? When? Who found it?" Macallister demanded.

"Washington has already sent agents from our New York office to recon the car, and a forensics unit will be at the location in fifteen minutes."

"How'd they find it?" I asked, repeating Macallister's question.

Lewis leaned forward to his monitor, narrating as he read, "We got an E-Z-Pass hit at the Holland Tunnel. Heading into the City."

"Yeah. New Jersey side. There's no toll if you're heading out of the city. But if you're heading in, you pay cash, or you use E-Z-Pass. Can't pay by mail," Macallister commented, somewhat helpfully. I remembered that he was originally from New Jersey. He'd know the area.

With an annoyed look at Macallister, Lewis continued, "And since that seemed impossible since there are a ton of tolls between Maryland and New York, they put a priority on the camera images from the tunnel tolling overpass in Jersey City. Those cameras are just for security, not for tolling, like Agent Macallister said. They matched the security camera images with the E-Z-Pass timestamp. Black Audi, exactly as described, sole female occupant. Different plate on the back bumper."

One of the several laser printers scattered throughout the operations center whirred, and Jordon, closest to it from his seat at the big table, rolled over and picked up the colored sheet of paper. He squinted at the image for a second, then wordlessly passed the picture to me. I instantly recognized the face through the windshield. Anastasia Volkov.

A second sheet of paper slid into the printer's tray, and again, Jordon passed it to me. The back end of a black Audi. Maryland tags. Volkov had slipped out of Walter Reed before the sun came up and had traveled, undetected, into New York City just after lunchtime. Unbelievable.

Lewis finished recounting the Washington report, "An APB on the car and the plate was sent to the New York Police Department and to our New York Field Office. Why they didn't tell us at the time is unknown. Doesn't matter, not much we could do from here.

"Anyway, NYPD found the car on a routine patrol. Some hotshot with a BMW had called the cops because he couldn't get out of a parking spot. An Audi jammed up against his front end."

"Where?" Zimmerman asked.

"Uh, Front Street? It's—"

Macallister, once again a fountain of local knowledge, cut off Lewis. "It's near the Brooklyn Bridge. NYPD got cameras everywhere in that neighborhood. I bet we can find her. But, shit, it ain't gonna be easy. She's got another fucking huge head start on us!"

12

SAME DAY, SAME TIME —
CROSSING THE BROOKLYN BRIDGE, NEW YORK

TO THE WEST, THE SETTING SUN had taken on a fiery orange color, casting a pinkish-reddish-orangey glow on granite-and-limestone-clad towers and the chunky metal cables of the 135-year-old Brooklyn Bridge as Anastasia Volkov ambled from the island of Manhattan to Brooklyn. The raised, wood-planked center pedestrian lane of the bridge was crowded with commuters and tourists, and the ponytailed-figure was virtually indistinguishable in a sea of people.

After working her way down the stairs at the eastern terminus of the pedestrian walkway in Brooklyn, Volkov headed south in the chilly, darkening evening, grateful for the overcoat that she had pilfered from the hospital. Eight short blocks and one very long block later, she found herself gazing at the sign for the Brooklyn Heights Public Library, currently housed in a church after its original location was converted to high-priced condos and before construction on a new building had begun.

All she wanted—no, needed, and required—was internet access in an anonymous place. *This will do nicely*, she thought.

With the library closing at 6:00 PM, she had to hurry, and she scampered inside to find a public computer. There were none to be seen in the downsized, temporary facility.

Noting the ponytailed woman ferreting around the interior, an elderly desk clerk had called out, "Ma'am? Can I be of assistance?"

Volkov painted her face with her friendliest smile. "I was hoping to use a computer briefly. Do you have anything I can use?"

"'Fraid not," the man replied. "We have a laptop loan program, though."

"Perfect," Volkov grinned.

"Can I see your library card?"

The grin vanished from her face, and Volkov stammered, as innocently as she could, "Oh, no, sorry! I left my wallet and phone back at the hospital, and I only just realized that after walking across the bridge. It will take *forever* to walk back. I was hoping to send a quick email." She flipped Carolina Barrington's ID casually but quickly at the aging clerk, who squinted at it, the letters too difficult to read, and the image on the photo a blur as the woman tucked it back into a plastic bag containing what appeared to be surgical scrubs.

Apprising the nice, young, casually-dressed doctor in front of him, the clerk smiled, "Oh, well, that's not a problem. A quick email," he repeated, as he gestured to the PC monitor at his desk.

"So much appreciated. How can I thank you?" Volkov babbled as she quickly opened a browser screen, selected incognito mode, and logged into a Gmail account. In a matter of seconds, she dashed off a note and clicked on the *Send* icon, closing out the browser screen with a flourish and a big smile. "Thank you. *Lifesaver!* Really appreciate it."

Before the clerk could reply, Volkov bolted to the door, the clerk thinking in her wake, *These young people are in such a hurry these days.* Eyeing the computer screen, he shrugged and went back to his tasks.

Three hours later, walking slowly, Volkov shivered, a combination of cold, and fear, and frustration. *Too long in one spot*, she thought, lips clenched tightly together in frustration. *I have to move on.*

The tiny hairs on the back of her neck tingled. *Settle down*, she commanded herself. *Wait! Patience!*

Volkov considered the email she had sent from the library clerk's computer.

The message was simple enough. And within that message, she herself had set the timetable:

> *I'm outside the Brooklyn Heights Public Library. 109 Remson Street. Come get me as soon as you can. I will wait 'til midnight. Flash your high beams four times when you are here. The Wolf.*

Midnight.

She had sent the message just before 6:00 PM. A six-hour wait. A six-hour window, which would be a reasonable enough time for the email to be received. It couldn't be helped.

But still, it was three more hours to wait. Three more hours before she would discover if the fail-safe plan was still active. And, three more hours for the FBI to find her, as she walked around the block, occasionally ducking into an alleyway.

This is a terrible plan, she chastised herself.

But I have no other options.

She sighed, pulled the overcoat tighter against her chest, and walked, reminding herself, *No! I have plenty of other options. I am the wolf. Give it time. If he doesn't show, I'll do it alone.*

SAME DAY, 9:42 PM — SHEEPSHEAD BAY, NEW YORK

PULLING UP THE BACK-RIGHT hem of his brown leather jacket, Dmitri Tretriaki pulled his billfold from the back pocket of his jeans. Squinting in the dim light, he extracted two twenty-dollar bills from an unsorted, wrinkled mess of notes, and he laid the Jacksons on the polished mahogany bar top.

"Early night?" the barkeep commented.

"Yeah. I think so, Dean," Tretriaki responded. "Keep the change."

The bartender nodded with just the tiniest bit of a faint smile, not one for emotion. In a single, practiced motion, he swiped up the bills with his left hand even as his right hand passed a cloth unnecessarily over the spot where the bills had laid atop the wood.

Tretriaki shoved his wallet back into his jeans and stood, brushing absently at a lock of longish, blond hair at his forehead. He paused, looking down at the bar. "Shit," he muttered, grabbing at the display-down iPhone that he had almost left behind.

He flipped the device over and checked the screen, scanning the notifications.

"Shit!" he blurted loudly. The bartender watched as Tretriaki's face blanched before the blond rushed outside.

Settling into the driver's seat of his Mercedes sedan, Tretriaki re-read the short email. He hadn't recognized the email sender's name, but the signature was unmistakable:

I'm outside the Brooklyn Heights Public Library. 109 Remson Street. Come get me as soon as you can. I will wait 'til midnight. Flash your high beams four times when you are here. The Wolf.

That was a message to be ignored at his peril.

✳ ✳ ✳

A few minutes past midnight, inside a quiet, darkened apartment in Brighton Beach, New York, Dmitri Tretriaki tilted a clear vodka bottle first toward his visitor's glass, then to his own, the liquid dribbling over a few tinkling cubes in each glass.

"Sorry again for the wait," Tretriaki whispered, as he poured. Setting the bottle down gently on a polished wood table, he brushed a truss of long blond hair from his tanned face, exposing his whitened teeth as he smiled at his guest.

"Of course, it's nothing," his visitor replied, kindly. "I'm happy you finally checked your email. I was getting cold, despite myself. And I was worried that, perhaps, you didn't, well, exist anymore. It's been a very, very long time since this was all set up."

"Indeed. I've wondered, often, whether that email account would have a message. I've checked it dutifully for years. That was my only assignment. And, as you know, anything you need is yours. What the wolf wants, the wolf gets," Tretriaki purred obsequiously.

"Thank you," Anastasia Volkov replied, sipping at the vodka, taking care not to swallow too much after her seventeen months of forced abstinence from alcohol. It was delicious, nonetheless, a slight burn in her throat followed by a mellow glow in her gut. She allowed the drink to relax her.

Dmitri Tretriaki waited for his visitor to give him his instructions; she merely stared into the abyss of the glass of clear liquid as she slowly swirled the vodka to and fro. Finally, she sighed, murmuring, "They'll be waiting for me. But it cannot be helped. And I can defeat them, don't you think?"

She glanced up at Tretriaki, who didn't dare respond verbally but nodded slightly. Taking that as affirmation, she continued, "Oh, yes, I know their ways. I can make a plan from here, yes? And, he would do it for me. We've both suffered for long enough."

She raised the glass toward her lips, adding, "Let's go get my father."

With that, Anastasia Volkov, christened at birth as Irinushka Petrikov, tossed back the remaining vodka in one authentically Russian gulp.

14

WEDNESDAY, NOVEMBER 14, 2018 — FBI BOSTON FIELD OFFICE, CHELSEA, MASSACHUSETTS

I WOKE WITH A HAND ON MY shoulder. The hand belonged to Agent Amber Jones. Through drooping, crusty eyelids, I wondered what she was doing in my bedroom, standing over me.

With a start, I realized that I was not in my bedroom. I was still in the dimly-lit operations center in Chelsea. Sitting in one of the ubiquitous, imitation Aeron swivel chairs. I wondered what the sensation on the left side of my mouth was, hoping it was not drool.

As casually as I could, I stretched my shoulders back, and then ran both hands through the hair on my scalp, conveniently passing my left wrist by my mouth. It *was* drool. Gross. I hoped no one had noticed.

Unfortunately, I was wrong. *Again.*

"Hey. You have a nice nap?" Agent Jones asked as she passed me a handkerchief. "You dozed off. Not that you missed anything. I woke you up because, um, you were, um . . ." She let that hang.

I finished her sentence. "Drooling. Right. Got it. Thanks."

"No problem."

"Any updates?"

She shook her head back and forth, saying, "Not really. No. Not since the review of the NYPD cameras found her on the Brooklyn Bridge."

"That was the last sighting? Our New York field office got nothing more? NYPD got nothing?" I asked.

"Unfortunately, yeah, the hit on the Brooklyn Bridge was the last one," Jones replied. "The field office coordinated tightly with NYPD. They got two hits near the car, in the Seaport Area. One by the Titanic Memorial Park. One at DeLury Square. Then there were three sightings near New York-Presbyterian hospital. Then the last visual. At the bridge," she recited.

"And she had changed her outfit between the hospital cameras and the bridge. Have we got anything from the agents at the hospital yet?"

"No," answered Connelly, who, apparently while I slept, had created another list on one of the whiteboards in the operations center. This time, instead of potential destinations for Volkov, she had recorded actual physical sightings of our missing jailbreaker. "We have four, or six, maybe, of our agents in the hospital, questioning everyone they can find. She goes in wearing the scrubs. She comes out wearing black pants and an overcoat, carrying a plastic bag."

I shook my head in disbelief. "That was yesterday afternoon. No one reported anything missing? What time is it now, anyway?"

"Seven-thirty," Jones stated, angling her watch toward me.

I can't believe I fell asleep during an investigation, I thought. *Real professional, Special Agent Porter. In the midst of a manhunt with FBI, NYPD, and probably Homeland Security. Ugh.*

I shook off the nap cobwebs and my insecurity. I needed sleep. If the rest of the squad stayed up all night, so be it. I wheeled my chair closer to the worktable as Jones added, "That last camera sighting was at sunset yesterday, on the bridge. She's been off-grid for about fifteen hours. Each minute that goes by, the search radius gets larger. Even if she managed to walk out of Brooklyn, she could be miles away. Assuming she didn't double back on the bridge. Duck into a bus. Hail a cab."

"Yeah," said Zimmerman brusquely, impatiently. He looked annoyed as he added, "and we know she might have some money. One nurse at the hospital reported that she was missing a credit card from the wallet in her purse. The purse was in her locker. No cameras in the locker rooms, obviously. She said she remembered having more cash too. It's possible Volkov took not only the card, but she also nabbed some cash too."

"She's smart enough not to use that stolen credit card unless she absolutely has to. She knows that once the card is reported missing, we will flag it, and a second or two after it gets swiped, we will have that location," I countered.

"But if she's got a few bucks in cash, and she's got herself a cab ride," Zimmerman pouted.

I wanted to say, *Yeah, well, duh, that's obvious*, but I bit my tongue, having learned my lesson yesterday to keep my opinions to myself and to focus on the facts. "Have we worked up a profile yet?"

Macallister actually laughed. "A profile? Of course. Fucking useless, though. First off, we know her story is bullshit. And second, we know that she knows all our tricks. All our methods."

"We're missing something," I said. "Let's bullet point it. Connelly, you wanna scribe again? You got nice handwriting."

"We're gonna need a bigger board," Brenda Connelly chuckled as she pantomimed drawing a whiteboard marker from her holster. Grins from around the table, as I thought, *We've gone past the point of work to foolishness, or we are just getting reengaged. I wonder which?*

An hour later, Connelly had filled a second whiteboard with her careful, multicolored characters, writing, then erasing, then writing again as we fleshed out a wordy picture of our target.

Anastasia Volkov. Female. Presumed to be age 32. Unable to verify age.

BACKGROUND.
   Alleged, proved to be false: Ukrainian orphan. Adopted by American family.
   Verified: Computer science graduate, MIT, with honors.
   Hired at FBI in 2008. New intelligence analyst training at Quantico, 2008, top of her class. How did she get past the FBI background check?

OPERATION E.T.
   Assumed but not proven she texted the terrorists during the operation.
   Proven that she called Petrikov after FBI learned how to track the
      terrorists.
   Proven that she called the lead terrorist after she called Petrikov.
   Proven that she murdered Vanessa Raiden.
   Proven that she attempted to murder, or confront, Ben Porter.

PRESENT DAY.
   Proven that she escaped Walter Reed and last seen on the Brooklyn
      Bridge.
   Potential targets:
      Boston – Ben Porter
      Boston – home for supplies
      Petrikov
      Petrikov's apartments, homes, or accomplices

Together, we studied the list. Macallister, who had been reasonably well-behaved as the squad had cooperated to build out the profile, leaned back in his chair, crossed his arms over his chest, and stated, "You forgot the part when she blew up my car."

Laughter from around the table. That story had become somewhat legendary within the **FBI**. After the discovery of Raiden's body, I was pretty shaken up, and I needed to tell someone what Raiden had told me: that she suspected an insider, either Appleton or Volkov, had been in contact with the terrorists from within our Chelsea building. Macallister and I had gone to a local pub to talk it over away from the possibly prying ears of the two suspects. When we left, Macallister walked me to my car, and when he pushed the button on his key fob to unlock his car a short distance away—it exploded.

Goes to show the lengths that Volkov went to eliminate the tracks of those who she figured knew about her treachery.

Laughter aside—not to mention also setting aside the fairly humorous postscript of Macallister's difficulties when he tried to make an insurance claim to replace his burned-out Range Rover, a process that did not go well for him since the car was destroyed in such odd circumstances, which, of course, he could not explain given the cloak of confidentiality wrapped around the case—something else gnawed at me.

"You know, Macallister, you got a point there," I said quietly. The chortles around the table fell silent as we got back to work. "*You* may also be a target. Your name, I'm afraid, should be on that list too."

Macallister nodded his agreement, and Connelly uncapped her weapon—er, marker—and wrote *Boston – Bradford Macallister* as an entry in the "potential targets" list.

We stared at the board. Finally, Zimmerman opined, "And one more target. Unknown." He air-quoted unknown. I thought that was pretty obvious, but I agreed that it was good practice to acknowledge that our profile was far from definitive.

Appleton had remained quiet during our exercise, occasionally flitting from the operations center to do something else but consistently dropping back in to watch the profile take shape on the whiteboard. She was engaged as everyone else; after all, Volkov had been a standout figure in Appleton's field office, and having a star turn traitor didn't look all that good for Appleton herself. I sensed this was not only a point of professional pride to resolve this case, but that it was also very personal to the SAC.

She rose from her chair at the far end of the worktable, furthest from the whiteboard, and, placing her hands on the table and leaning forward, commanded, "Okay. That's our profile. You're going to split the targets and take responsibility for each one. Dig deep. Protection, counter-measures, anticipation."

One-by-one, she made eye contact with each of us as she gave us our assignments, speaking slowly and clearly.

"Zimmerman. Jones. You're on Boston. You're gaming out what we do if she comes home. What we do to surveil her home and her local contacts. What Porter and Macallister do to stay safe. Put a team together.

"Connelly. Jordon. You got Petrikov. We closed up his properties, but you need to get surveillance on all of them. On all his known associates."

Scanning the faces to make sure that there was no confusion, she zeroed in on the senior agent. "Macallister. You all report to Macallister.

Every detail. Put the picture together. Macallister reports to me on a priority basis. Got it?" Heads nodded. We had a plan to act on.

Appleton circled the table so that she stood opposite me, and with her hands on her hips, lobbed the impossible at me. "Porter. You're the one agent who worked with Volkov during Operation E.T. You're on the unknowns. Start from today and work backward. Could she flee the country? Does she hole up somewhere? Does she link up with potential accomplices from the E.T. case? Maybe," she glanced at the whiteboard list, "you're missing a target. Miles Lockwood. The owner of the boat. The guy that foiled her last plot. Maybe she goes after him for revenge. Start making a list of *everything* and *everyone.*"

The SAC spun smartly on her heels and disappeared. The agents who had been paired up leaned into Macallister and began to strategize their assignments. I leaned back in my chair, once more staring down the whiteboard as if it would give me a new clue. But I got nothing, except a feeling that I had an unreachable goal that might only be solved with a bullet in my back, or a bullet in Volkov.

I greatly preferred the latter.

15

FOUR WEEKS LATER:
TUESDAY, DECEMBER 11, 2018 —
FBI BOSTON FIELD OFFICE, CHELSEA, MASSACHUSETTS

AT 5:20 AM, I WOKE, SENSING something amiss. I carefully opened one eye.

I saw a red dot at the center of my vision.

I opened the other eye. Same dot.

Laser gunsight. Aimed at me. I knew it was her. Behind the gun. *Volkov.*

I froze. I could feel the sweat. Clammy. Wet. My heartbeat raced. I closed my eyes and waited for the shot.

It would not come. I would be spared for another day. For this morning, like almost every morning, it was that same, recurring dream. And the red dot would turn out to be merely the power indicator on the phone at my bedside table.

It sucks to live as a target.

Especially when you knew that the potential shooter that was aiming at you was a wily and cunning mastermind who had successfully lived a double life for years, who was accustomed to being invisible, and who not only fooled the FBI from the inside, but also eluded them from the outside.

A month.

A solid month, and Anastasia Volkov had vanished, since last being spotted by a camera on the Brooklyn Bridge. She was gone, into the vast anonymity of…

Of where? Of New York? Boston? The United States? The planet? We had no clue.

Therefore, we circled the wagons, so to speak, and did what we could. The Bureau was great. We took care of our own. No expense was spared with a protective detail for both Macallister and me.

But, after the novelty wears off, in a matter of days, really, the circle of protection around you morphs from a comforting security blanket into a stifling straightjacket. Every step you take, every outing to a store for a six-pack, every commute to the office, becomes a burden.

Will this be the day I'm attacked?

Weekends were the worst. The first weekend, I tried to keep it normal, but after Saturday, trying to get some benign errands done, I felt like an idiot, with my two protective agents with their earpieces and collar microphones leading and trailing my every move. I stayed put on Sunday. Not only were the outings awkward, but I also felt guilty, too, subjecting my fellow agents to the inconvenience of spending their weekends with me.

After that first weekend, I decided simply to work. And I would spend Saturdays and Sundays at the office. Some of those days were, admittedly, less productive than they could have been, with searches on the internet that turned into trips down rabbit holes I didn't know existed (like when I retraced Volkov's steps in New York, and delved deep into the history of not only the Brooklyn Bridge but also the other bridges that crossed the waterways around New York City and the tunnels that cut under the dirt at the bottoms of the rivers, including the Holland Tunnel—incredibly fascinating stuff if you have the time, which I did).

But if weekends were the worst, the Thanksgiving holiday was the absolute pits.

My family lives in nearby Rhode Island, about an hour's drive from Boston. And I have a big immediate family: my parents plus an older sister, Grace, and a younger brother, Joe. And a concept that I avoided, but which the Bureau and my protection detail most definitely considered, was that now every member of my family was a target too.

That made Thanksgiving dinner *really* tough. On my immediate family, and especially on my mom, who was already petrified that her middle child had become a gun-toting FBI Special Agent and who now required constant security, but also on the aunts and uncles and cousins and friends who would stop by. And yes, it was tough on me too. I know that's selfish, but, for me, the difficulty was the guilt. I didn't want to put them, or anyone, in this situation; this place where you have this unknown, unseen threat that clouds your every waking and sleeping hour.

It. Sucked.

Macallister became my confidante and my go-to. It was tough on him too. But, if we were together, it halved the security requirements and gave a bunch of agents a break. He understood the pressure that I was feeling first-hand and empathized with the guilt. We hung out a lot together. Which was somewhat ironic, considering that when I was working as a nobody, before the Operation E.T. case, I hated him.

Now he was, almost by default, my best friend. And we shared the gallows humor of two people in an untenable situation—in a way, we both wanted Volkov to come out of hiding and make her move. And if and when that happened, we both wanted to come out alive. Obviously.

In the meantime, the investigation, however, went nowhere.

As the days and weeks passed, we become less convinced that our theories were accurate.

We would meet as a squad daily, at 8:30 AM, review the prior day's work, and plan for the new day. Often, the reports were perfunctory. "Nothing new" became the standard refrain. It was frustrating.

In addition to the 24/7 perimeter around both Macallister and me, we had human and electronic surveillance on Volkov's condo complex locally and Petrikov's penthouse apartment in Manhattan. The 235-foot expedition-style motor yacht, where we had apprehended Petrikov over a year ago, was under guard in a US Navy facility in Norfolk, Virginia, and his smaller vessels, and all the vehicles that we could track to his ownership, had been confiscated by the government. We had agents and the NYPD patrolling every area that Petrikov had frequented, including his old haunts in the Brighton Beach and Sheepshead Bay neighbor-hoods on the perimeter of the New York City borough of Brooklyn. And finally, in nearby Cohasset, Massachusetts, we had agents tailing Miles Lockwood's every move, sometimes surreptitiously, and some-times overtly, just to demonstrate to Volkov, if she was watching, that we were watching too.

Yet, Anastasia Volkov remained at large. Unseen.

Equally invisible, even to our squad in Boston, was the mastermind of it all: the Russian immigrant who had bankrolled the Operation E.T. terror threat, and who we had arrested in September 2017.

"He's untouchable," SAC Appleton assured the squad at this morn-ing's meeting, continuing, "Petrikov might as well be a ghost, hidden away behind the tightest security imaginable. In an undisclosed location."

"Great," I replied. "All the more reason for Volkov to focus on us. On me. How about you tell us where Petrikov is, we leak that tidbit of info to the press, and we go wait for her there? Get this over with."

"It doesn't work like that, Agent Porter," sniffed the SAC. "Besides, if you can't find him, neither can she. Petrikov is *infinitely* untouchable."

Right, I thought, once more wisely keeping my opinion to myself before going all sarcastic on the SAC—which would not be a good career move, probably. *She adds "infinitely" to untouchable, and that's supposed to inspire us with some level of confidence?*

I didn't feel reassured in the slightest.

16

SAME TIME — IN THE AREA OF MOUNT TABOR, VERMONT

TO OUTSIDERS, THE STATE OF Vermont was arguably best known for Ben and Jerry's ice cream brand, but "real" Vermonters might question that. "Flatlanders" came to Vermont for the ice cream or maybe for the maple syrup. Flatlanders were also described as "leaf peepers" who make an annual migration north for the spectacular fall foliage or are transients from Connecticut, Massachusetts, New York, or New Jersey who drive north on weekends during the winter ski season. And, while some Flatlanders might have owned vacation homes in the state and might tag their fancy four wheel drive SUVs with a distinctive green Vermont license plate, they were not *real* Vermonters.

Real Vermonters have lived in the state for generations, and while they might have appreciated the dollars brought to their bucolic home by the Flatlanders, what they really appreciated was the pure beauty of the state, its bountiful natural resources, and its thousands of square miles of untouched forests.

The United States government also appreciated those miles of forest, but for a completely different reason.

Solitude.

And solitude meant security.

Continuing across the Massachusetts border, at almost the southern-most and western-most corner of Vermont, US Route 7 runs north in the western half of the state until it terminates a few miles south of the Canadian border. It's a long, winding, 176-mile journey, in parts a divided highway but mostly a rural-feeling two-lane road, as it skirts the ski areas of southern Vermont, runs past the college town of Middlebury, and northward toward Canada through the heart of bustling Burlington.

About forty-eight miles from the Massachusetts border, or an hour's drive on a mostly two-lane road, Route 7 passes through the tiny town of Mount Tabor. Population: about 255. Significant source of municipal revenue, according to a 2018 study done by Vermont Public Radio: a speed trap on Route 7.

While the leaf-peepers might learn, the hard way, to slow down passing through town, the campers and hikers heading to the Green Mountain State Forest knew to brake to turn onto Brooklyn Road in order to reach the trailhead maintained by the US Forest Service. The Forest Service vehicles, often either a Chevrolet Suburban SUV or a Ford F-150 pickup truck, marked with the green-and-yellow logo of the Forest Service, were, therefore, a familiar sight in the little town.

And, when one of those inauspicious Chevrolet Suburbans had cruised past the trailhead on a Tuesday in April 2018, one might have assumed it was traveling for routine forest work. It would have taken an especially astute observer to notice that this particular Forest Service-logoed SUV was equipped with especially dark window glass, or that the clearance from the tops of the wheel arches to the tires was significantly tighter than usual due to the weight of the heavily-armored vehicle and, perhaps, due to the weight of the manacled occupant seated in the caged rear area.

Anatoly Petrikov, held as an enemy combatant to the United States, had been transferred from his prison cell in Manhattan in the bowels of the FBI Field Office in New York City to a new location: a clandestine, off-the-books, highly-secured government campus, well-hidden deep in the thick and virtually impenetrable Green Mountain Forest of southern Vermont.

Petrikov had not been a model prisoner during his seven-month stay in New York, after being transported there by a Black Hawk helicopter upon his arrest on Tuesday, September 26, 2017, when a daring squad of FBI Critical Incident Response Group (CIRG) agents had stormed his 235-foot yacht, at anchor in a Long Island, New York bay, and forcibly removed the fat oligarch from his comfortable bed in the middle of the night.

With the evidence compiled by the FBI, Petrikov had been implicated in a plot to detonate two nuclear dirty bombs in New York and Chicago. The trail of evidence ran clear across the Atlantic Ocean to Turkey, where the plot had originated, and Petrikov's virtual fingerprints were impossible to dispute: money transfers were backtracked that purchased the supplies and vehicles to effect the plot and were detailed by banking records; texts and calls to burner phones to his accomplices were exhaustively traced; and recorded security camera video evidence placed Petrikov near the scene of the murder of one of his own operatives.

Unfortunately, with that murder, Petrikov effectively silenced the one individual who had first-hand knowledge of the plot. Four other smaller players remained in custody, but their value was minimal. They were hired thugs, told exactly what to do and when to do it, and while they had pled guilty in exchange for sentences as prisoners as opposed to enemy combatants, they brought little evidence of value to implicating Petrikov.

Petrikov had immigrated to the United States from Russia as an eight year old in 1960 with his mother, who subsequently disappeared. The FBI's painstaking investigation found that his involvement with crime had been ongoing since as early as the late eighties or early nineties, as the Bureau unarchived old files and belatedly discovered a suspicious link between Petrikov and the Russian-leaning crime group that operated out of Brighton Beach, New York. For months, as investigators dug into files, interviewers would sit with Petrikov, asking question after question. The handcuffed prisoner would respond in guttural Russian (with curses, according to the translators) or with lies, meant to send the investigators off on useless tangents. It had been taxing and frustrating work for the interviewers and investigators alike.

The evidence that the Bureau had continued to assemble, despite Petrikov's penchant for deceptions, was considered incontrovertible.

Petrikov had assembled his outrageous wealth with the illicit trade of precious stones, outright bribes, and extortion. The Bureau reinvestigated the death of Petrikov's wife, Irina, in 2015 and deemed it "suspicious." The couple had given birth to a daughter, named Irinushka, who had disappeared in 1996 as Petrikov rose to prominence in the New York arm of the Russian mafia. The investigators concluded that she was dead, theorizing that the daughter had been killed by either an internal faction of the mafia in retribution for something Petrikov did, or, quite possibly, slain by her own father so that he could eliminate a potential future bargaining chip against him.

The Russian oligarch was considered a psychopath. A brutal, calculating, cold man who feared nothing—and who certainly had no fear for the long arm of American law enforcement.

With no fruition coming from the sessions in New York, a decision was made to move the criminal to a secure location as the case was built around him, without his cooperation, and he was moved to the secret facility in Vermont.

Arriving in Vermont in April, Anatoly Petrikov couldn't believe his luck. He had a window. And, though partially obstructed by a tall concrete wall and eventually by the leaves that filled in as spring warmed, he had a rather nice view of a forest and, in the distance, a twinkling lake.

Now, in December, the early winter snows had covered the drooping evergreens with a glistening coat of white ice, and the surface of the lake no longer twinkled with wavelets but glared with a thin, frozen sheen. Despite not having been in his homeland of Russia since boyhood, Petrikov felt quite at home.

The accommodations were a far cry from the luxurious master suite on his yacht or the sumptuous penthouse in New York that he once occupied. But, for the stoic oligarch, the room would be a comfortable place to wait as he watched the seasons change outside his window, waiting for his compatriots to come and free him, as he knew they would.

His room was furnished with only a bed and a writing desk, accompanied by a reasonably comfortable chair. Like the larger pieces, the chair was bolted to the floor but swiveled partially left and right. A small partition partially shielded a sink and toilet from view, not that anyone would care to watch Petrikov defecate.

There was a single steel grill in the ceiling by the window which blew warm or cold, depending on the season, and a second steel grill over the steel door to return the exhaust air from the room. Adjacent to the return air grill was a black dome, a camera, for certain.

Meals were delivered through the opened steel door by an unspeaking, armed guard, always with at least one, usually two, guards visible in the darkened corridor outside the room. The food was fresh and nutritious, if not uninspired.

He knew the camera watched him, for the door would open after he finished eating so that the armed guard could remove the tray, the leftovers, and the plastic utensils. Some days, to amuse himself, he would dine especially slowly, to see if they rushed him. They never did. If he ate quickly, gobbling up the food, the instant the plate was clean, the door would open, and the mute guard would reappear.

He had, of course, no communication to the outside world. He could request books, which he did frequently, and he was given months-old newspapers to read. To keep his brain sharp, he had asked for a chess set. He would play solo for hours, moves and countermoves, working out strategies. And, he requested a pull up bar, which had been installed with bolts into the ceiling by the door, so he could exercise on his own. He remained quite large, but he was not at all soft or weak.

The monotony of the interviews in the concrete-block-walled holding rooms had been replaced with hours of inactivity, staring out the thick, presumably bulletproof, pane of glass that afforded the welcome natural light into his cell. The prisoner was allowed to leave his quarters once daily for fresh air outside. He was manacled and escorted by two unspeaking armed guards in full tactical gear. The trio of walkers would complete several circuits of a walled, windowless but roofless courtyard, and then Petrikov would be returned to his room.

When he was out of the room, he knew it was cleaned and searched. The searchers were always careful to return things to where he had left them. The chess pieces may have been moved slightly, but they remained in their proper squares.

Until this morning.

Petrikov was nothing if not observant. He had made his fortune, after all, both by reading the intricacies of precious stones and by studying the faces of those who examined them. Had he cared to, he could have been a formidable poker player; his expressions generally remained placid and controlled. After all, he had once mingled with the glitterati of New York, and as Tony Petrikov, he had guffawed and charmed his way into the uppermost social circles of the City with his charisma and infectious belly laugh. He was skilled at noticing the tiny details, no matter how random they seemed.

A guard change was not unusual; the unspeaking sentries came and went weekly. During his months at the facility, he noticed a new face once a week. He had lost track of the actual day of the week, but no matter; he could still count to seven and very soon after arriving to his new quarters, somewhat for lack of anything better to do, but more just because of his innate curiosity, he began to keep a mental count of the days and the guards.

When a new, unsmiling face had delivered his morning meal, he had given it no thought. Business as usual; it was rotation day.

But when he had returned from his afternoon daily exercise with the tactical team, and when Petrikov had examined his chess set, he knew something was afoot.

As usual, Petrikov had been taken outside for his circle of the walled courtyard. It was a bitterly cold, mid-December day. The sun cast weak, midwinter warmth into the yard under a bluebird, cloudless sky. The trio made their circuit silently as usual, puffing moisture-laden miniature clouds of breath as they exhaled.

Petrikov enjoyed the cold. It reminded him of the freezing night in December that he finally rid himself of his wife, the cheating, botoxed bitch that he had carved into little pieces and then dumped into the Atlantic Ocean. He had brought along her two ridiculous, tiny dogs; fluffy, white, yapping annoyances that he had tied together with a weight and dropped over the side of his boat into the cold Atlantic waters. As the helpless little animals had struggled to remain afloat, he had watched with mirth as one would splutter to the surface as the other dipped below the inky swell, pulled by the relentless tug of the weight Petrikov had attached to their tied-together leashes. As he reveled in their slow-motion drowning, he had puffed a cigar that night, and the puffs of breath in the cold air today appeared, to him, as little clouds of cigar smoke.

He was in a reflective and happy state of mind, remembering that pleasing night when he was returned to his quarters. The heavy steel door clanged shut behind Petrikov. With a metallic snick, the bolt slid home.

Petrikov inspected his room, standing stock-still. Only his eyes moved, at first, until he spotted something different. And then, the corner of his mouth curled into an almost imperceptible grin.

Because he saw, positioned on their little squares, every single chess piece faced the window.

chapter 17

SAME DAY, 4:53 PM —
FBI BOSTON FIELD OFFICE, CHELSEA, MASSACHUSETTS

THE SQUAD HAD ASSEMBLED, once again, in the operations center, a place where we were surrounded by a stunning amount of information technology that had failed us miserably in the one task that we had: locating Anastasia Volkov.

But this time was different. The operations center was packed with agents and analysts alike. I couldn't find even find a seat at the large conference table, so I stood. Macallister had gotten a seat, as had Zimmerman. He had probably shoved someone out of the way to nab it.

The field office agents and staff had been summoned to the room with urgency by a frantic Louis Lewis. When the Information Analyst was excited or flustered, his spiky hair seemed to protrude higher and straighter. I had noticed this at sporadic times over the past month while working with him, but never dared to mention it. Lewis had slipped nicely into the technical assistance role that Vanessa Raiden had played, and he never complained about the increased workload, though his excitable outbursts were sometimes, in my opinion, unnecessary.

This late afternoon, though, his eyes told a different story—behind his purple-framed eyeglasses, those eyes were wide with discovery.

Even Special Agent in Charge Appleton had made an appearance. Lewis had actually called her office and demanded that she come down to the operations center. The SAC looked annoyed or bemused; to have her attention commanded by an Information Analyst was typically unprecedented. It's not like she had nothing better to do; even with our squad plugging away on this case, the SAC, of course, had plenty of other cases under review out of her field office.

Whatever words Lewis had spoken to her must have gotten her immediate attention and leaped to the top of her priority list. The SAC had been deferentially given the chair at the very middle of the huge table. I waited for the big reveal once she had taken her seat.

With the field office assembled, annoyed, mostly, at this interruption to their end-of-the-day routine, Lewis finally stood from his stool at his workstation and addressed the crowd around the massive conference table. Suddenly under the pressure of the stares that he himself had invited, he stammered, "Uh. Yes. Yes. Um, thank you for coming. It's, um, it's—"

Appleton leaned back in her chair and crossed her arms over her chest, her cold eyes drilling Lewis. The SAC was well-known for her dismissal of anything that wasted her time. Lewis apparently got the nonverbal message, composed himself, and started over.

"Yes. It's come to my attention today that we've seen abnormal traffic at our system firewall. To our servers here in Boston. From the outside, of course. Now, this is not unusual. We are subjected to attack, digital attack, daily. Hourly. But this is different."

"It started last night," Lewis continued. "I didn't know about it. I didn't see the pattern, the increased activity, until about noonish, one-ish, this afternoon, when this change in the normal network traffic was escalated to my attention. But once it got my attention, I went back to see when it started. The first ping was at precisely 9:00 PM last night. This, alone, would be nothing serious or alarming, but since then, it grew steadily in intensity and in frequency."

Zimmerman interrupted. "Whadya mean, you didn't see it? Then you noticed it?"

Lewis shrugged and explained, "Like I said, we get this sort of stuff every day. The technical staff monitors it all day, of course. But once it got to a certain level, it got kicked up to me. It's not like I, personally, sit around watching traffic at the firewall all day, waiting. But when it was escalated to me, it became my priority."

"Oh," Zimmerman huffed, reclining back in his chair.

"Anyway, by midafternoon, around two, the traffic had gotten heavy enough to be alarming, and I sent a message out system-wide to see if other field offices were getting the same types of attacks. I wasn't keeping track, like a map or something, which was probably a mistake. I shoulda been thinking that way." Lewis' voice trailed off.

Appleton immediately jumped in. "*And*? I don't like where this is heading."

Lewis straightened his shoulders and replied, "Over a little while, I got a bunch of negative responses. What I should have looked for, and it's obvious now, I guess, was nonresponses. By the time I realized that, I started making phone calls. Then I called all of you."

He paused. The suspense lingered, unnecessarily, and I was sure Appleton was going to explode. And by explode, I mean get colder than cold itself—which history had proved was not something one of her underlings wanted to experience.

"The attacks have reached a crescendo level on our servers. Our abilities to communicate externally are being limited by the sheer volume of the incoming hits, which are meant to accomplish exactly that. If you've sent an email, for example, you won't notice, but it's not going out right away. If you direct-message, same thing—the recipient won't get it right away. It's all delayed. Even most of our phone lines, which work through internet protocol, are affected. You can still dial out, of course, but if you pick up a handset for a call, there's a moment of silence while the system looks for an open line. Incoming call volume has dropped.

"I tell you this because once I realized that I was not getting responses to the messages that I sent that normally would have been returned right away by my counterparts, I resorted to our back-up POTS lines."

"What the hell are potslines?" Macallister snarled, clearly out of patience for the technical explanation.

"Plain Old Telephone Service lines," answered Lewis. "Analog. Got it? Old school."

"The point, please. Now!" Appleton demanded.

"Right. Not a single field office nationwide, other than us, was being hit. However, our satellite offices—the four resident agencies in a direct radius around us, here in Boston, are the only ones nationwide under attack. Exactly the same symptoms. *Exactly* the same timing."

Lewis reached back to his workstation and tapped a few keys. On a large monitor overhead, in view from anyone at the table, a map of the area appeared on-screen. In the center was a large red dot, marking our office's location just outside Boston. In quick succession, four smaller red dots appeared on the map: the Boston division satellite offices in Bedford, New Hampshire, and in Providence, Rhode Island, and here in Massachusetts, to the northwest, Lowell, and to the south, toward Cape Cod, Lakeville.

I had remained silent for the duration of this explanation, but upon seeing the map, it was instantly obviously to me. *How did Lewis not see this earlier?* I wondered, before I announced my conclusion to the room, "That is *not* a coincidence. We're surrounded. Looks like an attempt at isolation."

"Exactly!" Lewis proclaimed. "But," he paused before asking plaintively, "for . . . what?"

"Whaddya mean, for what? We're under some sort of digital attack, obviously!" Macallister yelled, a complete contrast to Appleton, who remained mute and unmoving.

Lewis shook his head. "Yeah. It's some kind of attack, for sure. But other than slowing traffic, it' . . . it's . . . Well, it's harmless, pretty much. And that's what I don't understand."

He pulled off his eyeglasses in frustration and rubbed the bridge of his nose, elaborating on his confusion, "It's not some sort of denial-of-service attack. We don't see any attempts to actually enter the system, and nothing has penetrated the firewall. Our systems are all functioning, just slower than usual. But..."

His voice faded, and Appleton, exasperated, hissed, "But what? You called us here because our systems are slowed to the point of non-responsiveness, but you don't know why? What, exactly, is happening? In plain words. Now."

Louis Lewis shrugged, "We're being isolated because someone is pinging madly at our firewall. But why? I have no idea."

I had an idea, pinging around in my mind. But, unfortunately, then, I wasn't able to articulate it. And my lack of clarity would make for a very, very stressful night.

18

SAME DAY, 9:05 PM — OUTSIDE OF MOUNT TABOR, VERMONT

WELL AWAY FROM URBAN light pollution, stars shone brightly where they could be seen through the gaps of the tree canopy of the Green Mountain Forest. The waxing crescent moon would set shortly, just after 10:00 PM, though what little light it still reflected was obscured by the heavy evergreen foliage. Temperatures hovered around 27°F, though, with a fourteen-mile-per-hour steady breeze, it felt more like a brisk fifteen degrees to the four men, dressed head-to-toe in black, who padded softly through the thin cover of snow on the pine-needled ground.

They had parked their vehicle, a nondescript, white Ford F-150 crew cab pickup truck with a yellow New York State license plate, at a turnaround clearing toward the end of US Forest Service Road 30, near the banks of a meandering creek called the Lake Brook. Leaving the F-150 behind, they would first aim south, paralleling the Lake Brook, and then cut west to skirt around Griffith Lake, before having eyes on the secluded stronghold tucked into the woods that was their target.

The four-man team was led by Carlos Chiloé Guerrero. A dark-haired, brown-tanned Chilean with pockmarked, weather-beaten skin, the pugnacious South American was no stranger to the cold or to the terrain as he led the attack team through the Vermont woods. A native of Patagonia, Carlos had slipped into the United States sixteen years ago across the US-Mexican border, eventually finding himself assimilating into the Latino community in the Bronx, an area north of Brooklyn in New York City. He learned that his unique talents in thoughtful violence made him a useful commodity to the shadowy community of crime in New York.

In the Vermont woods, far from the scrubland of Patagonia, the 3.18-mile journey, as the crow flies, would work out to be closer to five miles, as Carlos and his men trudged toward their rendezvous with Dmitri Tretriaki.

Four weeks prior, before a weak sun dawned on a chilly December morning in Brighton Beach, Anastasia Volkov and Dmitri Tretriaki had sped from the New York area in Tretriaki's Mercedes sedan. Volkov expected that it would only be a matter of time before the FBI found the black Audi, and once they had that clue, they would pore through camera footage looking for their escapee. The Bureau's agents would also zero in on Petrikov's accomplices; patrols and inquires through the Brighton Beach area would increase exponentially. But the FBI would not identify Dmitri Tretriaki as a suspect.

When Tretriaki had flashed the high-beams of his Mercedes four times outside of the temporary library facility in Brooklyn, it was Volkov's first introduction to a man who had a remarkably similar life to her own, with, of course, the exception of incarceration at Walter Reed.

By the early 1990s, Anatoly Petrikov's profile was on the rise in Brighton Beach, and his charisma and polished appearance had positioned him as an apprentice of sorts to the *vor v zakone*. The "*vory*" was *the* crime boss of the *Bratva*—the New York arm of the Russian mafia. In 1996, Petrikov had ascended to the top. The immigrant had become the *vory*.

Fearful of their daughter's safety, Irina Petrikov spirited their ten-year-old daughter Irinushka out of Brighton Beach. With the help of the *Bratva*, her father arranged a new identity for his one and only offspring; she would become Anastasia Volkov, her new surname selected because of its loose translation as "wolf," so similar to her mother's maiden name of Borisyuk, a derivation of the Slavic word *волк*, or boris—a wolf.

Volkov was sent to central New York State, where she was raised by a kindly Ukrainian couple in the shadow of Cornell University; her exposure to the Ivy League school spurred her education, and she thrived, eventually matriculating to MIT.

Unbeknown to the girl, Petrikov's predecessor as *vory*, Vyacheslav Ivankov, had similar concerns for his illegitimate son, and the two Russian crime bosses, despite their differences, made a pact: the children were off-limits. They would become each other's safety net, just in case. It was a permanent, if not a specialized truce, sealed with vodka and blood, between the two men, a shared paternal bond that created an unusual parity.

Ivankov's son remained in Brighton Beach. The community may have been aware of his mother's connection to the *vory*, who was arrested for extortion in 1995, allowing Petrikov to assume his place atop the *Bratva*, but the insular society paid the bastard child-boy no attention, and Dmitri Tretriaki grew up invisibly among his peers.

He had but one link to his past, a single word: *wolf.* If he needed help, he knew how to contact the wolf. And, of course, if the wolf communicated with him, it would be his duty to respond.

After slipping out of the Brighton Beach neighborhood, Tretriaki and the wolf had traveled north and encamped in Ithaca, New York, where the pair had plotted a plan to find and free Anatoly Petrikov. And for that, they needed two things—high-speed internet access, which was easy to come by in the college town, and a team. Enter: Carlos Chiloé Guerrero. Their man, who was currently traipsing silently through the Vermont pines, who had been hired to help liberate Petrikov.

Guerrero would not work alone. He had sourced three men to bear the weapons that they would need. And, perhaps more importantly, he would have help from the inside.

Anastasia Volkov's computer brilliance had not only located Anatoly Petrikov, spirited away in the Vermont woods, thought to be invisible by the FBI, but had also penetrated the compound's personnel assignment system.

For Volkov, tapping at a keyboard in Ithaca, it had been a simple task once inside the system: a quick substitution of a name and a photo for the guard who had been scheduled to begin a rotation yesterday, and Dmitri Tretriaki would slip into the compound in plain sight.

But first, Volkov had one more task to complete that she estimated would ensure their success.

chapter 19

SAME DAY, 11:18 PM —
FBI BOSTON FIELD OFFICE, CHELSEA, MASSACHUSETTS

IN BOSTON, LEWIS HAD USED the POTS lines to sound the alarm, and though our communications to the outside world had been slowed, we were still in business—and the FBI doesn't operate only from nine to five.

At the Bureau's Washington, DC headquarters, computer analysts in the forty-thousand-square-foot Strategic Information and Operations Center (SIOC) had been feverishly working to trace the source of attacks on the Boston Field Office and its four proximate satellite offices. With over 1,100 telephone lines and sixty miles of fiber optic cable (that the public knows about), the resources of SIOC were immense. But, since Lewis's outreach late afternoon, the combined computing power and analysis had made no progress.

For the FBI Boston Field Office, the problem was not so much the communications systems, but more the question of *why?* The attacks at the firewalls, at first sporadic but now constant, appeared to be benign. Was the field office the subject of some experiment by a hacker somewhere, trying to work out some sort of scalability question? Or were the attacks meant for a more nefarious purpose that we had yet to see?

No one had a clue. Not us in Boston, not the technicians working in the SIOC in Washington.

Little by little, agents and staff drifted from the building. The urgency of the response had been tempered by acclimation. Nothing was really happening, other than an inconvenience to our communications systems, which as the night wore on, we didn't really need, anyway.

I decided that I, too, was superfluous, and I flagged down Macallister, asking, "Sir? I'm not really doing anything. I'm gonna head home."

"Yeah, sure," the Senior Supervisory Agent agreed, "Me, too. Fucking protection detail. Go get 'em for both us, okay?"

"Yessir," I replied, but I didn't move, stopped in my tracks by two words. *Protection detail.*

And then my phone rang.

It was 11:18 PM when my personal cell phone buzzed in my pocket—an unusual time for a call to a number that was known only to my few friends and to my family.

The name displayed on my phone's screen was anything but meaningless to me, and my gut instantly churned.

It was my sister, Grace.

"*Ben! Thank God you answered!*" she screamed in a high-pitched, frantic tone.

I locked eyes with Macallister as I shot, "Grace! What's happening? Are you okay?"

"BenIdon'tknowwhattodoyou'vegottohelpme!" Her words fired into my ear as one.

"Grace. Grace! Please slow down. Start over. What is happening?" Macallister, obviously seeing the concern on my face and hearing it in my voice, leaned in.

My sister inhaled deeply and then, marginally calmer, whispered, "The power went out in my house. Like an hour ago. I was already in bed. I didn't think it was a big deal until I got up and looked out my windows. There were lights everywhere, Ben! Lights in all the houses around me!"

Grace lived outside of Providence, Rhode Island, in the small town of Bristol. She commuted into the city daily where she worked at the Citizen's Bank headquarters. Her tidy, Cape-style home in Bristol was her pride and joy, within walking distance of the waters of Narragansett Bay, but somewhat unfortunately located near the town's sewage treatment plant. The former feature she loved; the latter, she tolerated, since it meant she had more privacy, with a good-sized woody setback to the plant, and no backyard neighbors. I tried to visualize the situation; there would normally be no lights to the rear of her home, but across the street and to the sides, there should be. I rationalized, as calmly as I could, "Grace, maybe it's a tree limb down or something. Or a problem on the street. Did you call the electric company?"

"Fuck, Ben, do you think I'm stupid?" she spouted. That got my attention. For my sister to drop an f-bomb, the situation was dire. "I tried. I couldn't get through. I'd get a dial tone, and then it would disconnect. I tried to call nine-one-one. It didn't connect. I tried the electric company again. My phone line was dead. I called you from my cell phone. This isn't right!"

My heart skipped a beat.

Phone lines *and* power lines out. Could this be related to what we were seeing here in Boston and at our satellite offices?

Since we had identified my family as potential targets for Volkov a month ago, we had a combination of local police and FBI protection details around them—until last Friday, when the details had been deemed unnecessary due to the vague nature of the threat and the inaction thus far. I cursed myself for not following up more frequently with my sister. Trying to remain coolly collected, I intoned, "Okay, Grace, I get it. Don't hang up. Stay on this line. I'm actually still at work. Let me see what I can find out."

I jabbed the *mute* icon on my phone display as Macallister said, "What the hell was that about?"

Pointing at Lewis's overhead monitor with the map of the attacks, I barked, "Bristol. Rhode Island. My sister. Grace. Power out, but only at her house. Not surrounding houses. Phone line dead. No protection detail since last week. We gotta get somebody out there! Please! *Now!*"

"This is *not* good," Macallister replied, wildly looking around the room and settling on Lewis. "Can you get us an open line? Bristol PD and Providence, our office. Wait. What's closer, Providence or Lakeville?"

I looked again at Lewis's map. "Providence, maybe by a hair. But I don't fucking care! We gotta get someone there!"

"Bristol police, first," commanded Macallister.

I stepped slightly away as Lewis grabbed a handset, and I unmuted the call with my sister and put it on speakerphone. "Grace. We're getting in touch with Bristol police. Any change?"

Her breathing was fast, irregular. "Ben," she whispered, "there's a car outside now. It's, like, a big truck. Like an SUV. Dark color. Lights off. It wasn't there a minute ago!"

There was a quiet pause. I froze. The room froze.

Though the tiny speaker on my phone, we could just barely hear Grace whimper, "Ben. . . I'm scared! Please help me."

Her voice trailed off, and then, suddenly, the screen display changed. The call had been ended. But not by me.

She was gone.

I lowered the phone slowly, not realizing initially that I was holding my breath. My gut churned. I stared at Macallister, willing the words that I didn't want to speak to form on my tongue. "This could be... could it be... it's her. It's her, isn't it?"

I stopped speaking for a moment. *This* was what had been nagging at me earlier. An electronic attack. Initiated by the one person we were looking for. I finally blurted, "It's gotta be Volkov!"

Macallister's face went white as he nodded glumly.

How did we not reach this conclusion earlier?

Shit.

20

EIGHTEEN MINUTES LATER — VERMONT

THE FEW LIGHTS ON THE outside of the secret government compound shone brightly, the only source of illumination now that the moon had disappeared. The temperature had risen slightly, and with it, a humid haze had developed that obscured the stars.

Volkov's extensive online research on the facility, once she had gained remote access to the FBI's systems from her new lair in Ithaca, had indicated that there was no perimeter security. No trip lines, pressure sensors, infrared cameras, or even fencing. The seclusion and secrecy were enough, apparently, for protection; indeed, the compound was not intended for a high-security application, being more of a safe house than a prison. Nevertheless, the FBI did prepare for Petrikov's residency: a clearing had been cut in the woods for a two-way, high-speed satellite transmitter/receiver; a second clearing closer in afforded a liquid-cooled diesel generator with a large-capacity, above-ground fuel tank; and the structure itself had been enclosed with an eight-foot-high concrete wall with a single mechanized steel gate, eight feet wide, for vehicular and human access.

Roster lists showed that six agents were assigned to the facility, along with two Army servicemen who worked as a cooking and general cleaning team. A new agent was rotated into the roster once per week, to contain agent burnout and boredom; therefore, each individual agent assigned to the facility worked six weeks before being relieved.

Once on-site, the agents worked in pairs and stood six-hour watches. At all times, two agents were in a ready state, on active duty. A second pair of two agents were in a stand-down state, still armed but not on active patrol. During daytime hours, the stand-down pair assists the ready agents; during nighttime, the stand-down pair was permitted to doze but remain dressed and armed. Finally, two agents were off duty and could rest.

The servicemen were on call from breakfast at 7:00 AM until they had prepared and left out dinner at 5:00 PM, though their schedules were far more fluid, as long as the meals were hearty, and the place was kept tidy.

The structure itself was shaped like a squat U, with the open end facing northwest. The kitchen, storage, and mechanical spaces, including a single-vehicle garage, occupied the left leg of the U; opposite were bunkrooms and a common space for the agents and servicemen. The bottom of the U included three fortified "guest" rooms. Only the center room was occupied.

Arriving late the night before, magically assigned to the roster by Anastasia Volkov's computer wizardry, Dmitri Tretriaki's identification badge included his photo but, of course, not his actual name, reading, instead, Franklin Testani. He had hoisted his rucksack onto his assigned bunk and, feigning exhaustion from the long ride to Vermont, he had racked out immediately, to rest up before commencing his shift, and orientation, at 6:00 AM.

Tretriaki/Testani stood his watch until noon, when he was allowed to stand down, armed and ready but not on active duty. He continued his orientation to the facility with his partner, including conducting the usual inspection of the prisoner's quarters during his exercise time. At 6:00 PM, he went off-watch, until midnight.

He slept for a few hours, then woke, waiting, somewhat impatiently and nervously, for the prearranged time.

In the dark woods outside the compound, Carlos Chiloé Guerrero and his three-man team were also wide awake, checking their watches, also waiting.

* * *

SAME TIME — BRISTOL, RHODE ISLAND

Inside her tidy, Cape-style home, Grace Porter shivered uncontrollably. She was alone. Petrified. Frozen in place.

She had briefly considered sneaking out the back door and making a run for the darkened woods behind her house, but she couldn't bring herself to do it. Especially after the black SUV had appeared on the street outside. She hadn't seen it arrive, so she couldn't know if the driver and any passengers still were within the vehicle, or if someone had exited the vehicle and skulked around her house.

For the past twenty minutes, she had been jabbing at her iPhone, alternating between cursing the device, and praying for it to connect to her FBI-agent brother.

Outside, the black SUV remained motionless on the street.

She looked at her phone again.

11:40 PM.

She pressed her thumb on the top line of the "recent calls" list. *BenBro.*

To her astonishment, the screen changed to a call screen, with the counter ticking up. *Please please please please*, she begged.

"Grace! Are you okay?"

Ben Porter's voice shouted through the phone, with only three seconds showing on the log. To her immense relief, he had answered right away. Whispering, she murmured, "They're still out there, Ben!"

"Okay, okay," her brother's voice soothed. "We're in contact with the Bristol police. They'll be there in—" he paused.

"Ben?"

"Sorry, wanted to check. We are having comms issues here. The police will be there in minutes." He paused again before asking, "Grace, did you hang up on me, earlier? What happened?"

"No! I thought you hung up. The call just ended. Dropped. I've been trying to call you back for the last twenty minutes. It just wouldn't go through!"

"Wait, what? Explain that again," he requested.

"I kept trying to call out, but nothing happened. I checked and I had, like, all the bars, but it just wouldn't connect."

"Grace, hang on." She heard muffling and then, distantly, her brother's voice, asking someone, "Where the fuck are the police? And can she jam a cell signal? Short-range?"

"Ben!" Grace yelped. "I heard that! Who's *she?*"

"Just hang in there, Grace. The police will be there shortly. Stay on the line. Don't answer the door. Don't move. And don't hang up!"

✳ ✳ ✳

EIGHT MINUTES LATER — VERMONT

Carlos Guerrero's men, outside, were in position. Two men, just out of the bloom of light that glowed from the steel entrance gate fixture. Two men, at the corners of the structure.

Dmitri Tretriaki, inside, was ready, standing in the bathroom, armed with the FBI's standard-issue Glock Model 22.

One minute.

Thirty seconds.

Now.

The inside man moved before the outside team, who would wait, primed, for the signal—which, when it came, would be obvious. Exiting the bathroom, the inside man walked into the bunkroom, where his partner was preparing for their midnight watch, strapping on his utility belt. Dmitri Tretriaki squeezed the trigger on the Glock, firing a single bullet into the agent's head. The shot was silenced, thanks to the suppressor that he had smuggled in within his rucksack.

One agent down, four agents to go. Plus the two servicemen.

Tretriaki stole silently down the hall, to the base of the U-shaped structure. He might find the on-duty guards there. He might not. He would have to improvise. But his target—the switch in the lower hall that operated the mechanized entry gate that was shown to him during his orientation tour earlier in the day—must be activated in forty-five seconds for the plan to be fully intact.

Reaching the corner of the hall, he peeked—to find an empty corridor.

Twelve seconds to go.

Lightly, he strode to the panel, thirty feet away.

Six.

At the panel. *Three.*

Engage the switch. Outside, the entry gate began to slide open.

"What are you doing?" demanded one of the on-duty agents, who had materialized in the corridor.

Before Tretriaki could answer, with impeccable timing, the lights went out.

One hundred ninety-two miles away, in Ithaca, connected through the high-speed satellite link, Anastasia Volkov deactivated the electric power to the compound.

Outside, two men sprinted for the partially open gate. The second pair followed behind them from their flanking positions off to each side, a precaution in the event that an agent was standing behind the gate and caught the first two men on their incoming run.

As the infiltrators breached the open gate, the automatic transfer switch sensed the power loss and began the power-on procedure for the diesel generator. Though liquid-cooled, and therefore significantly quieter than an air-cooled model, its start-up was still noisy, and it began to clatter to life.

Inside, Tretriaki, having the advantage of knowing the blackout was coming, had raised his silenced Glock and squeezed off two shots, dropping the accosting agent.

Two down.

Now at sensing the diesel motor running at its operating RPM, the automatic transfer switch tripped, disconnecting power from the outside mains and switching to the generator circuit. The lights outside the compound flared on; inside, whatever had been lit, relit.

This was the riskiest part for Tretriaki, for he could easily be mistaken for an agent by the infiltrators. He stood stock-still in the entry corridor, his Glock on the floor, his hands outstretched above his head: a prearranged, simple signal to the team to identify himself. His right hand was clenched into a fist. His left forefinger and middle finger were conspicuously outstretched, indicating that two men were down.

The first two-man infiltration pair banged through the entry door to find Tretriaki frozen in his pose. With a nod, Carlos Chiloé Guerrero acknowledged their compatriot, who remained still. The attack team would take over.

With the element of surprise and with the distraction of the generator, they found the first pair of stand-by duty guards, who upon seeing the lights blink off then on, and hearing the generator outside, had rushed from the common room. The infiltrating team took them down in a swarm of bullets from a pair of M16A1 fully-automatic assault rifles. Once inside, stealth was not a priority.

Four down.

At the opposite side of the U, the two Army servicemen, startled awake by the unmistakable chatter of the automatic weapons firing, bolted from their bunks, clad in only skivvies and sweats, desperately seeking their own Army-issued pistols. They were too late. Their door burst open, and the second infiltrating pair sliced open the servicemen with a barrage of bullets. The Army men dropped, lifeless, to the floor.

One remaining.

The final agent, though realizing the futility of his situation, served until his end. He valiantly tried to get to the common room where the compounds communications gear was located, so even if he couldn't stop the attack, he could sound the alarm. Sneaking into the entry hall, he saw Tretriaki, still in his hands-up pose, but the agent mistakenly assumed the imposter was one of his own. His error was fatal to him.

Tretriaki dropped to his knees, snatched up the Glock, and snipped off a final shot.

All down.

"Follow me," Tretriaki commanded, and he led the squad to Petrikov's doorway.

Inside, the oligarch was dressed. He had bundled the chess set in a spare shirt, which he handed to Tretriaki, saying, with his head inclined in a bow, "A most pleasing game. I shall look forward to the next one."

Dmitri Tretriaki laughed. "I, too. But perhaps it should wait?"

Straightening, Tretriaki extended his right hand, which Petrikov accepted with a bone-crushing, typically Russian handshake. Formally addressing the big Russian with his full name, Tretriaki stated, "Anatoly Petrikov, I'm honored to take you to your daughter. She's looking forward to seeing you, at long last."

"My daughter? She did this?"

The six men began the long walk back to the F-150, in no particular hurry, for they would have plenty of time before the compound missed its 9:00 AM morning check-in call.

Petrikov beamed with paternal pride.

✳ ✳ ✳

SAME TIME — BRISTOL

Grace Porter heard the squeal of sharply-braked tires outside her home, and she cautiously raised her eyes above the windowsill. Two Bristol PD squad cars had stopped abruptly, scant inches from the front and rear of the black SUV, having arrived from opposite directions in a classic pincer formation.

In a blur of color, blue-and-red strobe lights alit on the rooftops of the two squad cars, their alternating colors painting Grace's reflection in the window.

Still connected by cell phone to her brother, Grace Porter sighed with relief. "They're here, Ben! They're here!"

"Fantastic. But don't move. Let them sort it out."

Outside, on the street, four Bristol police officers cautiously stepped from the two squad cars and surrounded the black vehicle, weapons drawn. The front driver's and passenger's doors opened slowly; two pairs of hands extended. Both hands held something; on the passenger side, facing Grace's view, she caught the flicker of a gold reflection in the headlights of the squad cars.

Confused, she watched as two men slowly exited the black vehicle, and seemingly began to converse, casually, with the police.

✳ ✳ ✳

SAME TIME — BOSTON

"Grace, what's happening?"

My sister had gone quiet. On the operations center screens, it appeared that the firewall attack continued unabated, yet my cell-phone connection to Grace remained uninterrupted. I heard rustling, then, "The lights came on, Ben! The power's back on!"

In our operations center, we stared at each other. None of this made sense.

"Grace, what's happening?" I repeated.

"The cops and the guys on the street, they're talking."

"They're what?"

"They're chatting. Talking. There were two men in the black SUV. They're all talking."

At that moment, Lewis bolted from his seat, a telephone handset to his ear. He angled it slightly and yelled, "They're ours! Providence dispatched two agents to watch over the house. The house was dark, so they figured she went to bed, and they just waited like they were told to do."

"Told to do by *who*?" barked Macallister.

"Duty agent in Providence. Says he got a message from SAC Appleton. The message to dispatch."

Appleton shot from her seat. "I sent no such message."

Macallister and I spun and faced each other, meeting each other's wide-eyed stare. Simultaneously, we both gulped, knowing, now, that the assumption that we feared earlier was likely correct.

"But," I mumbled, "if this was Volkov, what the hell just happened?"

Macallister grunted, "Yeah. And if it was her, she's up to something. But I got no fucking clue what. And I don't like it one bit."

"She's playing us," I offered.

Appleton inclined her head in agreement as Macallister concluded, "And, as usual, she's way ahead of us. What's next? How the fuck are we gonna track her down?"

And that, of course, was the problem. We seemed to be always playing catch-up.

CHAPTER
21

WEDNESDAY, DECEMBER 12, 2018 — FBI BOSTON FIELD OFFICE, CHELSEA, MASSACHUSETTS

WE ACCOMPLISHED EXACTLY zero for the rest of the night.

The Bristol police and the agents that had been dispatched from our Providence office established a perimeter around Grace's home. I checked with her by phone one more time; she had calmed down and was going to try and get some rest.

I approached Appleton, her normally cold composure softened with concern. "Can we get protective details out to my parents? My brother?"

"Already done," she replied. "Lewis got me a line and it's happening."

"Thank you," I whispered. "I'll call them and let them know."

"Fine. Make it quick. We have work to do," commanded the SAC, the softness replaced by a look of direct focus.

I stepped to the perimeter of the workroom and made a quick call to my parents, waking them, scaring them, but telling them to be on the lookout for one of our cars and asking them to relay the message to my brother. I did not tell them why, nor did I elaborate on what had happened earlier at their daughter's home. They would go ballistic. I didn't need that.

I could sort that out later.

For now, my priority was on the case. After a month in hiding, Volkov had surfaced. Assuming it was, indeed, Volkov, behind this.

The tension in the operations center had been like a roller coaster. When Lewis had called the staff in at the end of the day yesterday, we were on edge, but as the immediacy of a threat waned, as did the tension and the attendance, as agents trickled out.

Naturally, the tension spiked as soon as Grace called me, but only Macallister and I represented our squad. He made sure to change that, and he called them back into the office.

By 3:00 AM, the squad had reassembled in the operations center. Lewis's hair was flatter, and Lewis's network traffic monitoring screens were normal; he explained that the firewall attacks started to taper off.

Still, we were just as confused as before. We wanted to pin this whole thing on Volkov, but we had no proof. We had no data. We had nothing. Except theories.

"Was it a warning?" Connelly asked. Familiar with the South Florida drug trade, the former undercover agent had far more experience than any of us in the field.

"Could be. Or a test. To see if she could get into the systems," Jones ventured.

Lewis snorted. "But she was *in* the system! *We* didn't send agents out to Grace Porter's house."

"If it was her," countered Zimmerman. "You can't know that."

"Who the fuck could it have been?" growled Macallister. "She starts tapping at the system last night, when she knows we are minimally staffed, builds up the pressure, and uses that as a distraction so she can get in. Then she sends the message to Providence. But why?"

Rejoining the group, I sat; the eyes rotated to me. I may have jumped to conclusions a month ago, but today, I felt absolute confidence. I leaned forward, my elbows on the table, and began, "It had to be her. I don't know why, but here's how I know it was her."

I had their attention.

"First, and foremost, who would target my sister? Isolate her? Had to be Volkov. She would guess my sister would be a soft target. She's poking me, indirectly."

Zimmerman crossed his arms on his chest, in defiance, but the remainder of the squad nodded or murmured their agreement. I continued,

"Macallister is spot-on. The attack on our firewall was a diversion. All she needs is one of those millions of attacks to be successful, and she logs onto the system. In fact, the log-in isn't an attack. It's just a simple remote log-in made invisible by all the traffic around it. No one else could pull that off.

"She cuts the power to my sister's house. I don't know how she pulls that off, but if she can get into our system, she can pop into the local utility.

"She does the same with the phone line. The land line. But, I'm not sure how she managed to temporarily stop the cellular signals from connecting, but she failed, at least partially, at that."

"It's easy enough," Lewis interrupted. "And she didn't fail. I doubt she was jamming the airwaves. That would require someone nearby. She can spoof the same effect remotely. All's she's gotta do is hijack the SIM."

"Pots and sims. Could you people speak fucking English, please," grumbled Macallister, mirthlessly.

"A SIM is the little card that goes in the slot on the side of your phone," Lewis explained. "Stands for Subscriber Identity Module. It's basically your phone number, which is tied to your device identification. If a hacker, like Volkov, has access to your mobile carrier's network, they just reassign the SIM to a new number. You phone stops being able to make calls."

Confirming that Macallister was nodding his understanding, Lewis continued, "She played Grace's phone like a puppet. She allowed a call to Agent Porter, then she hijacked the SIM temporarily, then she re-activated it and bam, Grace can call out again."

"But why?" Macallister asked.

We had no answers, only questions.

I felt useless. And I was exhausted. So, I made a simple two-item list: I would call Grace in the morning, and then I would find Anastasia Volkov.

At least, that was my plan, then.

CHAPTER
22

AT 6:00 AM, I ASKED FOR A quick escort home. Two agents came with me so I could shower and change. On the way back to the office, I bought them both expensive coffees at Starbucks. It was the least I could do.

For me, I had an extra-large—sorry, venti—black coffee. No sugar, no milk, no whatever. Just straight fuel.

By 7:30 AM, I had checked in with the agents in Bristol; they reported to me that Grace was sound asleep. A new crew of agents would be on-site shortly to relieve the overnight team.

In the operations center in Chelsea, as I waited alone for the squad to trickle back in from getting their own breakfasts and pick-me-ups. I sipped my black coffee and examined the fake wood veneer on the surface of the conference table, following the veins in the wood, absently tracing them with a finger, and imagining that one of those veins would lead me to Volkov.

It was the calm before the storm.

In the darkness of night, we had no answers, only questions. But we're the FBI. That's what we do: answer questions. Investigate.

As the squad got to work at the big conference table in the operations center, Lewis brought us up to speed on the electronic investigation. The Washington, DC-based Cyber Division would be assigned to assist in the forensic analysis of the electrons. Boston would still have the lead in the boots-on-the-ground investigation, now adding in Bristol and Providence. Our team was about to get much larger.

But for now, at 8:00 AM on a Wednesday morning, we conferenced, floating one idea after another.

Connelly had been speaking, laying out another theory, "Let's say that was a test. She got to judge the reaction time both here and in Providence. She got to see how long it took to get agents out, under a reduced communications scenario, from Providence to Bristol. She got to see if Lakeville would be assigned or if the call would stay with Providence. She saw how we reacted. How the local police reacted. It's like it was a dress rehearsal."

"Plausible," concluded Macallister. "But let's say Grace was a trial run, and she's setting up for the big game. She's shown us her playbook. Let's say she's going for Porter, next. She's just wasted her best play. The diversion play."

At the sound of my name, I jerked my head up, in a moment of absolute clarity, and I parroted Macallister's words, "Diversion play."

The squad examined me; I could sense that my eyes had gone wide, and my lower lip was drooping. I composed myself enough to utter just two words, "Diversion. Petrikov."

They stared at me, and I drawled, "Her big play? It's not me. It's Petrikov."

Silence.

Broken by Macallister, who motioned toward the telephone positioned at the middle of the conference table. "Someone get me Appleton."

Lewis complied wordlessly, pressing the appropriate sequence on the keypad to direct-dial the SAC's office, then jabbing at the speakerphone button. The second the connection was answered by an assistant, Macallister hollered, "Priority. Senior Supervisory Special Agent Macallister for the SAC. Now."

"One moment, sir," replied an evenly-composed voice. I wondered how many times a priority call was made to the Special Agent in Charge. Probably more times than I imagined.

"Appleton."

"Ma'am, Macallister. Agent Porter has proposed a new theory. It is possible that last night's activity was a test, a dress rehearsal. For a bigger play. For a play on Petrikov."

"Go on," encouraged the SAC.

"If it was Volkov, and we can't prove that yet, obviously, but it stands to reason, she was testing our reaction times. Testing her infiltration method. Testing her diversion. We need to get this out to wherever Petrikov is. Make sure they expect it. Or get us there to brief it."

"I see. That would require authority from the very top, in that we would obviously be disclosing his location and breaching the wall that thus far has protected that knowledge. Which is on a need-to-know basis."

"I'd say we need to know. With respect, of course." Macallister, usually gruff and short, was being very professional. I was somewhat surprised, and by the SAC's response, I got the feeling she was too.

"I agree. The serious nature of this deserves additional analysis. Give me a few minutes. I'll run it up." She clicked off the connection. Macallister looked pleased.

Seven minutes later, Appleton burst through the operations center entrance, uncharacteristically gracelessly. Her dramatic entrance got immediate attention.

Without waiting, without sitting, without fanfare, the SAC breath lessly gasped, "Porter. That was your theory? That last night's exercise was a test? For a play on Petrikov?"

"Yes, ma'am," I quickly replied.

"You were wrong."

My heart sunk. Wrong again. I let my eyes cast downward but caught myself. I looked straight at the SAC. Her face was inscrutable as she announced, "It wasn't a test. It wasn't a rehearsal. It was the main event. It *was* a diversion. Someone grabbed Petrikov last night. He's gone."

CHAPTER

23

AS THE DAY WORE ON, and our spirits wore down, we learned what happened in Southern Vermont. We had five dead agents. We had two dead Army servicemen. All at a secret facility that was so compartmentalized, even the president wouldn't have known about it, and yet it was still discovered and breached.

It was a disaster.

And it was easy to conclude it had been orchestrated by Volkov. Or so we thought.

Her electronic attack on us appeared to be a diversion, though one for no purpose, since we didn't know where Petrikov was imprisoned. Perhaps she didn't know that we in Boston did not have a "need to know" status for his location. Or perhaps she wanted to taunt us, to boast about her reach.

Not only had she penetrated our local systems to send agents from Providence to Bristol, petrifying my sister, and me, in the process, but she also had apparently inserted someone into the secret facility. The roster records showed a Franklin Testani starting a six-week service rotation effective at 6:00 AM yesterday morning, arriving late the night before. No such agent existed in our system. The records appeared and were taken as legitimate. Identifications had been checked when the departing agent had left the facility and as this Testani had entered. The file substitution had been made at 9:00 PM, exactly when the attacks had begun the day before on our firewall in Boston. The file had been swapped under the cover of the very first attack.

The audacity was astonishing.

The Bureau had helicoptered teams to the facility, landing a few miles away at a US Forest Service Campground. They found the dead agents, spent casings, footprints in the snow, and a partially-open gate. They discovered, from the built-in control module on the generator, that the power to the facility had gone out just as we were sending the police to my sister's house in Bristol. The generator was still running when the agents showed up. The power had been cut remotely, and the working theory was that that was a diversion to help allow an infiltration.

What the agents did not find was a Russian oligarch, wanted as an enemy combatant for crimes against the United States.

The Black Hawks were landing and taking off in the tiny hamlet of Mount Tabor, nearby, and circling above, swarming, looking for their prey. And finding nothing.

It was a shitshow, and it was only beginning.

"Agent Porter." A whisper. The operations center was buzzing with activity, none of it particularly fruitful. The whisper was a little disconcerting, especially since the whisperer's spiky blond hair was brushing against my head.

"What's up, Lewis?"

"Agent Porter," the Information Analyst repeated. "You gotta check this out. Grab a chair and roll it over to my workstation."

I was already sitting, and my imitation Aeron swivel chair had wheels, so I propelled myself with little short steps over to Lewis's hive; he took his usual backless, ergonomic stool, which looked terribly uncomfortable to me.

"I think she goofed. She left a trail. And it's really unsettling." He was clicking and typing, and his screen was changing, and I had no clue what he was doing or what he was getting at. But, having learned to keep my mouth shut, I waited. The screen stopped changing, and he pointed at a line of code, "See that? Okay, that's the message identifier for the instructions that Providence said they received from us. Once we got fully back on-line, I wanted to trace the source of those instructions."

"Yeah, I remember that message. Providence said we sent them the message to send agents out to my sister's house. You're saying you can identity the sender?"

"Exactly. Here's the message. It shows that Appleton sent it."

"So what—we knew that." I blurted. "If Volkov has the chops to get into the system, she could have made it look like anyone sent it. She probably picked the SAC so it would get immediate action without upstream verification."

"Right. Totally agree. But here's the thing. To do that, she's got to get into Appleton's account in the system. And therefore, she can get Appleton's ID so that the receiving end of the message doesn't kick it back out as invalid. Follow?"

"Yeah. And?'"

"Well, here's the thing. She didn't close out the account. Maybe she forgot. Or maybe she was working on the thing in Vermont and got distracted. The SAC's account is wide open," Lewis blubbered excitedly, the tempo of his words picking up. "Anyone can read it. Including me."

I leaned in toward the techie, "I think you are treading on some very shaky ground here, Lewis. You need to tell her, and you need to lock it. There's some super-sensitive stuff in there. This is national security, man. You gotta fix this," I hissed.

I was getting agitated and nervous. If Volkov could get into Appleton's account, what else could Volkov get access to?

Lewis was unfazed, stammering, "I know, I know. But I was curious, so I took a quick look around."

"*What?*" I blurted, in astonishment.

"Shhhh!" Lewis admonished. "I know, I shouldn't. But here's the thing. Since the account was open, I wanted to see if I could back-trace how Volkov opened it, so I was digging around at the electronic signatures."

I glared at the Louis Lewis. He had crossed a line, and I was ready to call Macallister over. This was a huge deal, a massive breach of protocol, not to mention an equally massive violation of national security.

But Lewis stood his ground, and he stated firmly, "Agent Porter. I know I shouldn't have been poking around. I think the ends justify the means, though. Hear me out, please."

The hairs at the back of my neck prickled uncomfortably. I was a little hung up on Lewis poking around in the Special Agent in Charge's account. Yet, I could see the sincerity, the emotion, in Lewis's eyes, even through the purple frames of his eyeglasses. I capitulated and nodded my tacit agreement that he should proceed.

With a quick head-bob, Lewis quietly said, "Remember when we built that list of Volkov's background and current potential motives?" I nodded yes, silently. I didn't like where this was going.

Lewis continued, "In her background, we talked about how she got hired with a huge, obvious gap in her history. Like she just appeared at MIT before getting hired by the FBI?"

"Yeah, I know," I agreed. "It doesn't make sense. And her adoptive family, who turned out to be imaginary, fake. How that didn't get flagged as bogus by our background checks, we still don't know."

"Exactly," confirmed Lewis.

I shook my head back and forth. "But. We've got a team in Washington trying to figure out who got her through those background checks. They've come up with nothing, correct?"

"Yeah, they got nothing. For one simple reason. The single hiring approval file that they need is missing. They know it's out there, because of a gap in the file number audit sequence. You can't mess with that sequence. And it indicates that there is a missing file. But they haven't found that file. You know why? Because it's hidden in Appleton's account. No one can get to it, except someone with access to Appleton's account. Which is one person: Appleton herself."

Lewis paused, swallowing, and gushed, "Except now, with the account open, *I* have access to Appleton's account. The file is in that account. Which means: it was Appleton. *She* signed off on Volkov. *She* signed off on the background check. *She's* in on this whole thing!"

chapter 24

"HOLY SHIT, LEWIS," I whispered.

I couldn't believe it. That meant . . .

I couldn't even go there. Appleton covered for Volkov? That meant that Appleton knew what was going down during Operation E.T., and that meant—wait. Appleton originally told Macallister and me to back off, back when we had started that investigation. But—if she was in on it with Volkov, they must have estimated that I would just fuck it up. It would go nowhere. But they'd have cover since someone had been assigned to it. Then she must have realized that she could control it, with Volkov's help, and she let it play out.

Involuntarily, I stood and started to pace a lap around the giant conference table, my thoughts racing in lockstep with my footfalls. Maybe Appleton facilitated Volkov's escape from Walter Reed. In fact, come to think of it, Appleton didn't let my squad know that Volkov had escaped until midmorning, something like four or five hours after she went missing.

And the SAC's actions? She had appeared to be one of us, one of the good guys, and yet she's in on the whole thing? Watching it, opening doors when needed, carefully directing the investigation? No wonder she had insisted that the search for the mole who was responsible for allowing the FBI to hire Volkov had been moved to DC; it kept it out of our offices here, where the chain of evidence started, and it would have allowed Appleton to keep tabs on the investigation remotely, and block it when needed. No wonder that she isolated Petrikov from our questions, hiding him away at a place we didn't know existed. It made perfect sense.

My heart was pounding as I slumped back into the seat at Lewis's workstation.

I stared, unseeing, at Lewis's screen.

What do I do now?

I turned to Lewis. "Suppose Appleton is logged on, right now. Can she see that her account is open?"

"Probably not. It wouldn't look any different to her. Now, if I sent a message on her behalf or something, she'd see that someone spoofed her. Obviously, I'm not going to do that."

"Right. Don't move a muscle; don't change that screen. We gotta get help."

"Yeah, man, I know!"

I rotated the chair slowly, as casually as I could, and I scanned the room for Macallister. The senior agent was nowhere to be found. Agent Zimmerman had been watching Lewis and me from the worktable with an odd stare, no doubt wondering what we were conspiring and what had inspired my oddly-timed lap around the table. Agents Connelly and Jordan had apparently left the room at some point. Agent Jones had her head bent over a laptop.

I picked Zimmerman. He was already looking at me.

"Zimmerman," I called, "do you know where Macallister went?"

"His office, I think."

"You mind going up there and asking him to come in here? Like, now?" I didn't want to leave Lewis's side.

Unsurprisingly, Zimmerman balked at my request. "Just call him. I ain't walking up there. Or you do it."

I stared back at the uncooperative agent, and as sincerely as I could, I pled, "Wilson. Please. No phone call. Just go get him. In person. As fast as possible."

Agent Jones lifted her head from the screen in front of her, clearly wondering what precipitated this exchange.

Zimmerman's eyebrows had raised at my use of his first name, something I'd not done before. I guess he received the message, and he slowly stood, smirking. "Okay. You got it. You want a coffee too? Danish? Anything else?"

I didn't appreciate the sarcasm, but I didn't give a shit. Zimmerman would get the drift soon enough.

A solid fifteen minutes later, Zimmerman and Macallister strolled through the door. They both looked pissed off.

I'd been sitting with Lewis, wordlessly, for the entire time. Occasionally, he'd shake his mouse, to keep the screensaver at bay. And occasionally, I would notice Amber Jones glancing over at us; if it was curiosity or concern, I couldn't tell. Just as Zimmerman and Macallister made their appearance, Don Jordon and Brenda Connelly walked through the entry, both bearing tall paper coffee cups. I motioned at them, and they ambled in the direction of Lewis's workstation. In slow motion, it seemed to me. I was about to explode.

I took a deep breath. The more eyes on this, the better, and I waved Jones over too.

The entire squad made a semicircle around Lewis's back as I rolled off to one side. The other techs in the operations center began to take notice.

"What the fuck, Porter?" Macallister led, with his typical introduction.

"I'm handing it to Lewis. Everyone, pay attention."

Lewis began, retelling the sequence as he had explained it to me. Not a word was spoken by the squad as the evidence against Appleton unfolded.

It was Senior Supervisory Special Agent Macallister who made the arrest, at 4:58 PM, on Wednesday, December 12, 2018, less than twenty-four hours after Anatoly Petrikov was sprung, or kidnapped, or whatever, from the custody of the FBI.

The phone lines had burned through the course of the afternoon to Washington as Macallister put the pieces in place. He, like me, was devastated. Jennifer Appleton was a colleague we had trusted, who we thought we knew, who we thought was one of us.

Macallister had asked—no, requested—that I accompany him to Appleton's office, "Porter. You're doin' this with me."

"Why?" I had whined.

"You broke it. You and Lewis. But Lewis is not a Special Agent. And," Macallister added, more gently, "because it's your duty."

On the walk to her office, Macallister grabbed two other agents, who I recognized but who I was not friendly with. The four of us filed into her office unannounced.

Macallister somberly stated, "Ma'am, it is my unfortunate duty to place you under arrest."

Appleton's normally ice-cold stoic demeanor held, but her eyebrows raised slowly. "For *what*?" she demanded.

"Ma'am. For crimes against the United States. For treason." Macallister pulled a card from his pocket and began to read, verbatim, with careful precision, her Miranda rights. Appleton sat in her large, executive-style desk chair, fidgeting her left hand against a silver bracelet on her right wrist, but otherwise remaining immobile. When he finished with the card, Macallister sighed, "Ma'am, respectfully, would you please stand up, and place your hands behind your back."

Appleton complied, rising elegantly, almost majestically, from her seat. From her full height, as she clasped her left hand over her right wrist behind her back, she stated, clearly, "I don't know what precipitated this, but this is a mistake."

She looked at me directly. "Agent Porter. I'll remind you that I got you here. I trusted you. And now you're involved in . . . in . . . in *this*?"

I dropped my gaze to the floor. I couldn't meet her stare. I didn't say a word.

On one hand, I felt terrible. On the other hand, as I listened to her plea, it made me angry. Furious.

My temper quickly got to my tongue, and I snarled, "Involved? *Involved?*" The volume of my voice began to raise, even as I felt Macallister's hand on my shoulder. I ignored him. "I'm involved because I am *incensed* that my SAC—my *former* SAC—had partnered with—no, that's not strong enough. That you aided and abetted a treasonous criminal act. That you *enabled* Volkov. And that you involved my family and—"

"Enough," Macallister commanded. "Porter, shut up." One of the other agents handcuffed Appleton, and Macallister stepped aside. He would not grab her elbow and try to guide her; he would do this by the book and not lay a hand on her.

Head held high, the former Special Agent in Charge, FBI Boston Division, Jennifer Appleton, gracefully but with manacled hands, departed her office with Macallister at her side.

PART TWO

JANUARY THROUGH JULY 2019

CHAPTER
25

TUESDAY, JANUARY 1, 2019 — LOS ALTOS HILLS, CALIFORNIA

NEW TENANTS HAD MOVED into the rented mansion in Los Altos Hills, California, just before the Christmas holiday. A visitor might have observed unlikely housemates: a giant, big-bellied Russian immigrant man, with flabby jowls and a captivating, garrulous laugh; a lithe, olive-skinned young woman with flaxen, long, straight hair; a dark-haired, brown-tanned Chilean man with pockmarked, weather-beaten skin; and a tall man, a tanned face topped with a flowing truss of long blond hair.

But the new tenants of the mansion invited no guests.

In fact, the big man and the woman never left the confines of the gated, fenced, rented mansion property. They didn't dare. They were fugitives from the Federal Bureau of Investigation. The names and their likenesses were on the FBI's *Ten Most Wanted Persons* webpage and in law enforcement offices across the United States.

Only the Chilean and the blond ventured beyond the gates, individually, never together, running errands in a white Ford F-150 crew cab pickup truck, collecting foodstuffs at a supermarket or selecting excellent wines and vodkas in a liquor store. In this suburb of San Francisco, no one would give them a second glance as they kept a low profile and chose their destinations at random, rarely shopping at the same location.

With disciplined tradecraft, the group carefully concealed them-selves. Visibility was not an option. But the most exposed part of their journey had been successfully completed.

In December, rolling down an obscure gravel Forest Service access road, Petrikov, Tretriaki, Guerrero, and Guerrero's three men had jam-packed themselves into the five-seat F-150 crew cab pickup truck. Comfort was not a priority; their drive would take less than two hours.

Guerrero's three infiltrators had been dropped at the Albany International Airport for an early-morning 6:00 AM flight back to New York City. They had been paid well, but, regardless of the money, they knew to keep their mouths sealed if ever asked about their brief journey to the Green Mountain State. The *Bratva* would be unforgiving, and they would meet death swiftly, if they talked.

The three anonymous men disappeared into the terminal. Their assignment was complete, and they would return to obscurity in the vastness of New York City.

Petrikov had stretched his bulk across the backseat of the crew cab, invisible behind the tinted glass of the rear-door windows. Tretriaki took the wheel and Guerrero napped in the shotgun seat as the trio drove the three hours west to Ithaca, New York, the same town that the daughter had been raised, one where she felt at home and knew her way around.

Volkov was ready to leave her hideaway in Ithaca, a third-floor walkup apartment above a bagel shop, only a five-minute walk down College Avenue to the Cornell University engineering building basement, with its super-fast, fiber-optic internet connectivity, where she had posed as a teaching assistant—an easy credential to fake, especially with her local knowledge of the area and her expertise with computer jargon.

She had already packed her meager possessions as well as the few things that Tretriaki had brought from Brighton Beach. Without access to Petrikov's offshore accounts, Tretriaki had traded his Mercedes for the F-150 and a bit of cash to tide them over. The weapons and the men had been sourced from the *Bratva* with a promise to pay later; the IOU would, of course, be satisfied, for the word of the *Bratva* is its bond, especially when backed by the former *vory*.

And so, it was on an unseasonably balmy Wednesday in December, after roughly twenty-two years apart, that father and daughter had reunited, the big oligarch enveloping his daughter in a hug. But the moment was fleeting.

Upon disengaging herself from her father's embrace, Volkov had stepped into the backseat of the F-150, saying, "We've got a long drive. Plenty of time to catch up. Let's go!"

Happily, Petrikov had slung himself up into the high-riding truck. Not only was he free of the FBI, he was with his daughter, at long last.

With Guerrero behind the wheel, the nondescript, white pickup had headed west, 2,821 miles to their destination.

Speed would attract attention. Exhibiting what would be consid-ered "normal" behavior would help conceal them in the unremarkable pickup truck, chosen not only for its blacked-out windows, but also for its ubiquitousness on the American roadways.

Thus, there had been no hurry to make the cross-country drive cannonball-worthy, and forty-two hours of driving time became a leisurely, eight-day journey. They took turns piloting the pickup, with Volkov driving only at night, and always on an interstate, keeping to the right-hand lane and attracting no attention. During the daytime, Guerrero or Tretriaki would take the wheel, occasionally exiting the interstates to break the pattern and roll sedately down the more scenic local roads.

With three drivers, there was no need to stop for sleep. Fueling stops were made at service plazas on the interstate highways, with Guerrero always paying for the gas, always with cash.

By the time they were halfway across the nation, using their last prepaid burner phone's wireless hot spot and a MacBook Air that had been liberated from the Cornell campus, Volkov had successfully opened a new bank account and had been able to tap into Petrikov's hidden, offshore accounts in the Cayman Islands. Now flush with the ability to access cash, Volkov transferred the funds to pay off the loan from the *Bratva,* to her father's delight.

They made a detour to Denver so that Volkov could purchase two new computers and several new phones. Guerrero bought a toothbrush; Petrikov, two bottles of expensive vodka. Tretriaki watched, stunned, as he realized that the new life that he stumbled into had virtually no credit cap. Brighton Beach was fast becoming a distant memory, and he looked forward to the proper beaches of the California coast.

"Why California?" Petrikov had asked early during the trip. "Where are we going?"

"I think it's time we put some distance between Boston and me. And between New York and you," his daughter replied. "And I've got an idea. I worked it out during my, um, stay in Bethesda. I had a lot of time to think. With no access to anything, I really focused."

"And?"

"Our last mission. Why? Sum it up, briefly," Volkov requested.

"Is this some sort of game?" her father grumbled.

"No. Or yes. Whatever. Consider it . . . an exercise. Humor me; you'll understand."

Petrikov smiled. For twenty-two years, his contact with his daughter was mostly through emails, sporadic at best. They would change email addresses regularly, and the content of the messages would be vague. Occasionally, one would misinterpret the other's intent or tone. It made for a taxing, almost business-like, relationship.

When Volkov had written to her father that she was going to work for the FBI in one of those roundabout email chains, at first, Petrikov assumed he misunderstood. He had risked a phone call to clarify, their first discussion since she had left central New York for the MIT campus in Cambridge. She had laughed, saying, "Imagine the access I'll have. To computers. To files. To data. I bet you'll find a way to make it useful!"

Bringing his attention back to the game she wanted to play in the westbound F-150, Petrikov thought for a moment before responding, "Briefly, I'd sum it up as a mission for profit with the added benefit of revenge."

He was treading on delicate ground. She picked up on it right away. "Revenge?"

Before she could dig further, he quickly added, "Sure. For my opera-tive. Remember him? Victor Wolford. He took part for the money, of course, but he was a bitter man. He felt he had been wronged because of the diamond scam. I leveraged that bitterness into his cooperation.

That's why we added Chicago. We could have destabilized the markets for my profit by detonating a single device in New York City, but he wanted Chicago. I agreed because I figured it would be beneficial. It would make a bigger impact in the press and in the panic that would follow, than only one bomb."

Careful to keep his face placid, Petrikov examined his daughter, and to his relief, she seemed to accept his explanation.

After a moment, she asked, "And if you could do it over? What would you do differently?"

The oligarch laughed, his belly shaking, the frame of the F-150 shivering with the motion. "I get a do-over?"

"Sure," chuckled his daughter.

He collected himself. She was serious.

"We're not just going to California to get distance from the East Coast. You've got something in mind."

"Of course. Like I said earlier, I had plenty of time to think it through. But I'm curious. What would you do with your 'do-over'?"

"The same thing, only with a different trigger and a more limited scope. I wouldn't try and destabilize the entire financial system. That was a mistake. Despite my incarceration, my offshore accounts have done quite well over the past year and a half. I'd just be hurting myself.

"No, I would target something with precision. But I would do it in a way that I could have far-reaching effects. And, since I have your magical do-over, I'd make it repeatable." The oligarch sat back, smiling, before looking over at his daughter and saying, kindly, "But now I have no need. I have you, my little Irinushka. We can hide wherever we want on the globe. I don't need a do-over."

His daughter returned her father's smile. "But what if I told you that you *could* have all those things? Because I can give you that magical do-over."

CHAPTER
26

DESPITE THAT TEASE, halfway through their east-coast to west-coast cross-county drive, Anastasia Volkov did not elaborate on her magical do-over. Petrikov had no choice but to sit back and to enjoy the ride, hidden from view by the F-150's black-tinted rear windows.

The fugitives had stopped outside of Salt Lake City, Utah, arranging with the anonymity of a made-up username on the internet for an Airbnb rental at the base of the Park City ski area. Only Tretriaki and Guerrero were able to take a break from the monotony of the road; two men remained unknown to law enforcement, a fact confirmed by Volkov as she browsed the internet using the MacBook Air and a cell phone hotspot.

While the two men stretched their legs and strolled, separately, of course, down the picturesque Main Street, lined with nineteenth-century brick buildings constructed with the proceeds of the nearby silver mines, Petrikov sat alone on the balcony of the rental, enjoying the brisk, cool, dry air at seven thousand feet above sea level.

Inside the rental, Volkov had relaxed in the living room of the townhouse, reclining on an overstuffed sofa with her feet up on a large coffee table, laptop computer perched on her thighs. Using the name of a Cornell professor who had happened to leave her wallet behind in the engineering building one evening in early December, and armed with the professor's date of birth, driver's license number, home address, and credit card numbers, Volkov was in possession of enough data to create a parallel identity. The professor would be none the wiser that she suddenly had a Utah bank account and debit card.

Searching online with the computer, Volkov had found the perfect California rental home. The Cornell professor would electronically sign the papers to lease a fully-furnished mansion in Silicon Valley. But the professor would never know about it.

Once settled in the mansion in Los Altos Hills, Volkov had selected a second-floor bedroom. Arranging her computers in front of a north-facing window, she had gotten to work. She had everything she needed right in front of her, and she focused intently on her task with no desire to leave the residence.

The mansion that they had holed up in was comfortable enough. The black, scrolled-wrought iron driveway gate led to a brick-paved drive and a two-car garage within the two-story residence with a terra-cotta roof, barely visible through the lush, irrigated greenery that disguised a perimeter wire fence. Outside, an expansive patio led to an in-ground pool.

The first-floor windows looked into the property.

The second-floor windows afforded views of the scrub-covered hills that rose to the west, bisected by Interstate 280, and, from Volkov's north facing windows, looking across Arastradero Road, she could see the monolithic, low, gray structure that was headquarters to a company called Tesla.

A worldwide brand, Tesla designs and manufactures electric cars. Arguably, Tesla pioneered the space, creating the first mass-market, if not pricey, electric vehicles. Here, in Silicon Valley, a Tesla had been a familiar sight since the launch of the company's first significant production car, the Model S, in 2012. Since then, expanding not only its types of models on offer but also its distribution radius, Tesla had put over a half-million all-electric vehicles on the roads of the planet.

Volkov had gone mostly silent, asking for her team's patience as she programmed and tested. "I don't want to get your hopes up," she had said to her father, on New Year's Eve, December 31, 2018, "but I think I can make it work. I know I can make it work. But once you understand, you'll be more impatient, and that will be really distracting to me. And I know you'll be impatient anyway. Just let me work."

"You realize that the longer we stay here, the risk of the FBI finding us, sitting in one location, elevates daily," her father cautioned. Petrikov had been bored and essentially a prisoner in the house. With his name and likeness plastered in law enforcement offices nationwide, he didn't dare leave the compound. But he had nothing to do, except sip his vodka . . . and wait for the magical do-over that his daughter had promised.

His daughter grinned. "Yes, of course. And that is why the first order of business is to leave a trail."

"What? Why would you want to leave a trail? To here?" Petrikov asked, the concern evident in his voice and on his face.

"Hardly. Where do you want to go?"

"I don't understand. Stop speaking cryptically." Petrikov's face reddened in confusion. Volkov knew not to push it further.

"Relax," she said. "Let's see . . ." On her screen, she pulled up a map of the United States of America, and with her finger, she traced a path from Boston, generally moving in a southwest direction. "First stop for Ben Porter. Where should he spend his New Year's Day? How 'bout . . . Atlanta?"

CHAPTER
27

JANUARY 1, 2019 — CHELSEA, MASSACHUSETTS

SOMEONE WHO WAKES BEFORE dawn on New Year's Day is probably looking for an aspirin.

Not me.

Ever since Anatoly Petrikov had vanished on December 11, I'd had a feeling of unease. Certainly, that was rooted in the scare that my sister had suffered. That *had* to have been initiated by Anastasia Volkov. But we had no proof.

All we had, thus far, was a new Acting Special Agent in Charge: Bradford Macallister. My former supervisory agent became the big boss. The head honcho. The man in charge.

His first decree as Acting SAC was to provide for my security, and for that of my family. New, high-tech alarm systems were installed, courtesy of the Bureau, in my parents' home, my siblings' homes, and in my little, first-floor, one-bedroom apartment in the center of Chelsea. Perimeter cameras could be monitored by the techs working in the operations center. Panic buttons were linked not to a typical alarm monitoring service, but directly to the FBI. Doors and windows were reinforced and fitted with sensitive alarms.

It reassured me not in the slightest. For if Anastasia Volkov could breach the security at a top-secret government facility in the middle of the Vermont woods, surely she could figure out how to hack an alarm system.

I slept with my loaded Glock, and I didn't drink or party. Not even on New Year's Eve.

And so, as I made a pot of coffee in my little galley kitchen, it was not for a hangover cure, but merely for comfort. I'd watch ESPN or something, in front of the fireplace, and relax on a day off.

Naturally, my Bureau-issued phone rang as soon as I poured my first cup of coffee.

It was Macallister, snapping orders in short, staccato sentences. "Porter. Grab your go-bag. Meet the squad at Logan Airport. I'll text you the location. There's a Bureau jet waiting for you. Wheels-up in thirty minutes."

"Where am I going? What happened?"

"Petrikov is in Atlanta, Georgia. You'll be briefed on the plane." Click.

My five-person squad huddled in the narrow cabin of a Bureau-owned Cessna Citation X jet. Zimmerman and Jones had grabbed the two seats on the left side of the plane; Connelly and Jordon snagged the two ends of the three-person sofa-type seat on the right side. The junior guy—me—got the middle seat.

Huddled together, we listened as Macallister briefed us through the high-speed data-and-voice link to the plane. "12:52 AM. Security camera at the Navy Federal Credit Union in Stockbridge, Georgia. Blurry image of Petrikov outside the building. He was with another man who was using the ATM, inside."

Jones asked, "How did we get the data?"

"As you know, among other surveillance, we have liaised with the National Security Agency, to have their supercomputers analyze video and search for Petrikov's and Volkov's facial recognition tags. The NSA processed the image at 4:37 AM. A tech there downloaded the actual video feed at 5:02 AM in order to review it in person. NSA sent notice of a match to DC at 5:16 AM, and I got it at 5:28 AM. I arranged for the plane and called you all at 5:40 AM." Macallister paused. "It's now just before 7:00 AM. We've delayed flights at Hartsfield–Jackson Atlanta International Airport, so that we can thoroughly scan the terminal. We've got police on the ground. We've got agents from our Atlanta field office spreading out in the area, interviewing people. Full-court press, people. Let's circle the noose."

Zimmerman grunted, "All those boots on the ground, and you're sending us there? What are we supposed to do, exactly?" I looked at him; he did not appear to be well. *Ballsy move,* I thought, *questioning the SAC 'cuz you've got a New Year's headache.*

Macallister's response was noncommittal, though. "You're on the fastest plane we've got. Seven hundred miles per hour. You'll be there in just over an hour. Cars waiting for you on the tarmac. The more people we have on this, the better the chances of us finding Petrikov."

By the end of the day, it was obvious that Petrikov slipped the net.

When we had arrived at the location of the camera, less than thirty-minutes drive time from the airport, we had found a beehive of activity. Just off I-675, in the Atlanta suburb of Stockbridge, the Navy Federal Credit Union building fronted a busy street, even busier with the lights of massed patrol cars and interspersed, unmarked FBI vehicles. Teams had been assigned to review the records of a cluster of motels nearby, while others were tasked to interview staff at the dozen or so fast-food restaurants in the area.

Meanwhile, the NSA had put a priority rush on identifying the man that had used the ATM, inside the credit union building. His name had turned out to be Clyde Brady, a former Navy enlisted man who was the night manager at the Taco Bell across the street. He said that he didn't remember seeing a large, fat man outside while he used the ATM; he had gone there alone.

As my squad conferenced, with Macallister on a video link, in the Bureau's Atlanta Field Office, we ran through our findings and our options.

"Roadblocks. We should have put up roadblocks around the entire perimeter," Zimmerman asserted.

"Impossible. We got the hit almost five hours after the camera timestamp," countered Jones.

"Maybe he spent the night at one of those motels. Maybe he's got an accomplice other than Volkov, who we don't know to look for in the security camera feeds, who checked in and got the room key. Maybe he drove away under our noses," theorized Zimmerman.

"And maybe he wasn't there at all," I said. "Here's the problem. Other than the Bureau, law enforcement, and the folks who look at our web page, this guy is basically invisible. We stifled all the press back in 2017, so we didn't cause a panic. We certainly didn't announce that a high-value prisoner escaped from our custody in December. His face has never been on the news in this context. And therefore, the public doesn't know to look for him. We've been conducting a manhunt in isolation."

"Yeah," replied Macallister, "that *is* a problem. That's not exactly true; we announced in December that we were looking for two suspects. We *did* get the word out."

"Sure, but an announcement is hardly compelling. The public doesn't know what he did. And I get it, they can't. But that ties our hands too. Public attention span is limited. They're not going to remember what we put out in December."

Macallister considered that for a moment. "Alright. Here's what we're gonna do. With Appleton under arrest, the mole hunt seems to be concluded. We'll go public on Volkov on infiltrating the FBI. The public relations people will have to spin it, of course, but they'll get the word out. And we'll go more public on Petrikov. Wanted for treason, or something.

"You're right, Porter. We gotta be more visible."

There were affirming nods around the table. Macallister wrapped up his instructions, "Stay in Atlanta for a while. Turn over every stone. If we can get even a hint of a thread from that location, we can follow it. *Someone* there must remember a gigantic guy with a Russian accent."

"Getting the word out is key," Connelly stated with confidence. "After all, no one can remain invisible, forever."

I wasn't so sure. If anyone could do that, it was Anastasia Volkov. She remained invisible, inside the FBI, for years. And if she was working with Petrikov again, she was already way ahead of us.

I didn't share Connelly's confidence. In fact, I wondered if Volkov was playing us. Again.

CHAPTER
28

TUESDAY, APRIL 30, 2019 — LOS ALTOS HILLS, CALIFORNIA

ON THE LAST DAY OF APRIL, dining with the three men on the patio of the rental mansion in Los Altos Hills, Anastasia Volkov laughed, "Do you think they know, yet, that they are chasing a digital ghost?"

"Where did you send them this time?" Guerrero inquired.

"Brownsville, Texas."

"Texas, huh?" Tretriaki said. "First Atlanta in January, then west to Oklahoma City, Oklahoma, in February. Where was March, again?"

"Outside of New Orleans."

"Right," Tretriaki continued. "Pulled 'em back south. Now you're taking them further south. Same technique?"

"Yep. I find a street-facing camera that's operated by a government or quasi-government entity, which the Bureau would have immediate access to. Actually, via the National Security Agency. They will have been looped into to do the data crunching. Anyway, I find an image of, um, a larger man that's realistically close to my father's profile. I drop my father's facial recognition tags into the camera feed, but I blur the actual visual that the camera has recorded. I wonder if they've noticed that each hit is when it's raining and dark. Maybe they'll assume that he reduces his vigilance in the dark, or sneaks outside. Doesn't matter. They'll never get a clear image, but they'll trust the computer," Volkov explained. "Next one at the border of Mexico. Maybe they'll think he's gonna try to cross it."

Guerrero and Tretriaki laughed, but Petrikov only scowled. "You're playing a dangerous game. How much longer?"

It had been four months. Four long months that Petrikov had been holed up in the Los Altos Hills house.

Occasionally, a box from Amazon had arrived, addressed to the Cornell professor. And occasionally, Volkov had reclined outside on the patio, soaking up the California spring sunshine, chatting pleasantly with the men, but never divulging a word about her secret work in the second-floor bedroom.

And once, beyond the scrolled-wrought iron driveway gate, the men had been bewildered to discover an idling, flatbed delivery truck, bearing a white Tesla Model X.

Volkov had only smiled a thin grin before requesting that the shiny new car be parked in the garage, out of sight, meant to be left untouched by the men.

Until, finally, on the night of Tuesday, April 30, to answer her father's question, she replied, "You know what tomorrow is?"

Guerrero had slurred, "Wednesday," through a mouthful of food, grinning a lopsided smirk at his quick wit.

Volkov had rolled her eyes and, looking at her father, overruled the South American, "It's Wednesday, but it's also May the first. May Day. In the motherland."

Petrikov had beamed, "The day to celebrate the working class. Our Russian Labor Day. Why?"

His daughter, finished with her meal, had stood, saying quietly as she left the table, "Exactly. Let's celebrate *my* work. Why don't you all plan for a very nice meal tomorrow night, inside for our privacy, and after, we'll have a little talk. And maybe a demonstration."

The May Day celebration meal was extravagant. It had been Tretriaki's turn to shop, and he had spent Petrikov's money on Kobe beef, several bottles of highly rated wines, and, from a specialty liquor store in San Francisco, a special bottle of authentic Russian vodka.

After the plates were cleared and the glasses topped off for an after-dinner drink, without fanfare, Volkov leaned forward and began, "I read an article in *Wired* magazine back in 2015. Two hackers had figured out how to connect remotely into a Jeep Cherokee. Using the car's built-in infotainment system, they could control the radio, the air conditioning, and the windshield wipers.

"But that's just a preview. They could also control the electronic brakes and the electronic transmission. With a reporter from the magazine in the Jeep, driving at speed on the interstate, they shifted it to neutral and let it coast to a stop."

She paused, noting she had their undivided attention.

"At that point, they could only steer the vehicle when it was in reverse, and so they didn't really have total control. But it was a test case. Widely reported, it brought attention to the issue of the connected car. Automakers had to build in security to their systems because these two hackers were able to do this over an IP address. Internet protocol, by the use of the car's built-in cellular connection that allowed data to flow to and from the car via the manufacturer. And that was back in 2015.

"But now, imagine how far the technology has progressed," she concluded.

Volkov went silent, letting the concept sink in. Tretriaki was the first to step up with a question, "Why do I sense this has something to do with the Tesla in the garage?"

"What does the Tesla have which the Jeep in 2015 doesn't have?" she asked, a reply in the form of a question.

She waited a beat, not letting the men steal her thunder. "It has Autopilot. The car can drive itself, under certain circumstances, without input from the driver. It has electronic steering, electronic acceleration, and electronic braking. It's all drive-by-wire. It has a complex array of sensors to 'see' where it is going. And it can control all of those things autonomously."

She stood.

"Or," she smiled, "*I* can control all of those things. Remotely. Wanna try it out?"

chapter 29

WEDNESDAY, MAY 1, 2019 — LOS ALTOS HILLS, CALIFORNIA

THE AFTER-DINNER DRINKS were abandoned, untouched, on the table.

Under the harsh glare of an LED bulb in the overhead garage door operator, the white Tesla Model X glinted; heretofore undriven.

The men knew that whatever Volkov had been working on, somehow involved this vehicle. She'd sat inside the car for hours at a time, sometimes in the driver's seat, but more often in the capacious back seat accessed by the high-tech and captivating gull-wing rear doors. But the car had never left the confines of the garage, and for the first time since its delivery months ago, the overhead door slid upward, and the charging cable was disconnected from the flanks of the electric Tesla.

Tretriaki snagged the driver's seat, anxious to try out the slick and sleek SUV. Guerrero grabbed the shotgun position.

Petrikov folded himself through the gaping gull-wing and dropped his bulk into the back seat, commenting, "This is exciting. I finally get to leave this fucking house."

Volkov, however, remained standing outside the car. "Aren't you coming along?" her father asked.

"Nope," she laughed, "not this time. Someone's gotta drive."

Silence, as the men, confused, tried to interpret that comment. Tretriaki dropped his hands to his lap, releasing his light grip on the leather steering wheel.

"No, that's okay," chuckled Volkov as she handed Tretriaki an iPhone. "You can drive. But when this phone rings, answer it. It's already set up with the car's Bluetooth, so when I call you, you'll be able to hear me on speaker." With that final instruction, Volkov turned and disappeared from the garage, skipping back up the two steps to the interior access door to the mansion.

After a moment of familiarization, Tretriaki placed his foot on the brake, shifted the car into reverse, and guided the silent car into the quiet night.

The only noise heard was the groan of the mechanized gate swinging open, and the tires of the Tesla crunching over the uneven brick pavers in the driveway.

The iPhone blared its ring; Guerrero hefted the device and accepted the call. As Tretriaki searched for volume control, Volkov's voice thundered from the vehicle's outstanding audio system, "Take a left out of the driveway and then take a left to head toward Interstate 280."

"Which way on 280?" Tretriaki asked as he pushed the accelerator pedal, the electric car responding to his touch with instant torque.

"I don't care. Which way do you want to go?" replied Volkov.

"How about west? Toward San Francisco."

"Fine with me."

A few minutes later, the white Tesla came to a stop at the end of Arastradero Road, and with his right turn signal engaged, Tretriaki turned the vehicle right and aimed for the underpass and, beyond, the I-280 West entrance ramp.

With no warning, the Tesla slewed into a hard right, accelerating up the I-280 East ramp at an alarming speed. "What the fuck!" yelled Tretriaki as the steering wheel moved under his hands. He jammed his right foot onto the left brake pedal as hard as he could, pushing the pedal to the carpeting, and yet after the briefest hesitation, the Tesla continued its surge onto the divided highway.

In the back seat, Petrikov's body tensed, and the big man's face flushed as the roadside signposts flashed by the windows, faster and faster as the car shot up the ramp. He gulped and whispered, "Irinushka! What? Why?"

Guerrero, sitting shotgun, was less reserved, yelling, "What the fuck? Anastasia?"

"Amazing acceleration, don't you think?" commented Volkov amiably, her voice clear over the speakers. "Sit back. I decided you should go east, by the way."

Stunned, the three men were unable to speak. The Tesla cruised serenely, silently, in the right lane, and began to overtake a slow-moving box truck. Tretriaki dropped his hands again, to his lap, as the left turn signal began to blink, and the white SUV gracefully slid into the left lane to pass.

Collecting himself before the other two men, Guerrero stuttered, "But . . . but . . . How can you see where you're going? I mean, where we're going?"

"Autopilot sensor arrays and cameras," replied the disembodied voice. "Stock equipment. It's all very sophisticated. And because of Autopilot, and because the car is all drive-by-wire, it's actually quite easy to control. I'm sitting at my desk. I've got three monitors showing me data and video, and I've got an Xbox video game controller to steer, brake, and accelerate."

"You're driving this thing like a video game?" Tretriaki gulped.

"Yep. That was almost the hardest part. Getting familiar with the feel of the controls. I logged a lot of hours on the Xbox. For practice, of course."

"Hang on," Tretriaki said. "I slammed on the brakes when the car shot up that on-ramp. Nothing happened. I know enough about cars to know these things have mechanical brakes. Why didn't it stop?"

"Try it," the disembodied voice prodded from the car's speakers.

Tretriaki tapped the brake pedal, and the car slowed for a moment, allowing the box truck to the right to move ahead of the white SUV. In the back seat, as the car slowed, Petrikov had begun to unclench his jaw and relax, but then, with no warning, no turn signal, and with a gut-pounding force of acceleration, the Tesla shot forward and immediately cut into the right-hand lane, narrowly missing the front of the box truck and eliciting an angry blast of horn from the truck driver. Petrikov gasped, and he began to pant, petrified.

Over the Bluetooth connection, the three men heard Volkov's laugh. "Sorry 'bout that. I didn't mean to cut it so close. You've still got your foot on the brake?"

"Yeah," Tretriaki admitted.

"Right. You have some braking ability. But I use the computer to cut off the power to the hydraulic system that pressurizes the mechanical brakes, and they become ineffective. The electric motors easily overpower what little pressure remains. And I can control the electronic regenerative braking for my remote driving." She paused, and the men saw the signs for exit 16, El Monte Road, approaching. Volkov added, "You're getting off here."

The Tesla settled itself into the right lane, leaving the truck quickly behind, and then smoothly decelerated on the hard right curve of the cloverleaf-designed junction at El Monte Road. Slowing briefly to allow right-of-way traffic to continue, the SUV merged into a line of cars and then slipped onto the ramp for I-280 West.

"Can I drive, please?" Tretriaki begged.

Volkov laughed. "Sure. Your turn."

The vehicle jerked slightly as Tretriaki resumed control. With his hands on the wheel and feet at the pedals, Tretriaki audibly inhaled, then exhaled.

Guerrero's right hand, clenched tightly on the door pull handle, didn't relax, as he asked, "Are you going to do that . . . that driving thing again? Without warning? Can you just warn us, please," he begged, voice nervous and quaking slightly.

Volkov giggled, "No. You have control. Head back to the house, please. Enjoy the ride. I'm out." The audio connection went silent.

In the back seat, Petrikov's rapid breathing slowed.

The three men didn't say a word during the short drive back to the rented mansion, where they pulled the SUV into the garage, the overhead door rumbling down, and hiding the shiny, white car from view.

The rear gull-wing door articulated itself open, but Petrikov, deeply settled into the back seat, didn't move for a long moment. Finally, his breath still coming in labored bursts, he reached out his left hand to Tretriaki, who helped the large oligarch from the Tesla.

In between short breaths, Petrikov growled, "I need a drink. And an explanation."

CHAPTER

30

TRETRIAKI LED THE BIG RUSSIAN back to the living room in the rented mansion. Guerrero had darted ahead to pick up Petrikov's abanonded after-dinner drink, and the Chilean met the two men at the entry to the room.

Without a word, the Russian accepted the proffered glass and downed it in a single gulp. Soothed, Petrikov's breathing returned to normal, and he ambled to the bar to pour himself a fresh drink. All the while, he pointedly ignored his daughter, who was reclining, primly, in a club chair, legs crossed, bearing a peaceful expression with a hint of a grin.

Petrikov considering the vodka bottle before tipping it toward his glass, filling it once more. This time, instead of slugging it, he swirled the liquid around aimlessly, contemplating it before resting his bulk back into the sofa across from his daughter.

Licking his lips, he spoke efficiently, "That was *very* impressive. But *very* disconcerting. I did not enjoy it. Explain. Please."

Volkov uncrossed her legs and slid forward so that she was perched on the edge of the club chair. With her elbows demurely resting on her knees, Volkov launched into her explanation, "First, let's talk about the inherent trust that consumers put in their devices and in the technology that they use. Your everyday citizen is completely interlinked with the online world. For one, they bank online. Therefore, every detail about their banking and credit card records can be accessed online. They correspond online by email, text message, and sometimes video calls using

Facetime or Skype. All transmitted over the internet. And on top of that, a vast majority of the first-world population now carries a smartphone. Those things are insidious. They're everywhere. And they're used for everything I just talked about, and then some. Social media, for example. People post every detail about their daily lives. From their phones or on their computers. It's *all* connected to the internet!"

"People are like sheep," Guerrero commented. "No one thinks about security. They just do what everyone else does."

"Yeah, and then they throw their hands up and say, 'how could this happen to me?' when their identity is stolen, right?" Tretriaki added.

"Exactly." Volkov took a sip from a glass of water before continuing, "And the crazy thing is, people assume it's all secure. But it's *not*! Every day, someone, somewhere, is trying to find a weakness. Constantly probing. But the average consumer doesn't care about that. They just want the immediate convenience of a connected world. And that isn't just limited to computers and smartphones. It also includes automobiles."

Her audience was rapt as she blasted a series of rapid-fire rhetorical questions, "Did you know that General Motors has sold over ten *million* cars with an always-on internet connection? That *every* Ford that will be sold next year will have built-in internet connectivity? That certain German cars have 300 *gigabyte* hard drives that record vehicle diagnostics, infotainment, and location information?

"And this—"

Volkov paused, for dramatic effect, "this brings us to our Tesla.

"Tesla has built in two ways to access their cars. First, each car has the capability to receive over-the-air software updates. The car is set up to receive those updates only through Wi-Fi. In other words, let's say an update is ready. You get a message, and then you connect your car to your Wi-Fi network at home. Then it updates.

"Then you've got mobile access. This is the convenience that is expected by a buyer. What I was talking about before. This is so you can, for example, lock or unlock your car with an app on your phone remotely. You can do a lot more through your phone, with the Tesla app. The car has an always-on, mobile broadband connection. Got it?"

Heads nodded around the room. Petrikov took a small sip of his vodka before resetting the glass down on the coffee table in front of him.

Volkov continued, "What I did was to sort of merge those systems. I figured out a way into the mobile broadband connection. I had to get into Tesla's servers to do that. That took a long time. But, once in, I can force a little packet program through the mobile connection into the central firmware system, that normally would be accessed only by Wi-Fi, and tell the central computer's firmware system to open a permanent link to the mobile broadband connection.

"The rest is easy. Once the central computer is open to mobile broadband, I can control it through that mobile broadband connection. I sent it another packet program to facilitate my control so that I would get the data I needed off the car's systems to be able to drive it through a two-way connection.

"In fact, Tesla did much of this for me."

"What!" exclaimed Petrikov. "They're working with you? Why didn't you tell me? They could find us. They could—"

"No, no, no," interrupted his daughter, before her father got any further with his objection. "Not literally. Indirectly. Tesla wants to give its owners all sorts of ways to interact with their vehicles. Not only do they make it as easy as possible for you to link your smartphone to your car, they've gone further. For example, later this year, an owner will be able to summon their car to come to them, and it will self-drive itself to their location. That feature is supposed to release soon. But they've already got a feature where you can tell the car, via your phone, to initiate a firmware update. That's the mechanism I needed to install my packet. Tesla already set it up so a mobile phone, through a mobile connection, could do those things. I just sidestepped them for my own purposes."

"I don't get it. You controlled the car through the phone you gave us?" queried Guerrero.

"No. That was just so I could talk to you. Simple as that. My driving connection, if you call it that, is through the cellular system that already exists. If you didn't have a strong cell signal, I wouldn't be able to do it."

Her father leaned forward, taking a small sip from his glass. "But you can do it from anywhere? The proximity was just convenience, no?"

"Correct. You could have been in Boston. I could do the same thing."

"With any Tesla?" demanded Petrikov.

Volkov reclined in the club chair and crossed her legs. "Unfortunately, no. Not yet, at least. That was the proof of concept. Now I have to scale it. Figure out how to identify other cars and to get into their onboard systems. With this car, I had an advantage; I could hack its brains and get the addresses and identifiers I needed from it directly."

She uncrossed her legs and planted both feet on the floor, again leaning forward earnestly in the chair. "That's the next step. And, I'm afraid, more difficult. Because now, I need to figure out how to hack someone else's vehicle."

Petrikov chuckled slightly, his laugh becoming more enthusiastic until he cackled, "What you did was amazing. What you could do next will be . . . unprecedented! Imagine the possibilities!"

The oligarch downed his glass of vodka, and, wiping his lips, concluded, "I can't wait!"

chapter 31

ABOUT A MONTH LATER:
LATE ON SUNDAY AFTERNOON, JUNE 2, 2019

IN THE LIVING ROOM OF THE Los Altos Hills mansion, Anatoly Petrikov paced back and forth, much as he had been doing for the past month or so. Waiting. Annoyed. But having no choice but to continue waiting, and pacing.

His daughter had tantalized him with her incredible, unprecedented hack of a car, and yet now, a month gone by, she remained in her room, rarely coming out, taking food back to her desk and not conversing with her housemates.

Petrikov had enough. He had been, for all intents, a prisoner in this house, a fugitive on the run. He was ready for action. For results.

He laboriously climbed the stairs to the second floor and barged into his daughter's quarters.

At the sound of the door banging open, she muttered, "I can't do it."

Anastasia Volkov's head was slumped into her arms, crossed on her desk, keyboards and laptops shoved messily aside. Her father's heart sank at the sight of her dejection. With a hand lightly resting on her shoulder, her father kindly said, "Talk to me. How can I help?"

Lifting and twisting her face to her father, Volkov rolled her eyes. "No offense, but I'm not sure you can offer the kind of help I need."

Petrikov smiled. "Tell me, anyway." He pulled over a side chair and settled his flab into it, the chair's spindly wooden legs creaking under the strain. "Explain," he commanded, setting his glass of a late afternoon vodka pick-me-up onto his daughter's messy desk, a signal that she had his full attention.

Volkov straightened, inhaled, and ranted, "I was making great progress. I didn't think it would be this hard. I just don't have the bandwidth, the capacity. It's like this.

"Each car's mobile broadband connection is always on. It's always communicating with the cellular towers. Tiny packets of data, just to let the system know where it is and that it can receive. Just like any mobile phone.

"Once I figured out what to look for, I could find them easily."

She pointed out the window at a red Tesla Model 3 that happened to be driving by. With Tesla's headquarters just beyond the scrub, this was a common sight. "That one . . ." Pointing at a line of code on a screen, she finished her sentence, "is probably this one. Or," she traced on-screen, "maybe this one."

"What's the problem? You figured out how to identify the car. Can't you just narrow it down and send it your program?"

"I could, probably, if I had the computing power and the connection power. I just don't. Here's the first problem. I need way more computing power and bandwidth to narrow down which packets sent over the cell network belong to a car I want to target. Simplistically, I need to know when a packet sent over the network is a VIN. Vehicle Identification Number. Then, and only then, can I establish my credentials in order for it to think I am the so-called Tesla mothership, and the car will trust me to send it instructions."

She grimaced. "And there are two basic problems with that. One, I need brute force computing power to scan the signals. Physically. I'd have to write an algorithm or something to identify the correct data packets to quickly establish, or, well, fake, that I am Tesla.

"The second problem is time. With the car in the garage, it was easy. It just sat there and waited. But a moving car is different. If I lose it because of distance, because it transits to the next cell tower coverage area, I have to start over from the beginning."

Shrugging, she confessed, "I thought that since we were here, next to a sea of Teslas, I could do it and find one to hijack. But it takes too long. Either the driver gets in and then drives out of range, or one coming into range gets to where it's going and stops. No one has just circled the block a whole bunch of times. Because that's what it would take. And that's not realistically gonna happen."

The daughter fell silent while her father stared out the window, to the area where the now long-gone, red Tesla had been.

Petrikov finally spoke, at first softly, but with tempo and tone becoming faster and louder, "To me, it appears you need to clone yourself. But what if you could clone yourself? Would that be enough to be the brute force you need? Because you already have the programming figured out, don't you? You need to get the, what'd you call it? The bandwidth. Right?"

"Sure," she replied. "But cloning me is a far different order of magnitude than programming. Don't you think?"

Petrikov chuckled. "Not literally."

He thought for a moment before asking, "I've been thinking about this for a month. But I want to hear your perspective. What's the end game? What can we do with this?"

His daughter leaned back in her chair and brushed a strand of hair from her olive-toned forehead. "Oh, the possibilities are endless. If you could do this on scale, you could control a swarm of these things. They would do whatever you wanted. Go wherever you wanted. The sky's the limit!"

Standing and grabbing his glass off the desk, the big man began to pace the room, his highball of vodka cradled in his left hand as his right hand punctuated his sentences, "Those possibilities." Fist punching the air, upward. "A swarm. An excellent word. So descriptive." Right hand swooping through the air, sideways. "You know what I want to do? Just for fun? To see if it really works. Let the swarm snarl traffic." Finger slicing at throat. "Stop 'em dead. Park 'em on a bridge, maybe." Pause, the pacing stopped. "In Newport. Rhode Island. You called me, just as our last adventure started to go bad. I was looking at a big suspension bridge. Stop a handful of these things on the bridge at rush hour. Both directions. No one can get by." Pacing resumed. "And not just there. Bridges all over the country at once. Imagine! Gridlock! It would be *so* entertaining!"

Petrikov stopped talking and stopped pacing, and his daughter laughed, "Really? That's it? All this work, and you want to be entertained by gridlock? Surely there's a way to profit, or at least to leverage this for something more than a traffic jam!"

Nodding, her father lowered himself back onto the creaky chair. "I'm sure I could come up with something better, yes. But we're not there yet, are we?"

"No, I'm afraid not. Not without the bandwidth, more people, and more resources."

"Exactly," Petrikov agreed, finally tipping back his glass and swallowing the clear liquid in a single, triumphant gulp. "And I know just the person who might be interested in helping—who has both the technical know-how *and* the financial ability."

PART THREE
AUGUST 2019

CHAPTER

32

TWO MONTHS LATER:
SATURDAY, AUGUST 3, 2019 — 9:15 PM — BURLINGTON, VERMONT

FBI SPECIAL AGENT Abdul Hamid accepted the two red-checked, waxed-cardboard paper trays from the street-cart vendor. The off-duty agent flashed a bright smile, his teeth appearing exceptionally bright against his dark Middle-Eastern complexion as he eyed the two pairs of sliders, each pair nested in an unruly gaggle of greasy but delicious-looking fries. Just what the evening called for.

Quantico, Virginia, was a long way from this northern Vermont city on the shores of Lake Champlain, and on his first real getaway from his post-Quantico job at the FBI Albany, New York, Field Office, Hamid was ready to party.

He'd done the three-hour drive from Albany earlier today accompanied by his buddy Alberto "Al" Rodriquez, a recently-minted Information Analyst who had been assigned to Albany Field Office six months ago. The Al-and-Abdul show, they had decided, would take the Fools by storm.

The pair had decided, last minute, that a late-summer road trip was in order. Searching the internet, Rodriquez discovered an advertisement for the 12th Annual "Festival of Fools," just one-hundred-and-fifty miles away, promising street food, live music, a variety of entertainers, and, hopefully, probably, a fair number of cute, fun-loving, single girls. They booked a room for Saturday night at a worn-down, dated Hilton in Burlington, near the shore of Lake Champlain. They hoped that they wouldn't have to use it.

Finding Rodriquez reserving a wood-and-iron bench under a tree strung with hundreds of little, white lights, Hamid sat, handing one of the slider trays to his friend. "Whadya think?"

Grinning, Rodriquez answered, "Half-assed."

"Come again? I stood in that line, and that's the gratitude you got?"

Still smiling, Rodriquez repeated, "Still half-assed. No beer."

"No, actually, what's half-assed is you," Hamid poked, feigning indignation. "Listen. Remember I told you about my NAT roommate at Quantico? Ben Porter. My buddy Ben would have had a beer waiting for me. A nice, cold beer with a nice head of froth. That would *not* have been half-assed."

"That's a great story, bro," Rodriquez responded with a healthy measure of snark, adding, "But you can't get beers on the street. We gotta go over there." He pointed at the outdoor bar opposite and lectured, "Now, your turn to listen. Let's eat first. Then you can buy me a beer over there to make up for your shitty, insolent attitude."

Hamid laughed, and the pair dove into their sliders, wiping greasy fingers on disintegrating napkins as they carried on their good-natured ribbing.

Crumpling what was left of his last paper napkin into a loose ball, Hamid tossing the wad into Rodriguez's equally empty, also decimated red-checked tray. "Two points, man. Nice shot," sneered Rodriquez.

Before Hamid could respond, they both heard the sharp chirp of tires on pavement. Recognizing that sound from his TEVOC driving training at Quantico, Hamid's head swiveled to the left, his senses engaged.

The two off-duty FBI men would be witnesses to the terror that followed.

A white Tesla Model X with green Vermont license plates had swerved into the pedestrian-only street, blasting past the barricades and bouncing bodies like sacks off the car's white flanks. High-pitched screams of terror were countered by the thumps and grunts of people being mowed down by the fast-moving SUV as it shot by the pair of stunned men and clipped a little girl standing by the slider cart that Hamid had walked from only minutes before.

With a whine of its high-torque electric motors, the Tesla suddenly accelerated even faster, arrowing its dented, bloodied flanks and cracked windshield at the parked fire truck that blocked the intersection at Bank Street.

In a flash, the Tesla's hood was under the truck's body, and then the A-pillars that supported the Tesla's windshield and roof met the steel frame of the firetruck. With a screeching squeal, the roof and greenhouse of the SUV were shorn from its body, leaving a trail of mangled metal and millions of bits of shattered tempered glass.

For an instant, there was only silence, punctuated only by the creaking and popping of the twisted metal, and by the weak moans and cries of injured.

Hamid and Rodriquez sprang forward, rushing into the stricken crowd, helping victims and putting the basic medical skills they had learned at Quantico to use, as armed policemen ran to the scene and the sirens wailed louder by the second.

CHAPTER

33

SAME TIME — PLATTSBURGH, NEW YORK

IN A DARKENED ROOM, lit only by the glow of computer monitors, Anatoly Petrikov's belly began to shake; he couldn't hold it in, and his garrulous laugh filled the space as he choked out, between peals, "Well . . . that . . . that . . . that was *extraordinary!*"

Clutching at his gut, the oligarch couldn't stop laughing, and an involuntary tear dribbled down his right cheek. In the dark space, no one noticed as he wiped his eye.

"Finally!" he muttered. "Action! And progress. And success."

His guffaws subsided to chuckles as he recalled the long, and oftentimes extremely boring, two months of time since he was a passenger in a remotely-operated Tesla, back in the Los Altos Hills.

The cross-country drive east, from California to New York, had been far more arduous than their leisurely journey from Ithaca to Silicon Valley seven months earlier. This time, they had been on a schedule.

By July 1st, they had packed up the mansion, loading Volkov's array of computers, couched in waterproof boxes, carefully into the bed of the pickup. With the white Tesla loaded on a trailer behind the white Ford F-150, the driving was taxing and relentless.

The drive had taken three days. And it was three days of great risk. No longer shielded from view by the tall fence that surrounded the mansion in Los Altos Hills, the two fugitives remained in the F-150's back seat, only occasionally risking a trip to a restroom. The three men and one woman had been irritable and exhausted by the time they reached Plattsburgh, New York, a town of about twelve thousand people in upstate New York, only twenty miles from the Canadian border.

The proximity to the Canadian border had been important. Naturally, Petrikov and his daughter had assumed that they were not only on a law enforcement most-wanted list, but that they were also both on a border watch list. Petrikov and Volkov had been in captivity long enough to have had their biometric details scanned—fingerprint, face scans, retinal scans, and DNA samples, and departing the United States had been an impossibility.

The three men they were to rendezvous with carried legitimate passports, but it had been decided that they would make the trans-Atlantic journey by air into Canada and cross into the United States by a more casual method.

By car.

The men would fly into the Montréal–Trudeau International Airport and would then drive south, using their carefully-sourced passports at the ten-lane United States border crossing at Douane. The men would have had nothing to declare; the inspection of their rented Ford Explorer would be cursory and quick, for their bags contained nothing illicit and their appearance, three young European men with accents, touring Canada and seeking a casual road-trip to see New York City, would arouse no suspicion.

It was what was in their brains that had mattered.

Unit 29155 had dispatched three of their most talented hackers, and those three men sat alongside Anastasia Volkov in the darkened room in Plattsburgh, listening as Petrikov's laughter faded away.

As the *vor v zakone* of the Brighton Beach *Bratva*, Petrikov often had dealings with Mother Russia. But he had been disgraced, in the eyes of the motherland, by his involvement in a scheme to sell one of the Kremlin's finest jewels, a three-hundred-carat diamond known as "The Creator."

His plot to detonate two dirty nuclear bombs in New York and Chicago had been driven by a desire for profit and a wish for revenge.

Revenge on all those small people who had slighted him, who had dismissed him as a pot-bellied pretend con-man. And therefore, to Petrikov, the plot had one more potential blessing: it would put the megalomaniac back on the map.

Though the plot had failed and had never been made public, it had nevertheless percolated as a story in the international intelligence community; too many people had been involved to compartmentalize it as a well-kept secret, and the story attracted a great deal of attention in Moscow for its audacity.

When Petrikov had reached out to Mother Russia in July from Los Altos Hills through his old channels, not only did he ask for help, but he also made sure the Russians understood his leadership in the 2017 plot. The Kremlin was suitably impressed. The man was down, but not out. He had attempted a brazen terror plot, failed, but then he had escaped the custody of the FBI, he had traveled cross-country undetected, and with his daughter, he had cooked up something unimaginable.

Once his bona-fides had been established with the Kremlin, it had taken only a week for Petrikov to make the deal, using a VOIP (voice over internet protocol) connection made untraceable by the efforts of Volkov on one end, using a series of Tor cutouts, and by the inherent security on the other end.

The order had come from the very top—Russian President Vladimir Vladimirovich Putin had approved sending three men from his elite group of spies, hackers, propaganda artists, and specially trained, fiercely loyal combatants known as Unit 29155.

Immediately upon encamping in the Plattsburgh house, this rental again courtesy of the Cornell professor, at the outskirts of the State University of New York at Plattsburgh, the now four-person team of three Russian hackers and Anastasia Volkov began to attempt the unthinkable: to download Volkov's program into any Tesla vehicle.

A medium-height, dark-haired, dark-eyed man from Unit 29155, who spoke perfect English with only a very slight Russian accent, introduced himself and his compatriots, "I am Vitaly. I am in command of the team. With me are Georgiy and Fedor. First names only, of course."

They settled into their work with cup after cup of black coffee, and with sustenance brought from the outside by Tretriaki and Guerrero. The team's three-week hackathon was both exhilarating and exhausting. Vitaly and Volkov agreed to focus their efforts on a Model X, since the architecture of the firmware would match the vehicle in their possession. Trial by error, as line of code after line of code written, tested, rewritten.

For Petrikov, it was more tiresome waiting, and the oligarch's temper grew shorter and shorter. Early successes of the programming team were toasted with Stolichnaya. Early setbacks were mourned with Stolichnaya. Petrikov complained to Tretriaki, "Find me something more suitable to drink. We're going to be here a while." Tretriaki searched the internet for nearby distillers and successfully appeased Petrikov with a local vodka.

The oligarch's mood brightened considerably as the sun set on Saturday, August 2, three weeks after the group had assembled in Plattsburgh, when Volkov announced, "Our programming protocols are complete. We are ready!"

"When do we begin?" Petrikov demanded.

"Now," his daughter replied. "However, one of the shortfalls that we had months ago still exists. Our experiment requires that a vehicle must remain in operation, for about fifteen to twenty minutes, within the service radius of a single cell tower. It might be some time until that criteria is met."

Petrikov nodded as he took a seat in the darkening room, alongside Tretriaki and Guerrero. No one bothered to turn a light on as the sun set to the west.

Working their keyboards quietly, the team identified the signals of several Model Xs in their three-hundred-mile search radius, an area chosen completely at random.

Within minutes, they zeroed in on a promising target: a Model X on-network and moving slowly, only nineteen miles away, across Lake Champlain in Burlington.

Scraping the VIN from the vehicle's mobile broadband handshakes with the network, they learned this particular Model X was brand new, having been delivered only days before to a buyer in Burlington, Vermont. Suzanne Cahal would never know how much to regret buying that beautiful, high-tech, shiny-white, eco-friendly, luxury SUV with its unique gull-wing doors, nor would she discover that a search for a parking spot would take her life.

"Initiating initial vector via the modem," Vitaly announced.

On the monitors, they began to assemble the data stream from the target. Location and speed data were compiled quickly; the target appeared to be traveling in a circular route around the Church Street Marketplace.

The first packet program was sent successfully.

The target made a second circuit, retracing its route. "What's it doing?" Guerrero asked.

"Ten to one it's looking for a place to park," wagered Tretriaki, familiar with the search for a spot in Brooklyn.

The first program had loaded into the Tesla's onboard computer, and the vehicle was ready to receive the second program.

"Initiating final stage. Autopilot gateway module. Establishing Autopilot root persistence," Vitaly intoned, as progress indicators on-screen neared 100 percent.

The target turned right onto Cherry Street and began to slow near the intersection of Church Street.

"Radar sensors through Autopilot Electronic Control Unit transmitting. Parking aid sensors ECU feed active. Waiting on cameras."

The three waiting monitors had begun to flare with data; first, the onboard diagnostics of the vehicle on the left-hand screen, then the sensor arrays and data streams on the right-side screen. Volkov held the Xbox controller at a darkened center screen; the three Unit 29155 men tapping furiously at their keys as the firmware update to the Tesla's brains was completed. "Now!" Vitaly shouted.

"We have it!" Volkov exclaimed, as her center screen infilled with the color image from the Tesla's built-in, forward-facing camera. She squeezed the right trigger on the controller, inadvertently bringing her right hand down. At her command, the image jerked to the right as the target swerved to the right, and the speed indicator clicked higher.

"You're on a sidewalk! Look at all those people!" Tretriaki yelled.

Volkov attempted to jockey and swerve the vehicle to avoid pedestrians, but to no avail, for the area was tightly packed, twinkling lights above and throngs of people in the view from the Tesla's camera. "No!" she screamed, "No! I have no braking!" Her left hand crushed the left rear trigger on the controller, to no effect, as a small human figure was catapulted over the sightline of the camera.

Keying furiously, trying to find the gap in the data stream, Vitaly updated, "I found the glitch. It's coming back online—it's back!"

In her panic, Volkov squeezed the incorrect trigger. The right-rear trigger. The accelerator trigger.

The target surged, closing the distance to a stationary, red firetruck in seconds.

In an instant, the screens rapidly began to go dark. First the camera feed, then the diagnostics, and finally the source signal: *CONNECTION TERMINATED*.

With a gasp, Volkov dropped the Xbox controller.

Behind her, Petrikov's belly began to shake; he couldn't hold it in, and his garrulous laugh filled the space as he choked out, between peals, "That was *extraordinary!*"

THE NEXT NIGHT:
SUNDAY, AUGUST 4, 2019 — PLATTSBURGH, NEW YORK

ANASTASIA VOLKOV SAT, ALONE, in the darkened room where the operation had been conducted the night before.

The only light in the room was from the LCD monitor of a MacBook Air; her fingers played lethargically over the trackpad below the back-lit chiclet keyboard.

Story after story . . .

All featured prominently on the home pages of news outlets worldwide.

CNN.com. APnews.com. BBC.com. UPI.com.

The newspapers who still had print editions tried to capture the event in a carefully-composed headline.

The *New York Times* somberly proclaimed, "Tragedy in Vermont."

The *New York Post* alliterated: "Freak Fiasco at the Fools."

And from the hometown *Burlington Free Press*: "The Festival of Fools Canceled; Torn Asunder by Heartbreak." A subtitle asked, "Will this be the end of the Festival?"

Volkov clicked through to the article.

BURLINGTON, VT, AUGUST 4, 2019. The city is silent.
In solidarity, as one, the musicians packed up their instruments.

The huskers put away their props. Staff and patrons alike cooper-
ated to clear the tables and to clean up the litter. The Church Street
marketplace, only last night a thriving, exciting place of discov-
ery, of family fun, and of revelry, is all but abandoned, save for
a heavily-barricaded area where investigators comb through the
wreckage of a fatal, horrific accident.

The home page of the Festival of Fools event website has been
replaced with a black screen, with simple, sans-serif block letters
announcing: "The 12th Annual Festival of Fools is canceled, and
we mourn."

Flags throughout Burlington and the State of Vermont are
lowered at half-mast. The somber tolls of church bells have replaced
the shrieks of sirens that screamed through the night.

Fourteen victims are described to be in area hospitals in con-
ditions varying from stable to serious. Five fatalities have been
reported, the most recent an eight-year-old girl who died from her
internal injuries overnight. Names of the victims have not yet been
released by the authorities, and the counts thus far are unofficial.

Sources reveal that the Tesla Model X involved in the accident
was recently purchased by Burlington artist Suzanne Cahal, a
figure covered in these pages in the past as her critically acclaimed
artwork rose to prominence. It is unclear whether the artist was
in the vehicle at the time of the incident.

As the investigation continues, questions are being asked. Why?
How did this terrible event happen? Why was perimeter security
lax enough to allow a vehicle to pass into the Festival grounds?
Can the Festival continue?

Burlington may be silent now, as the city grieves as one. The
quiet will pass, the questions will be answered, but the wounds
may never heal.

With a sigh, Volkov slowly, with more deliberate precision than
necessary, folded the screen of the laptop closed. The last light in the
room was the glowing bitten-apple logo on the rear of the laptop screen,
until it, too, went dark.

Volkov caught herself holding her breath. With a soft whoosh, she blew the air from her lungs through her lips, and she whispered to the empty room, "What have I done?"

A WEEK LATER:
SUNDAY, AUGUST 11, 2019 — PLATTSBURGH, NEW YORK

THE WHITE TESLA MODEL X with California license plates had been attracting a great deal of curious interest for its similarities to the vehicle that had been involved in the Vermont accident a week before. Since the Model X was superfluous, now, the Cornell professor who owned it, on paper at least, had sold it five days ago, on Tuesday, to a local car dealer at a substantial discount.

At the same time the attention getting Tesla was being driven from the rented house at the outskirts of SUNY-Plattsburgh to the dealer's lot, an unremarkable, rented Ford Explorer had passed back into Canada, to be returned at the Montréal–Trudeau International Airport. The three occupants of the vehicle had cleared Canadian immigration without issue. Boarding their Rome, Italy-bound flight, the men from the Explorer had reclined in their economy class seats and slept, their luggage of benign personal belongings safe in the cargo hold below them, and a message for their superior hidden in their brains.

Anatoly Petrikov could barely contain his glee, his sixty-seven-year-old body energized with a rush of enthusiasm he had not felt in decades. *This* was *it*.

The message he had sent to Vladimir Putin, via the three operatives from Unit 29155, was simple.

Petrikov would grant the code, the technology, and the method to Putin. Not in exchange for a fee, though. Petrikov figured he had enough money, squirreled away, untouchable, in the Caymans.

No, his compensation would not be monetary. It would be asylum.

For all that he had to offer, all he wanted in return was transport to the motherland, for him, for his daughter, and for their two accomplices, should they desire it.

Neither Tretriaki nor Guerrero had attracted attention. In Plattsburgh, they had donned the T-shirts and Birkenstocks of summer graduate students. They could return to New York City if they wished, or they could accompany father and daughter to Russia to start a new life there.

For the oligarch, though, there was no choice. In Russia, he would be far from the reach of the F B I. He would be able to do whatever he wanted since he alone had the key to the kingdom. Or, more precisely, the password to the computer that held his daughter's code.

And he would have his daughter. And with her at his side, surely Putin would grant him a seat at the table. Imagine! Petrikov, shoulder-to-shoulder with Putin, in the splendor of the Kremlin, plotting mayhem at the arrogance of the West with this fantastic breakthrough.

In her bedroom, Anastasia Volkov did not share her father's excitement.

For a week, she had listlessly played with the MacBook, refreshing the websites with fewer and fewer new stories as the headlines had petered off. The news cycle was ruthless; the accident in Vermont had captured the nation's attention for only a few days, before being replaced with the endless parade of political and economic news, sports scores, and celebrity sightings that fed the voracious appetite of clickers and commentators and tweeters and bloggers.

Though the national press had relegated updates on the story to the below the fold, so to speak, or to a small font in the hyperlink, the *Burlington Free Press* had been relentless with their updates, and Volkov found herself more often than not on that website's clean, white-back-grounded and uncluttered home page.

The banner logo of the site normally spelled out "Free Press" in blue and "Burlington" in black, but with a blue dot capping the lower-case "i." The dot had been replaced with a tiny blue ribbon as a memorial.

The stories on the accident at the Festival remained placed at the upper left corner, the most prominent location on the page, and follow-ups were scattered about as the *Free Press* assembled a picture of what had happened on that Saturday night.

Volkov was horrified by the damage that she had wrought, by her hand, with the Xbox controller.

She had struggled with these emotions. Only two years prior, she had been a willing, complicit partner in a plot to detonate two nuclear bombs—*nuclear bombs!*—in two major cities. The casualties, had they been successful, would have counted far, far higher; the property damage would have been exponentially greater.

Yet, this time, it had been much more personal. It had been *her* hand on the controller, at the virtual wheel of the Tesla. It had been *her* squeeze that had launched the projectile on its arc of destruction. It had been *her* code, *her* idea, that had made it all possible.

The bomb plot had felt so . . . detached.

This felt so . . . immediate. So intimate. So . . . *individual.*

It was the little girl. Volkov imagined an eight-year-old, braided-pig-tailed princess, who had been dancing on the brick pavers, her tiny feet pattering with the excitement of a late night with . . . Loud music! And athletic, awe-inspiring acrobats! And yummy food, the tastes, the treats! And the funny comedians, with their crowd-pleasing jokes (a few of which she didn't understand, but, whatever!).

And then the hood of the Tesla, at Volkov's command, had lifted that innocent little girl off her feet, her thirty-nine-pound body no match for the five-thousand-pound mass of the metal monster.

And it had killed her.

Ashley Whitby.

She had a name.

Her name had been released, along with the other victim's names, as next-of-kin had been notified, somberly, by Vermont State Police, their caps in hands, their eyes downcast, their presence and their mission unwanted by neither messenger nor recipient.

Ashley Whitby.

Volkov slammed the MacBook closed, and she squeezed her eyes tightly shut.

CHAPTER
36

THREE WEEKS LATER:
FRIDAY, AUGUST 30, 2019 — MORRISTOWN, NEW YORK

THE KREMLIN HAD AGREED to Petrikov's offer, and after three excruciating weeks of hiding in Plattsburgh, it was finally time to put plan into action. It was time to leave the United States.

Father, daughter, and friend relaxed in the gentle, westerly breeze, sitting on the open tailgate of a white Ford F-150 pickup truck, parked in a grassy field perhaps fifty feet from the seawall at the edge of the Saint Lawrence River.

A mile and a half to the northwest.

That was all that lay between them and freedom. Freedom from the FBI Most Wanted list. Freedom from looking over their shoulders at every venture outside, in public. From searching for surveillance cameras when in public, with heads down but while trying to act nonchalant. If there were cameras here, in this spot, that they had not seen, by the time the FBI got the footage, they would be long gone. Because, in less than an hour, the big man and the woman would board a small, twenty-three-foot runabout, and with the friendly upstate New Yorker that they'd met through a Craigslist posting, they'd go watch the Tall Ships Challenge "Parade of Sail."

This would be the last stop of the 2019 Tall Ships Challenge Great Lakes Series itinerary, that had started in June, in Toronto, and zigzagged back-and-forth across four of the five Great Lakes, with ports of call in both the United States and Canada.

A parade of nine vessels would sail into the Canadian town of Brockville, Ontario, almost opposite Morristown, to the delight of shoreside spectators and on-water observers. The friendly New Yorker had advised his passengers that they would be careful to hold to the United States side of the narrow Saint Lawrence River, but they would still have a wonderful vantage point to watch the majestic vessels, led by the iconic Canadian tall ship *Bluenose*.

Their captain for the outing, the gregarious Tom Morris, was a distant descendant of Gouverneur Morris, for whom the town was named and who was one of the signatories of both the United States Declaration of Independence and the Constitution. The present-day Morris, a lifelong resident of the tiny village, would be careful to respect his forefather's legacy and would not stray his vessel into Canadian waters.

Except, perhaps, just this one time.

For a stunning sum of cash, ten thousand dollars, all he'd have to do was allow his twenty-three footer to pass close enough by a similar Canadian vessel. Close enough so that his two passengers could step comfortably from one boat to the other. From one nation to the other.

Unseen and unnoticed amid the spectacle of the Parade of Sail.

Morris had been reluctant, at first, when the scheme had been proposed to him by the charterers who had reached out via Craigslist, in response to his advertisement for boating expeditions, a little side-hustle for extra cash in the summertime. It had been a slow summer, though, and the dreaded lake-effect snowstorms would start soon enough.

And the story had been compelling to the soft-hearted, overtrusting Morris. After years of searching, a Canadian father had finally been reunited with his daughter, who had disappeared from his life twenty-three years ago, abducted by a stranger in the teeming throng of New York City during a family vacation to see the City at Christmastime. The daughter had no passport. The father just wanted to bring her home.

It was innocent enough.

The pair had arrived in an unostentatious pickup truck driven by a friend. They were a tad early, and so they decided to enjoy the view and the gorgeous late-summer afternoon while parked on the grassy lawn abutting the docks where Morris kept his boat.

The friend had wandered to the little nearby restaurant to order some take-out snacks for the outing, offering to pick something up for the captain who, in turn, had suggested that he accompany him to help carry the items to the boat.

Left to themselves, father and daughter conversed quietly.

Anastasia Volkov had not been herself, her father thought, since the test of their breakthrough in Burlington, almost a month ago. He wrote it off to exhaustion, to burnout: the months and weeks and hours of programming, coding, sitting, all the while being unable to take a break and circulate in public. That alone was enough to weigh heavily on Petrikov's spirit, and he wasn't the one staring at lines of code on a screen.

Eleven days ago, Volkov had begun the laborious process of transferring the code from the various laptops to a single, two-terabyte Kingston flash drive, a marvel of miniaturization that cost well over a thousand dollars. The tiny USB drive was currently nestled in a soft, black cushion within a shiny, alloy case, that looked, perhaps, very much like a container of mints, tucked in her father's pants pocket.

Grazing his fingers over the fabric that comprised that pocket, his belly splayed in his own lap as he perched on the F-150's lowered tailgate, Petrikov whispered to his daughter, for the hundredth time, "Are you ready? Are you okay?"

Volkov, for the hundredth time, rolled her eyes and answered, "Sure."

She stared across the Saint Lawrence River, tiny wavelets twinkling in the sunlight like millions of diamonds.

Her father attempted a pep talk. "I don't understand. The glumness. In a few hours, we'll be in Canada. One step closer to freedom. A significant step from the FBI. And we'll be together. And yet you pout."

Twisting her face toward her father's, Volkov snapped, "Are you kidding? I *pout*? How do you think that little girl feels? She's not pouting. She's *dead*! And! Did you see that article on the *Free Press* website? The one where they wrote about the driver? The artist? She was *decapitated*! Her head was *literally* sliced off by the fire truck!"

Petrikov laughed heartily. "Decapitated. I did see that. Fabulous. Wonderful. What a way to go."

He paused, examining his daughter's face, then exploded, "Are *you* kidding? What did you expect? This was *your* idea! *Your* concept. Was it for some sort of amusement park ride? You *knew* that we would have this power. And yet you now question why?" Petrikov snorted.

"It's different now," sniffed his daughter. "Yes, of course. I knew all that. I didn't expect that it all would have happened the way it did. I should have been more careful. I should have taken it slower."

Her voice trailed off as she looked down at the grassy earth below the tailgate. "The last time, I wasn't directly involved. I was in the background. This time, though, it just felt so . . . specific."

Petrikov shook his head, his jowls wobbling. "Oh, please. Did you not anticipate the consequences? You knew exactly what you were doing. What those *consequences* would be."

"I did, but I didn't. I guess I just didn't expect . . . *this*."

"Just like your mother," Petrikov grumbled, muttering.

"What?" his daughter demanded.

Annoyed, Petrikov growled in a fierce tone, "You heard me. You're just like your mother."

Now incensed, his face flushed with anger, the oligarch stared at his daughter, his eyes slitting, his words spitting, "Your mother. Sleeping around. *She* knew what the consequences would be. But she did it anyway. Well, fuck her. Fuck her and all her fucking fuck buddies. I got the last laugh, didn't I? I sliced her up and dumped that cheating bitch's body into the ocean. But what fun it would have been, to put her in that Tesla and to slice her fucking head off with a fire truck!"

Anastasia Volkov leaped from the tailgate, her shoes touching the earth in two puffs of dusty poofs as she pirouetted to face her father. "*You* killed her? *You? YOU?*"

Petrikov, red with rage, said nothing, his teeth clenched together and his eyes barely visible through his fierce scowl.

His daughter took a step backward.

She whispered, "It wasn't the *Bratva*. You've lied to me all these years. It was you!"

Bowing her head, her shoulders sagged.

Petrikov's furor subsided as quickly as it had started. "Irinushka," he murmured, stringing out the syllables softly, lifting his hands, palms up.

His daughter spun away from him and bolted.

The fat man, the friend, and the captain waited by the pickup truck. The woman did not return. Finally, the father whispered, the sadness gravelly in his throat, "It will be only me. She had told me this before, you know. She was afraid. She said she might get cold feet. But I will come back for her."

"Then there is no need to do this, is there?" Tom Morris objected, confused and hesitant. "She's the one without the passport, right? Isn't that what you told me?"

The burly man scowled at the New Yorker. "I paid you. And I don't want to be here any longer. Are you proposing to renege on our agreement?"

The venom in his voice was palpable, and Morris cowed, "Oh no, no, of course not. And you say you've got a passport, right? What's the harm, in that case?"

Petrikov's demeanor visibly softened. He looked inland and then turned his head toward the Saint Lawrence River. "Yes. That's correct. Let's go."

Though it occurred to him, Morris didn't have the guts or perhaps the fortitude to ask to see the big man's Canadian passport, so blinded was he by the thought of an easy ten K for only a quick boat ride. The three men proceeded to Morris's boat, the friend coming along to say goodbye and to help cast off the lines.

Moments later, leaning on the pickup truck's massive front grill, Dmitri Tretriaki watched as Anatoly Petrikov, standing at full height next to the Craigslist captain, motored toward the throngs of boats gathered to watch the majesty of the tall ships as they hove into view off Brockville, Ontario, Canada.

The oligarch never turned back, never altered his stance. Only his fingers moved, grazing against the outline of the small, tin box stashed in his pocket.

CHAPTER
37

DMITRI TRETRIAKI HAD A SINGLE assignment, whispered to him as he had walked with Petrikov toward Tom Morris's waiting runabout. Forced close to the fat oligarch by the confines of the metal rails bordering the narrow ramp that led to the dock, Petrikov had hissed, "Find her. And kill her. If you can't, tell the *Bratva* to do it for you. Do not fail. Understood?"

Tretriaki had wanted to wipe the spittle from his ear lobe, but he had not dared, instead murmuring his single word response, "Yes."

Easier said than done, Tretriaki thought, leaning against the massive grill of the F-150.

He alighted the familiar sidestep of the Ford and started the big truck's motor, shifting the vehicle into drive and aiming the snout of the white truck southeast. He would follow Main Street for less than a mile before picking up US Route 37 South to begin the long, six-and-a-half-hour drive to New York City.

"There's no way," he muttered out loud to himself. Finding her would be impossible. She had the ability to become a ghost, to disappear from the grid.

He would try, of course, and he'd make the effort to put out feelers through the *Bratva*, on the slim chance that someone would know her, and on the more hopeful chance that someone would ultimately report his diligence upward and word would get to Petrikov, somehow, that Tretriaki was not shirking his responsibilities.

Within moments, he changed his mind. It would be far easier than he expected. For there she was, walking slowly down the last stretch of concrete sidewalk before it ended at the outskirts of Morristown.

With his left forefinger, Tretriaki clicked on the passenger's side power window button as he stepped lightly on the brake, slowing the F-150. Matching his speed with the sluggishly-walking woman, he called, in a friendly tone through the opened window, "Wanna ride?"

Volkov studied the rolling pickup and the face within.

She halted.

Tretriaki swerved the truck to the shoulder and braked hard, expecting her to run the opposite direction. Instead, and to his surprise, she casually ambled toward the side of the truck.

With her face barely visible above the passenger side windowsill, she peered at Tretriaki, a blank look on her face.

He smiled and leaned slightly toward the window, keeping his left hand visible on the steering wheel but leaving his right hand resting on the shifter. "He's gone," Tretriaki announced. After a beat, he added, "C'mon. Get in. Let's go back to the City."

Volkov appeared to consider the invitation, eyebrows scrunched, until she shrugged, and grasped the handle to swing open the door. As she clambered into the height of the pickup truck, she mumbled, "Okay."

Pulling the seat belt across her chest, she clicked it in place, laid her head back, and closed her eyes. "Let me know when you want a break from driving," she said softly.

"Sure," replied Tretriaki, shifting the truck into drive and pulling away from the dusty verge at the side of the road.

As he followed the on-screen map in the truck's center stack, he considered his options. *Try to kill her now? No. Too difficult. And with what?*

He thought through his options, his mind moving faster as he accelerated the F-150. *I'll do it in New York. We'll go back to my apartment. She'll lie down to sleep. And I'll suffocate her. It'll be quick and easy.*

Satisfied with his plan, he decided to let her rest for only a short while. Then, to her annoyance, he'd turn up the volume on the radio. He'd keep her awake so that she'd be tired by the time they arrived in Brighton Beach.

Years ago, he had been instructed that he may never ignore a message from the wolf. Now, he'd have to kill her. But then, his obligations would be fulfilled, and he would no longer have to wonder if the wolf would reach out again.

There would finally be closure.

SIX HOURS LATER:
JUST AFTER MIDNIGHT — BRIGHTON BEACH, NEW YORK

THE LIGHTS HAD APPEARED BLURRY, surrounded by fuzzy halos, as the F-150 sped toward the Verrazzano-Narrows Bridge and the final stretch of the journey to Brighton Beach. Tretriaki had rubbed his eyes and blinked several times. Perhaps it was the anticipation of home, but the three-hundred-and-eighty-one-mile drive from the Saint Lawrence River had dragged on, seeming to take far longer than the six hours and change that had elapsed.

Reaching his apartment building in Brighton Beach, Tretriaki had found a curbside parking spot for the pickup truck. Volkov didn't appear the least bit tired. She had driven much of the middle stretch of the drive, allowing Tretriaki to take the helm only an hour before. She had not slept, but instead spent the time quietly gazing out the windows as they had driven through New Jersey, the congestion and lights and traffic building, even at this late hour, as they closed in on New York City, the city that never sleeps.

"I'll take the sofa, of course," Volkov stated as she crossed the threshold at the doorway to Tretriaki's apartment. "But first, how about a nip?"

"That's about how we started, right?" chuckled Tretriaki, recalling the night in November when Volkov had summoned him, as he tossed his duffel bag on the floor. Volkov, of course, had no luggage.

"Mhmm," Volkov agreed.

Tretriaki filled two glasses from the vodka bottle that was nicely chilled in the freezer, exactly as he had left it.

The pair clinked glasses and tossed the clear liquid back in a single motion. Volkov set down her glass gently. "That's it. I'm done. I gotta get some rest."

Looking at Tretriaki carefully, she added, "Thank you. We'll sort this out in the morning. But thank you." She smiled a genuine-looking smile.

He grinned back at her, toothily. "What the wolf wants, the wolf gets." He bowed with an exaggerated swoop, and Volkov laughed.

Tretriaki had retreated to his bedroom but had not undressed, slipping under the covers fully clothed. He had listened carefully; outside the partially open door, he could hear Volkov rustling about, first in the kitchen area returning their empty glasses to the stainless-steel sink basin with the tap of glass on metal. Then, soft thumps as sofa cushions had been tossed to the floor as she arranged herself to find some sleep.

He had waited.

Wide awake.

The digital clock on the bedside table indicated 2:30 AM, and he wondered, *That can't be the time. Spring forward, fall back? Spring back, fall forward?*

When he was last in this room, it had been November. Now, it was late summertime and Daylight Saving Time. *Was it an hour earlier or an hour later?*

It doesn't fucking matter, he decided.

Soundlessly, he stole from the bed, taking a pillow with him. *I'll jump on her and smother her. I'll knee her in the gut when I jump. Knock the air out of her lungs, and I'll suffocate her.*

Tiptoeing from the room, he carefully navigated the gloom of the darkened living room. Volkov was prone on the sofa, face-up, her left arm laid peacefully across her chest, her right arm dangling to the floor.

Tretriaki approached, angling toward her legs. He crouched on one bent knee, and using the coiled spring of his leg, knee, and thigh muscles, he launched himself toward his prey.

Volkov was ready.

She straight-armed her attacker with her left arm, pushing him off balance, and he collapsed into the coffee table, crashing into it and crushing the flimsy, originally flat-packed table, flat to the floor.

Twisting her body off the sofa, the agile woman leapt atop the fallen man, bringing the carving knife that had been grasped in her right hand up and then down with a vicious thrust into the exposed neck of her attacker.

Like father, like daughter.

Except, Volkov didn't slice again into her target. Instead, with Tretriaki subdued and gravely injured, she pushed at him as she pushed herself away.

"Did he tell you to do that?" she growled. "His last orders?"

Tretriaki could only groan.

Volkov didn't wait for an answer, instead whispering, "That pig lied. To me. To my past. To my mother." She paused, licking her lips. "Now it's my turn to chase *him* down."

With a quick glance around the apartment, she decided on the table lamp next to the sofa, and she lifted the lamp with its heavy, ceramic base and brought it down onto Tretriaki's skull with a dull *THWACK*, cracking both base and skull.

Immediate danger at bay, she found Tretriaki's duffel and dumped its contents on the floor. Rummaging through the apartment, she selected a few items: a laptop, his wallet, stuffed with cash and credit cards, some linked back to the accounts in the name of the Cornell professor, a towel, and a few T-shirts. From the kitchen area, a Ziploc plastic bag.

Examining the still body of her former ally once more, she grabbed again at the knife, and carefully, precisely, sliced off Tretriaki's right thumb. *I might need that thumbprint*, she thought. *One never knows.* She dropped the digit into the plastic bag and sealed it.

As Tretriaki, once her savior and now a subdued foe, bled unconsciously to his death on his living room carpet, Volkov swiped the key fob for the Ford F-150 and slung the duffel over her shoulder.

The wolf disappeared across the threshold of the apartment and into the Brighton Beach night.

PART FOUR
SEPTEMBER 2019

chapter 39

TUESDAY, SEPTEMBER 3, 2019 — FBI BOSTON FIELD OFFICE, CHELSEA, MASSACHUSETTS

"WE GOT A BODY! And a print!" Acting Special Agent in Charge Bradford Macallister screamed as he charged into the conference room.

Macallister blasting through the door with the words "body" and "print" was a shot in the arm of a stalled investigation. A dose of caffeine. No, way more than that. Like an injection of adrenaline. Or of climax. Or of the most exciting, enthusiastic, insanely uplifting moment. A hit!

Well, you get the point, right?

I sure did. We needed something new. We were due. Because for nine long months, we had uncovered exactly . . . nothing.

Nice months of searching for Anatoly Petrikov and for his presumed accomplice, Anastasia Volkov. The two most-wanted fugitives on our list. Outreaches to the public to police departments nationwide. Scouring facial recognition databases for sightings. Looking for tenuous leads that led us everywhere and chewed up the shoe leather.

Atlanta. Oklahoma City. New Orleans. Brownsville. We had chased the shadow of Anatoly Petrikov across the southeastern and southern United States until early May. The sightings were tenuous, at best—blurry, dark, and rain-streaked images from security cameras but confirmed by the facial recognition algorithms to be Petrikov.

Yet, we were no closer to putting our hands on him, and by September, we had become convinced that he had slipped across the border in Brownsville, Texas. He could be in Mexico, or, really, anywhere on the globe.

Likewise, Anastasia Volkov remained a ghost. Invisible. With her talents, she, too, by now, could be anywhere.

The Operation E.T. squad had gathered, today like every other day, as usual, at 8:30 AM in our glass-doored conference room. Though our squad was getting a great deal of support from the Bureau at large, and though we were but one cog in a very big machine, the case had gone nowhere.

The problem with a hunt that long is that it becomes stale. You trod the same ground over and over again, looking at the same clues, the same data, hoping that some anomaly that you hadn't thought of before would jump out at you. Even the static nature of the posted perp photos becomes a problem; after a while, looking at the same picture again and again, you simply don't notice it.

The FBI, however, is relentless. And big. We have over thirteen thousand agents, supported by over twenty thousand other professionals, including the highly-trained intelligence analysts. Amid that powerhouse, three squads in DC, two in New York, and our squad in Boston had been assigned full-time to the case, now broadened in scope to encompass the disappearance of our two prime suspects.

We had gotten nothing from the disgraced Jennifer Appleton. She fiercely proclaimed her innocence. But she had no proof. The digital record couldn't possibly lie. People can lie, though.

Appleton had volunteered for three separate polygraph tests, an unprecedented decision, and one sure to backfire on her. It is possible to defeat the lie detector, which relies on patterns of reactions to questions, measured in pulse, respiration, perspiration, and blood pressure. The former SAC passed every polygraph test. Appleton had fervently denied that she overrode the background checks when hiring Volkov. And, Appleton had rejected the notion that she had any subsequent involvement, or participated in any conspiracy, with Volkov.

Unfortunately for Appleton, she was well-known throughout the Bureau for her ice-cold, stoically unflappable demeanor. If there was anyone who could beat the lie detector machine, surely it was her.

Appleton remained under house arrest at her home in Salem, Massachusetts. The sentiment in the office was that she should be in jail, but the Department of Justice weakly agreed to her lawyer's declarations that she was not a flight risk, that she was a patriot, and that she ultimately wanted a full trial by jury, where she would have the opportunity to demonstrate her innocence.

In the meantime, like I said, the investigation was unproductive.

The security camera recordings at the Mount Tabor, Vermont, facility had been erased, no doubt, we thought, by Volkov, covering the tracks of whatever hitmen she hired to break out her benefactor and coconspirator.

Dogs, men, and machines had scanned the area around the facility, only to find a few scattered footprints leading to a Forest Service access road. At the terminus of the road, tire tracks had been found; the tires were common and used on several types of vehicles, but the stance of the tracks and the turning radius established a high possibility that the getaway vehicle was a Ford F-150.

An F-150. Which, by the way, was the best-selling pickup truck in the United States. Really narrowed it down, right?

Oh, and the US Forest Service owned a slew of them. The tracks in question could have been caused by one of their trucks on a routine inspection of the area.

Video surveillance in rural Vermont was basically nonexistent, found only in sporadic homes and businesses in the area. With a widening search area, door-to-door, the FBI found no images that were useful. The concept was considered a dead end.

Our last conclusive sightings of our suspects were grossly stale: Volkov on the Brooklyn Bridge, back on November 13, 2018, and Petrikov, in Mount Tabor, Vermont, on December 11, 2018.

And so, it got our immediate, undivided attention when Macallister burst through the door, yelling, "We got a body! And a print!"

CHAPTER

40

MACALLISTER SHRUGGED OFF his suit jacket and plopped into an imitation Aeron chair. The toll of the go-nowhere investigation and additional responsibility of being the Acting Special Agent in Charge was visible on his face. Normally tanned, especially after summertime, he was pale, having spent hours upon hours holed up in the building.

And I chose the word "plopped" for a reason. Macallister had put on some weight over the past nine months. His gym-toned frame was now, well, not so toned. I could sympathize.

The flabby Acting SAC looked at the five of us, one by one. Zimmerman, Jones, Connelly, me, Jordon, seated in that order around the veneered-wood table.

"Our office in New York. They got a high-priority call—not email, not system generated, but an actual phone call—late last night. Or early this morning. Here's the gist of it.

"Landlady in Brighton Beach. Outside of Brooklyn. Called NYPD to report a terrible smell from one of her apartments. Second-floor walkup. Said she hadn't seen the tenant in months. Since—get this—since the middle of November. The tenant had prepaid his rent for a year—a year!—and told the landlady he had gotten a new temp job and would be gone for a while. He gave her a key to the apartment, which she obviously had already, but that meant she had permission to enter. Got it?"

Heads around the table nodded, and Zimmerman verbalized, "Yeah. I see where this is going. Landlady can just go in. Whenever she wants."

I wasn't certain that was helpful or relevant, but I didn't say so.

Macallister continued, "The New York Police Department doesn't give a shit about smelly apartments. They blew her off. Not their problem. And, this is yesterday, so it's Labor Day. A holiday. They don't want to deal with nonsense calls like this one. They want to go home, to their barbeques and some beers.

"So, guess what? Landlady goes into the apartment. This, by the way, is all reconstructed from the notes from the cops when they finally do arrive, so it's probably not exact. But it's close enough."

With his audience mesmerized, he sniffed and went on, "Landlady finds a rotting, dead body. Now she calls 9-1-1, and now NYPD dispatches. The homicide squad responds. There's been a fight, tables smashed, lamps broken, that sort of shit. Oh, and the dead body on the floor and a bloody, icky carpet. And the smell. One detective barfed, apparently."

"I hope you're gonna tell us the dead body is Volkov. Or Petrikov. With a lead-up like that," I begged.

"'Fraid not." Macallister shook his head. "Oh, and aside from having a gaping knife wound, the body, a male, is missing its right thumb. Sliced clean off.

"Now, all this ratchets up the attention meter. NYPD had the place crawling with cops and forensics within the hour. The place is searched, top to bottom. And guess what they find?"

No one said a word.

Macallister leaned back in his chair, crossed his arms, and proclaimed the answer to his own question. "They found two glasses in the sink, with a bit of vodka in each glass. Dead guy's fingerprints on one glass, and on the other glass. . . Anastasia Volkov's."

No one said a word until we all started talking over each other at once, voices suggesting, "We gotta get down there." "Need a team out there! Close it down. Bridges, tunnels, roads." "Put an APB on Volkov. New York, New Jersey, Connecticut. How much of a head start does she have this time? What's the search radius?"

Macallister shouted, "Whoa! Shuddup! One at a time." The squad quieted, fidgeting, as Macallister said, "NYPD is, of course, linked in with our Criminal Justice Information Services system. They ran the prints through CJIS. The victim had no record. But Volkov's print, obviously, is in there, and that got an immediate ping. NYPD called us, but we also got the notice through the system."

"Why didn't we see that, as soon as it hit the system?" Jones asked.

"You probably did. It came in early this morning. It's probably mixed in with all the other shit that came in over the long weekend."

Connelly shook her head. "It doesn't matter. Even if we saw it the second it came in and immediately started a search, it wouldn't have mattered. Or if we saw it before we started our meeting at eight-thirty. Listen, I've got some experience with dead bodies. They start to really reek from decomposition in a day or so, but it depends on a lot of factors. Landlady called it in on, what, Monday afternoon?"

"Yeah," confirmed Macallister.

"That body could have been killed on Sunday. Or Saturday. Or, outside chance, Friday. Which means, if Volkov was the killer, she's got a two or three day lead on us!"

"Yeah," repeated Macallister. "And when she called it in, the landlady said it had been stinking for a while. We got both an NYPD Coroner squad and an FBI Evidence Response Team on-site. They'll work up an estimated time of death. But, yeah, Volkov has got a substantial head start."

He paused for a moment before concluding, "And the FBI New York Field Office is on high alert. They are putting search squads out, they are going door-to-door, and NYPD is all over this. Total cooperation. This is being run as a manhunt for a potentially dangerous suspect. Schools in the area are being locked down, public places closed, all over Brooklyn. But you know, and I know, that there is probably zero chance that she hung around, or that she's still in that area.

"Nevertheless, she's popped back on the grid. She's alive, and we will find her. Questions?"

He leaned back as the squad started hurling questions at once.

"Wait!" I shouted as loudly as I could, launching myself to my feet. The room slowly went silent.

"What about my sister? My family? We gotta get protective details back on them!"

Macallister's face went sheet white, and the room went stone-cold silent.

Jones reacted first, grabbing the handset of the telephone perched at the center of the conference table, and she barked, "Get me the Providence office. Right away. We got an emergency. I need an immediate response."

The call would be too late. For Volkov, we soon would learn, was already at my sister's tidy home in Bristol.

CHAPTER
41

AS JONES AND MACALLISTER hovered over the conference table phone, now set to speaker mode so that the Acting SAC could verbally authorize the Providence satellite office to engage protective details for my family, I had stepped to a corner of the room to text my sister, brother, and parents.

Knowing that my sister Grace had been a previous target of Volkov's, I started with her, tapping out,

```
Grace where r u
```

I counted to myself, nervously waiting. *One. Two. Three . . .*

I could feel a bead of sweat on my forehead as I mouthed *twelve,* when a reply bubble appeared on my screen.

```
At home why
```

Looking over my shoulder, Connelly was reading my screen. I was not the least bit bothered by the lack of privacy. I needed my squad on my side. Connelly blurted, "At home? On a Tuesday? Why? Shouldn't she be at work?"

Good question. I thumb-typed

```
Why not work?
```

and pressed send.

The reply was almost instant:

```
long wknd, extended it and took the day
off. why
```

I thought for a moment. That seemed odd. My sister didn't take days off. She loved her work, the rigor of it and the responsibilities that she had taken on with gusto and with dedication.

I set that aside and focused on the moment at hand. I didn't want her to panic, but all the same, I wanted her to keep her guard up, to stay aware. After a few false starts, I composed a message that I thought met both of those criteria:

```
There's been a new development and out of
caution, we're sending a couple of guys
out to watch over you.
```

I angled the screen to Connelly for a second opinion. She nodded her agreement, and I pressed send.

The reply didn't come quite as fast as the others, but when it bubbled on-screen, I was not surprised.

```
Ugh when will this end. OK thanks. I
guess
```

My fiercely independent sister was not happy. I was more concerned with her safety than her happiness, though, at this moment, so I replied,

```
Please check in periodically. I think it
is almost over. I'm trying! We all are.
```

Her reply was as curt as curt could be:

```
OK
```

I did a double-take, looking at the screen. She rarely used the two-letter, all-caps version of "OK." She thought that was rude and abrupt, and therefore she would spell out "okay." She'd texted the abbreviated version twice in quick sequence. Not only that, Grace almost always signed off with her nickname for me. I would have expected *okay BenBro*.

She must be really pissed off.

It couldn't be helped. The protective detail would be there within the hour, and I also had to get in touch with my brother and parents. I grabbed an imitation Aeron and pecked out a message to my folks and a second message to my brother.

No sooner than my thumb had lifted from the *Send* icon, I was on my feet.

"I'm going down there," I announced. "My sister's texts. I dunno. Something is off. Something doesn't feel right."

Macallister, too, leaped to his feet, grabbed his suit coat, and flung it over his shoulder. "I'm going with you."

We bolted from the conference room, the Acting SAC's protective detail shouting their objections. Despite the new, potentially temporary title, Macallister remained a Special Agent at heart. And, it was clear that we both had the sense that Volkov would retarget Grace, where she had left off in December.

Reaching the building's garage, we jumped into my black Dodge Charger—which, ironically, had once been assigned to Volkov—and sped for Bristol, seventy miles away.

The growl of the Dodge's big engine didn't drown out the voice in my head. *Volkov has always been one step ahead of you, Ben. You're too late.*

SAME TIME — BRISTOL, RHODE ISLAND

THE NONDESCRIPT, white Ford F-150 pickup truck parked curbside would attract no attention on a leafy, shady side street on the outskirts of historic Bristol, Rhode Island. The tidy, Cape-style home that backed up to a woody area often hosted vehicles with out-of-state tags, usually Massachusetts, but sometimes Connecticut. The yellow New York plates on the pickup might stand out, but more than likely not; tiny Rhode Island was peppered with cars from beyond the Ocean State.

Sitting comfortably cross-legged inside the home on a perfect white couch with seashell-embroidered throw pillows in a unique greenish, turquoise-y color, Anastasia Volkov laid Grace Porter's iPhone beside her, saying, kindly, to her host, "I'd expect that the cavalry will be coming. This should be over soon."

Opposite, Grace Porter perched nervously on an ottoman.

The night before, when she had walked toward her house, returning home from a neighborhood Labor Day barbeque, she had noticed the F-150 parked on the street outside her Cape, but she had guessed it was just one of the party guests.

She had been wrong.

There was an intruder inside her home.

And, after a few moments of strained conversation, if one could have called it that, she had deduced that the olive-skinned, flaxen-haired woman who had broken into her home was her brother's nemesis.

The two women had spent the night together in forced company, the visitor apparently not requiring sleep as she kept watch over the homeowner.

As captivities go, it had been . . . pleasant. Volkov was an ideal guest. She had brought take-out for dinner, not that Grace Porter had an appetite, and two bottles of rosé. This morning, one remained corked and stashed in the fridge, and the other bottle sat mostly empty on the Carrera marble countertop in the kitchen.

The visit had begun awkwardly—aside from, of course, the inherent awkwardness of having an uninvited stranger invade one's home. Volkov had demanded her hostess's phone and passcode and then changed the settings to disable that passcode to enable her unfettered access to the device. Volkov had focused mostly on the messaging app, scanning the little bubbles to get a sense of Grace's texting style—mostly lower case, which actually took a bit of an effort due to the auto-capitalization algorithm built into the device's firmware, a few abbreviations here and there, and no emojis except in unusual and spare circumstances.

With that task complete, Volkov had asked her hostess to get comfortable, to relax, and to listen.

For she had come to apologize.

"I know this is going to sound self-serving," she had begun last night. "But I'm here to say that I am sorry. That whole thing in December? The power outage, the phone troubles, the agents on the street. That was my doing. And it was necessary, at the time, for reasons that I regret now."

Grace shook her head sideways, whispering, "I don't understand."

Volkov smiled thinly. "Of course not. As they say, it's complicated. And since we've got nothing better to do, and since I am tired of running, and because I have a new sense of motivation, while we wait, I'll tell you my story."

For the next three hours, Grace Porter had sat in rapt attention, Volkov pausing her story halfway through to open one of the bottles of wine. It had taken Grace a moment to realize what was happening, as she shared a companionable drink with a person who she had thought was trying to kill her, and who had once tried to kill her brother.

Volkov's story had been compelling. From her banishment, for her own safety away from her father's mafia connections in New York, to her involvement in her father's plot to destroy New York and Chicago, and to her capture and incarceration, she had spilled it all.

Volkov had spoken with obvious regret about her attempt to chase and shoot Grace's brother, the FBI staffer-turned-agent who had disrupted the plan. "I was caught up with it. I wanted to protect my father. I wanted to reunite with him, to be able to be myself instead of pretending to be someone who I was not," she had murmured sadly. "But if I knew then what I know now, I would have gotten out long ago."

Grace had wondered if Volkov could cry on command, or if the tears were real when Volkov told her about the death of her mother. "I was told it was the *Bratva*. A deal gone bad. My father assured me he had done everything he could do, but he had been too late. But then he slipped. It had been *him*. The lying, fat pig. It's always been about him, putting himself first. He manipulates. He cajoles. He gets what he wants." She paused to wipe a tear. "Well, not anymore!"

Eventually, Grace had dozed off, her visitor keeping watch, knowing that the body in Brighton Beach would be discovered and the single clue that she had left behind would be passed on to Ben Porter. She knew their ways, their playbook.

Lifting Grace's phone once more, Volkov reread the thread of texts that she had sent to Ben Porter, pretending to be Grace. Volkov hoped that the string of messages had accomplished her objective; she had carefully composed them to be slightly different from Grace's usual style. Volkov expected that Ben Porter would send agents to establish a security perimeter around his sister.

And Volkov was already inside that perimeter.

For Volkov, this would be the safest way. Grace Porter would be her shield, and therefore would protect Volkov from being mowed down in a hail of bullets.

Certainly, the FBI had every right to shoot on sight.

But Volkov preferred the opportunity to explain herself to the FBI. This time, there would be no lies. No half-truths, no deceptions. She would tell them about her father, and about the code that he had on that USB flash drive in his pocket. Volkov leaned into one of Grace's greenish, turquoise-y pillows and wondered, *Will they give me that chance? Would omitting Grace's usual sign-off be the tip-off that was needed to bring Ben Porter himself to Bristol?*

Volkov's hands clenched tightly together as she asked herself, *Will Ben Porter believe me? Why should he?*

CHAPTER
43

"ARE YOU FUCKING KIDDING ME? No, her house—not her work location!" Macallister had fumed, the spittle drenching the bottom edge of his phone as he blasted the duty agent in the Providence office.

The message had gotten confused. Providence had sent agents to the Citizen's Bank headquarters building, less than a half-mile from the satellite office, a short, seven-minute walk across the bridges over the Providence River. Arriving at the thirteen-story building twenty minutes after the Acting SAC's call from Boston, the two agents wasted a solid half hour trying to find my sister, before they, and the bank staff, realized that she was nowhere to be found in the building, had not called in, and had not indicated to her supervising manager that she would not be at work on this Tuesday after the Labor Day holiday.

Macallister had been infuriated when the duty agent had explained the situation. The hapless agent promised that the field agents understood the immediacy of the assignment. The duty agent assured the Acting SAC that they would be in Bristol in under thirty minutes.

I had focused on the road, pushing the powerful Dodge as much as I dared, my training at Quantico giving me a new-found confidence. The last time I drove this car, this fast, it was over two years ago, and it had seemed like such fun. This time, not so much.

I had not spoken as I concentrated on the road, trying to keep that nagging thought at bay which kept invading my consciousness: *What if we're too late? What if Volkov is already there? One step ahead.*

The two FBI cars arrived in Bristol at the exact same time; the flashing headlights of the Providence agents' Chevy Tahoe directly in front of me, coming south on US-114, as I headed north, having blasted down US-24 before racing across the Mount Hope Bridge and carving a squealing right turn onto my sister's leafy street.

With the chirps of hard braking and with the thumps of slamming doors, Macallister and I, and the two agents from Providence, converged on the street. There were no sidewalks in this part of town. Other than a Ford pickup truck parked with its right-side wheels on the grass one house away from my sister's home, there were no vehicles visible except for Grace's Subaru, parked as usual in her driveway. My sister's tidy Cape, with its manicured yard and carefully-positioned potted plants flanking the front walk, looked normal.

Phew.

I felt a tiny bit foolish as I led the group of agents up the walkway to the front door.

I knocked, tilting my body to the right so I'd be visible through the sidelight from within.

I heard the metallic *snick* of the deadbolt as the knob inside the door was twisted, and the bolt slid from the recess in the jamb.

The door swung open to reveal my sister, standing, dressed in black leggings and a purple hoodie sweatshirt, with Anastasia Volkov behind her. Volkov's left arm wrapped around my sister's waist, and her right arm was extended, her right hand clutched a carving knife.

Grace's expression was placid.

Volkov's face was blank, but her eyes were bright, carefully focused on me.

I froze.

I heard rustling behind me; Macallister undoubtedly pulling his Glock from his chest harness under his suit coat.

In slow motion, with careful, deliberate movements, Volkov rotated the knife so that the tip of the blade pointed downward toward the threshold of the door. Holding it delicately with the tips of two fingers, her forefinger and her thumb, she made it apparent that it could not be used as a weapon. She extended the knife toward me, dangling it, daintily.

Volkov finally spoke, in a normal tone of voice, but carefully and distinctly. "Ben. I am not here to harm Grace. She can attest to that. I came here to apologize to her, for bringing her into our . . . dispute. I should not have done that. She should have been off-limits."

I accepted the knife from Volkov's outstretched arm and could see, from the corner of my eye, her grip on my sister's waist loosening, but I remained still.

Volkov took one small step back and to the side, away from my sister, the outstretched right arm now reaching up toward the ceiling, as she also brought her left hand up slowly, her body now completely exposed.

Hands raised, she stated, "Arrest me. But give me the chance to talk. To explain. Please."

I gently pushed Grace in the opposite direction, away from her, as I stepped over the threshold and put my body between Volkov and my sister.

Behind me, Macallister now had a clear shot, his Glock aimed, at a ridiculously close range, between Volkov's eyes. There was no possibility he would miss.

Not like I did two years ago.

But the FBI does not do that. We do not act impulsively and recklessly. And so, Volkov's capture was orderly, by the book. She was handcuffed and read her Miranda rights. She was given a chance to express that she understood those rights, which she did.

Volkov complied when she was requested to sit, hands manacled behind her back, on a sturdy chair, to wait for transport. She held her head high, and she was polite, deferential.

The Providence agents called for help from the Bristol Police Department, who brought over a squad car with an enclosed back seat, and Volkov was relocated from my sister's house to wait in the police vehicle. Within an hour, an armored vehicle had arrived, dispatched from Providence, this time to the correct location, and Volkov was secured for transport. Macallister had decided to take her to Boston.

In what would turn out to be a stroke of brilliance, Macallister decided that her name would not be disclosed to the transport officers or even to the Providence agents. On the spot, he decided her name would be Ann Karin.

I wasn't sure if that was a veiled reference to the novel *Anna Karenina* penned by Leo Tolstoy, but, honestly, I thought that a nod to great Russian literature would be a stretch for Macallister. Whatever. It was a good move. In fact, it would be a great move.

Before we followed the transport vehicle back to Boston, Macallister and I took a few moments to talk with Grace. And what she told us was astonishing. To the point of being completely unbelievable.

CHAPTER

44

GRACE REMAINED CALM and collected. I was proud of her.

Seated at her sunny, perfectly-clean breakfast table, Macallister and I listened as Grace told us what transpired the night before.

My sister's memory was typically excellent, and she carefully laid out the sequence of events, starting with finding Volkov inside her home, to their conversation with a bottle of wine at hand, to the morning's text messages.

I was shocked when Grace said that Volkov had been "nice."

"You're kidding, right? You know this is the woman who tried to kill me? And tried to kill Macallister while she was at it."

Grace looked at my boss. "I didn't know that part. But, yes, she told me that she chased you. That she tried to kill you. She said she was caught up with it. That she now wanted to get out."

We spent an hour or so with Grace, Macallister leaving first so that I could have a private moment with my sister. I assured her it was over, that the protective details would no longer be needed, but if she wanted them, she could have them. She had laughed and declined, independent as always. Later I found out that she showered, dressed, and drove to work, apologizing that she had been late before diving into her assignments and to the long weekend backlog, made longer by her forced morning off. I actually think that she was relieved; it was closure, of sorts.

Macallister and I headed back to Boston, leaving behind an Evidence Response Team combing Grace's house, and, street-side, a flatbed truck that was loading the Ford pickup truck with New York plates to transport it to our offices for analysis.

As we drove, this time, at a more leisurely pace, Macallister and I debated the nuances of our discussion with Grace.

"Volkov is up to something," Macallister stated with confidence. "There's no way that she showed up at your sister's house with a bottle of wine to confess. To turn herself in. This has to be another one of her diversions, this time using herself to really distract us while she's got something cooking remotely."

"Totally agree," I replied, as Macallister's phone rang as we rolled off the Mount Hope Bridge.

A moment later, he put the phone down and reported, "The pickup truck. Ford F-150. Which, if you'll recall, is the same type of truck that the evidence team speculated was used as a potential getaway vehicle in Vermont when Petrikov disappeared. The F-150 that was parked outside your sister's house was registered to a Dmitri Tretriaki. Who, before you ask, is the dead guy in Brighton Beach. And guess when he registered it?"

"Wait. Don't tell me. Um, November 2018? Right after Volkov escaped?"

"Yup. He had to have been an accomplice. Maybe he turned on her, so she offed him. Or maybe she was just done with him."

"Her body count is really adding up," I snorted sarcastically.

"Yeah. And then she turns herself in. Doesn't add up one bit," Macallister summarized.

"Go back to the Brighton Beach guy. He got a record?" I asked.

"Not that I've heard so far. Sleeper, maybe?"

"Yeah, maybe," I concurred. "Makes you wonder. If she's got one sleeper out there, how many more does she have? And, don't forget we still got one *big* missing piece out there as well. Where the fuck is Petrikov?"

"I have no idea," Macallister said in a defeated tone, shaking his head sideways. "I get the feeling she's going to tell us more about Petrikov. But it's not like she's a credible witness."

"And do you get the sense she's going to send us on some wild goose chase? I think you're onto something, Macallister. She didn't turn herself in for nothing. She's up to something, and while we dick around with her, that something is going to come up from out of nowhere." I gripped the steering wheel of my Dodge tighter and stepped on the gas. I wanted to get back to the office and figure this thing out.

SAME DAY, 4:00 PM —
FBI BOSTON FIELD OFFICE, CHELSEA, MASSACHUSETTS

MY STOMACH HAD BEEN GROWLING with unease while my heartbeat pounded with anticipation. I'd been waiting for this moment for over two years. I'd finally have a chance to be face-to-face with the woman who tried to kill me.

Macallister and I had discussed the plan on the drive back to Boston. "She was one of us," he had started. "And she's clearly a mole. An operative of some kind, for Anatoly Petrikov. And because of that, I'm gonna throw out the playbook for this one."

Typical Macallister bluster, I had thought, before asking, "What do you mean?"

"Well, normally, interviews are conducted in holding cells, and there is a specific protocol that we gotta adhere to. How we select the interviewer, how we conduct the interview, even the order that questions are asked. We gotta script those questions in advance. The Department of Justice will review 'em. Ensure that no detail is overlooked. Ensure that the questions are not leading the witness. Ensure compliance with the law."

"Yeah," I had agreed. "And what makes this one any different?"

"She's a mole," Macallister had repeated. "The rules don't apply. Plus, I bet she knows where Petrikov is hiding, and we need to get that out of her. We don't have time for the usual procedure. We gotta talk to her before Washington and Justice overthink this thing."

I had been swept along with Macallister's enthusiasm, especially when he had added, "I'm gonna be conducting the interview myself. With you at my side."

The interview of Anastasia Volkov, or, as she appeared on our records, Ann Karin, began at 4:00 PM and was conducted in a small, windowless room adjacent to our operations center. The room was already equipped with the necessary audio/visual connections that could broadcast a Secure Video Tele-conference (SVTC). That meant that no time would be wasted setting up a holding cell with those audio/visual connections, and time wasted was time for DC and the DOJ to get involved and to gum up the works.

Macallister took precautions, though. If there were others involved within the Bureau other than Appleton and Volkov, he wanted to be as careful as possible to make sure that Volkov's arrest didn't leak. Each person observing the interview would have to register with our operations center and would be cross-checked with a list of preapproved observers that Macallister had made. Lewis would maintain the list and oversee that no one outside the list would know the real name of the interviewee. After all, Ann Karin was not on our fugitive list, nor a name to be found anywhere in our records.

All the same, Macallister covered his ass by making sure that a handful of higher-ups in DC would be admitted into the circle of confidentiality. Macallister's list was short. My squad, a handful of people in Chelsea who were already briefed on the Appleton case, and, in Washington, the Director, the Deputy Director, and the General Counsel.

The chosen few would be able to watch the interview via the SVTC, as would our squad and team in Boston. Lewis linked in one of the secure conference rooms within the Strategic Information and Operations Center (SIOC) at the Hoover Building in Washington.

As a final measure, Lewis would use his technology to wash out the interviewee's face on the video feed as well as altering the voiceprint.

Macallister wanted her presence in our office to be locked down as tightly as possible.

I wasn't nervous in the slightest when Volkov was brought into the room to sit across a small table from Macallister and me. The cameras on all four walls of the room were perfectly visible, and Volkov glanced up at them and nodded. She, of all people, a former Intelligence Analyst herself, knew what they were for.

I half expected Macallister to start in a sinister tone. "*So* . . . we meet . . . *again,*" exaggerating and drawing out the syllables as he spoke.

Instead, Volkov began the interview herself, crossing one leg over the other casually, if not a little awkwardly due to the imbalance of having her hands, resting on the table in front of her, shackled together with cuffs, by stating plainly, "Thank you. Thank you for not killing me earlier. Like I said, I have a lot to explain. And I'm not going anywhere. Are these necessary?" she asked, raising her manacled wrists off the table slightly.

"For now, yes," Macallister replied, not giving an inch. "Frankly, I'm not even sure where to start. So, let's start with the one question I really want answered. Where's Petrikov?"

"Russia. Probably Moscow."

Macallister snorted, rolling his eyes slightly. "Really? And did you have a hand in that?"

"Of course."

"You were responsible for his escape?"

"Yes. By the way, where's Appleton?" Volkov asked, purposely scanning the little room with a slow head movement to accentuate her question.

At that, Macallister chuckled under his breath. "Appleton? Your coconspirator on the inside? You really expected her to be here?"

Volkov shook her head sideways. "The file was a fake. You haven't figured that out yet? Appleton has nothing to do with this. Back then, I didn't want her on the hunt for me. She's very good. I couldn't risk that. So, I planted the file. The same way I planted the files that got me past the background checks."

This time, Macallister made no attempt to stifle his laugh. "You expect us to believe that? Tell me, quickly, as we have a lot more to discuss, how you managed that."

"When I was at MIT. I was intrigued by the challenge, and way back then, it was a lot easier to hack into a system. Of course, the security measures have been improved ten-fold, a hundred-fold even, since then—but once you're in, you can keep up with those changes. You can keep a door open, so to speak."

"Let me get this straight," Macallister snorted. "One day, at MIT, you decided that you wanted to be part of the FBI. You hack into our system to get yourself hired. And ever since, you've granted yourself access, from the outside?"

Volkov smiled. "That's exactly correct, Macallister. You've got a knack of catching on fast. *But*," She paused for a moment, then said, "you're off slightly on the sequence. I figured out how to hack in, and then we decided it might be useful, so then I inserted myself."

"Who's *we*?" I blurted.

"My father and I."

"Your father?" I repeated.

"Yes. Macallister asked where he was, before. I believe you boys know who he is, actually. Anatoly Petrikov."

Dead. Silence.

Macallister and I actually turned our heads to look at one another, stunned.

Volkov, clearly enjoying the moment, once again raised her wrists off the table and pled, "We have *a lot* to talk about. Please?"

46

I THINK ANASTASIA VOLKOV knew that the request to remove the handcuffs would not be granted, at least not right now. She placed her wrists back onto the edge of the table, uncrossed her leg, and planted both feet on the floor.

Leaning forward in the chair slightly, she stated, "My real name is Irinushka Petrikov. I was born in 1986, to my mother, Irina Borisyuk, and father, Anatoly Petrikov. Back then, he sometimes went by Tony.

"Anatoly Petrikov was a prominent member of the Little Odessa mob. The Russian mafia, operating in the United States. The *Bratva*. In 1996, when I was ten, my mother feared for me and sent me to central New York to hide me from the *Bratva*. But I stayed in touch, carefully, with my parents. They arranged to pay for my education at MIT.

"And, after I graduated MIT in 2008, we—my father and I—decided that the FBI would be an excellent vantage point to oversee what you knew about him. From the inside, I could keep an eye on him. Because, by then, he had been disgraced. By the whole diamond fiasco. He wanted to regain his footing. Put himself back on the map, so to speak. Having me on the inside was a strategic decision too."

She took a deep breath. "My mother died in 2015. Killed by the *Bratva*, or so I was told."

Shaking her head, she looked down at the table, then back up again, at Macallister and me. "After I escaped from Walter Reed, my first priority was to go get him. My cover was blown, obviously, here at the Bureau. He was all I had left.

"I got him out, I showed him what I could do, and then, just before we were going to both go to Russia, he let it slip. His temper, as always, got the best of him. *He* killed my mother. *He* is the traitor. And that is why I am here."

Macallister studied Volkov's face for a moment, and then stated, "Complete nonsense."

I wasn't so sure. I mean, that was quite a story, especially the part about Petrikov being her father, and I sided, a bit, with Macallister. Certainly, it all seemed far-fetched. Yet she told the story with such earnestness and confidence.

Of course, she also tried to kill me, with earnestness and confidence.

As my thoughts wavered, Volkov's eyes never left Macallister's stare. She was not backing down.

In the silence, I examined her. As fit as ever, her flaxen hair flowed to her shoulders, unfettered by her usual ponytail; the elastic had been taken from her, in the event she tried to use it as a weapon or to assist in a suicide. She wore a simple, gray, short-sleeved, crew neck T-shirt, atop faded jeans. No belt, also confiscated. Her Adidas Stan Smith tennis shoes, sans shoelaces, of course, were a brilliant white. Brand new.

I was curious, so I asked. "Where'd you get the shoes? The clothes?"

Macallister turned to me and scowled. "What?"

I didn't respond and continued to maintain eye contact with Volkov, who answered, "I bought them. In Brooklyn. With Dmitri's credit card. You've traced him by now, of course," she stated.

"Did you kill him?" I asked.

"Yes," she replied simply, before elaborating. "But I had to. He tried to kill me first. Orders from my father, presumably."

"When did he, um, the person you claim is your father, give those orders?"

"Probably just before he stepped on the boat to cross the Saint Lawrence River into Canada. That was," she brought both hands up to scratch her chin, "Friday. Five days ago. He would have been met by the Russians, given a Russian passport, flown to Rome, and then to Moscow. They would have had a passport for me too."

"Right," I confirmed. "Your father slips up and tells you, by accident, that he killed your mother. You get cold feet or something. Decide not to go with him. And you come back to New York to kill this Dmitri . . . for what? Because you needed money? To buy new shoes? I don't get it."

"No. Dmitri was with us. In fact, Dmitri is who I contacted after I snuck off the Brooklyn Bridge. You saw me there, right? I missed spotting one camera until too late. I was more careful after that.

"Anyway," Volkov continued, "Dmitri was my sleeper, my point of emergency contact. On the *Bratva* payroll, compensated to do nothing but wait. And when I activated him, he helped me put together the team to break out my father. He was the man I inserted into the facility, so we could open the door from the inside. The door was not connected to the network, so we had to have someone on the inside. I got him in the same way I got myself in, the same way I tainted Appleton. Which was meant to be a distraction. She's innocent."

It made sense. There were six agents at the facility. Five bodies were recovered. One disappeared, the one that had been assigned to a shift the night before Petrikov's escape. An agent who was a ghost in our computer systems, who we had no data on whatsoever, except for a name that showed up on the shift records. I confirmed, "The man you put inside the facility was this Dmitri? An accomplice?"

"For sure. I put him in as Franklin Testani."

I looked at Macallister. We had never released that name. He was shaking his head, "No. I don't buy it. This guy, he's your guy, but you end up killing him. Another one for the body count. Where does the count stand, now, anyway?"

She groaned, "Oh, I don't know. I'm guilty, for certain. But the count will go a lot higher if you don't believe me. And that, too, is why I am here. It has to stop. My father has to stop."

"Sure," I said. "One item at a time. The count. Let's run through it."

"Okay, like I said, I am done with the running. Done with the lies." She leaned back and, in a matter-of-fact tone, recited, "Vanessa Raiden, one. Dmitri Tretriaki, two. The five agents and two servicemen at the facility, that's nine. Plus, the five in Vermont. So, fourteen total."

"Whaddya mean, the five in Vermont?" Macallister interjected. "Not that I'm interested in helping you, but that's a double-count. You already listed the five agents."

"Not at the facility," she said softly. "In Burlington. I don't remember all the names. One was the driver. Suzanne Cahal. And one was the little girl. Ashley Whitby."

Volkov's voice had trailed off.

She snapped back to attention, and in a much harsher tone, she exclaimed, "Look. We're gonna be here all night. The handcuffs. Please. And maybe a glass of water. Or a coffee?"

"I'm ready for a break." Macallister stood. "I'll send in coffee and water. And I'll take care of the cuffs."

I stood a second after my boss spoke. I was not ready for a break. In fact, I had a thousand more questions. Now was the time to ask them, not to take a coffee break.

I did what I was told, however, and I dutifully followed Macallister from the interview room. The time to disobey orders, however, would be later. Only I didn't know that, yet.

MACALLISTER AND I JOINED MY squad at the operations center workroom, set-tling into the far more comfortable imitation Aeron swivel chairs circled around the familiar, giant conference table. On-screen, we watched as a male agent and a female agent entered the interview room. The female agent removed the cuffs as the male agent set down a paper cup of water and a paper cup of coffee, no lid. Both agents retreated to opposite corners of the room and remained standing. I noticed that both had removed their holster harnesses, and they were unarmed.

Pointing at the screen, I asked Macallister, "No weapons? What's up with that?"

"In case Volkov tries something funny. We can lock her in there, but she'd have hostages. I don't trust her in the slightest."

"No kidding. That story is bullshit," pontificated Zimmerman, puffing out his chest.

"Agreed," Connelly concurred, before calling over to our Intelligence Analyst Louis Lewis, "Hey Lewis. What she said, about manipulating the files? Planting Appleton's file? Is that doable?"

"No way," Lewis replied confidently, removing his purple-framed glasses and polishing them with his tie, a garish affair that was not fastened around a standard, collared dress shirt but knotted at the neck of a concert T-shirt. The techies got away with whatever they want to wear.

But, despite his questionable choices in attire, Lewis had been a solid contributor, and I thought his analysis was robust when he repeated, "No way, not a chance. She'd have to change all the audit records too. You can't just insert a file. It would stand out if the audit records around it were out of sequence. And to sequence the audit records would take hours and hours and days of work, and by the time you were done, you'd probably be out of sequence again. I mean, sure, anything is possible, but the odds of doing it and not missing a single step out of literally thousands, millions maybe, are really slim."

As he was speaking, I had opened my own laptop and was inputting the two names that Volkov had added to her hit list. Our system was able to run a phonetic search, so I wasn't concerned about spelling when I typed *suzanne cahill* and *ashley whidby*.

A search in our Guardian files came up empty, but a search within the National Incident-Based Reporting System (NIBRS, a collaborative effort between branches of law enforcement to capture details on every single crime incident) appeared successful. Both names, with slightly different spelling, were associated with a vehicular accident in Burlington, Vermont, back in August.

Lewis had rolled over and had been looking over my shoulder, and as I rotated the laptop so that Macallister could read the file on-screen, Lewis brought the same information up on one of the big screens so that the squad could see it too.

The report detailed a horrific, midsummer traffic accident at an artsy-type festival in Burlington, where an out-of-control vehicle apparently smashed through a crowd of people, killing four bystanders and the driver of the car. "She did say five in Burlington, right?" I asked.

"Yeah," confirmed Macallister, as I kept reading.

The incident had been handled by local and state police but . . . wait! A name I recognized. I read, out loud, a single sentence buried in the report, "*First responders were also assisted with victim triage by off-duty personnel who happened to be on-site, FBI Intelligence Analyst Alberto Rodriquez and FBI Special Agent Abdul Hamid.*' I know Abdul Hamid!" I exclaimed as I reached for the worktable telephone handset.

"Who?" Jordon asked, monosyllabic as usual.

"He was one of my roommates at Quantico," I answered, as I dialed the FBI Albany, New York Field Office, hoping that my friend was still at work.

He was, and he was gregarious as usual. "Hey, Ben! Good to hear your voice! What's up, man?"

"Hi, Abdul. Business call, I'm afraid. You're on speaker with my squad and with my SAC. And probably others too."

"Thanks for the heads-up, man. I'll be discreet. No stories about—"

I cut him off. "Seriously. Abdul. Not now. This is a big case. *Lots* of ears." I paused and, thankfully, Hamid remained mute. Some of those stories need not be told. "Listen, I'm reading a file that has a tangential relationship to something I'm working on. Operation Eleanor Thornton. You've heard of the case, obviously. A suspect associated with that case has just told me that she killed five people in Burlington, Vermont, and then she recited two names that were among those listed in an accident report that—"

It was his turn to cut me off. "Yeah, I was at that. Man, I remember that night like it was yesterday. Horrible. Absolutely horrible. This Tesla ripped through a pedestrian street. My buddy and I were there at a summer festival and watched it happen. We helped to treat some of the injured as best we could. Nightmare." He cleared his throat. "Anyway, your suspect, and it doesn't matter who your suspect is, couldn't have killed anyone. Unless she was the driver of the car. And the driver's head got literally ripped off when her car crashed into a fire truck. Decapitated."

Hamid, true to form, then editorialized, "Pretty hard to talk, now, if you lost your head, back then. You know?"

Despite the gruesome nature of the discussion, there were smiles around the table. Volkov had fucked up. Not only had Lewis definitively contradicted her claim that she was able to substitute Appleton's personnel file, now Volkov herself had claimed to be part of an accident in Vermont. She couldn't possibly have been part of that scene, and by trying to insert herself in it, she had just removed any shred of credibility that she still had.

CHAPTER
48

WATCHING ON SCREEN, we waited until Volkov had finished her coffee, leaving the water untouched on the table.

Dismissing the two agents still on guard within the room, Macallister and I retook our hard seats. Pleasantly, Volkov said, "Thank you for the accommodation," motioning her now unshackled hands back and forth and then to the empty coffee cup. "The coffee hasn't changed. Still as bitter as usual."

"Hmmm." Macallister wasn't going to be pulled into small talk.

He looked at me.

"I ran the names you mentioned. From Burlington," I announced.

Volkov nodded. "Of course you did. The car accident." With her now-free hands, she air-quoted *accident*. "And now you think that affects my credibility. That I must be lying about that, so, logically, what else am I lying about? I get it."

I peeked over at Macallister, who met my glance with a tiny shrug. "Pretty much, yes," I confessed. As usual, Volkov anticipated us uncannily. Maybe if we played her game, she'd slip up, so I added in a conciliatory tone, "I know, and you knew, that would be the progression. And I know that you will cook up an explanation. Care to dish?"

"Cook. Dish. Clever, Ben. I like that about you." She smiled.

I didn't.

"Okay, now we're getting to the meat of it all. Do you like how I continued your little word-play, Ben? Cook, dish, meat!" She giggled. Macallister and I sat, like chess pieces, frozen, as she recomposed herself and began to speak again. "Now, I know you're going to dismiss this, just as the techs in the ops center have probably dismissed my claim that I inserted Appleton's file. 'Impossible,' they'll say. 'Out of sequence,' they'll say. But, it's child's play when you're the one who *created* the code that *assigns* the audit sequence." She cocked her head, modestly. I was unimpressed by her false humility but intrigued by her statement, though I didn't say so.

"Which brings us to Burlington. *I* drove that Tesla. Remotely."

Macallister laughed out loud, unable to contain his astonishment at that outrageous claim.

Volkov didn't react; she sat, passively, her face stone-like. Serious.

I wanted to hear her play it out, so I asked, "Remotely? Like you rigged it like a stunt car in a movie? Why?"

She shook her head as she said, "No." Leaning forward, she claimed, "I hacked it. I figured out a way in. Teslas are drive-by-wire. They can drive themselves, pretty much. I hacked their system so I could take control of the car."

"This is ridiculous," Macallister spat, interrupting her. "I'm well aware I don't know shit about technology. I get that. But there is no way you hacked Tesla. I've read the news stories. We ran a case study on it too. There's no way," he repeated.

"Right," Volkov replied evenly. "Like there was no way to hack Equifax. Or Capital One. Pretty big entities, eh? Tesla is no different than Ashley Madison. Or, wait, how 'bout the Federal Bureau of Investigation? Where I cut my teeth and learned how to do it."

She leaned forward, her hands planted side-by-side, flat on the small table. "Listen to me, and listen carefully," she said. "*Any* computer system, unless it is physically air-gapped from the rest of the connected world, can be hacked! And anyone who denies the possibility has a serious case of hubris."

She leaned back.

I leaned toward her. "I don't follow. Let's say I believe you, for discussion's sake. You hacked into a car. You were able to control it remotely. You still haven't told us why."

"Good question, Ben. Thank you for your patience, for playing along. You see, what Agent Macallister has forgotten is this. That case study he mentioned? *I* wrote it! That was *my* assignment. In 2015, based on an article I saw in a magazine, which *I* brought to his attention.

"That was my inspiration," she continued, after taking a breath. "I wanted to see if it could be done on a modern vehicle. You see, back then, they could hack into it and control features, even control the transmission. But they could not steer. Today, with a Tesla that can steer, with Autopilot, it seemed feasible. And it's been done before. A group in China called the Tencent Keen Security Lab hacked a Tesla Model S in 2016. And after I escaped Walter Reed, when I was doing my work to figure out how to do it myself, I saw an online article in *Jalopnik*, in April, that Keen did it again earlier this year."

She stopped long enough to shift her weight in her chair.

"And as for the *why* . . . because, at the time, I was with my long-lost father. I wanted to impress him. To work with him. To finally have a family. To redeem myself, sort of, from the fiasco of the bomb plot. Which *you*—you, Ben Porter—got in the way of."

"Okay," I interrupted gently, "let's agree that you've got some serious family issues. And let's say you've reunited with your dad and the two of you are going to take over the world, do some seriously scary stuff. What's a car got to do with it? What's whatshername Sue in Vermont got to do with it?"

She sniffed. "That was my test case, in the real world. I had already accomplished my objective with a Tesla I owned, bought with my father's money. With the computers I bought with his money. But I was able to achieve that because I had access to that particular Tesla. Suzanne Cahal's Tesla was the first one, and the last one, by the way, that I was able to control on the spur of the moment. We figured out the code and the connection."

"We? You and your father?"

"Yes, and Dmitri, and Carlos, and Unit 29155. *That's* who you need to hunt, Ben. *They* have the code now, thanks to my cheating pig of a father."

Macallister blew out his breath in one, long exhale, saying, "Oh boy. This is way past any level of believability. I'm done. We're done. Let's pick this up again tomorrow. And, Volkov, tomorrow we are going to start at the beginning. Perhaps then you will be a little more forthright, because we've got you on one murder for sure. Vanessa Raiden. We've got you on conspiracy. Treason. If you'd like to avoid spending the rest of your miserable life at, oh, I dunno, Guantánamo Bay, maybe you'd consider speaking some truths."

Macallister stormed from the room, leaving me alone with Volkov, a breach of protocol on his part, but a dramatic exit, nonetheless.

Volkov was nodding, muttering toward me, "He'll never get it. But you, Ben, you might. Please don't give up on me. I have a lot more to say. My father, the Russians. They have the code. And they can do terrible things with it!"

I snorted and stood as two agents, male and female, came into the interview room, bearing a set of handcuffs, and with their weapons drawn and aimed. The female agent cuffed Volkov, and the pair marched her to the exit.

As I watched them leave, I considered Volkov's parting comment, thinking, *If she's telling the truth, how do we verify it? Because this is an incredible tale.*

And then another thought popped into my head. *And if she's lying, as she's done so many times before, what is she really up to?*

49

BY THE TIME I REJOINED the team around in the operations center conference table, Macallister was grinning cheerfully.

"What are you so happy about?" I asked.

"This is so predictable. She's jerking our chains. Why, I don't know. Probably to stay out of jail. Or, as we've theorized, so we're focused on her while Petrikov strikes. I mean, while 'her father' strikes!" He laughed at the absurdity of Petrikov being Volkov's parent.

"Well, that should be easy enough to establish," I commented. "DNA test. We have all her data on file already. We have Petrikov's data, too, from when he was in custody. That's our first step, right?"

Macallister laughed again. "You really believe that shit, Porter?" Zimmerman and Connelly also chuckled. Jordon and Jones remained stoically quiet.

I licked my lips nervously, before contradicting the SAC. "Umm. Yeah. Well, no. Really, at this point, I don't know what to believe." My voice had trailed off under Macallister's withering stare. I concluded with more confidence than I felt, "But we gotta test the claim."

Macallister rolled his eyes. "Yeah, right. First thing tomorrow. Someone get on that. But the priority has to be on penetrating the smokescreen."

"The smokescreen?" queried Zimmerman.

"Yeah. This has got to be one of her smokescreens. By her description, Petrikov was last seen on the Canadian border. But we last saw him on the Mexican border. Which is it? Well, I'll tell you. It's a smokescreen. Make us waste our time in Canada. Listen, she's way ahead of us. She didn't come in here for a confession." The Acting SAC air-quoted "confession."

He paused, and then added more somberly, "But what she's forgotten is that now we have *her* in custody. We can take our time with the process. We're going to dust off all the questions we had while she remained mute at Walter Reed, and we're gonna start with those. And, for the first time, we're gonna get ahead of her!

"And get this!" Macallister was on a roll. "She's gonna stay *here*. Not get spirited off to some facility that we aren't told about. Don't you see? Appleton kept that quiet. 'Compartmentalized on a need-to-know basis,' she had said. Bullshit. Compartmentalized so that her crony Volkov would eventually be able to spring the big bossman."

Macallister walked toward the exit before stopping to turn back toward us. "Yesterday, we were searching for two subjects. Tomorrow, only one. Petrikov ain't in Russia. And I'd bet he's not in Canada *or* Mexico. He's here, somewhere, and she's covering for him. And here's how we're gonna find him. First thing tomorrow, here's how we start.

"Lewis. Tear that Ford truck apart. See where it's been. Every location, every fucking inch it's been driven. Backtrack it."

"Zimmerman. Has that Dmitri guy ever owned a car before? Find it, or them, and track 'em down. Confiscate 'em. Bring 'em in. See where he's been. Go back five, ten years.

"Connelly. Humor Porter and get a DNA test in the works.

"Jones. Work with Connelly to get Petrikov's biometrics, and then run 'em again through our systems. Go back to each of those sightings. See if there are any patterns. Because if she says he was at the Canadian border, he probably wasn't at the Mexican border. Figure out which one it is, or if it is just more bullshit on both."

Macallister took a deep breath. In the old days, before he was Acting SAC, when he was fit, he probably would have continued to barrel on, unstoppable in his tirade of orders. Because he wasn't done yet, barking out his instructions: "Jordon. You're on Dmitri's financials. Paint a picture. Where did he get his money? Where did he spend it? Work backward. Volkov said she killed him then used his credit card to buy clothes, shoes. Funny, but that's probably the only truth she's told. Start there."

The Acting SAC stopped. He looked at me. "Porter. Go to Bristol and take your sister out to dinner. Expense it. Celebrate. Because this nutcase Volkov is out of our hair, finally!"

Calling over his shoulder as he strode from the operations center, he yelled, "And I'm going home!"

The squad dispersed, the operations center techs who were not on duty that night switched off their screens, and I sank back into one of the familiar swivel chairs, thinking over Macallister's plan of action.

It all made sense, on the surface. But still, something bugged me.

Okay, I thought. *We do all that, and it's going to establish when and if Volkov has told the truth.*

Or will it?

Is she clever enough to anticipate what we would do? Of course, she is.

I closed my eyes. *And that's the problem, right? She knows our playbook. So, if this is a smokescreen, we're walking right into it. Again.*

Without reaching any conclusions, I looked at my phone and checked the time. Tempting as it was to spend some of the Bureau's bucks on a swank dinner, it was, realistically, too late to get to Bristol. Instead, I texted my sister:

> Grace, how's it going. Are you okay?

My phone bleeped.

> better than ever! going to bed soon.
> your friend left a bottle of vino and i
> had some to celebrate

I laughed to myself. Grace had told us that Volkov had broken into my sister's home yet brought take-out food and two bottles of wine. Good for my awesome sister to crack open one of those bottles for a nightcap. I texted back,

```
The SAC wants me to take you to dinner.
On him. Also to celebrate. You free
tomorrow night?
```

The reply did not come instantaneously, as usual, and I started to sweat. I was relieved that my concerns were unfounded when I eventually read,

```
sorry, no. and no questions! i have a
date :)
```

A second bubble appeared a half-second later.

```
raincheck?
```

I smiled as I tapped out,

```
Sure. Love you!
```

I smiled even more broadly when her response popped up.

```
love you too BenBro!
```

I settled back, thought for a moment, and, looking at my phone again, I scrolled through my contacts list and tapped on Abdul Hamid's personal cell phone number.

He answered right away. "Dude! What the eff was that all about? Who was listening in?"

I laughed. "Everyone. My squad. The Information Analyst team here. The Acting SAC, Boston office. This thing is huge."

"You okay?" he asked, in a concerned tone, catching onto the serious nature of my tone.

"Yeah. Trying to fill in some gaps. Can you tell me more about that accident? Like what you saw? The car, the driver?"

"Sure, yeah. It was brutal. Big SUV. A Tesla. The fact that it was electric made it even more scary, really. No gunning engine, just a whine, sort of, as it careened down what is basically a really wide sidewalk, a pedestrian street crowded with partiers. The car literally lifted people off the ground and tossed them aside. Erratic driving. Insane. If the thing didn't auger into the side of that fire truck, who knows how many more people would have been killed or hurt."

"Awful," I agreed, googling the incident on my laptop and scanning the headlines. "What's the story with the driver?"

"I don't think anyone really knows for certain. Obviously, they can't question her. And the FBI wasn't involved, at least not directly. It was handled as a local traffic accident. Horrendous, for sure, but there was no reason for us to look into it. Really, the only reason we opened a file on it was because I happened to be there with my buddy from the Albany office."

"Rodriquez, right?" I asked.

"Yeah. You'd like him. Good dude. We both kept up with the case, obviously. We both were asked to answer questions from the police periodically. Which we did, of course. Tried to help them out.

"Anyway, going back to the driver. From what I gathered, talking to the police investigators and reading the stuff online, the driver was a local artist. She hit it big in New York City. The critics loved her, apparently. She sold out shows, made a ton of cash. Became the talk of the town in Burlington. You know, local success story. Starving artist gets her big break."

"Wow," I commented. "Sounds like she had it made."

"Yup. And then, the theory goes, she snapped. Had to produce the next show, the next great piece of art. Too much pressure."

Scanning an article online, I was unconsciously nodding my head in agreement, saying to Hamid, "I'm looking at stuff on the web right now. Says the value of her art tanked after the accident. No one wants to be associated with it."

"It's a really sad story, isn't it?"

"Yeah," I muttered.

In a stronger tone, I asked, "Listen, this suspect we have here. Like I said, she claimed responsibility. After we spoke to you, she claimed she controlled the car remotely. Any chance that's possible, from what you saw?"

"No way, man. I saw the driver through the windows of the car. She looked, well, insane. I could see her face. Her eyes were wide open. And her mouth was open like she was screaming. Like she had totally lost her shit. Like she had gone batshit crazy. That's what I told the cops too."

"Right. I saw that in the report. Hey, I gotta go, but thanks. Let's figure out how to get together one of these days."

"You got it, Porter. See ya around. Call anytime. Later."

The phone in my hand went silent as I considered what he said, thinking, *You'd look insane, too, if your car was driving itself, with you in it, out of control and slamming into people.*

But, all the same, Volkov's stories seemed, well, insane. *Because they were, obviously. Insane lies,* I concluded. Macallister was right. She's up to something, again. And tomorrow morning, we are on the case, with a plan, to finally get ahead of her.

Reaching that conclusion, I went home and slept soundly.

Had I known then how wrong I was, I doubt I would have slept at all.

chapter 50

EARLIER THE SAME DAY:
TUESDAY, SEPTEMBER 3, 2019 — OTTAWA, ONTARIO, CANADA

ANATOLY PETRIKOV HAD BEEN promised that today would be the day.

Finally.

Four days of anticipation.

But, today, Petrikov had been able to move on from that sense of nervousness. Today was the day to be cheerful.

The big Russian cradled a mug of a coffee drink nicknamed a Raf, a shot of espresso steamed with cream and sugar. It was his favorite way to start the day. And here, it had tasted better. More authentic, perhaps.

Possibly, he thought, because the drink had been mixed by a Russian, on Russian soil.

Or, at least, what was legally recognized as Russian soil, here at the Embassy of the Russian Federation in Ottawa.

Four days ago, when Tom Morris's twenty-three-foot runabout had brushed against the side of a single-engined, eighteen-foot Boston Whaler motorboat, the big Russian had taken one careful step. This close to freedom, it wouldn't do to fall into the waters of the Saint Lawrence River. It might have caused a commotion and attracted attention, for sure, but it might have also caused damage to the two-terabyte USB flash drive he carried in his pocket.

That, too, would have been disastrous.

But Petrikov had made that single step gracefully, or at least as gracefully as one could be with his bulk, as he accepted the outstretched hand that belonged to the familiar face of Vitaly Nikolaevich Rodionov.

Aboard the little Boston Whaler, rocking back and forth from the sudden transfer of this new weight into it, turning his back to Tom Morris, Petrikov had embraced the medium-height, dark-haired, dark-eyed hacker who spoke perfect English with only a very slight Russian accent, that he had bid farewell to only three-and-a-half weeks ago.

"I didn't expect it to be you, again," Petrikov had said in Russian, as the men released their embrace.

"At your service," Vitaly Rodionov had replied, also in his native tongue. "You've become quite a topic of conversation, you know. We're happy to see you and to begin anew."

Petrikov had glanced at the helmsman of the Boston Whaler and recognized that face, too, another one of the men from Unit 29155. Anxiously, he had tried, to no avail, to remember the man's name, and for cover, hoping that he would not seem impolite, Petrikov had commented, "We are missing one."

"Georgiy is waiting with the car. It is just Fedor and I for now. You are missing one, as well. Where is your daughter?"

"She elected not to join me."

Rodionov's eyebrows had raised in concern. "That was not the arrangement. And that creates a potentially treacherous situation."

"I understand, of course." Petrikov's head had dipped, his eyes downcast, and he had muttered, "I did what I had to do. She will not survive the night, I'm afraid."

Now, Rodionov's eyes had narrowed as he processed that comment. "My condolences for . . . your loss. But . . . the code?"

Petrikov had tapped the tin case in his pocket.

"I see," Rodionov had said, then adding, "Make yourself comfortable, please."

Petrikov had offered a thin, insincere smile as he seated himself on the gunwale edge of the Boston Whaler's hull, tipping the little vessel inadvertently with his massive weight. Rodionov had subtly moved opposite to counterbalance as the motorboat made its way to its dock in Brockville.

Around them, the parade of sail had continued, the US Border Patrol vessels and the Canada Border Services Agency boats on duty oblivious to the transfer of a single person from one nation to the other, and equally unaware of the tiny flash drive in that person's pants pocket.

Arriving on Canadian soil, the three men had departed the Boston Whaler and joined a fourth, Fedor, who had been waiting behind the wheel of another rented Ford Explorer.

"To the airport, yes?" Petrikov had inquired with anticipation.

Rodionov had laughed. "No. Far too dangerous."

Petrikov's crestfallen face had clearly transmitted his disappointment; the big man had made no effort to hide his confusion. "What? That is not acceptable. That was not the deal!"

"It cannot be helped. But I assure you, where we are going is good enough. For now."

Sipping the Raf, Petrikov recalled that the drive from Brockville to Ottawa had taken less than an hour and a half, and during it, Rodionov had outlined the plan, telling his guest that they would be quartered, for the time being, in the safety of the Russian Embassy in Ottawa, and that no expense would be spared in the oligarch's comfort.

He had been truthful, and the past days passed pleasantly enough. The food was excellent and bountiful, and the vodka was authentic.

And in moments, he would be escorted to an underground room, where he was told the Embassy maintained a secure communications suite, impenetrable to the bugs that the Canadians, in cooperation with the British intelligence agency MI5, had attempted to plant when the Embassy building was constructed in 1956.

In the Ford Explorer, Rodionov had explained, "I am not merely a computer hacker. I am the senior-most information technology officer of Unit 29155. I report only to President Vladimir Putin. He would like to speak to you directly. That is scheduled for Tuesday morning. In the meantime, you are free to do what you wish, within, of course, the confines of the Embassy grounds."

Petrikov was ready, as he slurped down the last of the Raf at the sound of a knock on the ornate, mahogany door to his suite. He would discuss matters with Putin, and then he would, in a moment of drama, slide the flash drive, in its alloy case, slowly across the table.

Then he would become a hero of Russia.

CHAPTER
51

ONE WEEK LATER:
LATE AFTERNOON, TUESDAY, SEPTEMBER 10, 2019 —
CARTWRIGHT, CANADA

A WEEK LATER, after a grueling, thirty-three-hour, nonstop drive from Ottawa, Anatoly Petrikov found himself outside of the village of Cartwright, located in the southeastern area of Canada's Newfoundland and Labrador Province, with a new Russian passport in the name of Pyotr Petrovich Shirshov.

As far as the Canadian authorities would know, he was an oceanographer.

With the short notice required, there had been no time to create an immigration record that would be unassailable to inquiry, and a risky decision had been made. Rather than wait, Petrikov, with his newly-issued identity, and Rodionov would be flown out of the country, departing the small, single-strip airfield outside of Cartwright.

The passport had been hastily created, using the name of a deceased Russian oceanographer, with Petrikov cast as his son. The dates and the backstory would not line up, but the chances of the Canada Border Services agent doing the leg-work to determine that, on the face of this routine helicopter transfer to a Russian research ship, would be slim.

Waiting for the helicopter, Petrikov reclined in the back seat of the rented Ford Explorer and closed his eyes.

The call with President Vladimir Putin a week ago had exceeded Petrikov's expectations and dreams. Sitting side-by-side at a polished, figured walnut table with Rodionov, facing a video screen with the eye of a camera below it, Petrikov had glowed as Putin expressed his admiration for the successful experiment in Burlington.

The president, in person, had reiterated his promise that Petrikov would be granted asylum in Russia, protected from the clutches of the United States government, as a quid pro quo for the code that his daughter developed.

As Petrikov absently fiddled with the small alloy case that laid on the table in front of him, Rodionov had asked about the daughter. "Our sources do not report that your daughter met her demise, as planned. Are you certain this will be taken care of? And if not, are you going to request asylum for her too?"

"No," Petrikov had stated flatly. "No asylum. Even if she has somehow survived."

Putin spoke with a direct, firm tone, "And if she has, somehow, survived, you understand that I will not hesitate to order her removal." The president of Russia paused, then added, "In plain words. Her death."

"Yes. I understand," agreed Petrikov, without hesitation.

"In the event that she is alive, she, too, has the ability to unencrypt the code that you intend to provide, correct?" Putin had probed.

"She does, but she is not here, nor will she be invited to sit at my table ever again," Petrikov had proclaimed. Looking first at Rodionov, then at the camera, at Putin, Petrikov had demanded, "We have an arrangement? The drive for my asylum?"

Putin spoke a single word: "Da." *Yes.*

As he had dreamt, Petrikov had slowly opened the little case and, with a thumb and forefinger, lifted to USB stick from its cushioned repose. With an almost-inaudible *click,* he set it on the table, and with his forefinger, he slid it in front of Rodionov.

Idly gazing at the expanse of the gray, weather-beaten asphalt airstrip at Cartwright visible through the window glass, Petrikov considered this final hurdle, this final step to take. As he waited, he marveled at how he had managed to reach this moment.

Two years ago, he had raged as his carefully-constructed scheme for profit and revenge had been undone, ultimately costing him his freedom and exposing his daughter's long-kept secret identity.

He had no regrets.

Thanks to that daughter, he had been freed of his captivity, and again thanks to his daughter, he had been given a gift, her wonderful technological breakthrough.

And then she had turned on him.

She didn't understand.

She, apparently, was too much like her mother. Blind to the genius of Anatoly Petrikov. Too close-minded to appreciate his penchant to see beyond the present, to plan audaciously, and to take the risks that would become fruitful rewards.

The mother saw only his appearance, bloated and distasteful, and she—she alone!—chose to cheat. *She* chose to turn her back on him. And though he had ignored her indiscretions, preferring to focus on his work and his wealth and his power, *she* had taken it too far, and *she* had paid the price, her body long since disintegrated beneath the surface of the Atlantic. The boat anchor that weighed down her corpse, and the lead weight that dragged her dogs downward to follow her, would be the only markers of the grave.

The daughter chose what to see. She saw only a death. She did not understand the treachery of her mother. She could not fathom the reasons why; she only could see the end result. *A shame*, thought Petrikov.

He had enjoyed their months together. But it was her decision, and she—she alone!—chose to run.

Imagine what she would see now.

She, like her father, would be surrounded by her countrymen. She, like her father, would be on the cusp of greatness, as they prepared, together, for a final experiment, a final test, that was not only blessed, but also encouraged, by none other than the president of mother Russia.

Imagine what she would have understood now.

Alas, she was gone. She made her choice.

Her loss.

Petrikov's reverie was interrupted by the clatter of a gray-painted Kamov Ka-226 coaxial rotor, light-utility helicopter touching down on the cracked asphalt pad. On either side of the Explorer, Petrikov and Rodionov opened their rear passenger doors. Crossing to the rear tailgate, they removed their luggage: a duffel bag each and, for Rodionov, a large case with a diplomatic seal. Inside, the case contained the four laptop computers that had been set up by his team before they departed the Embassy.

Petrikov carried the USB drive, a comforting if not almost-unnoticeable weight in his pocket. It was a backup, now with the code unpacked and transferred to the laptops. All the same, he was happy to still have it.

Halfway between them and the helicopter, its blades rotating to a slow stop, a Canada Border Services agent waited, his shadow long in the late-afternoon sun.

Having been instructed to act with authority, Petrikov reached him first, and proffered his passport with a curt, "Good afternoon," in Russian-accented English.

The agent reviewed the small folio and gave a cursory glance at the photo, then at the flabby face in front of him. "An unusual method of transport to your ship, would you say, Mister . . . Shirshov?"

"It could not be avoided," Petrikov replied, with a feigned tone of indignation. "Nor is it my preference. I typically do not travel in such an . . . undignified manner."

Rodionov passed his credentials to the agent, asking, "Yes, of course, this is unusual. You were briefed ahead of time, no? Is there a problem? We are running out of daylight, and making the ship before nightfall would be far more preferable, if you don't mind."

The agent examined the second passport, shrugging his shoulders. He had, indeed, been briefed. A Russian scientist and his assistant were to be airlifted to a waiting Russian research vessel. The agent had been instructed to ensure that what Border Services had been told by the Russian embassy was what would transpire on the tarmac.

Closing both passports, the Border Services agent passed them back to the two waiting men, saying, "Have a nice flight," as he eyed the odd-looking, double-rotor, double-tail chopper.

Within minutes, the twin Rolls-Royce 250C series turboshaft engines had reached their take-off revolutions, and the drab gray helicopter lifted off Canadian soil with a slight wobble before twisting and turning toward the east, headed out over the Labrador Sea.

Inside, his belly fat jiggling with the rattle of the chopper, Petrikov grinned as he looked down on the steel-gray water as Canada receded in the distance. He was free. Free of the FBI, free of the United States, and finally free to implement the plan that he had outlined to Rodionov during the drive from Ottawa.

Petrikov's grinned widened. A plan that would use his daughter's gift in a way most unexpected.

CHAPTER

52

AFTER A RATTLING, SHAKING, one-hour-and-twenty-three-minute flight aboard the Ka-226, Petrikov's grin became an outright leer, as he gazed down upon his salvation, his freedom, and his asylum. It was not Russian soil, to be certain. But it was Russian property, and, unlike the embassy building in Ottawa, bordered on all four sides by sovereign Canadian territory, this particular piece of Russian property floated on international waters, one hundred and fifty-six miles from Cartwright and Canada.

The round-trip journey from the ship, to Cartwright, and back was at almost the outer limits of the Kamov Ka-226's 375-mile range, and the two pilots breathed a sigh of relief as the wheels of the chopper were chocked on the wide, open helipad at the front of the dark navy-blue-painted ship.

As the rotors wound still and the engines ticked over quietly, a crewmember opened the cabin door for Petrikov and Rodionov, and the two men clambered down onto the deck of the ship. A figure clad in a black naval officer's uniform waited at the edge of the pad; as the newcomers approached, the figure doffed his cap in a formal manner, and said, with a slight bow, "Gentlemen. I am Captain Borodin Maxim Stepanovich. Welcome aboard the *Yantar*."

The three men shook hands, and the newcomers followed the captain from the helicopter deck as he introduced them to his vessel, "*Yantar* was launched in December 2012, and is three hundred and fifty-four feet in length. Our crew numbers about sixty, though we have accommodations for additional personnel. We operate as an ocean-going research vessel, but we have, shall we say, other capabilities." As the men made their way aft on the ship's narrow side passage deck, Captain Stepanovich was pointing upward at the two tall masts that bristled with antennae and, further back, a giant, teardrop-shaped, white dome. At the very back of the ship, yellow-painted cranes sprouted at odd angles, poking from the blocky, white superstructure like tentacles. The captain concluded, "From the outside, she may not be the most elegant ship on the oceans. But we have a far different view from the inside."

Captain Stepanovich led his two guests through a doorway in the side of the superstructure, and the trio disappeared as the sun set below the western horizon.

After a crewmember had shown the two visitors to their nicely appointed cabins, and they had been given some time to wash and to put away their sparse belongings, a steward escorted them to the captain's table in the mess hall.

As they dined, the captain outlined their itinerary, as if he were their cruise director on an ocean liner. "We will return to our home-port in about eight-and-a-half, perhaps nine days. Murmansk. Are you familiar with it?"

"On the Barents Sea, yes?" Rodionov offered.

"Indeed. We will pass to the east of Greenland and to the west of Iceland, eventually skirting the northern coast of Scandinavia. When we are close in, we will reactivate our AIS transponder. You know what this is?"

Petrikov had no need to guess. He was intimately familiar with the Automatic Information System, an internationally adopted means of location data that was communicated between vessels so that each vessel, as well as shore-based stations, could be tracked electronically. But, Petrikov wondered, "what do you mean, 'reactivate'? You are a research ship. Are you not required to transmit your location at all times?"

The captain narrowed his eyes slightly, picking up his fork, waving it, saying, "Perhaps. As I said before, we have other capabilities. And since I have been told you have been authorized to explore those capabilities, I will explain.

"Currently," he continued, "we have a decoy transponder being used on a sistership that departed Murmansk yesterday. It will wander back and forth offshore slightly. We will rendezvous with it and then turn our system back on. A little subterfuge to keep the American watchers busy. You understand?"

His guests nodded.

"Once in Murmansk, we will take on the men and the equipment that you need. During our journey there, I am told that you—" the captain motioned to Rodionov, "will begin familiarizing yourself with our capabilities, to ensure that we are adequately prepared."

"I need to order specialized equipment for delivery to the ship. How much time do I have once we are in port?" Rodionov asked.

"Perhaps two weeks. Will that be adequate?"

"Yes."

"Then the schedule appears to be workable," Captain Stepanovich concluded, raising his glass in a toast. "We shall be back at sea on the first of October."

CHAPTER
53

SEVEN DAYS.

Seven days.

See that? That repetition? That's the thing about investigations. They're oftentimes repetitive. And, therefore, oftentimes, you feel like you're banging your head against a wall, for no good reason.

Well, not that there's any good reason to bang your head against a wall, come to think of it.

We had questioned Anastasia Volkov, claiming to be Irinushka Petrikov, but hidden in our records under the guise of Ann Karin, for seven days.

The story got more complex, of course, as she had the time to fill in detail after detail. To her credit, I suppose, she was consistent with every single detail, every single time, every single retelling to every single interviewer.

While it was repetitive, one of the advantages of conducting a series of interviews was that we would get the ability to analyze if and when a witness changed their story. Volkov's story never changed. And, as they say, it was a doozy.

The first eye-opener popped up less than thirty-six hours after we took Volkov into custody. Agent Connelly had demanded an expedited DNA test, to compare Petrikov and Volkov, a concept so farfetched that no one in the Bureau had ever considered it. Connelly's report was conclusive: "DNA lab results are back. 99.9 percent accuracy. Petrikov is Volkov's father."

Upon learning that news, Macallister had ranted, "And now we have a potential motive. She's covering for him, for her father. She claims she parted ways with him on the Canadian Border. But I'd bet that's yet another deception engineered by Anastasia Volkov. Or, rather, by Irinushka Petrikov. Her father is still somewhere in the States. And she's acting as his decoy. That Tesla thing and the Russia thing are bullshit. They're smokescreens. And when there's smoke, there's fire. Volkov is hiding something. Probably her father. Find him!"

After seven days of nonstop investigation, we were no closer to succeeding at that task than we had been back in December, when Petrikov disappeared from the Vermont facility. The squad assembled in the operations center, and Agent Brenda Connelly stood, once again, at the whiteboard, carefully scribing an outline, a synopsis, of what we had learned so far.

"Okay, here we go, again," I started in. "November 2018, Volkov escapes Walter Reed and meets up with Dmitri Tretriaki in New York."

Connelly wrote quickly and cleanly, and Jones picked up the narrative, "Volkov camps out in Ithaca with Tretriaki, and she uses her backdoor access to the FBI systems to locate Petrikov in Vermont."

Waiting for Connelly to ink another bullet point, Jones continued, "Tretriaki and Volkov build a team with the help of the *Bratva*. When they are ready, she plants Tretriaki in the Vermont facility and initiates the firewall attack on our office, while using Grace Porter as a decoy to slow our reaction times."

"And that's where it doesn't add up," I quickly stated. "You'd think she would know, if she had access to our system, that we didn't know, here in Boston, where Petrikov was."

Macallister snorted, "Yup. Smokescreen. She's lying."

"Yeah, but learning that from the system is like looking for a double negative," I countered. "How does she look for something we don't know? It's a reasonable assumption for her, that she assumed we'd have tabs on Petrikov."

"Nah. Smokescreen." Macallister leaned back and smugly crossed his arms.

Jones recommenced her retelling of Volkov's statements, "She told us about a cross-country trip to California. She told us how she had created a parallel identity for a Cornell professor and used that identification to rent that home in California, and later, a second place in Plattsburgh, New York."

Agent Jones paused to let Connelly catch up, before Jones continued, "And then she claimed that she created a parallel identity to Petrikov's face and planted it in four places in four months, using it to draw us out to those places so we would search there. That was my task, to check those out. Here's the interesting thing: each sighting was at night, in the rain, and the camera visual was blurry because of the lighting and the weather. But the facial recognition results are spot-on. With hindsight, it is possible to conclude that those images were spoofed."

"Exactly," Macallister agreed. "All smokescreens. Part of the pattern."

Connelly turned to another whiteboard as Jones picked up the narrative, "Let's stick with the timeline. Okay, in California, Volkov, via the Cornell professor's ID, ordered a white Tesla Model X. That checks out. In Plattsburgh, she, or rather the Cornell professor's alternate identity, sold the Tesla. Volkov recited bank account numbers and gave us the dates of transfers from offshore accounts in the Cayman Islands that she said would link back to her father."

Connelly kept writing at the board as Jordon chimed in with a summary of his investigation, "Her description of her travel matched the location history the Ford F-150 had retained. Matched up with credit card transactions in Denver, Utah, and California. Matched up with the location records of Dmitri Tretriaki's cell phone."

Lewis had pulled the tracking history from Dmitri Tretriaki's F-150, and Agent Don Jordon had literally gotten in a car and followed the electronic breadcrumbs. His investigation took him from New York City to Vermont to Ithaca, New York. Jordon decided not to drive cross-country, instead picking up the trail in Plattsburgh, New York.

Then Jordon found himself on the shores of the Saint Lawrence River, in a little place called Morristown, New York, where a local named

Tom Morris confessed to taking a large man partway across the river, allowing him to step on a Canadian craft piloted by two men, where he disappeared. Morris had set aside the ten thousand dollars in cash that he had been given, saving it for when he'd need it in the winter, and he forfeited it to us.

The lawyers at the Department of Justice were not quite sure what to do with Tom Morris; he had committed a crime, but he was a cooperating witness to a far larger investigation. They were going to work on a deal.

As Jordon and a team of agents dug deeper in Morristown, they had found a photograph of Petrikov and Volkov sitting on the open tailgate of a white F-150, in a distant background, through a window, with the Saint Lawrence River beyond. It was a selfie taken by a bartender with a customer who had left a generous tip after the bartender had comped a few drinks while the customer waited for a take-out food order. That customer? Dmitri Tretriaki, now deceased.

Zimmerman had run down the names that Volkov gave us of the team that Tretriaki and she had hired to help with the operation in Vermont to free Petrikov. One of the men, Carlos Chiloé Guerrero, had used a passport in that name to return to his native Chile. The DOJ was attempting to negotiate an extradition order. The other three men remained at large, invisible, so far, to law enforcement.

And yet, even though her exacting memory recalled all these details and times and places and gave us a roadmap of her travels, and had, perhaps more importantly, given us a last known location for Petrikov, giant holes remained.

The Canadian Security Intelligence Service and the Royal Canadian Mounted Police cooperated with our inquiry to trace Petrikov after he allegedly crossed into their jurisdiction. We had a date, we had a time, and we had a location to start, but we got nothing, despite their best efforts, from the RCMP. There was no record of anyone matching that description on a flight to Rome, as Volkov had claimed, or as far as anyone could tell, to anywhere. The Canadians would continue to review airport security tapes on our behalf, but that detail, to Volkov's confusion, didn't pan out, and her story began to fall apart.

The most fascinating, or fantastical, depending on your viewpoint, part of her story was her claim that a secret Russian hacking team had assisted with the coding.

"Unit 29155" was a group well-known to the United States intelligence apparatus. It was hardly a secret; as recently as last month, its existence was reported in the mainstream press. And yes, it operated, to the best of our knowledge, as an ostensibly sub-rosa arm of the Russian government. Yet all the same, we could find no evidence of a group of three Russian hackers driving into the United States.

Looking at the whiteboard, and at Connelly's last entry of "Unit 29155, Russian Hackers," Macallister rose and stabbed a finger at the board, smudging the carefully-printed letters. "Let's start there, today."

He stalked to the interview room where Volkov was already waiting. I dutifully followed. The squad would watch on the video feed.

Volkov ran her right hand through her long hair as we entered the small room, tucking loose strands behind an ear.

Macallister dove right in. "Let's start with your Russian hackers. No trace of them. Not in our records. Not in the Canadian records. Ghosts."

"They used false identification, of course," Volkov protested. "Let me see the tapes of the border crossing at Douane. I'll identify them."

"Right. The hackers. The hackers who helped you get remote control of a Tesla," Macallister responded in a sarcastic tone. "Here's what I don't get. *Why?* You say that you, Petrikov, and a bunch of Russian hackers holed up in a basement. Where was it? Plattsburgh. Holed up in Plattsburgh, so you can drive some woman's Tesla into a crowd."

Macallister snorted and steepled his hands over his expanded gut. "I hate to say it, that's kind of a lame terror attack, don't you think? The Russians have nothing to gain by it. Petrikov has nothing to gain. *You* have nothing to gain. Yet you take credit."

He shook his head and repeated, "Why? What's the end game?"

Volkov's shoulders sagged, and her head slumped. "I don't know," she whispered.

"Riiiighhht," Macallister said, drawing out the word. "Of course, you don't. Porter, run it through again, please."

"Yessir," I replied. "Volkov consolidated the code onto an encrypted flash drive. The only two people in the world who have the password credentials are Volkov and Petrikov. And, Petrikov was the last person in possession of said flash drive."

"So," Macallister picked up the question, "what's he going to do with it? And you claim that you don't know. Of course, you don't."

Volkov's face reddened, in anger or in angst, I couldn't tell, as she answered, "We once talked about a swarm. You could control a bunch of these things at once if you had the bandwidth. Which I didn't have. He talked about it once, suggesting bridges. Maybe causing gridlock or something, all over the country."

"A traffic jam, huh? Another real winner of a terror attack," Macallister replied in a tone drenched with snide.

I added, "But, don't forget, she doesn't have the bandwidth. Hey," I asked Volkov, "where do you get the 'bandwidth'? Where does Petrikov get it?"

Volkov sighed. "From the Russians. From Unit 29155."

"Sure," spat Macallister. "Let's call whatshisname, Putin. Maybe he's in on it too."

"He is."

Macallister stared at Volkov, stunned at her audacity, and called her on it, "He *what*? Are you fucking kidding me?"

Volkov looked down at the table. She slowly ran her right hand through her hair, and as her hand passed her forehead, she brought her gaze up to stare directly into Macallister's eyes. She spoke a single, deliberate word, "No." After a beat, to let that sink in, she continued, "My father has dealt with the Kremlin for decades. He was the *vory* in New York. His diamond dealings? You think that was all on the up-and-up?"

She laughed softly. "Oh no, the Kremlin has long since been involved. Russia is very creative. Probably the long winters. Lots of time to think, to plan. Russia meddled in the United States elections in 2016, of course. Remember?

"And Russia has meddled elsewhere too. Madagascar, for example. Their 2018 elections. And why? To protect the Kremlin's interest in the diamond trade, among other things."

Looking at Macallister and me one at a time, she concluded quietly, "Putin has an adventurous spirit. He does not hesitate to try new ideas, and he is not constrained by the media and by the second-guessing like the politicians here in the United States. He has no need for any sort of false humility. He can do what he wants, and he was intrigued by the concept of hijacking a vehicle from afar. And I have no doubt that he remains profoundly involved."

As she finished her sentence, she had locked eyes with Macallister, who stood and shoved his chair back in one fluid motion, snapping, "And I have no doubt that you are full of shit. Smokescreen after smokescreen. These interviews are going in circles."

Macallister stormed from the room.

I followed, but I paused at the exit, turning to face Volkov. I looked at her one last time before spinning on my heels.

I realized I had just spun my own body in a circle. And the motion made me think, *We are both dismissing this too fast.*

I had to come up with a way to slow it down. Because the problem with spinning in circles is that you get dizzy. And then you fall down, flat on your face, and say, "What just happened?"

Which was exactly what was going to happen to us.

54

WEDNESDAY, SEPTEMBER 11, 2019 — FBI BOSTON FIELD OFFICE, CHELSEA, MASSACHUSETTS

I ARRIVED AT THE OFFICE the following morning after a sleepless night, lugging a cup of coffee so big it could have been called an urn. The blessed effects of the caffeine had begun to take their effect by the time I walked through the door of the operations center, wondering, *Who was the first person to think to pour hot water over a ground seed of a Coffea plant? I mean, why would you do that? Because it's brilliant.*

I sipped my coffee, recalling the conclusion of the interview the night before, *Stop spinning in circles. Start by breaking the circle into two halves.*

On the one hand, we had the vast piles of evidence painting Volkov as a criminal. I mean, not only did she infiltrate the FBI under a false identity, she was also a conspirator in a treasonous plot against the United States, and our evidence indicated that she was responsible for the murder of Vanessa Raiden, an event that she admitted. She had also confessed to killing Dmitri Tretriaki, and we had her fingerprints on a broken table lamp, a knife that was used to cut off his finger, and on a glass found in the apartment. In other words, hard evidence that she had been involved in another murder.

Of course, on the other hand, we had her sudden appearance at my sister's home in Bristol, where she surrendered to the FBI willingly. In a series of exhaustive interviews, she maintained her story—not just the details about her travels since her escape from the Walter Reed medical facility in Maryland almost a year ago, but also on the Operation E.T. case, where she filled in the missing details on the intricacies within that plot.

Everything she told us checked out.

And therein lay the problem.

It's occasionally called "threat bias." It's sort of like when you identify a threat, you begin to amplify your response to that threat, until you focus only on that threat. You don't see anything else. You develop tunnel vision and you try to slot your responses into your preconceived biases against the threat.

My coffee cup felt a little lighter as I sat, sipping and thinking. I decided it was time to examine my bias against Volkov. I pulled a notebook from my backpack and drew a big circle on the blank page, thinking, *I can break this down further than two halves.* I divided the circle into four quadrants, and I filled in each quadrant with my observations and questions:

> *Quadrant A: Volkov spent literally years working beside us, within the secretive confines of the FBI, and had convincingly played a part which was an outright fabrication. How could that person ever be trusted? Because everything they told us, before, checked out. Until it didn't.*

> *Quadrant B: How could we know if her confession was nothing more than an extension of her initial deception? How could we be certain that she was not acting as a willing accomplice, again, for her father, as he plotted something beyond our reach, using his daughter as the sacrificial lamb to appease our appetites?*

> *Quadrant C: Was it that she could not tell us where to find Petrikov? Or, was it that she could tell us, but would not?*

> *Quadrant D: All she has given us is nothing but a travelogue. We have verified where she has been with hard evidence. But what we cannot verify is her claim that a mysterious Russian group called Unit 29155 had helped her hack a Tesla.*

With one last gulp, I slurped down the dregs of my coffee and looked at the last quadrant that I had filled in, thinking, *verify*. I'd begin with the last word. *Tesla*.

✳ ✳ ✳

By late September, fall was primed to arrive in Boston. The sticky summer heat was gone, and the leaves on the trees would soon start to turn brown, before dropping to the ground.

Meanwhile, I had started with Tesla, and I went to the source.

The engineers at Tesla had refuted Volkov's claims.

After the accident in Vermont, which had initially been widely reported in the media, Tesla's engineers had examined the car. Similar incidents had occurred in the past, including two notable accidents in Florida. In the first accident, in 2016, a Tesla driver had been killed when his Model S ran into, or more correctly, *under* a semitruck carrying a load of blueberries. In that case, Tesla proved that their Autopilot system had been in use, improperly supervised by the driver. In early 2019, another Tesla driver, also using the Autopilot system improperly, perished when his Model 3 collided with a truck.

Upon learning of the Burlington tragedy, the company had immediately cooperated with the Vermont State Police investigators. The Tesla engineers examined the wrecked Model X's computerized logging system. Autopilot had not been engaged by Suzanne Cahal. And, the log records indicated that her hands were on the wheel, gripping it tightly, but that she had let go of the steering wheel at sporadic times as the SUV careened through the festival-goers.

"But yes," Volkov had complained, when we redirected this line of questioning to her, "the system won't show that Autopilot was on. It wasn't. *I* had control of the car, through the telematics."

I had suggested to Macallister that we request custody of the Tesla Model X involved in the Burlington accident, now in a State Police storage facility in the Vermont capital city of Montpelier. Macallister had grunted that he'd put in the request.

Volkov had begged for a computer, offering to retrace her steps, to both show us how she penetrated our systems and to start to recreate her hack of the Tesla. To his credit, Macallister ran that request up the flagpole, to the director, who had been continually briefed on our investigation and knew that Volkov, not the fabricated Ann Karin, was the person in our custody.

"Not at all advisable" had been the response from Washington. Under no circumstances would Washington dare permit her access to any sort of computer, concerned with the chaos she could cause once online again.

She had offered to disclose her access method to the engineers at Tesla, explaining that she had located a weakness, buried among millions of lines of code, "You won't understand. Simplistically, it's basically a typo. When the car is pinged, it responds. To respond, it must open the correct port. Call it, for discussion purposes, port four hundred. The car sends its response, and then the code is supposed to close the port. It doesn't. It closes port *forty*. See? It's just a seemingly innocent mistake in the code. But, with that port remaining open, I can send my packet program."

Lewis had hedged that this was feasible, but the engineers at the company, when we passed this theory onto them, were unconvinced. *Impossible*, they had claimed. *It doesn't work like that.*

✳ ✳ ✳

That research took time. Excruciating time. It was the last day of September when Macallister and I took our usual hard seats in the stuffy, uncomfortable interview room for the umpteenth time, and when Volkov wasted no time starting in with a request of her own.

"What's the harm in me talking to Tesla engineers? I speak their language," Volkov pled. "The risk that I am worried about is this concept of a swarm. If the Russians can figure out how to do this en masse, they can create a swarm of these things, turn them into weapons. You dismissed me. Like all they could do was to cause a traffic jam. There's *so* much *more* potential than just that!"

Her voice had risen, but she modulated, "All it takes to prevent it is a simple patch to the code. Before the Russians succeed and create the swarm."

At the first mention of the Russians, Macallister appeared to tune her out, muttering, "Same old line of bullshit." I doubt he was even listening when she referenced them a second time.

But I wavered, thinking, *What's the harm in connecting her with the engineers?*

Macallister interrupted my thoughts, and in a brusque tone, he stated, "The Russians. The same ones who you allege spirited him across the Canadian border, made him invisible, and who now possess this code you've written. Yet, despite all that intimate knowledge, you still conveniently claim that you have no knowledge of your father's whereabouts or his intentions?"

"Yes."

"Therefore, we are merely to wait? For him to resurface somewhere? Or for him to trigger his next scheme?"

Volkov responded in a clear tone, "That's what I'm afraid of."

I thought that was an odd statement. And it triggered a sense of fear in me too.

Fear can be an excellent motivator, and sitting there, watching Macallister stew at what he obviously considered to be a Volkov smokescreen, I suddenly realized what I had to do.

I'd have to light my own fire. Put up a smokescreen of my own.

I had a plan. And I knew who I had to talk to.

PART FIVE
OCTOBER 2019

ANATOLY PETRIKOV WAS accustomed to the trappings of power, and with his bulk prominently positioned in a tall-backed, black-leather chair overlooking two orderly rows of men and computer monitors in the information warfare suite aboard the Russian Naval Research vessel *Yantar*, the oligarch certainly projected authority and supremacy.

Petrikov was pleased. He had been enjoying this view for seventeen days, since the navy-blue research ship had departed Murmansk Harbor, a few days later than her captain had predicted, on the morning of October 3rd.

When *Yantar* had arrived at the ship's home port in Murmansk, Rodionov had required a full two weeks to procure the specialized equipment that he required to make the plan, first suggested by Petrikov during the long drive from Ottawa to Cartwright, into a reality. The wait in Murmansk had been necessary and unavoidable.

Once clear of Polyarny and into open water, the captain instructed the navigator to switch off the vessel's AIS transmitter. The research ship would be invisible to maritime traffic, though on clear days, she might still be spotted by one of the many surveillance satellites orbiting the globe.

That was a risk *Yantar* would have to accept.

The research ship had played this card in the past, to the point where *Yantar* had begun to attract the attention of foreign intelligence agencies. The ship had been spotted in several odd, perhaps suspect, locations over the course of her previous voyages: in 2015, she loitered off Guantánamo Bay, Cuba. Two years later, in 2017, she began her year staged in the eastern Mediterranean Sea, above an undersea telecommunications cable originated in Israel. Then she crossed the Atlantic later in the year to assist in a search for a missing Argentinian submarine.

Theories abounded. Was the ship a bona-fide research vessel that was also equipped with search and rescue (SAR) personnel and equipment? Or was *Yantar* built for a more sinister purpose, for clandestine surveillance and reconnaissance, under the guise of her research vessel classification?

To Anatoly Petrikov, comfortably seated in the tall-backed, black-leather chair in the vessel's main-deck information warfare suite, the answer to *that* question was obvious.

In the two tidy rows before him, eighteen of Unit 29155's technicians were seated at workstations. In the front row were two groups of four men, each clustered before three screens. The second row was occupied by ten men in pairs; each pair worked in front of four screens. The men focused on their monitors and conversed only sparingly through their headsets. At the far end of the space, from Petrikov's perspective, three giant, flat-screen monitors angled to face all occupants. The left screen displayed a chart. The middle and right screens were off.

Seated similarly at Petrikov's right shoulder, Vitaly Rodionov spoke quietly into his own headset, occasionally nodding and tapping at a tablet held in his right hand.

A third high-backed command chair, to the right of Rodionov, was vacant, reserved for Captain Stepanovich.

Except for the location, the assembly of men and computer equipment resembled a video gamer's conference or, perhaps, a military headquarters.

It was a little of both.

There are almost four hundred telecommunications cables that cross the oceans of the globe, snaking across the bottoms of the seas and totaling a staggering 750,000 miles in cumulative length. These circuits carry the vast bulk of international and intercontinental communications, from simple phone calls and internet traffic, to the backbone data transfers of the giant multinationals like Google and Facebook, and to the highly-encrypted communiques between companies and governments alike.

Copper wire has largely been replaced with fiber-optic cables. Simplistically, these are strands of glass similar in diameter to a human hair, bundled together in an insulating sheath of copper, surrounded by a plastic or nylon coating reinforced with galvanized wire. In lab conditions, a single fiber-optic filament can carry more than ten terabits of data per *second*.

Shoreside, these cables are heavily reinforced, often not only jacketed for protection, but also buried deeply for security. But once offshore, due to the expense of fabricating and laying miles upon miles of cable, these lines merely rest on the seabed, ranging in thickness from the size of a garden hose to the diameter of a beer can.

Therefore, once offshore, security for the cables is guaranteed only by the depth of the ocean. And, despite myth, sharks and other marine predators typically don't bite at the cables because they are simply too deep in the water.

They are not too deep, however, for a pair of Russian-made, Konsul-class, autonomous, deep submergence vehicles, like the two being launched in alternating sequence from the stern davits of the Russian Naval Research Vessel *Yantar*.

After leaving the shores of Russia behind, *Yantar* had, at first, retraced her inbound course to the north of Scandinavia, then motored south-west, turning to aim between Greenland and Iceland. But once off the tip of southern Greenland, the ship headed south. The journey was well over 3,500 nautical miles. It had taken over two weeks for the ship to travel from Murmansk to a location one hundred and twenty-nine miles south-east of the island of Nantucket, the nearest landmass.

The ship had been loitering in this location for the past sixteen hours, and it was projected that it would be in position for at least one more full day, if not two.

It was the riskiest part of the mission.

And the location had not been chosen at random.

For there, at the bottom of the ocean and separated by only a few thousand feet, three undersea fiber-optic cables cross each other: Facebook and Google's Havfrue/AEC-2, Century Link's Atlantic Crossing-1 (AC-1), and a third cable known as TAT-14.

It was the latter of the three that Unit 29155 was interested in.

The TAT-14 trans-Atlantic cable terminated in Manasquan, New Jersey, a beach-front community only forty miles south of New York City. The cable featured four pairs of fibers and could carry a designed capacity of 9.38 terabits per second. It was owned and operated by a consortium of telecommunications companies including British Telecom, Deutsche Telekom, Verizon, Sprint, and AT&T. The cable connected almost directly into critical communications networks.

It would take several days of nonstop work by the alternating autonomous subs dispatched from the surface by *Yantar*'s deck crew, with a parallel process in coding and monitoring by the men toiling in the information warfare suite, as they labored to tap the cable so that Unit 29155 could intercept the network traffic.

Yantar had been uniquely designed for this type of operation. Below the ship's waterline, two azipods could rotate as needed, giving the fixed-pitch propellers on each pod the ability to steer thrust in any direction. In addition, the ship was equipped with two thrusters at her bow. As a result, Captain Stepanovich could ensure that *Yantar* hovered in a fixed position above the TAT-14 cable, while Rodionov quietly exhorted his team of technicians to make the final connections to enable the tap.

Meanwhile, Petrikov watched anxiously. A few days more, and he would finally watch his plan unfold.

CHAPTER
56

MONDAY, OCTOBER 21, 2019 — SALEM, MASSACHUSETTS

IT HAD BEEN THE LAST DAY of September, in the interview room with Volkov and Macallister, when I had reached the conclusion that, in order to possibly crack this case, I would need to spark a fire of my own and to operate under a smokescreen of my own creation.

Easier thought than done.

On a Monday in October, the fall chill was in the air, and the leaves in Boston had begun to drop from the trees, three weeks after my epiphany. It had taken me a week of stonewalling by the bureaucrats in Washington before I took a new tack, and I came up with the lie that got me what I needed. Getting the background for my lie prepared and then approved consumed the better part of the next two weeks.

I kept asking myself, *Do the ends justify the means?*

I rationalized it. *If nothing came of this line of inquiry, there would be no issue. No harm, no foul, right?*

Macallister had almost caught me, and I felt guilty lying to him as I slipped on my suit jacket and dropped the key fob for my Dodge into my pocket. "Where are you headed?" he had asked, innocently.

Better tell the truth on this part. Besides, I already put the authorization for this trip into the case file, to cover myself. "I'm going to Salem," I had stated in a matter-of-fact tone. "I'm going to interview Appleton."

Macallister had done a double-take, "For what?"

"I have some questions for her on the sequencing in the Operation E.T. case. I have a list which got approved by Washington. To double-check Volkov's claims on the timing. I'd like to confirm that Appleton's recollection matches up exactly with hers."

Vague enough, I had hoped.

Macallister had bought it. Cross-checking the details over and over bored him. "Better you than me on that assignment," he had taunted as I headed for the bank of elevators.

My reasoning for questioning the disgraced SAC were wholly fabricated.

I had wanted to talk to Jennifer Appleton about Anastasia Volkov.

I had never visited the former Special Agent in Charge's home before. Had no reason to. Had no desire to. I was surprised.

Jennifer Appleton had glided through the halls of our Chelsea building like a witch. While she was fair, she was also quick to curse any mistakes, procrastination, or posturing. No matter your seniority in the ranks, you did not dare to cross Appleton.

Therefore, I had expected a dark, forbidding castle with thunder-clouds above. And with a moat surrounding it, teeming with sharks or, as Number Two may have proposed, with mutant sea bass. I have a pretty active imagination.

I did not expect a bright-white, antique, two-story colonial, simple in design, perfectly restored, and impeccably maintained.

Appleton had, of course, been expecting me, and she greeted me at her door kindly and politely. She was dressed in a subtly-patterned, mostly light gray, some light blue, sweater above black capri-type pants. Her feet were bare.

I think she chose the capris to ensure that I noticed the much uglier bracelet on her left ankle: the ungainly black band of the GPS- and radio-enabled tracking anklet assembly that ensured that she did not leave the confines of her house arrest.

Exhibiting her standard powers of observation, and despite what I thought was a quick-as-a-flash glance at the anklet, she caught my look, commenting dryly, "Really not my color. I've gotten used to it, but as you remember, I'm sure, I don't think I am supposed to be sporting it."

I looked her in the eye, "That's what I'd like to talk about."

"Not about the case? You had some questions about the details. Standard operating procedure to check twice. That's what they told me."

"No, ma'am. That's what I told them, otherwise I doubt I would have been allowed to speak with you. I sent them a list of my questions and told them those would be the only questions I would ask."

"I'll answer those questions, nothing more," she stated firmly. "Agent Porter, while I may be under suspicion, I will not risk my innocence by cooperating with you in a line of questioning that is not authorized."

"Of course," I replied. "I'd expect nothing less. May we review the questions?"

Appleton's face clouded. "Was that some sort of attempt to trick me?"

"No, ma'am. I do have questions about the case, which I will ask. But I have nothing to gain by being less than transparent. Perhaps, after we finish with my list, you'll allow me some latitude to, well, ramble?"

"You can ramble all you want, Agent Porter. Unfortunately, I have little else to do. Your list?"

We arranged ourselves on tastefully-upholstered opposing chairs in her living room, and I balanced my laptop on my knees. Diligently, I began in on the list that I had carefully prepared, and that had been blessed by the bureaucrats. One item after another, and I was unsurprised that Appleton's memory of the timeline during the Operation E.T. case coordinated with Volkov's statements as she had disclosed what had gone on in the background. I watched Appleton's face for reactions as I posited questions for which she could not have an answer for unless she was in cahoots with Volkov.

The interview went as expected: Appleton correctly answered the questions that she should have been able to, and demurred when I asked something that only Volkov would have known.

Of course, Appleton was smart enough not to incriminate herself by answering a question about a detail that only Volkov knew if, indeed, the disgraced SAC really was a coconspirator with Volkov.

Which, I had come to conclude, she was not.

And that's why I was in Salem.

I had reached the end of my preapproved question list when I said, "That's it. That's the last of the questions I can ask."

"I hope my responses were helpful. Shall I show you out?" Appleton replied.

I made no move to get up. Instead, I closed my laptop and zipped it into my backpack. Leaning forward in the upscale chair, I planted my elbows on my knees and spoke softly, "Volkov has maintained that she planted the file that incriminated you. On the day that she initiated the operation to spring Petrikov from the Vermont facility. You'll be interested to learn Petrikov is her father."

Appleton's eyebrows raised slightly. *That* nugget had to be a shock to her. But she did not speak or otherwise react, clearly realizing that I had wandered outside the scope of my approved inquiry.

I continued, "Subsequent DNA testing confirmed Petrikov's paternity. Which, of course, possibly establishes a motive for Volkov. At the same time, the subsequent audits and reaudits of the incriminating file, the one that shows you signing off on Volkov's employment and overriding the background check, also shows the correct sequence and the correct approvals."

I leaned back, crossing my arms across my chest. "Yet Volkov would have the technical expertise to be able to pull that off. If you believe her current story, in which she claims she hacked the FBI system to employ herself, she would have been able to do it again to pin you. And if you believe the other part of her current story, that she has accomplished a technical feat that everyone says is impossible, it actually gives her claim that she planted your incriminating file even more credibility."

Appleton listened wordlessly, unwilling to engage verbally in the conversation, but her eyes remained focused on me. I took that as a sign to continue with my monologue.

"Here's my theory," I said. "Volkov planted that file for two reasons. One, to remove you from the hunt. And two, as a decoy. To confuse us. Same as she distracted us by targeting my sister that night. Same as she subtly sidetracked us during the Operation E.T. case. Same as she used my sister again as a distraction when she turned herself in, so that we would not come in with safeties off. Volkov is skilled at planning these kinds of diversions, so the question is, did she allow herself to be taken into custody as yet another diversion while Petrikov works out his next play?"

Appleton did not respond to my sort-of rhetorical question. I didn't expect her to. And it was time to lay it on the line, "I think that's a stretch. Petrikov makes his move, and she must rely on him to spring her from our custody? *She* is the person with that capability, not him. *She* can't do it from the inside. So, let's say she is being truthful. She framed you, she, at first, helped her father, but now has a change of heart, and she wants to unwind all of it. That's a possibility that none of us are looking at. And we should."

"You should."

My head jerked up as Appleton finally spoke. I stared at her.

The former SAC whispered, "Agent Porter, you got your start by going with your gut. It's telling you something now." She paused and then continued in a normal volume. "I cannot encourage you to follow this theory without appearing to be doing so for my own self-interest. I can encourage you, however, to pursue your idea for the nation's interest. For if what you are saying is correct, Mister Petrikov is up to something, and Miss Volkov might be able to help us. That is our charter: to explore the evidence, no matter what preconceptions we might have."

I smiled at her carefully-worded speech, dictated as if I might be wearing a wire. As usual, Appleton got her message across without compromising her morals. "Problem is," I said, standing, "much of the evidence points the other way."

"Perhaps," Appleton said. "Or perhaps it doesn't, but you are just unwilling to concede that you might be blinded by your bias."

As I drove back to Chelsea, I knew what I must do. And it, too, posed a great deal of risk. I'm a sworn Special Agent of the Federal Bureau of Investigation. Not some gunslinger operating outside the law, fearless of the consequences.

I had taken an oath.

I, Ben Porter, do solemnly swear that I will support and defend the Constitution of the United States against all enemies, foreign and domestic;

that I will bear true faith and allegiance to the same; that I take this obligation freely, without any mental reservation or purpose of evasion; and that I will well and faithfully discharge the duties of the office on which I am about to enter. So help me God.

Defend against all enemies. Petrikov was the enemy. Not Volkov. She was trying to help us. To help me.

It was time to lose the bias. But to do that, I would have to disavow my oath.

chapter 57

THE NEXT MORNING:
TUESDAY, OCTOBER 22, 2019 —
FBI BOSTON FIELD OFFICE, CHELSEA, MASSACHUSETTS

ON MY WAY INTO THE OFFICE the next morning, I knew what I had to do. But I also knew that the reaction that I expected would be less than enthusiastic. I promised myself, *Whatever they say, remember: Appleton said, go with your gut. So, go for it!*

I got myself fired up. *I can do this!*

With a confidence that was, at best, a veneer, I strode into the squad's usual conference room at 8:30 AM. I grabbed a marker, and on the whiteboard, I scrawled, in penmanship no match for Connelly's: *New theory: Volkov's entire string of claims is factual, and we face an imminent attack of some kind by the Russians.*

To punctuate my point, I announced, "We have to consider the possibility that Volkov could help us."

To say my pronouncement and my writing was not well-received would be an understatement. I shrank into a seat as the squad berated me with examples of the mountains of evidence against Volkov: a murder, an attempted murder, aiding and abetting a known criminal, and treason.

"Fer chrissakes, Porter, that's ridiculous!" Acting Special Agent in Charge Bradford Macallister exclaimed.

And, in every way, the squad was correct. Yet, I kept thinking about Appleton's words: *Concede that you might be blinded by your bias.*

"What happened yesterday with Appleton?" Macallister demanded.

I stammered, "Nothing new. She answered the questions as expected."

"Did she claim that she's innocent? That she was framed?"

"Yessir, but not directly. Only when I was at the door, when I arrived. Something about wearing the ankle bracelet unfairly, or something," I muttered.

"But she offered no proof? No new evidence?"

"No, sir."

Macallister stood and shrugged. "Look at the facts, Porter. Just look at the facts. I got another meeting to go to."

His exit started a parade. The morning conference disbanded and one-by-one, without the usual chattery gossip, my squad left me behind to stew.

That didn't go well, I complained to myself. *You're on your own, Ben.* But, maybe not . . .

One seat remained occupied. Louis Lewis, our Intelligence Analyst, remained behind.

After the glass door whooshed closed, he turned to me, "Porter, I've been wondering the same thing. Got all this evidence. But we've also got her claims that she's hacked us and hacked Tesla. Someone that smart would not be backing themselves into this corner."

I apprised the Intelligence Analyst. Tried to judge his sincerity. I led with a statement that both contradicted him and backed him up. "But you've said that our records are in order. That she couldn't get into our system. And Tesla said the same thing. Isn't that part of the evidence against her?"

"Yeah. But if she's truthful, then I'm just wrong. I suppose it could be possible. I just don't see how," he responded in a dejected tone.

"Is there any way to prove you wrong?" I queried, keeping any shred of hopefulness out of my flat tone. *Careful, Ben. Don't push it too fast.*

Lewis thought for a moment, head down. He pulled off his purple-framed glasses and polished them with his T-shirt, maybe buying time to think, or maybe as just a nervous tic. Finally, slipping the glasses on, low on the bridge of his nose, he raised his gaze to me. "We'd have to do exactly what she's been asking, but which the director has specifically forbidden. We'd have to let her show us how she got into our system *and* Tesla's system. How she altered the audit file sequence. I mean, if she could show us, then by extrapolation, she's showing us that we're wrong and she's right."

"I know. But it's risky It's a contravention of an order from not only the SAC, but also from the very top. From the director." I shook my head sideways, and tested, "Is there another way?"

"How 'bout taking it one step at a time? Just the first part. Let her show us how she got into our system. Establish one fact, first. Then literally yank the keyboard out of her hands before she could do anything scary, in case it's all a set-up."

"Would you be able to know exactly when she was in?"

"Oh, sure, absolutely. We could have, like, a safe word! I could yell, I dunno, *pastrami*, and you'd pull the computer away from her." Lewis was getting into the idea, getting excited.

This was progress. I had an ally. For a single test of my theory. I replied, "Okay. Figure out the logistics, and let's set it up for this afternoon." Lewis nodded, and I strode from the conference room.

Just after lunchtime, Macallister dragged me into an afternoon-long conference, and Lewis and I were forced to hold off a day. And that single day made all the difference. We'd be too late. A day late.

chapter 58

THE NEXT DAY, EARLY AFTERNOON:
WEDNESDAY, OCTOBER 23, 2019 —
ABOARD THE RUSSIAN NAVAL RESEARCH VESSEL YANTAR

INSIDE THE DARKENED INFORMATION warfare suite on *Yantar,* an early-afternoon October Wednesday at sea was invisible to the two tidy rows of techni- cians who toiled in front of their screens. Days had passed with the ship in its unique hover mode.

The night before, just before midnight, Rodionov had triumphantly announced, "It is done!"

The technicians of Unit 29155, and the crew of *Yantar* operating their two autonomous, deep-diving submersibles, had successfully tapped into the TAT-14 undersea telecommunications cable.

The operation had been conducted with the utmost precision. Nine thousand five hundred feet below the waves, the remote-operated arms of the submersibles installed a watertight, protective caisson around the TAT-14 cable. Within, using specialized tools that were built into the caisson and operated from the warfare suite of *Yantar,* technicians had stripped the protective jacket of the cable, millimeter by millimeter, in order to expose the fiber strands. Each strand was equipped with an optical splitter, a device that allowed more than 95 percent of the light flashing through the filament to pass through unobstructed. By the time the consortium that maintained the cable noticed the signal loss, *Yantar* would be long gone, the optical splitter removed, and the cable back to a 100 percent signal pass-through rate.

"I cannot believe this is possible," Petrikov had exclaimed, when he had been told of the tapping operation.

Rodionov had laughed, dismissing Petrikov's disbelief with an arrogant wave. "It is not only possible, but it is also acknowledged. Ten years before we commissioned *Yantar*, the United States could do this with a submarine called the *Jimmy Carter*. The US Navy denied it, of course, but a story reported by the *Associated Press* made the *New York Times*."

Eyes widening, Petrikov had asked, "But that means no communication through these cables is secure!"

"Not exactly. We don't have the ability to decode all of it on this ship. That would take computing power beyond what could realistically be installed on a vessel this size," Rodionov had clarified. Observing Petrikov's confused expression, Rodionov added, "However, we do not need to intercept data. We need to only send data into the networks onshore, and to receive only the packets specifically sent back to us."

Petrikov had nodded his understanding; the men of Unit 29155 had specific targets in mind, and, therefore, used the tap to send their discrete messages, and to then receive only what they needed.

Yet, given the hour of the successful tap, it did not seem expeditious to start their experiment, so they had waited for a more opportune time.

And that time appeared to be now, an early-afternoon October Wednesday.

✳ ✳ ✳

I-278 EASTBOUND, FORT WADSWORTH, NEW JERSEY

Chuck Towers was not a well-liked man. The sixty-year-old, gray-skinned criminal defense attorney with unfashionably long, gray hair, often fastened into a messy ponytail, was known for having unpopular clients, the kind of clients who are convicted in the courts of public opinion long before their jury trials for misdeeds like spousal murder, sex offenses, or white-collar crimes like bribery or extortion.

But Chuck Towers didn't care about public opinion. He concerned himself with only two things: that his miscreant clients could afford his attorney's fees, and that he could find enough mud to sling about in order to confuse juries about his client's guilt (and most of them, if not all, were guilty).

Neither money nor mud were in short supply in Chuck Towers's world.

After concluding a meeting with a client who owned a trash collection business on Staten Island and who had been accused of collusion with local politicians, a trivial case but one that paid well, Towers was running late for a golf game on Long Island as he piloted his dark blue Tesla Model S P100D onto the Verrazzano-Narrows Bridge.

The tourists who wanted a view of the Statue of Liberty and New York Harbor took the upper level. He was in a hurry; he would use the less pleasant lower level, his view through the Tesla's sloping windshield a narrow constraint of paved roadway below and the crisscross of steel lattice supporting the upper level above, as the concrete median slid by to his left and the staccato pattern of the vertical steel supports flashed by to his right.

The steel-and-concrete suspension bridge had originally been opened in 1964, with a single deck spanning the waters between Staten Island and Brooklyn. The engineers who designed the bridge had included a series of trusses that could accommodate a second roadway deck, which was added in 1969, and at present, thirteen lanes of I-278 passed over the 4,260-foot central span—over three-quarters of a mile—between the bridge's 650-foot tall towers near each end.

Less than ten seconds after transitioning from terrestrial roadway to concrete bridge deck, flashing over a gridded expansion joint flush to the road's surface, Chuck Towers sensed something was wrong.

✳ ✳ ✳

ABOARD THE RUSSIAN NAVAL RESEARCH VESSEL YANTAR

The updates were delivered in short sentences, always in a monotone, by the various members of the Unit 29155 team.

"We have established connectivity with nine targets within one mile of each other. Four westbound, five eastbound."

"External visuals?"

"Yes. Webcam. West side, looking southeast." From his perch in the rear of the information warfare suite, Petrikov studied the right-most big-screen monitor at the front wall of the space. It was a live webcam view of the eastern half of the Verrazzano-Narrows Bridge, including the Brooklyn-side tower, supplied by a helpful bed-and-breakfast inn located in Rosebank on Staten Island. Through the high-speed satellite uplink connection concealed in the teardrop-shaped dome atop her superstructure, *Yantar* could be online with the terrestrial internet; the subsurface cable tap would be reserved for the operation.

"Status?" Rodionov called.

"Less than a minute. Leading target visuals now."

While the center screen remained blank, the left big-screen lit with a camera view broadcast from the upper area of the windshield of a Tesla; the data icons on the bottom of the screen indicated that the source was a dark blue Model S P100D.

The technicians did not want to overwhelm their data feed with extraneous data, and they would be careful to control their targets in a systematic fashion. Rodionov stood at his seat, a conductor behind his orchestra. Petrikov had been joined by Captain Stepanovich, who had relinquished the con of his ship to a mate so that the captain could leave his bridge and watch the operation unfolding on the screens below deck in *Yantar.*

The technicians at the front of the room sat in two groups of four men, mimicking but doubling the setup in Plattsburgh, New York, three months ago. Unit 29155 now had the skills, the hardware, and the manpower to hijack several targets at once, and the ten men in the second row of the warfare suite were tasked to maintain these connections. Even with their fiber-optic connection to the shore-side cellular network, they were still limited by bandwidth. Had they been ashore, more targets would certainly be possible. For now, this would have to do.

The leading target was acquired by the Alpha team, the four men on the left-side of the front row. A secondary target was being tracked by the Bravo team. Seven subsidiary targets had been identified and the control programs installed; those subsidiary targets could be transferred to either the Alpha or Bravo teams by the technicians in the second row.

Rodionov glanced at a tablet in his hand and commanded, "Alpha—go!"

The Alpha "driver" squeezed his right-side rear Xbox trigger, and 286 miles away, Chuck Towers's sedan lurched faster.

The image on screen could have been from a video game as the Alpha driver swerved around slower vehicles, accelerating faster and faster as the target climbed the gentle incline toward the center of the Verrazzano-Narrows Bridge. "Focus!" Rodionov commanded. "It's soon!"

The driver's eyes never left the screen as he waited for what they knew would approach: a break in the concrete median that separated the eastbound and westbound lanes. There! In an instant, the driver found the opening, and with his right finger mashed on the accelerator trigger, he piloted his target precisely into the gap.

✳ ✳ ✳

I-278 EASTBOUND, CENTER SPAN, LOWER DECK, VERRAZZANO-NARROWS BRIDGE

The front bumper of Chuck Towers's Tesla bisected the far edge of the gap, slamming into the concrete median with such force that the left-side front tire assembly broke from the vehicle and hurtled into the windscreen of a bus approaching in the westbound lane.

The bus driver swerved to avoid the oncoming projectile and crashed into the guardrail in a screech of metal-on-metal-on-concrete, smoking to a stop and mangling the right side of the bus and partially disintegrating a large section of concrete guardrail.

The rail held.

The screaming of the panicked passengers subsided as they realized they would not hurtle into the abyss beyond the guardrail.

The screams resumed as the passengers realized that the car that had just crashed into the median in the opposite traffic lane had burst into flames. Flames that were dangerously close to their twisted and stricken bus. The passengers fled in terror.

No airbag was pillowy and yet sturdy enough to cushion the impact that Chuck Towers's pony-tailed head had made into the steering wheel and dashboard assembly of his car, and he was already dead when a forward section of the lithium-ion battery pack below his seat ignited.

The manufacturer, of course, understood the very real potential of "thermal runaway" that can occur with lithium-ion batteries and had designed physical firewalls into the below-floor battery system to isolate sections of cells. Those firewalls were intended to give a driver time to escape a crashed vehicle, but as such, could not prevent the thermal runaway process that started when the sedan had violently impacted the median. The battery self-heated, and as each cell ruptured and released its volatile contents, the adjacent cell would repeat the process. Within minutes, the firewalls would be useless against the chain reaction, and the blaze would begin in earnest as temperatures around the wrecked car would rise above 1,000°F.

✳ ✳ ✳

ABOARD THE RUSSIAN NAVAL RESEARCH VESSEL YANTAR

"Eastbound target two, Bravo team, go!" commanded Rodionov, in a calm, steady voice.

"Engaged!"

As the leading target had been piloted to its encounter with the center median, the center screen had illuminated with the camera feed from a silver Tesla Model 3 that had been only a few hundred feet behind the Model S.

On-screen, the flares of brake lights illuminated the interior of the Verrazzano-Narrows Bridge lower deck in an eerie shade of red. Ahead, traffic had clustered to the right-hand lanes, passing the still-smoking but no longer blazing wreck on the center barrier. Past the wreck, a handful of vehicles had pulled to the left, the good Samaritans who would stop and lend a hand.

"Hold back! Leave room for acceleration!"

"Copy."

The image dipped as the Bravo driver tapped the left brake trigger. "Wait . . . Wait . . . Now!"

Crushing the right-side accelerator trigger, the Bravo driver leaned in toward his screen, the technicians flanking him, ensuring that the vehicle's data streams flowed unobstructed. The camera image, duplicated above on the center screen, showed the gap between target and the smoking wreck of a blue sedan closing faster and faster until impact.

The center screen went dark.

On the right screen, the static webcam view of the bridge, Petrikov could see the first tendrils of smoke rising into the air near the lowest point of the suspension cables, toward the Brooklyn side. "Now what?" he asked, rubbing his hands together with giddy anticipation.

Rodionov, composed as ever, announced, "Targets three and four. Upper deck. Both westbound and within close proximity. Converge above as close as you can!"

With a flash, the left and center big-screens changed, this time showing the unobstructed view of sky and suspension cables above as two targets traveled onto the upper deck of the bridge, leaving Brooklyn behind.

Traffic on the upper deck still flowed freely, drivers unaware of the growing conflagration below them. The Alpha and Bravo drivers concentrated on their timing. They would not be able to use their vehicles to penetrate the concrete barrier between the westbound and eastbound sides; though the barrier was moved twice a day by a special machine to create an extra traffic lane as needed, it would be impenetrable by a vehicle.

On the upper deck, however, trucks were permitted, and the goal was to intercept a truck near the center of the span.

Bravo team got the glory this time, commandeering a black Model S traveling west just ahead of Alpha team's white Model X.

Bravo's Model S was pacing an eighteen-wheeled, tractor trailer, which was in the center westbound lane, the electric sedan matching the speed of the lumbering truck. Rodionov watched the data stream carefully, trying to time the intercept so that it occurred more or less above the accident on the lower deck below.

"Three . . . two . . . one . . . *NOW!*"

The Bravo driver aggressively pulled back on the right accelerator trigger, and the sedan surged to pass the semi. As the car came abreast of the truck's front bumper, the Bravo driver swerved the sedan into the path of the far larger tractor trailer. Predictably, the truck driver had no time to brake or to avoid the collision as the two vehicles mashed into a single mass, the Tesla skidding sideways at an angle before being overrun by the truck.

As the front end of the smaller sedan was being crushed by the truck's front tires, the trailer of the truck was swinging to its left, the driver's foot pressing on the brake pedal, all but useless against the momentum of the heavily-laden trailer. The truck jackknifed and the trailer detached from the tractor in a chaotic, slow-motion dance of leverage and force.

* * *

I-278 WESTBOUND, CENTER SPAN, UPPER DECK, VERRAZZANO-NARROWS BRIDGE

Nguyễn Bình hated heights, bridges, and traffic, in that order, but in the solid security of his white Tesla Model X, he felt as safe as he'd ever felt. Safety had been very much on his mind when the short-statured, always-smiling, dark-haired and brown-skinned pediatrician had bought the car six months ago. He wanted a vehicle that was big, substantial, technologically advanced, and safe enough for his soon-to-be-born first child.

The doctor glanced over at his wife, Thuy, who was contently cocooning her swollen belly, before returning his attention to the road and to the confines of the spidery steel cables of the suspension bridge.

As he crossed the threshold from land to water, he noticed a semi-truck passing to his left; he much preferred the more sedate speeds of the right-most lane. In the left lane, a black Tesla sped past the truck, then slowed.

As Nguyễn had carefully maintained his steady speed, up ahead, near the crest of the bridge where the thick suspension cables drooped to their lowest apex, the black Tesla made a sudden lane change, slicing in front of the truck. Nguyễn watched in horror as the truck collided with the black car. In a slew of motion, the trailer twisted to the left as the semi jackknifed.

Nguyễn slammed his foot on the brake pedal, confident that the marvelous, electric SUV's antilock brakes would stop him, and his precious cargo, well short of the skidding wreck ahead.

Nothing happened.

And then, panic.

The big white Model X jerked as its electric motors applied torque to all four wheels. The last thing the pediatrician heard was Thuy's petrified screams of abject terror as their car impacted the low-slung fuel tank of the tractor at a ludicrous rate of speed, far faster than Nguyễn had ever driven, and the front end of the Tesla, the windshield, and the passenger cabin collapsed under the crushing collision.

✳ ✳ ✳

ABOARD THE RUSSIAN NAVAL RESEARCH VESSEL YANTAR

Anatoly Petrikov rose to his feet and applauded, a standing ovation as all screens but one went dark.

That third screen, to the far right, repeating the real-time feed from the helpfully-positioned bed-and-breakfast webcam, displayed the now-massive inferno on the lower deck, flames spitting from the open trusses and supports, as the two vehicles and the evacuated bus on the lower roadway burned in an uncontrollable blaze. Above, an oily black plume of burning diesel fuel mixed with a growing second fire, as the thermal runaway fires in two lithium-ion battery packs combined, igniting the shell of a stopped truck atop the upper deck.

The visible traffic on the bridge had come to a standstill.

The Alpha and Bravo teams at the front of the space were also at a standstill, but behind them, the technicians of Unit 29155 were tapping at keyboards as they disconnected from their remaining five targets. The traffic jam would make it impossible for additional vehicles to be used to exacerbate the firestorm on the bridge.

As soon as he realized that the game was over, Petrikov demanded of Rodionov, "What is this? You have more targets. Use them!"

Rodionov demurred, "No. A handful of smaller accidents elsewhere are not necessary. We have proved the intent of the experiment. It will be several hours, possibly even tomorrow before we learn if the desired outcome was achieved. It is time to move on. With what we know now, we can plan for something far larger, far more coordinated."

The senior-most man of Unit 29155 smiled gently as he stood from his high-backed, black leather chair. "I'd say it was a most successful proof of concept. But it's not our decision what to do next."

Captain Stepanovich also stood, nodding at Rodionov. "Tell me the instant you've dropped the cables."

"Of course, Captain."

"I don't understand," Petrikov huffed. "We're done and moving?"

"Yes," Rodionov explained in his evenly-modulated voice. "We'll remove the tap itself with the submersible in order to remove any resistance within the cable, but we will leave the caisson in place. We will drop our cable links to the caisson into the water. We can use the submersibles to pick them up again, should we need them. It would take far too much time to disassemble the entire assembly, but no one will find it unless they pull up the cable. And that is unlikely to happen, ever."

Looking up at the webcam feed of the Verrazzano-Narrows bridge, Rodionov added, "Our satellite connection will be unaffected, so you'll be able to continue to enjoy the show. Coffee?"

Several hours later, *Yantar's* four 1,600 kilowatt diesel generators were producing the required power for the ship's two 3,400 horsepower electric motors, and the propellers on her two azipods below the hull began to spin at speed, pushing the ship south for the first time in days.

CHAPTER

59

SAME DAY, EARLY EVENING: WEDNESDAY, OCTOBER 23, 2019 — FBI BOSTON FIELD OFFICE, CHELSEA, MASSACHUSETTS

I HAD ARRIVED AT THE OFFICE that Wednesday morning in a foul mood. Macallister had kept me in a useless status conference for the entire afternoon yesterday. I suspected he was subtly browbeating me back into submission, back to the party line.

I had texted Lewis from the status conference,

```
We're on hold. Tomorrow.
```

His reply had been simply a thumbs-up emoji.

Macallister's distractions continued throughout this day, too. I was pissed off. I wanted to execute the plan. I didn't get the chance.

Before going home for the evening, I had felt I should check in with Lewis.

When I walked into the operations center, it was after 6:00 PM, and the majority of the staff had departed for the day. A handful of techs would be on duty through the night.

Lewis was reclining at his workstation, having eschewed his normal work-mode, backless, ergonomic stool for a more comfortable imitation Aeron chair. With his feet up on his desk, he gnawed on something long and skinny in his hand while watching a television news feed on one of his many screens.

I rolled over a chair to join him.

"Want some?" he asked, proffering the long and skinny thing toward me.

"Want some what?"

"Beef jerky. Delicious." He nabbed a plastic bag off his desk and waved it at me.

"No, thanks," I grinned. Patting my gut, "I'm still trying to get the weight off. Can't eat any of the good stuff."

Lewis scoffed, "Foolish. You're gonna die anyway, somehow, someday. You never know. I mean, look at that shit." He pointed at the television feed with the jerky stick, using it as a pointer.

The sound was muted, but the image was clear. A scroll across the bottom of the screen read, *Tragic multivehicle accidents close the Verrazzano-Narrows Bridge.* I knew where that was, it was one of the bridges I had researched in New York when we were tracking Volkov's escape almost a year ago. "What happened?"

With a mouth full of masticated jerky, he mumbled, "Not sure, really. They said there was an accident on the lower level and then a pile-up on the upper level shortly after."

Leaning forward, he tapped a button several times on one of the keyboards and slowly, the volume of a reporter's voice-over increased.

". . . and for the time being, the bridge is closed to all traffic except emergency vehicles, causing an unprecedented traffic jam and gridlock around the City as commuters seek alternate routes. Firefighters are battling two separate blazes, on both the upper and lower roadway decks, and sources tell us that, inside the confines of the lower deck, they are making very little progress. Fatalities have been reported, but officials have not disclosed details at this time, and it is unclear when the bridge will be reopened."

Tapping his keys again to mute the sound, Lewis swallowed his jerky and, licking his lips, said, "Crazy, huh? What are the odds that they got fires on both decks at the same time in almost the same place?"

I focused on the screen. Dusk was falling over New York, and the sky was a dark bluish-black. The still water below the bridge glinted a shiny, reflective black. I remembered seeing a photo of the bridge during my research, and the suspension cables were lit with bright strings of lights. In the television shot now, clearly taken from a news chopper, the lights were off. The bridge looked abandoned, save for a section in the middle of the center span where a fire blazed, flanked by the flashing lights of emergency vehicles on the upper roadway. Below, flames tickled, and smoke drifted from either side of the bridge's lower deck, and there the lights of the fire trucks and police cars were obscured by the trusses that the lower roadway hung from.

"What do you mean?" I asked Lewis. "Two fires? Same time?"

"Yeah. I've been watching this unfold for a while. Reporter said that the initial police reports came in one after the other. Happened earlier this afternoon. First there was a crash on the lower deck, and then a short time later, a crash on the upper deck. On the same bridge. What are the odds? Gonna cause a huge mess in New York."

Lewis waved the bag of jerky in front of me for a second time. "You sure?"

"Nah."

"Whatever. I'm done for the day. Going home. You open for our little test with Volkov tomorrow?" He pulled his legs off his desk and stood, stretching, still clutching the bag of jerky.

I hadn't moved, staring at the screen, a thought crystalizing in my brain.

Volkov.

"Yeah, umm . . ." I couldn't finish the sentence. Lewis stared at me.

Wait.

Volkov. Petrikov.

"No way," I said out loud. I realized that my mouth had drooped open, as I stared at the screen, and as Lewis stared at me.

I clamped my mouth closed as it hit Lewis too. He dropped the bag of jerky on the floor.

I verbalized the thought that had stirred in my head, "Volkov. Petrikov. Bridge. Lewis—this could be it!"

CHAPTER
60

LEWIS'S BAG OF BEEF JERKY lay abandoned, forgotten, on the floor of the operations center. The Information Analyst grabbed his backless, ergonomic stool, its casters bumping over the bag as Lewis positioned the stool in front of his workstation.

I barked, "You got access to Volkov's transcripts here somewhere?"

"Yeah, yeah, yeah, of course."

With a flurry of keystrokes, he found the appropriate files. I watched him click and type, wondering if my gut instinct was correct.

The data on the screen blurred to my eyes. There were folders for each day, and within those folders, files for each interview. There was no way I was going to read all of them. "Can you search all of them, at once, so we don't have to look at each one? It'll be faster that way."

"Yeah, sure. What's the search term?"

"Two words. *Traffic.*" He typed the seven letters. "And *jam.* J-A-M."

Lewis typed the three letters and froze. "Holy shit," he whispered. "You don't think . . ."

"Why? What do you think?"

"I was thinking a bomb or something. An attack on a bridge. But . . ."

"No. Just search it, please."

The inquiry took only a few nanoseconds. Lewis opened the first file that had come back as a hit, from an interview on September 10th, and we read it together, silently, on-screen:

MACALLISTER: So, what's he going to do with it? And you claim that you don't know. Of course, you don't.

THE SUSPECT: We once talked about a swarm. You could control a bunch of these things at once if you had the bandwidth. Which I didn't have. He talked about it once, suggesting bridges. Maybe causing gridlock or something, all over the country.

MACALLISTER: A traffic jam, huh? Another real winner of a terror attack.

PORTER: But, don't forget, she doesn't have the bandwidth. Hey, where do you get the bandwidth? Where does Petrikov get it?

THE SUSPECT: From the Russians. From Unit 29155.

"Holy shit," Lewis repeated.

My stomach sank.

This can't be . . . If only we had run out our plan to test Volkov yesterday. Could we have stopped this?

A reporter was on-screen, standing on the banks of New York Harbor with the bridge in the background of the shot over his right shoulder. "Turn it up," I commanded.

Lewis tapped at his keyboard once more, and the on-screen voice narrated as the image alternated between his face and the clearly pre-recorded helicopter footage.

". . . officials are tight-lipped about the accidents on the bridge. Sources at the Fire Department have told us that part of the problem is the type of blaze they are dealing with, apparently very difficult to extinguish due to the nature of an electric vehicle fire. 'Stubborn' was the word they used. We don't have any additional details at this time. However, a real concern, according to the FDNY, is the heat from two fires burning at once, and therefore the potential for structural damage to the bridge. Reporting from Brooklyn, this is—"

Lewis slapped the appropriate key, and the sound was muted once again as we both gaped at the screen.

"What did he mean, electric vehicle fire? What's the deal?" I asked Lewis, who was clearly taken more aback by the report than I was.

"That's new intel. I didn't hear that when I was watching the news before you showed up. Anyway. An electric car uses batteries. Lithium-ion. If they burn, it's bad news. They can cause something like a runaway fire. Very difficult to put out, since the cells can burst into flame and start the fire up again."

"You said earlier, 'what are the odds.' Well," I theorized, "what are the odds that the electric car burning on the bridge is a Tesla?"

Lewis shrugged. "Well, the odds are really good that it's a Tesla. It's not really a smoking gun."

I shot him a look, confused, and he hurried on, "Sorry. That was a bad turn of phrase, given the circumstances. What I mean is the majority of all-electric cars on the road these days *are* Teslas. Wouldn't be unusual."

"You think this is coincidental?"

"No. Not at all. But—"

I cut him off, blurting, "Let's see if we can find out."

I elbowed Lewis aside and picked up his desk phone handset as I flipped through the spiral-bound, plastic-laminated interoffice directory that was placed next to every phone. I dialed, punched the speakerphone button, and waited for the connection.

"New York FBI duty office. Peck speaking."

I recognized that name, but now was not the time for a trip down memory lane. "Agent Peck, my name is Agent Ben Porter. Boston Field Office."

Clearly, he didn't remember me. "What can I do for you, Agent Porter?"

"Consider this an unofficial inquiry. I'm following a hunch. You know any details about that accident on the Verrazzano Bridge?"

"Maybe. We got contacts in NYPD. They're reporting in sporadically, but it's not our investigation. What do you wanna know?"

"Is the electric vehicle that is causing problems for the Fire Department a Tesla?"

"Vehicle?" Agent Peck harrumphed. "More like vehicles. With an 's'. Multiples. Crazy thing, the cars involved are all Teslas. What are the odds?"

Lewis and I looked at the phone, wide-eyed and speechless.

"Hey Boston, you still there?"

"Yeah, yeah, yeah," I stammered. "Whaddya mean, 'they're all Teslas'? How many? I don't get it."

"Best as we can tell from the initial reports from NYPD and eyewitnesses before they were evacuated from the bridge is that the first crash was on the lower deck. Tesla. Hit the center median and caught on fire. Then in the opposite lane, a bus crashed into the outer guardrail. Then, from the same direction as the first Tesla, a second Tesla rear-ended the first crashed car. And then there were several fender-benders as traffic piled up.

"Upper deck, about three minutes later, a third Tesla cut off a semi-truck. The truck jackknifed and was hit by another Tesla. The fourth Tesla. NYPD gonna be all over the Autopilot thing, for sure. Crazy, huh?"

"Yeah, sure. Um, thanks, Agent Peck. We may have some interest in this, but like I said earlier, it's a hunch. Keep this off the call log for now, please, if you know what I mean."

"I can do that. Unofficial interoffice question. It's easier that way."

"I appreciate that, Agent Peck. Thanks."

The call over, Lewis and I sat for a moment, watching the silent images from the television news feed.

I broke the silence. "Traffic jam. Two different bridge levels, same time. Four Teslas. Knowing what we know, that *cannot* be coincidental."

"Agreed," Lewis said, succinctly.

I lapsed back into silence. *If* this was not coincidental, could it have been prevented? *If* I had talked to Volkov, yesterday, with Lewis. Could she have prevented it?

"Listen," I started. "If—and this is a very big *if*—this was orchestrated by Volkov's technology, they could do it again, right?"

"Out of the blue, yeah. Anywhere. Anytime." Lewis paused. "I'm not going home anytime soon, am I?"

"I don't think so. We gotta escalate this."

I reached for the desk phone again and dialed the extension for the SAC's office. Voicemail. Macallister had left for the day.

Pulling out my smartphone, and swiping for his contact card, I thought, *Macallister is not going to like this.*

The Acting SAC answered after three rings, "Macallister."

"Sir. This is Porter. Are you watching the news from New York?"

CHAPTER
61

SAME TIME: VERRAZZANO-NARROWS BRIDGE, CENTER SPAN

NEW YORK FIRE DEPARTMENT Battalion Chief Sean O'Connor, a tall, powerfully built, black-haired, Irish-skinned firefighter, raised the microphone of his radio pack to his Magnum, P.I. mustache, and ordered, "All teams. Fall back. Repeat, fall back. We are evacuating the scene. I repeat, we are evacuating the scene!"

"I'm sorry, but it's the right call," reassured the short, bald, pale man standing next to the monolith of a firefighter.

Their faces, even on this seasonably cold October night, were beaded in sweat, as they stood just clear of the superheated inferno blazing on the upper roadway deck of the Verrazzano-Narrows Bridge. The two men were lit by an eerie orange glow, the blues-and-reds of emergency strobes reflecting off O'Connor's gear and the bald man's glistening cranium.

O'Connor shook his head in dismay. Retreating from a fire was not in a firefighter's DNA. But, at the same time, he understood. Their first priority was saving lives, and here on the bridge, there were no more lives to be saved. A secondary priority was saving property, and the engineer from the Metropolitan Transportation Authority (MTA) Bridges and Tunnels agency had convinced the Battalion Chief that his men would be in peril very soon.

David Stein had been dispatched to the scene to observe, first-hand, the conflagration on the two decks of the bridge operated by his employer, and the senior-most engineer with the MTA did not like what he saw. In fact, this was one of his worst fears.

He had, of course, read the interagency reports and seen the media accounts of lithium-ion electric car battery fires. In one scary instance, a fire in a vehicle that had crashed into a concrete barrier in California spontaneously reignited several times, even after the vehicle had been removed from the accident scene. The difficulty of extinguishing these types of fires, though, was only one of his concerns.

The other concern was the heat.

Stein had recalled a 2004 tanker-truck accident where nine thousand gallons of heating oil caught fire and caused damage severe enough to close both directions of a heavily-traveled section of Interstate 95 in Connecticut. The heat from the fire was intense enough to crack concrete and to weaken steel.

At first glance, four car fires on the Verrazzano would not be as dangerous as a tanker-truck fire would have been. However, these were no ordinary car fires.

A single lithium-ion battery fire can reach temperatures of 1,100°F. And, normally, Stein had considered, while that was a high temperature, the bridge he was standing on could withstand a fire of that nature.

Concrete does not burn and is generally regarded as a fireproofing material; indeed, concrete is often sprayed onto the steel structure within a skyscraper for that very purpose. Steel melts at 2,500°F, a temperature far higher than even a lithium-ion fire.

The heat of a typical fire caused by a vehicle accident would, therefore, already be accommodated within the design parameters of the bridge.

However, four simultaneous, runaway lithium-ion fires had not been anticipated in the 1950s when the bridge had been designed, nor had the flammable nature of the tractor trailer's load of high-density polyethylene (HDPE) and fiberglass tubing.

Unlike concrete or steel, HDPE is highly flammable and will burn or melt at only 260°F. And, when the resins and plastics melt, they become a molten material that can flow and drip. A section of a concrete-and-steel highway bridge on Interstate 85 outside of Atlanta,

Georgia, collapsed to the ground after a fire fueled by HDPE was set below an overpass in 2017.

The fire on the upper deck would be unlikely to damage the steel suspension cables, but it would degrade the concrete deck of the upper level of the roadway, especially as the upper-deck fire was also being fed from below.

And, as David Stein calculated the effect of the doubly-intense inferno contained within the confines of the steel-and-concrete enclosed lower deck, he began to consider the very real possibility that the critical center section of the bridge's main span would become structurally compromised, especially since steel begins to lose its strength when persistently heated to 1,000°F. The heat in excess of that figure caused by the two sustained lithium-ion fires below, plus the two similar fires above, fed by molten HDPE which dripped into every crevice and crack from the upper deck down to the lower level, and the duration of it all, would put the span in danger of weakening substantially, even to the point of catastrophic failure and collapse.

On his watch, Stein would not take the risk of firefighters plunging 228 feet in the water below. He had given O'Connor the order to evacuate the men and the machines from the roadways.

The fire would burn until it exhausted itself and its fuel sources. And Stein knew that an uncontained fire would cause even more damage to his bridge.

But he had no other choice.

CHAPTER
62

ONE HOUR LATER: FBI BOSTON FIELD OFFICE, CHELSEA, MASSACHUSETTS

MACALLISTER HAD BEEN DINING with friends, and when I had called, the Acting SAC had stepped to the bar area in the restaurant to find a television. Apparently, from what I could discern from the muffled conversations that I had heard through his phone, there had been some disagreement when he insisted that the bar TV channel be changed from baseball to the news. Since the Red Sox had already been eliminated from World Series contention, and since the patrons of this Boston bar had little interest in the Nationals or the Astros, he had gotten his way.

As he watched, I had brought him up to speed with the theory that I had developed with Lewis. He wasn't buying it until I got to the headline: "Sir, I called the New York Field Office. They have intel that is not being reported on the news. Four Teslas were involved in the two crashes. Four cars end up wrecked on the same stretch of bridge at the same time?"

He had acquiesced that was an unusual coincidence, and he had reluctantly agreed to return to the office. I had known he would be in a very uncooperative mood, but I wasn't expecting a tyrant.

"Alright, whaddya got?" he demanded as he burst through the entry to the operations center, casually dressed in khakis and a polo shirt. He looked like a golfer, not a high-ranking agent of the FBI.

Step-by-step, I laid out my theory that Volkov had been telling us the truth, that her programming technology could have been exploited by Petrikov, and that our missing suspect could be behind the astonishing, had-to-be-infinitely-low-odds of four electric cars being involved in accidents on one stretch of bridge, within minutes of each other. Lewis had printed the transcript that we had read earlier, and I had highlighted three of the words she had used: *swarm*, *bridges*, and *gridlock*. As I passed the sheet to Macallister, Lewis brought up traffic maps of the New York City area from two different sources and displayed them on two different screens; the roadways around the city were traced in the angry bright-crimson shade that indicated slow-moving traffic, with several areas delineated in the deep dark-red of stalled or stopped flow.

Macallister skimmed the transcript and then examined the on-screen maps. "The Verrazzano, right? There's no traffic jam. It's green."

"Sir, it's closed to traffic. The algorithm doesn't know that, so it paints in green since there are no signals crossing it that would indicate otherwise," Lewis explained.

I thought that was self-evident, but I didn't contribute, noticing the reporter we had listened to earlier was delivering a new update; the word *LIVE* displayed in the bottom-left corner of the television feed. "Lewis, can you unmute?"

He tapped his keyboard, and we caught the close of the reporter's statement.

"*. . . and evacuated the bridge. As far as I know, it's unprecedented for the Fire Department to pull back from a blaze. FDNY simply does not do that. But that is exactly what seems to be happening here, as the fire trucks appear to be driving off the bridge in both directions.*"

The picture cut from the reporter's headshot to a view of the bridge, and as the camera zoomed to the center span, we could see blue-and-red lights moving slowly away from a towering column of smoke atop flickering, orange flames that pulsed from the bridge structure.

I looked at Macallister's face, it was placid. He barked toward Lewis, "Turn that off."

Then he turned to me with a sneer, "Porter. You're saying that Petrikov and his team of hackers from Russia hijacked these cars and crashed them into the bridge? And if that's what you're saying, what are you proposing?"

"I think we need to give Volkov another chance."

"No."

"Sir, think it through. Let's give Volkov the opportunity to prove, beyond a shadow of a doubt, that she is able to access our system from the outside. If she can, that adds credibility to the rest of her claims. One step at a time. That's all."

"No," Macallister repeated. "First off, the director said no access to computers for her. And second, has it occurred to you that's part of her plan? To get inside access to our computers? Another smokescreen from her devious mind with her deceptions and decoys?"

Standing my ground, I spat, "What plan? That doesn't make sense! She gives herself up into custody so she can wait for her father to trigger an attack so she can—*what*? Hack back into our system? If that's the case, she's already done that!"

"You're overcomplicating it, Porter. You're—"

I cut him off. "It's not overcomplicated. Let's say Volkov is telling the truth. Like I proposed a couple of days ago. She could have stopped this. You want this on your conscience? We owe it to our oath to research it. To test it. She could have—"

Macallister help up a single hand, palm outward, and snapped, "Enough! Porter, you're not only overcomplicating, you're overreaching. You are guessing."

"Yes, sir, that's correct. I'm guessing, and I'm going with my gut. Conceding my bias. Exactly what Appleton suggested I do!"

Oops. *I should not have said that*, I thought, immediately regretting my outburst.

Macallister didn't let it slide. "Appleton? You talked about this with her? That is a giant fucking breach of protocol. She's *with* Volkov! She's one of them!"

I bit my tongue. Literally. My tongue tasted the metallic tinge of blood, and I kept my mouth shut, as I wasn't quite sure what to say, and Macallister clearly took that brief pause in the cadence of the argument as either weakness or an admission. "Porter, you're on thin ice. I'm gonna give you a pass and pretend I didn't just hear that about Appleton, that you conversed outside the boundaries of the approved interview topics with her. And I'm gonna pretend that this theory of yours is constructed as a straw-man thing. That you are concerned with playing all the angles, despite the *overwhelming* evidence that Volkov is a murderer and a traitor."

"Yes, sir."

"Okay, then." Macallister seemed to calm down slightly. He took a deep breath and covered his ass, "If, and only *if*, it turns out that the car company can prove those things were not under the control of their drivers, I'll humor your theory. Got it?"

"Yes, sir."

"Thank you. Now I'm gonna go home." Macallister stalked from the room.

I looked at the silent television screen in dejection as the fire on the bridge continued to burn unabated. Those vehicles would be destroyed beyond recognition.

I slumped into one of the imitation Aeron chairs and considered my options. Lewis had sidestepped away from me and was focusing at his workstation, apparently unwilling to be dragged into the disagreement between the Acting SAC and me. I scanned the room. The usual nighttime techs, on duty, were unconcerned with a multivehicle accident in New York, far outside our territory. No agents, and none of my squad, were present, except for the reticent Agent Don Jordon, who always seemed to be hanging around, probably because he was unable or unwilling to converse with, well, anyone else.

Lewis spun in his chair to face me. "Porter, I just got an interoffice email. One of those general ones. NYPD has asked FBI to look into the bridge accident. It's a routine procedure. To confirm it is not a terrorist incident."

"Yeah. And?" I asked.

"That means that there's now an open file on it. That we didn't have to open. This could be helpful, you know. I think I should populate it with a note. To say that there may be another theory. 'Cuz if we're right, we're gonna get blasted for not taking action, and if we're wrong, we don't get penalty points for not exploring, how did Macallister put it? 'All the angles.'"

"Okay, thanks, good call on the note," I replied, relieved that Lewis was still with me.

Clearly overhearing our conversation, Jordon had ambled over and pulled up a chair next to me. And then he drawled, "Porter. Lewis. I think you're onto something. How can I help?"

OF ALL THE MEMBERS of my squad, Jordon was the one who I thought I knew the least. Zimmerman was brusque, Connelly was daring, Jones was calm and collected. But Jordon? He didn't say much. Other than assuming that he was maybe a little dim-witted, I had no real basis for forming an opinion about him.

And that's the problem with opinions, isn't it? We tend to make them based on first impressions or gut reactions. We don't take the time to do otherwise. We go with our biases. There's that word again.

And that's the problem with technology too. We just accept it. We don't take the time to question its security or if it can be used in a way we don't expect. We're not critical of it because we're blinded by convenience.

I had been blinded and biased by Jordon's languid Midwestern drawl, which, I would learn, had nothing, and everything, to do with his powers of analysis. He didn't think slowly. No, he thought carefully. He listened and only contributed when he thought through a problem or question, and only then when he figured he had something of value to add. He didn't speak just to hear his own voice or to give himself credibility by merely participating in a discussion.

And tonight, he had thought through a whole host of potential scenarios.

Lewis and I sat rapt as Don Jordon played out those angles, speaking slowly and almost rhythmically, "There's little doubt in my mind that we must give Volkov the opportunity to show us how she can access our system from the outside. This gives a layer of credence to the remaining open questions in her statements. It also gives us a layer to begin from.

"I posit that we consider that as fact, in order to explore this further. Let's also consider as fact that she successfully hijacked a Tesla. Finally, let's consider as fact that she has turned against her father."

Jordon paused and examined his two-man audience. "Where does that leave us?"

Lewis looked at me, deferentially. I knew where Jordon was going; it was the same conclusion that I had reached, and I was relieved that my theory was being explored by someone other than just me. "It leaves us with a conclusion that the incident on the bridge was no fluke. That it was coordinated by whoever has Volkov's code. And if you consider as fact, to use your phrase, that it is a Russian group, then it is highly likely that there will be a subsequent incident. Which puts us in the uniquely responsible place to attempt to stop any subsequent incident."

"Exactly," Jordon replied.

"But why?" Lewis asked. "What's the motive? Why would the Russians want to gridlock New York and damage a bridge?"

"Good question," Jordon acknowledged. "That would be another question for Volkov."

"No," I said, "she's already told us. Same interview. September 10th. It's further down on the page." I flipped through the transcript that I had printed and highlighted for Macallister to read, and with my right index finger, I pointed at the lines:

> THE SUSPECT: *Putin has an adventurous spirit. He does not hesitate to try new ideas, and he is not constrained by the media and by the second-guessing like the politicians here in the United States. He has no need for that sort of false humility. He can do what he wants, and he was intrigued by the*

concept of hijacking a vehicle from afar. And I have no doubt that he remains profoundly involved.

MACALLISTER: And I have no doubt that you are full of shit. Smokescreen after smokescreen. These interviews are going in circles.

"She said, 'he can do what he wants.' And then later on, in a subsequent interview, I remember wondering why she was so concerned. About Putin," I recalled, speaking as my colleagues finished reading the short passage from the transcript. "Putin is a scary dude. Volkov is correct. He does not have to deal with a constant barrage of questions and second-guesses by a free press. He has no real political competition, so he's very secure in his position."

Heads nodded, and I concluded my brief poli-sci lesson, "But what is not secure is Russia. It is weak on defense, and it is weak on economics. I read an article from the *New York Times,* dated over a year ago." I flipped open my laptop to find the file where I kept my notes on the case and on my research. I had even appended a comment to Volkov's case file with my citation. I read aloud, "September 20, 2018. The title was 'Subvert an Election,' by Scott Shane and Mark Mazzetti. Here's what they wrote: 'If Russia had only a fraction of the United States' military might and nothing like its economic power, it had honed its abilities in hacking and influence operations through attacks in Eastern Europe. And it could turn these weapons on America to even the score.'"

"Hacking, huh," Jordon commented. "Precisely what we see here."

"Yes," I agreed. "The authors of that article saw it too. They also quoted a great-granddaughter of the Soviet premier Nikita Khrushchev, now a professor of international affairs who is named Nina Khrushcheva. She was referring to allegations of Russia meddling in the 2016 United States elections, but still, what she said, as quoted by the *Times,* seems to apply: 'Putin fulfilled the dream of every Soviet leader—to stick it to the United States. I think this will be studied by the K.G.B.'s successors for a very long time.'"

"That's nuts!" Lewis exclaimed.

"Not really," I countered. "It's a different perspective toward life, that's all. Yet it all adds up. *If* Volkov did everything she said, and *if* Putin is behind this attack on the Verrazzano Bridge, then we can assume that this type of attack could be repeated."

"When? Where?" Jordon asked, somewhat rhetorically, adding, "Impossible to know, I realize."

"Then how can we stop it?" Lewis grumbled.

"By doing what we should have done yesterday," I stated flatly, with the resignation of knowing that, perhaps, we could have stopped the Verrazzano incident. "We've got to talk to Volkov. We're gonna put an end to this and do what it takes."

CHAPTER
64

"BEFORE WE BEGIN," I started, our heads bent close together, "I want to confirm that you both understand what I am proposing. We intend to contravene an order by the Acting SAC. And even if the ends justify the means, we could still find ourselves in a deep pile of shit."

"No," Jordon corrected, "without doubt, we *will* find ourselves in that mound of manure. But we need to take this step. I'm in."

"Me too," confirmed Lewis. "We gotta do this."

"Okay. If it goes bad, I will take the fall," I stated, with false confidence.

A moment passed, perhaps a symbolic one, as we realized what we had committed ourselves to.

I shrugged off my feelings of anxiety and asked, "So, how do we get to Volkov?"

"Easy," Lewis grinned. "I've been thinking about logistics since Porter mentioned this concept a few days ago. The holding cell is in the basement. You two go talk to her. I'll cover the cameras and the perimeter security." The techie rifled through several items that were on his desk and pulled from his neon green backpack a MacBook Air, a Samsung phone, and charging cords for each.

"Here's the plan. Give her this MacBook. It's mine. Not Bureau issued and not registered at all to our networks. I use it to go online only, and there's no password or anything of value on it. It will link up with the hotspot on the Samsung phone. Tell her to work her magic. I'll watch the firewalls and the access nodes from here."

"How will we know what she's doing?" I asked.

"Call my desk extension from your cell phone. Put it on speaker so both you and Jordon can hear it. And Volkov too."

"Got it." I stood and collected our goods, also checking that my Glock was nestled in its holster. I glanced at Jordon, who was doing the same.

We headed for the elevator bank, but before reaching the exit to the operations center, Lewis called, "Remember! If she gets in and starts doing something bad, I'm gonna yell the safe word, and you yank that machine away from her!"

Jordon blanched. "The safe word?"

"Yeah. Prosciutto," I said.

"No!" Lewis yelled. "Pastrami. *Pastrami!*"

Right. This was off to a meaty start.

That moment of punny mirth passed as soon as the elevator doors slid open on the lowest level. We could turn back. We did not.

Volkov's ward was not guarded by personnel, only by cameras, and Lewis had assured us that he had those covered. I didn't know exactly what that meant, but no alarms seemed to be raised as we approached the door to Volkov's quarters.

I knocked.

I'm still not sure why, as Jordon turned a key and swung the door open. Volkov was sitting in a chair, reading a novel or some type of paperback book. She barely acknowledged Jordon, but she did an obvious double-take when she spotted me.

"Now *this* is an unexpected surprise," Volkov said pleasantly, rising. She looked at the laptop that I carried in plain view, but then brought her gaze to Jordon's face. "I don't believe we've met, and I don't recognize you."

"This is Agent Don Jordon. Part of my squad," I announced. How does one make introductions in a cell?

Jordon kept his hands to his side. Protocol. He did not risk a handshake. Volkov knew the routine and did not appear to be offended as the two merely nodded at one another.

"Please, have a seat."

"Thank you, Ben. This is very unusual. What's going on? Do you want to sit? I can't offer much in here."

I scanned the room. A single chair, a single small table, a bed, and a partially enclosed bathroom area. Spartan but not unpleasant, I supposed, but I was not the one locked inside. "No, thanks anyway," I replied, standing next to Jordon.

"Listen," I continued after an awkward second, "I'm not sure how to say all this, so I'll be blunt. Your story is beginning to add up. We'd like to run a little, ah, test, and see if that can help establish, um, some credibility to other facets of your claims."

I purposely did not mention the incident in New York or the tiny detail that we had no authority to conduct such a test. I didn't expect Volkov to figure out the latter, but I was not the least surprised when she guessed with regard to the former, "Something's happened. Something parallel or similar to Vermont. And now you are starting to second-guess yourselves."

I didn't respond. Jordon, too, remained mute.

"I get it. You can't say anything. No problem. What's the test?"

Lifting the MacBook and taking the Samsung phone from Jordon's outstretched hand, I explained, "Vanilla laptop. It's set up to connect to the hotspot generated by the phone. Show us that you can get into our system."

Volkov nodded, "And how will you know when I am successful?"

I pulled out my phone and dialed Lewis's direct line. No sooner than I had tapped the speaker icon and placed the phone face-up on the small table, he answered. "Are you in place? Ready to go?"

"I see. Hello, Lewis," Volkov said, recognizing her former assistant's voice. "You're watching the firewall? The access points?"

"Yes."

"It's going to take some time, you know," she muttered as she flipped open the MacBook, its screen lighting up.

"We have all day," I replied.

"It's nighttime, Ben. Nice try. And don't think for a minute that I'm not wondering why you're here at this late hour."

I shot a look at Jordon, who blinked rapidly. *How would she know what time it was?* I wondered. One of the interview procedures, which trod close to an interrogation technique, was to keep the witness a bit disoriented by not allowing clocks and by conducting discussions at random times.

Volkov chuckled at my ill-disguised confusion. "I didn't know what time it was. The computer does, though." She pointed at the clock display on-screen and added, "But thanks for that interesting, if unhelpful, clue. Anyway, I have told you that I will be transparent, so I won't hide that discovery from you. Let's begin."

I watched, fascinated, as she began tapping at keys and at the trackpad, at first methodically, but then with increasing speed as she established a rhythm. After twenty minutes or so, Jordon signaled me to sit, and I plopped down on the hard floor, grateful to be off my feet for a moment. Fifteen minutes later, we traded positions. Then again, and again.

After roughly an hour of our forced game of musical chairs, concerned by not knowing what was happening, I asked, "Lewis, are you watching your firewall or whatever? What is she doing?"

"Yeah, of course," the information analyst replied over the Samsung speakerphone connection. "But really, I don't know how she gets around the firewall. Typically, a hacker needs to trick someone within the system to open malicious code, disguised in an email, or a Dropbox account, or similar. Then the hacker establishes a connection through the connection that the user within opened."

Barely slowing her keyboarding, Volkov laughed. "Hardly. And I know that the network blocks external IP addresses with a network abuse system. My method is more sophisticated. Many years ago, I coded a back door into the system. A trojan horse. But the network abuse system will block my IP address. I have to change that first. And for that, I have another back door into the C&C."

I looked at Jordon. He was equally confused and beat me to the obvious question, "The what?"

Lewis answered for Volkov, "Fascinating. That's very clever. The C&C is the command-and-control server. IP stands for internet protocol.

That's the address of the computer that she's using. You're going to spoof it, right?"

Volkov laughed again. "No. First I get into C&C and allow the firewall exception to whatever IP address I'm using. Then I use the trojan to allow me entrance." Volkov paused her work for an instant, admonishing Lewis, "You'll never see it."

"Oh," Lewis said, in a dull, defeated tone. That wasn't a good sign.

We lapsed into silence, listening only to the noise of the MacBook keyboard. Occasionally, either Jordon or I would say something to Lewis, just to ensure that the connection between us and him was still active.

Two hours, forty-two minutes, and forty-two seconds after we called Lewis, according to the on-screen display on my phone, Volkov announced, "I'm in. Lewis, check this port and this IP address." She looked down at her screen and rattled off a series of numbers.

I heard a long, low whistle, and Lewis whispered, "Holy shit. She's in. Totally undetectable. That's *genius*."

Volkov had pulled her hands away from the MacBook and had placed them demurely on her lap as she sat back in the chair.

I expected a verbal *I told you so*, or at the very least, a nonverbal look of smugness. Instead, Volkov maintained an attentive, professional attitude. With a poker face.

She was all business. And she appeared to be all-in when she considered me and asked, "What's next, Ben?"

CHAPTER
65

TALK ABOUT CONFLICTING emotions.

Volkov had not been lying. She had murdered Vanessa Raiden. And she had tried to murder *me*!

But she had also surrendered herself to us.

Don Jordon had been sitting on the floor when Volkov had said, "I'm in," and the agent had shot to his feet in an instant, his hand into his coat and onto his Glock.

My reactions were less impressive.

In fact, nonexistent.

I was not surprised that Volkov had managed to hack the system. And, given her demeanor during her month or so in our custody, when she had been pleasant and cooperative, I had expected her to respond to our test as she did. But, honestly, I had not gamed it out further.

Volkov patiently repeated, "What's next?"

On the spot, I blurted, "Hack into a Tesla."

She smiled. "Now that, you don't have time for. And with this?" She motioned with her chin toward the MacBook. "Not enough power or memory. I could recreate my steps, but it would take *days*. Weeks, really. I mean, I remember exactly what to do, but I don't think I can recall every detail immediately."

Her smile drooped to a thin frown. "Wait. That *is* why you're here. Because of another Tesla. My father has hijacked another, correct?"

I decided to come clean. After all, she was spot on, and we were here, in this basement cell, against orders, for one reason and one reason only: to prevent him from hijacking another.

"Possibly. That's our theory, at least. Obviously, we can't know if it was him or some sort of unlikely coincidence," I confirmed. "But there were four cars, actually. At roughly the same time. On a bridge."

"What did he do?" she asked, with what appeared to be genuine curiosity.

"We don't know the exact sequence yet. One hit a concrete median and then was rear-ended by a second. That was on the lower deck of the bridge. Then, shortly after, on the upper deck, going the opposite direction, a third cut off a truck, the truck jackknifed and was hit by a fourth."

She leaned toward me, her hands immobile on her lap, her expression resuming the emotionless poker face. "And?"

"The fires are still burning, and the bridge has been evacuated. You told us about a gridlock scenario. Looks like he pulled that off, and then some."

"Fire, huh?" Volkov's brow furrowed. "Of course! The batteries. Thermal runaway. That's gotta be the Russians. My father is not that clever or technical. And . . ."

She went silent and closed her eyes. I let her think. After three seconds, her eyelids popped up, and she exclaimed, "The timing! In order to do one right after the other, they've figured out how to control a few at once. Is this the first incident?"

"Yes. Though it's the first one we know of," I confessed.

"Probably. He wouldn't target a single vehicle again. He'd want to know if they could target several simultaneously. And if that's successful, he'll scale up."

"Could you stop him?" I asked, quietly and directly.

Her answer was equally direct, "Do you know where he is?"

I laughed, before saying sarcastically, "No. Do you?"

"Unfortunately, no. You've asked that before, and if I knew where he was going, I would have told you. But perhaps it doesn't matter. Now that we've gotten this far, and now that it would appear that you are finally accepting my truths . . . Maybe there's a way to stop him electronically, without finding him and going in, guns blazing. That sort of thing. And—"

Volkov paused yet again, working over the problem in her mind, then completing her thought, "And if we could stop him electronically when he triggers his next attack, we'd have a very good chance of determining his location."

"That's a very risky approach," cautioned Jordon. "We would basically have to wait for an attack. What if you couldn't stop it, once in progress?"

"I'm not sure that changes anything," I countered. "If we don't know where he is, we can't stop him from triggering an attack. We need to prepare our defense and wait for him to move."

"He loves chess," Volkov suggested, "and he loves the moves and counter-moves. I hope that you have not disclosed that I am still alive?"

It was a question, not a statement, and I confirmed, "Yes. You're here under an assumed identity. It's a very closely held secret."

"Good," she replied. "Then we have the advantage. He won't anticipate that move."

"How do we proceed? And if that's the outline, do you really think you can stop him?" asked Jordon.

"Yes," she whispered, before adding in a stronger voice, and directing her next question at me, "but are you ready to make a deal?"

That was a question well beyond my authority.

CHAPTER

66

8:00 AM, THURSDAY, OCTOBER 24, 2019 — FBI BOSTON FIELD OFFICE, CHELSEA, MASSACHUSETTS

LAST NIGHT, OR, RATHER, earlier this morning, Jordon and I had collected the laptop, phone, and cords from Volkov's room and locked her door behind us, with assurances that we would talk to the higher-ups about a deal.

Naturally, that was a bold-faced lie. The higher-ups had no clue that we'd even talked to her, much less let her demonstrate that there was credibility to her claims.

In short, we were fucked.

There was no possibility that we'd be able to carry on our exercise with Lewis covering the cameras and us evading detection in Volkov's holding cell. And, to carry that thought out one further step, there was no way we'd be able to remove Volkov from the cell and bring her elsewhere without someone noticing, like as soon as the next mealtime.

Yet we *had* to do something, as it was becoming increasingly obvious that Volkov was well-intended. I was sold, Lewis had been persuaded by watching her penetrate our firewalls, and Jordon was cautiously convinced.

Which is how Lewis, Jordon, and I found ourselves waiting in the Acting SAC's office the following morning at 8:00 AM, when a refreshed Bradford Macallister appeared to start a new day. Macallister had dressed in his usual Brooks Brothers navy-blue suit, with the jacket buttons straining against the push of his expanding belly. I averted my gaze.

"Gentlemen. Good morning," the Acting SAC intoned, without enthusiasm. "Are we picking up where we left off last night? Or are you onto a new theory? This is becoming tiresome."

The three of us had agreed that I would speak first, and, as rehearsed, I plowed in, "Sir. There is no new theory. We're still on the one we proposed last night. And before you cut me off, I'd like to bring two new pieces of evidence to your attention."

Macallister sat in his large swivel chair. He had replaced Appleton's severe, glass-and-chromed steel minimalist table with a burly, woody, mahogany-or-something traditional desk. "Fine. They better be two cold, hard facts. No theories. Got it?"

"Yes, sir. They are. First, as reported widely on the news this morning, and which I confirmed with a call to our New York office earlier today. The bridge has been closed for the time being. The fires are lingering, and there is concern that the structural integrity of the bridge was compromised. That is a fact."

"Yeah, I heard that. How is it related?"

"That, sir, would be a theory which we cannot prove . . . *yet*. We discussed it last night. That the odds of four electric vehicles crashing in close proximity in distance and time as very, very slim."

Macallister was nodding but smirking, and before he had the chance to blast another one of my theories, I pulled out my Glock and badge and laid them on his desk.

The smirk disappeared from his face, replaced by a quizzical look that I knew well.

Oh shit, here we go, I thought, as I forced my posture as straight as I could, pushing my shoulders back. I could feel sweat on the back of my neck and on my forehead.

"Sir. I am prepared to offer my resignation for insubordination. I did what we should have done a month ago. We should have allowed Volkov to establish her credibility. I allowed it last night."

Macallister rose from his seat, and with his hands planted on his desk and his body leaning forward, he spat, "Are you fucking kidding me?"

I held my ground. "Sir, I said there were two facts. The first was that the car accidents on the bridge, *if* they were not coincidental, which seems extremely unlikely, appear to have been purposely executed to damage or destroy the bridge. There is a second fact. Please hear me out."

He waited, face reddening and eyes narrowing. I'd seen that look before, but I was not deterred. "I tested Volkov's claim that she could access our system. As a way of establishing, indirectly, that her claims on the other feats of technology might be credible. Jordon and Lewis assisted me, but to be clear, this was my decision. Mine alone. And Volkov succeeded. She hacked into our system. That is a fact. She was successful and—"

The Acting SAC held up his right hand and growled, "Stop." He picked up his desk phone with his left hand and pressed several buttons. With the handset to his ear, he shot, "Zimmerman. My office. Now!"

"Sir, she succeeded. Which means—" I continued.

"Shut up, Porter," he rumbled, guttural sounds from the back of his throat. The scowl on his face was nasty and cold. He was as pissed off as I'd ever seen him.

And I was too. The fucking clown wouldn't even listen to me. Wouldn't even consider hearing out an explanation.

Zimmerman arrived, and Macallister instructed, "Take Porter to cell two. Quietly and quickly. Got it?"

"Yep," Zimmerman grinned. I didn't resist as he led me from the room. In a few moments, I'd be Volkov's neighbor. The Chelsea building was not a jail, it had been designed with only two holding cells for high-value suspects or transients. FBI Boston Division's prisoner facilities would be at maximum capacity shortly.

I didn't care. I wasn't going to let Petrikov get away with whatever he had planned without putting up a fight. I'd beat him once before. I wasn't ready to give up now.

The last words I heard spoken as my escort and I walked from the Acting SAC's office were Macallister's. "Lewis. Jordon. Which one of you is going to tell me what the fuck is going on here?"

CHAPTER
67

THE DOOR TO MY SOUNDPROOF CELL, identical to Volkov's, swung open about three hours later. Maybe more, maybe less. I didn't check my watch, which I had been allowed to keep, along with my tie, belt, and shoelaces. Zimmerman did request my phone, which I handed over without protest. He'd been smiling when he locked the door behind him.

Jackass.

I expected Zimmerman again, back to gloat, but got, to my astonishment, Macallister. He sat on the bed—a far cry from the stately pose he had struck behind his desk. I remained seated in the single chair, which, ironically, was way more comfortable than the rock-hard "soft" seating in the break-out spaces scattered about the hallways above.

"Porter," he began, "you have a bad habit of jumping to conclusions. We're gonna work on that, okay?"

That took me by surprise. I waited. He continued, "I spoke with Lewis and Jordon at length. Ballsy stunt you guys pulled last night. But I'll concede that it may have been the correct decision. Unfortunately, that leaves us in a very substantial bind. You follow?"

"No, not really, sir. Facts are facts. We tell Washington what she's capable of, they give us the leeway to conduct our investigation. Right?"

"You'd think, but no. Washington only sees the murder charge, the treason charge, and the mole. *Moles,* as in plural, if you count Appleton. Who, I will also concede, may be innocent, if what Volkov can do is as impressive as her work last night. Proving all that, however, is a different story. You think I'm stuck in my analysis? Try to change the mind of the pencil-pushers at the Hoover building."

"I think I understand, sir," I replied, hoping to move the conversation forward, but thinking that the agents who occupied the Edgar Hoover Building in Washington would have more sense than that. Unfortunately, I had no experience with them, and Macallister did. I'd have to follow his lead, and I asked, "So, what now?"

"Do you think another attack is imminent?"

"I have no idea," I answered. "Nor does Volkov. But I think we have to assume that there would be no reason that it would not be. That would be the safe assumption, at least."

"Correct." Macallister shook his head sideways, physically contradicting himself, before adding, "That gives us very few options. We cannot risk the time of investigating this like a normal case. Would you agree?"

"Yes, sir. Absolutely."

"Good. You're being placed on administrative leave. For insubordination." Macallister stood with a smile on his face.

What the fuck? Now I was really confused. I stood also, not knowing what else to do.

"I suggest that you go visit that friend of yours. You know, the one you saw a few days ago," Macallister said quietly. "Lewis tells me that the residence there is wired for high-speed internet access. Lots of bandwidth, or something, he said. On account of that resident's former occupation."

With a hand on the door handle, Macallister continued, "And Don Jordon might be bringing you a housemate. He's going to be tasked with moving a high-value prisoner to a new, undisclosed location. Got it?"

I made a nonsensical noise, attempting to convey something between dumbfounded and astonished, thinking, *Macallister is really proposing this?*

"Listen, Ben," the Acting SAC concluded, his hand immobile on the door handle. "I don't know how much time you'll have. From Petrikov's end, we can't know. From my end . . . a few days. That's all you've got, to find a solution that we can plug in place if Petrikov initiates an attack.

And if you can show me that solution, demonstrate it, we might be able to pull this off. Got it?"

"Yeah. Got it. But one question. Are you putting yourself on the line, with me?"

"I am. I was wrong, and I'm gonna fix it. You up for it?"

I smiled and replied with a single word, "Yes."

Macallister nodded, and just before he pushed down on the door handle, he whispered, "Good. 'Cuz you got two days. Three days, tops. Get it done."

He swung the door open. Zimmerman stood outside, key at the ready, Glock unholstered and in hand just in case there was any funny business. He sneered at me as he slammed the door shut.

I smiled and extended my right middle finger at the door, toward Zimmerman. *Jackass*, I thought, as I sat back down in the comfortable chair and began to work on a plan to get out of Boston without being tracked by my own squad at the FBI.

CHAPTER
68

I KEPT AN EYE ON my watch, and twelve minutes later, Zimmerman reopened the door. He had kept his Glock out and unholstered, like a cowboy.

Zimmerman escorted me directly to the parking lot. "You're outta here, Porter. No time for goodbyes," he blustered.

I laughed at him. Have I mentioned that I thought he was a jackass?

I usually left my Dodge in the lot at the Bureau, choosing an easy fifteen-minute stroll to or from my cozy, first-floor, one-bedroom apartment in a brick-faced, slate-roofed building in the center of Chelsea. That was no longer an option, and I found a parking space on a side street. I'd let the black Dodge signal that I was sulking at home.

I misled my neighbor into letting me use her Uber account. "Official business," I whispered. She knew, of course, that I worked for the FBI. She was eager to be in on the secret agent shit. Little did she know. . .

Former Special Agent in Charge Jennifer Appleton was not as tickled by the agent on administrative leave for insubordination who knocked on her door, but her mood changed greatly as I told her my story. "This could end very badly for you, Ben," she cautioned.

"I know, ma'am. But I am convinced, and if I am wrong, then I am screwed. And even if I'm right, I'm probably still screwed. But at least then I'll be satisfied that I tried."

"Well, it can't get any worse for me, and since I'm not harboring a fugitive, and since there's probably no statute that says you can't be here, you're welcome to stay. What's next?"

There's that question again.

I wondered if she would react as gracefully when I responded, "Um, it might get worse for you. Apparently, we have a friend en route. That fugitive that you don't think that you are harboring. She needs to use your internet connection. Anastasia Volkov."

Appleton rolled her eyes but remained unflappable as usual. "I see. Now that could get me in trouble. There's no other place?"

"This was Lewis's suggestion to Macallister."

"Lewis would know what is here. He arranged to wire it. Makes sense. And Macallister is going to run cover, I assume?"

"Yes, ma'am."

"How much time?"

I gulped and replied, "Macallister said two or three days, tops."

The doorbell rang, and we greeted our two visitors: Don Jordon and Anastasia Volkov. I half-expected to hear sirens and to see unmarked cars screeching to a stop in front of the handsome antique, but I heard only birds and saw only the falling leaves of an October day in New England.

Volkov spoke first, with her eyes straight ahead, looking into the eyes of the woman who she had framed. "I've made many mistakes, and I am sorry. I know that an apology will not be enough. I hope my actions will be enough. I need to undo the damage I've caused."

Appleton closed her front door and said quietly, "We'll see. I assume Macallister made you a deal?"

"No," Volkov responded. "He told me this was off the books. It's a risk that I have to take."

"Really?" Appleton said in surprise. "This is a black op, off the books? And you're still here?"

"Yes. You might understand. Or not."

"Try me," tested the former SAC.

Volkov folded her arms across her chest. "My father betrayed me, just like I betrayed you. And, like you, I didn't know about it until well after the fact." She paused to collect herself, then continued. "My father killed my mother. He'll stop at no end to achieve whatever he wants. He's a psychopath. He'd kill me if he had to, his only child. In fact, he tried to, indirectly. I will not continue to work for him or to work with him, even if he is my father. I'm done with that individual."

The room fell silent.

Finally, Appleton called the truce, stating in her normal tone of voice, unflustered as always, "Very well. We can talk about it later, some more. For now, that's good enough for me. And you've got a lot to do. You'd better get started."

TWO DAYS LATER:
SATURDAY, OCTOBER 26, 2019 — SALEM, MASSACHUSETTS

I FELT LIKE A criminal.

Fitting, right? *I am a criminal*, I thought.

I didn't look like a criminal. I had brought a bag of clothes with me in the Uber, and Appleton's home was a dignified hideout, with clean sheets and hot showers. The past forty-eight hours had been more akin to a stay-cation.

Except, of course, for the tension.

Oh, and the little, annoying fact that our little stay-cation was on borrowed time, before the barrels of the FBI would be trained on us fugitives.

I asked myself again, for the umpteenth time, *Will the ends justify the means?*

I wasn't having cold feet. I'd come this far, and I was more and more convinced that I had been correct to trust Volkov. She had been on a mission, resting or eating only occasionally, as she clicked and tapped and typed. Either she was playing the most complicated game of double-cross ever, or she was legit. It had to be the latter.

It had to be.

The problem was, without Lewis there, neither Appleton, Jordon, nor I really had any clue what Volkov was doing. It was a leap of faith for the three of us.

The waiting made it worse. Would she complete her coding in time? Would Petrikov launch another attack? And could she stop it?

Meanwhile, of course, I wondered what the other side was doing. No, wait, that would be *my* side. The FBI. *My* FBI.

Our only point of contact with Macallister was the Samsung phone that Lewis had slipped to Jordon before he escorted Volkov from the building to take her to a new "undisclosed" location.

Talk about a shitshow. When Macallister sent an encrypted memo to DC that our star suspect, Ann Karin, was a potential target and was being relocated off-site, Washington went ballistic, demanding intel and explanation. Macallister apparently handled it brilliantly, claiming that Washington did not have "need to know" status and citing as his basis Petrikov's escape from what had been considered a completely secure, invisible facility.

That bought us a day, probably.

Then, according to the brief messages that Lewis had been sending us via the Samsung, our squad had started asking questions. "Where's Jordon?" "What really happened to Porter?"

Zimmerman, naturally, was our biggest problem. He had a big mouth and a bad attitude, and he reveled in telling the tale of my brief incarceration. But, when Macallister refused to offer more details, and Jordon and Volkov did their disappearing act, Zimmerman felt left out, and he corralled Connelly and Jones to take his side. *They* started making inquiries to Washington, which stirred the pot again.

Macallister just stonewalled, but he also quietly told Lewis to send us a message: *You're running out of time, and DC will be turning up the heat.*

Unfortunately, that's when Volkov went cold. Literally. She passed out, probably from exhaustion and the nonstop computer work. She had to take a break.

And, once seated in one of Appleton's comfy club chairs, a mug of peppermint tea in her hands and her feet propped on an ottoman, Volkov confessed that she was unhappy with her progress, and lack thereof.

"This took me *months* the first time. The second time would, of course, be faster. But days? I can't do it. We need a new plan."

"Whaddya mean, a new plan?" I asked. "There is no new plan. We don't have any options."

"I understand, of course. But I think we're going about this incorrectly," Volkov responded in a confused tone. "What's the goal of what I'm doing?"

I shrugged, "To replicate your procedures from before, right?"

"But why? We need to think this through," she exhaled.

"I get it," Jordon drawled. "Why does she need to hack a car? How does that advance us forward? It won't stop any attack."

"Exactly!" Volkov exclaimed.

Appleton prodded, "How far have you gotten?"

As Appleton spoke, I had focused on Jordon's question. And it gave me my epiphany: *Why does she need to hack a car?*

"Wait!" I interrupted. "Jordon's right. You don't need hack it. You don't need to control it. You just need to know when someone else is controlling it. When someone else sends your code to it."

"Why? So, she can take control, instead?" Appleton asked.

I replied, "No! We don't want control. We just don't want *them* to have control. We need to *freeze* them, not *be* them."

Volkov shot from her seat. It was a miracle that her tea didn't spill on Appleton's pristine, probably pricey, carpet. "That's it. Genius, Ben!" She trotted back to her computers, clearly reenergized to the task at hand. She called over her shoulder, "And not only can we stop them, but we can also play our own little game with them!"

The three of us—Appleton, Jordon, and me—hurriedly followed her, and as she explained her plan, I felt, finally, elated. For the first time since this all started, we were going to be on the offensive.

No more playing defense, playing catch-up. We were going on the hunt. *We* would attack.

SAME TIME:
SATURDAY, OCTOBER 26, 2019 —
ABOARD THE RUSSIAN NAVAL RESEARCH VESSEL YANTAR

THE RUSSIAN NAVAL RESEARCH VESSEL *Yantar* had recommenced the unique hover mode, made possible by the ship's two azipod drives and two thrusters, four-hundred-and-fifty miles east of Jacksonville, Florida.

Three days ago, after dropping the communications lines to the TAT-14 cable caisson, *Yantar* had made revolutions at her relatively sedate cruising speed of 12.5 knots, rumbling in a south by southwest direction, passing well west from the island of Bermuda and remaining hundreds of miles off the United States eastern seaboard.

The research vessel's AIS transmitter had remained in the *off* position as the ship trundled south, but her sophisticated communications suite had remained active, with message after message alternating between sent and received from the both the Kremlin, and the Russian Navy headquarters in the gilded-spire-topped Admiralty building, located in the heart of Saint Petersburg, Russia, at the intersection of that city's three primary avenues.

The reaction from the Kremlin had been enthusiastic. The operation in New York had succeeded beyond expectations. Not only did it prove that Unit 29155 had the technological prowess to hijack several vehicles at once, but it also demonstrated that the cars could be used as weapons, punching well above their characteristics as passenger vehicles. The conflagration that the crashes had caused had wrought havoc beyond imagination on the bridge itself, its steel weakened and its integrity under question, forcing that the structure be closed to traffic for an undetermined length of time. Repairs would be complicated and costly, all while crippling for the transportation network around the largest city on the East Coast of the United States.

Based on the overwhelming triumph of the first experiment, the Kremlin initiated an immediate follow-up strike. For mission compartmentalization, during the three-day transit, Vitaly Rodionov had disclosed only the tap location to his compatriots on the ship. With the Unit 29155 team assembled in the information warfare suite aboard *Yantar*, he began a final premission briefing: "We will be operational in roughly twenty-four hours."

Anatoly Petrikov and Captain Stepanovich were seated in their usual tall-backed, black-leather chairs at the rear of the information warfare suite. The Captain asked, "The new cable tap is going as planned?"

Rodionov replied confidently, "Yes. Better than planned, in fact. We benefited greatly from the TAT-14 exercise. This tap will take far less time. Furthermore, this cable is only one mile deep. It is an easy target for our autonomous Konsul-class submarines."

"That may be the target of the deep-diving subs. But what is the target of the mission?" inquired Petrikov, in a pointed, direct tone, a grimace on his face.

Rodionov deflected the question, addressing Unit 29155 men gathered in front of him, "Moscow is uninterested in primarily causing loss of life or mass casualties. Instead, with this insidious, invisible weapon, they have selected a much more appropriate target. And, while a handful of people might perish, the impact to the might of the United States will be far, far greater."

Petrikov's fleshy grimace slowly transformed into a flaccid sneer. "That sounds promising."

"Indeed," replied Rodionov, smiling, as he enjoyed the moment of a dramatic, slow reveal. With a flourish of his hands, he proclaimed,

"We shall strike a blow that will be tragic for the United States, while being impossible to trace to Mother Russia."

Vitaly Rodionov's smile broadened as he proclaimed, "Our target is none other than the United States Navy."

71

THE NEXT MORNING:
9:40 AM — SUNDAY, OCTOBER 27, 2019 —
ABOARD THE HENNINGER-HEITZ ATLANTIC,
DEPARTING THE PORT OF NORFOLK, VIRGINIA

AT 9:40 AM ON A GRAY Sunday morning, high above the water on the bridge of his giant ship, Captain Manfred Boeckmann of the German shipping company Henninger-Heitz Logistics cut an imposing figure. Dressed impeccably, in sharp-creased black slacks and a crisp, white button-down shirt with a navy-blue tie Windsor-knotted at his neck, the tall, gray-haired, bespectacled German captain stood ramrod-straight. This was his domain. His presence commanded authority.

The captain hovered, as was his custom, one pace behind and to the left of the shorter, brown-haired, white-skinned Port of Norfolk Harbor Pilot Gordon Green, who had recently completed his six years of apprenticeship and who was carefully intent on his task at hand, while doing his best to ignore the imperious captain who peered over his shoulder.

Every commercial ship that transits the Hampton Roads—the approach of water to the Port of Norfolk, Virginia—must have a harbor pilot on board for both arrival and departure. The pilot's job is not to physically steer the ship; that task is done, as usual, by the ship's crew, and the captain remains in command. However, the pilot, with his or her intimate knowledge of the waters, currents, and effects of wind gusting

over headlands and swamplands alike, is responsible for guiding the
ship in or out of the harbor.

Captain Boeckmann had little confidence in the freshly-appointed
pilot. Green was clearly nervous as he directed the 787-foot-long,
104-foot-wide, uncreatively-named *Henninger-Heitz Atlantic* in a slight
north-of-east direction, south of the Newport News area where the ship
had been docked for the previous few days. The roll-on/roll-off cargo
vessel, referred to as a "ro-ro" in the maritime trade, could carry 5,495
automobiles; the ship had made several deliveries of German-built vehicles
to ports on the United States eastern seaboard and was just now beginning
her trans-Atlantic crossing back to Europe with just over a half-load of
mostly American-made vehicles, destined for European import.

A ro-ro is a blocky, ungainly vessel, whose primary purpose is to
jam as many items of rolling stock into her slab-sided hull as possible.
To accommodate the competing physics of her varied load capacity,
split through her eight decks based on an imprecise science of what is
loaded or unloaded, in what order, and when, a ro-ro is equipped with a
sophisticated water-ballast system, whereby seawater can be pumped into
large tanks deep within the ship's hull to provide a calculated measure
of stability to oppose the forces of wind and water on her towering, flat
sides. Even a slight turn at slow speed causes a ro-ro to tilt sideways,
and at sea, wave patterns and windspeeds are carefully monitored while
the ballast system is constantly adjusted to cope with the ever-changing
conditions that affect the vessel.

Pilot Green knew this, of course, and as a result, his rudder commands were almost hesitant, as he took great pains to guide the ship
slowly toward his reference point, the red bell #6 to the ship's left (or
port) side, which marked the beginning of a substantial thirty-degree
turn to the northeast direction, and which would leave the restricted
area around the United States Naval Station at Virginia Beach well to
the ship's right, starboard side.

Past the left turn around red bell #6, the *Henninger-Heitz Atlantic*
would make two more right turns before entering the straight-line,
twelve-mile stretch of the Thimble Shoals Channel, the deep-water
cut that cleared Hampton Roads and created the passageway for large

ships in and out of the Norfolk area at the southernmost extent of the Chesapeake Bay.

The Newport News channel that the *Henninger-Heitz Atlantic* was currently traversing was maintained to a depth of fifty feet, more than adequate for the ro-ro's draft of thirty-six feet. However, just outside the channel, the sandy shoals of the Hampton Roads were only twenty to twenty-five feet deep. Once the vessel made its final turn into the Thimble Shoal Channel, the dredged depth would remain at fifty feet, but an auxiliary channel to either side of the main channel offered a narrow buffer zone for smaller vessels, maintained to a thirty-two-foot depth. Straying outside the confines of a channel would instantly ground the ship—an outcome neither the pilot nor captain wanted on their respective records.

Within the confines of those channels, however, the large ships had the right-of-way over smaller pleasure and commercial boats, be they yachts out for a day sail or fishermen working the waters. Furthermore, large ship traffic was tightly controlled with cooperation by the Port of Norfolk as well as with the Naval Station in Virginia Beach; indeed, if an aircraft carrier was transiting the channels, the massive bulk of those vessels closed the channels to even commercial traffic such as Captain Boeckmann's ro-ro.

Video screens on the bridge of the *Henninger-Heitz Atlantic* displayed images from the bow and stern of the immense block of a ship, and radar and AIS were both used to establish electronic contact with nearby boats. Between scanning the displays, listening to the radios, and maintaining a visual watch, the channel transit was a stressful time for anyone.

Beads of sweat were forming on Pilot Green's brow, to the dismay of the taciturn Captain Boeckmann. In his clipped and precise, slightly accented English, the captain inquired, "Pilot. Any concerns? Any traffic? I saw the weather stations showing a brisk northerly wind in the bay. I trust you saw that recent update?"

"Yes, captain," the pilot confirmed. "Traffic is minimal. One contact well astern, behind us. Small pleasure fishing boat. Not commercial, based on the AIS signal. The contact has remained in our wake. It is of no concern."

Green took a moment to review the various displays before continuing, "The wind is not a concern here, either. I plan to use the wind to assist in the turn to the southeast into the Thimble Shoals Channel. We have no oncoming traffic, so we will have the channel to ourselves. And, this weather will deter the pleasure boats." Green's voice conveyed a confidence that he did not feel. Though he was in constant communication with the Harbor control and was certain that the channel would be clear, the weather was deteriorating, even as the first few drops of rain splattered on the ship's bridge windows as the leaden gray skies began to weep.

The beads of rain on the glass matched the beads of sweat on Green's forehead as the pilot began to calculate the amount of rudder to use to guide the massive ship around red bell #6, a critical turn. For, directly in front of the ship, dead ahead, lay the US Naval Station at Virginia Beach, bristling with warships at the docks.

This was a deadly place to miscalculate a turn.

72

9:45 AM — SALEM, MASSACHUSETTS

AT 9:45 AM, STILL TOILING IN Jennifer Appleton's home in Salem, Anastasia Volkov ran both her hands through her hair, rubbed at the bags under her eyes, sighed, and bent back again at her keyboard. The hours were obviously getting to her as she had worked through the night, coding a counterattack.

"I got you another coffee," I said quietly.

"I'm grateful. Thank you," she replied in a raspy whisper. She sniffed at the steaming rim of the simple, white porcelain mug before taking a sip. "Ahh . . . Good. Thanks again," she murmured. "Perfect."

I grinned, then asked the elephant-in-the-room question. "How's it coming along?"

"I'm not quite there, yet. Really close, but I need more time. I could explain, but that seems like it would waste that time."

"Agreed," I laughed. "And I probably wouldn't understand, anyway."

She smiled, looked at her screen, and took another pull from the coffee mug when Agent Don Jordon appeared, just as the Samsung phone rang.

The noise unnerved all three of us. Previous messages had been by text, notified by a pleasant ding. The blare of the "classic phone" ringtone was not only unexpected but also unprecedented. The screen displayed two words: *Unknown Caller.*

I stabbed the speakerphone icon and answered the call with a curt, "Yeah?"

Macallister's voice: "You're out of time."

"What do you mean?"

"Fucking Zimmerman," said Macallister. "He wouldn't let it go. He chewed on this all day Friday, and yesterday, he somehow got wind through Lewis's department that the network traffic from Appleton's connection that we set up had spiked. He put two and two together. He doesn't know you're there, but he told Washington, and Washington told me to go check it out. As a priority."

"Where are you?"

"We're just leaving the office. We've got three cars headed to Salem. Zimmerman called in Connelly and Jones—on a Sunday. He's got everyone fired up. You got thirty minutes. Thirty-five, tops."

"Maybe we hit the road," Jordon suggested. "Pack up the computers and bolt. We can figure out where to go once we're in the car."

"No. I'm close. I'll be ready," Volkov stated, ignoring my gift of coffee while not lifting her eyes from her screen and without pausing her flying fingers.

"Good," Macallister replied. "Because Washington sent one of their code experts up last night. To check out why Appleton is suddenly using so much bandwidth, they said. He's the top guy in the Cyber Action Team, part of the Cyber Division. Name's Cheng Chen."

Volkov paused her work long enough to look up, briefly. "I know Cheng. He's very, very smart. When the Bureau started the Cyber Division in 2006, he was one of the first people hired. He'll understand the code. He'll know how to use it if my father starts another attack. Question is, will they trust me that it's legit?" She bent back to her work.

Instead of answering her question, Macallister blurted, "Gotta go. Thirty minutes."

The connection dropped. Jordon said, over his shoulder as he trotted from the room, "I'm going to update Appleton."

I slumped down into a chair, asking Volkov, "You said thirty minutes was gonna cut it close. What does that mean?"

She didn't lift her head as she answered, "I figured out how to identify, isolate, and intercept any traffic sent to the weakness in the code that I identified. And now, I am working on a way to respond. But, obviously, I can't test it. I have no idea whether or not it's gonna work. If and when it happens."

"And the trouble is," I added, taking it one step further, "we can only prove whatever you've done works if there is an attack. And if there's not, we're . . ."

I let that hang until she finished my sentence, "We're fucked. They don't trust me, and they're gonna turn on you, Ben."

I groaned, "Might as well say it out loud, then. To save my career, and to absolve you, we both need a terror attack to happen."

"Pretty much," she agreed. "However, the odds are good that an attack does not happen, imminently. Then, with a little more time, I, for certain, can get the code done. And therefore, it's your job, Ben, to figure out how to sell this beyond Macallister. To Washington." She examined my face and concluded, "I'm on the programming. You're on the sales pitch."

She paused and added, "And you've only got thirty minutes to figure that out."

CHAPTER 73

9:50 AM — ABOARD THE RUSSIAN NAVAL RESEARCH VESSEL YANTAR

"TARGET VIDEO FEED established."

A moment after the unseen speaker in the information warfare suite within *Yantar* spoke, the center big-screen display lit with an unusual image: a giant, light-gray block of a ship, its squared-off stern towering high above flat waters below leaden-gray skies. The name of the ship was painted in big, block, black, all-caps letters on the stern and, in gigantically big, block, black, all-caps letters, on the visible side of the ship: HENNINGER-HEITZ ATLANTIC.

Occasionally, a drop of rainwater would dribble in a downward motion across the screen, obscuring the image for a moment before the drop skittered off the polished surface of the camera lens.

"How is this possible?" asked Anatoly Petrikov.

"Simple. We have two operatives in the area who rented a vessel for the day. They set up a couple of web-enabled cameras to broadcast, and we are picking up the signals via our satellite dome, topside. There's a second camera facing the other direction that we will use when our vessel passes the target," Rodionov responded.

"Not a very pleasant day, it seems, from the skies," Petrikov commented.

"That was helpful. Arranging a charter on short notice was difficult until the weather forecast turned. Then we had plenty of options. And the weather will work in our favor, later."

"And the target?" Petrikov inquired.

"Moscow has been tracking several options for a few days. This one appears to be ideal. It's carrying about a half-loaded cargo, which was not distributed strategically, according to our contact on the docks. The ship took on its cargo in Norfolk in haste; speed in loading was apparently the priority.

"Deck eight, the uppermost, highest deck, is empty. Seven and six are three-quarters full. Five and four are only half-full. The remaining lower decks are also perhaps half loaded."

Petrikov nodded as Rodionov consulted a small tablet screen in front of him before commanding, "Let's begin. Reconfirm cable tap?"

"Confirmed," a voice announced. "BRUSA cable, traffic normal, maximum designed capacity is 138 terabits per second."

"What does that mean?" Petrikov hissed.

Rodionov sighed. The fat man's questions were tiresome. "The cable name is BRUSA. Owned and operated by a South American company, it links North America to South America."

Petrikov interrupted, "But why South America?"

Rodionov caught himself before sighing again, though he wasn't certain that his eye roll went unnoticed. "Traffic via the cable is bi-directional. We don't care about South America in this context. What we care about are the seventy-five data centers in and around Virginia Beach that the cable is linked to. It's one of the highest concentrations of data centers in the world. And it is as close to our target as possible. Our latency will be almost nil, and our capacity only limited by the number of technicians we have working here on this ship. Now," he paused, before asking in a conceited tone, "may I focus on the operation?"

"Of course. Please proceed," replied Petrikov obliviously.

In a louder voice, Rodionov commanded, "Option count, please."

From one of the technicians: "At least nineteen identified so far. There may be more."

"Dispersion?" Rodionov asked.

"Multiple decks."

"How do they know that?" Another whispered question from Petrikov.

Rodionov muttered in response, "The GPS systems in each vehicle include an altimeter. The data packets include the height off sea level, and we can roughly approximate which deck the vehicle is parked on." Then, in his normal volume of voice, he directed, "We're starting on deck five. Acquire a target, please."

As with the Verrazzano bridge operation, Rodionov had split his unit into two primary teams of four men, both seated in the front row, in order to control two vehicles at once, with the technical backup and continuity provided by the men seated in the second row. Again, the Alpha team took command of the first vehicle.

Onboard the *Henninger-Heitz Atlantic*, decks five and four had been loaded in Norfolk and at the ship's previous port of call in Brunswick, Georgia, with preowned vehicles destined for Europe and beyond. Various international shipping companies specialized in this sort of cargo; from luxury SUVs to premium sedans, demand for well-maintained, American-owned cars was strong enough to offset the shipping cost of a car, especially when transported economically on its own wheels inside the cavernous interior of a ro-ro. One of those preowned cars was a red Tesla Model S P85D parked on deck five. And, like all Teslas, the car was never really "off" as it waited for a command from either a door handle or a brake-pedal-push, and the key card was, of course, stored inside the vehicle, as were all the keys for any of the vehicles on the big ship.

The displays within the Model S lit, ghost-like, upon a command sent by the Alpha team onboard *Yantar*. The vehicle's forward-facing cameras showed that it was parked nearly in the middle of the ship, and with a click of the right-side trigger held hundreds of miles away, a signal transmitted at the speed of light through an undersea cable, the electric motors of the car engaged.

For a moment, the sedan strained against the nylon straps that attached to tow hooks under its front and rear bumpers. Those straps, however, were meant to constrain the cargo against the gentle rocking of the ship's decks, and while the two straps together were rated for 12,000-pound breaking strength, they had only perhaps a 5 or 7 percent elasticity—and with the 345-kilowatt motors of the Tesla jerking on the 6,000-pound rated rear strap, it took only seconds for the nylon to snap.

The Tesla lurched forward, slamming into the rear bumper of a Lincoln Town Car, quickly overcoming that vehicle's inertia and shoving it against its retaining straps.

With the front bumper sensor arrays returning fault codes, the Alpha team driver resorted to piloting the vehicle using only the forward-facing camera, mounted high on the windshield in the rearview mirror assembly. Employing a series of forward-and-reverse transitions, the driver broke the vehicle free. It was now a potent 4,500-pound battering ram, with instant torque from its electric motors and an almost fully charged battery pack.

As Rodionov and his team monitored the progress of the *Henninger-Heitz Atlantic* toward her left turn at the apex of the Newport News shipping channel, the Alpha team herded one vehicle after another to the right side of the ro-ro, breaking the cars free one by one. Bravo team joined the exercise using a Tesla Model 3, parked further back on the left side of the ship.

Moving just one 4,500-pound car would have no effect on the massive ship.

Moving ten or twelve vehicles from their places on the centerline to one side of the ship, however, would transfer some fifty-thousand pounds of weight, five decks above sea level.

Rodionov, and his counterparts at the Admiralty building in Saint Petersburg as well as within the Kremlin in Moscow, had done the math. Without access to the ship's cargo manifest, they estimated that its full load was about 12,500 tons. At a bit more than half-full for this return crossing, her cargo weighed perhaps seven-thousand tons. Therefore, moving fifty-thousand pounds, or twenty-five tons, would barely be noticeable.

Unless, they reasoned, that weight had been pushed to one side, high enough in the hull.

And the ship turned in the opposite direction.

CHAPTER
74

9:58 AM — ABOARD THE HENNINGER-HEITZ ATLANTIC

"PASSING RED BELL NUMBER SIX; twenty-degree turn to port with five degrees of rudder, please," ordered Harbor Pilot Gordon Green.

The helmsman complied, and the big ship began a slow swing to a northeasterly course.

As she turned, her deep hull carved to the left, and as usual, her superstructure leaned in the opposite direction. To a person unaccustomed to the motions of this very large ship, typically that movement would be very subtle, but to Captain Boeckmann's well-trained eye and inner ear, it was extremely noticeable.

And the captain was concerned.

"Too fast a turn," the captain scolded. "Look at the list to starboard. Ballast, port side, immediately."

His ballast engineer complied instantly, pressing the buttons that opened the valves deep below the ship's waterlines that allowed seawater to flood into the port side ballast tanks. The effect was slow but steady, as the ship slowly returned to a more upright stance, despite the ongoing turn.

The pilot, chagrined, muttered under his breath, "Five degrees is too much rudder?" He straightened and addressed the captain, arguing, "Captain, the turn is required. And it is gradual. And nothing out of the ordinary. Please confirm your ballasting."

Annoyed at the pilot's self-defense, the captain only grumbled, under his breath, an unintelligible phrase in German, "Der Pilot rechnete nicht mit Wind. Täuschen." *Pilot didn't account for wind. Fool.*

✳ ✳ ✳

9:58 AM — SALEM, MASSACHUSETTS

"Hold everything! I'm seeing some traffic," Volkov had announced a moment ago, her coffee mug untouched beside her keyboard. Jordon, who had been standing by Appleton's front windows, awaiting the expected blue-and-red lights that would announce the arrival of our soon-to-be-probably-former squad, crossed to join Volkov, Appleton, and me.

To me, her screen had looked like gibberish, as usual.

"Network traffic through Tesla's nodes," she translated, "which they call Telsafi. They've got an app for it. It's how you can monitor your car from your phone; you plug in your Vehicle Identification Number and the credentials that go with it. And it's the method I used to establish contact. Very similar in the patterns that I used. Hang on."

No one had spoken as we watched her work, or hack, or whatever it would be called.

"Yeah," she added a moment later, "This could be something. There's too much two-way traffic for a normal check-in. At least, that's what I asked my system to notify me of, in case it happened. There's no way, of course, to watch every car."

"What does that lead to, please?" inquired Appleton.

"It means that something different is happening and — "

Volkov stopped speaking and was concentrating on her computers. She looked at data on one screen and turned to a second one, bringing up a map. With a flurry of keystrokes, a dot appeared on the map screen.

"That's odd," she muttered. "It's in the water."

"What is that showing us?" I asked.

"That's the location of the vehicle that I am tracking that is initiating this type of data connectivity. But it's not on land," she replied.

"That's the Chesapeake Bay area. Outside of Norfolk, Virginia. And Virginia Beach. I know it well," Jordon offered. "Lots of tunnels there. The roads go through tunnels because of all the ship traffic in that place. There's maybe three or four tunnels."

"They're attacking a tunnel?" Appleton exclaimed.

My eyes went wide. "Of course," I blurted. "The bridge in New York and now a tunnel. It's a confined area!"

"Volkov, can you confirm that?" Appleton demanded.

"Yeah, I think so," Volkov answered. "Now there's a second car too. Slightly different location, more to the east. Maybe a second tunnel?"

"Get me Macallister!" Appleton shouted.

"He's on his way here." I looked at my watch. "Maybe fifteen or twenty minutes."

"Call him anyway. We need to roll on this right away!" Appleton ordered.

I pulled out my personal phone, and for the first time in several days, I powered it on. The FBI now knew where I was, and, in fact, was on their way for a visit, so there was no need to keep it off any longer. And I needed Macallister's phone number. After all, who memorizes phone numbers anymore?

✳ ✳ ✳

10:02 AM — ABOARD THE RUSSIAN NAVAL RESEARCH VESSEL YANTAR

"Sir, the ship is proceeding northeast. The Norfolk Harbor Entrance Reach. Approximately three miles to the next turn."

"Thank you," Rodionov replied, consulting his chart. "We need to get more assets moving. The ship is making seven knots speed. That's less than a half-hour to the turn." Pausing again to scribble numbers on a pad, he ordered, "We need to double up. Alpha, you're on deck five. Alternate vehicles. Push the load to the opposite side. To the port side of the ship."

Rodionov consulted his small tablet screen and added, "Bravo, get me two contacts on deck seven."

Within seconds, the Unit 29155 team located two brand-new Model Xs on the seventh deck of the *Henninger-Heitz Atlantic*, and the process began anew. Now with doubled speed, alternating vehicles, the Bravo team began breaking vehicles loose on the half-full seventh deck, the highest loaded deck on the ship.

Below, the Alpha team began herding their group of vehicles, one by one, to the port side of the ro-ro, until one of them announced, "We have a problem. Our Model S is jammed in place!"

"There's almost three thousand cars on that ship!" Rodionov exploded. "Find another one!"

The tech team had isolated the data streams from nineteen Teslas scattered throughout the ship, and they quickly assigned a different Model S, this one the more powerful P100D series, to the Alpha team.

With the benefit of the vehicle's dashcams, Rodionov could see the load being slowly shifted, and thanks to the following charter fishing boat with its camera focused on the exterior of the big ship, he could also confirm that the ro-ro remained level, at least from the outside.

Raindrops cluttered the image more frequently, and whitecaps were visible on the water as the convoy slowly proceeded northeast, passing the Naval Station and heading toward Thimble Shoals.

✳ ✳ ✳

10:10 AM — ABOARD THE HENNINGER-HEITZ ATLANTIC

"Captain, loadmaster reports chaos on deck five!"

"Explain," demanded Captain Boeckmann of his First Mate, who held the ship's intercom handset to his ear.

"He can't explain. Cars are slamming into one another on deck five. He said it's like they're possessed," the mate garbled, knowing that his frantic tone would not be well-received by the captain, but not knowing any other way to repeat the loadmaster's equally-frantic tone and words.

The captain stepped back from his customary stance behind the Harbor Pilot and crossed his arms over his chest. "Impossible. Restrap them immediately. One must have been improperly secured and moved when we last turned. This is unacceptable."

The mate repeated the captain's orders into the handset, in a low tone but with eyes wide open. He shook his head. "Loadmaster says he cannot send deckhands into the area. Too dangerous."

"Not as dangerous as an unsecured cargo. Get down there and report back. Now!"

The mate spun on his heels smartly and dashed for the stairs that led below.

* * *

10:15 AM — SALEM, MASSACHUSETTS

To the confusion of her neighbors, three unmarked, black vehicles screeched to a stop outside of Jennifer Appleton's antique home. While sirens did not bray, the blue-and-red alternating lights were alarming enough.

However, the three windbreaker-clad figures who disembarked from two of the vehicles, "FBI" emblazoned in yellow on their backs, holding black pistols in plain sight, caused extreme consternation. Two neighbors dialed 9-1-1.

As the FBI team conferred briefly on the perfectly manicured grassy front yard, Jordon gave us staccato updates as he peeked through the preserved, wavy-glass windows of the antique home.

"Zimmerman, Connelly, and Jones. Guns drawn. That seems unnecessary." He paused. "A new guy. Appears to be Chinese. Mr. Cheng Chen, I presume." He paused again. "No gun. He's got a briefcase." Another pause. "Macallister's here. He's on the phone."

Yeah, I thought, *I know that because he's talking to me.*

"No, sir," I said to my phone, "We are not armed, nor are we going to resist." I figured I was on speakerphone, and that was orchestrated by Macallister for the benefit of the squad.

The connection remained active as two Salem police cruisers squealed into view, their rooftop lights also blazing and with their sirens howling, vibrating through the thin windowpanes. Appleton's quiet street was anything but.

"Hang on, Porter, let me deal with the locals first," Macallister barked.

Macallister had driven with two other men, agents I presume, based on their visible but still-holstered Glocks, who I did not recognize. This was becoming a bit of a tenuous situation. Armed agents and armed cops. I hoped Macallister would take charge.

"There's two more. This is definitely an attack!" Volkov yelled.

"I know! I don't recognize them. They showed up with Macallister," I shouted back.

"What? Wait. What?"

"Outside. Two more agents," I clarified.

"Not outside," she scolded. "Here. Or, well, there, on-screen. They've hijacked two more. They're on open water too. That can't be a tunnel!"

None of this made sense to me. Volkov was saying there were additional vehicles being hijacked, my boss is outside yelling at the local cops, and my squad is out there, too, with guns drawn and aimed. Were we fugitives, or were we agents?

I figured I had nothing to lose, so I called out, "I'm gonna try and defuse this shit. Okay?"

No one objected.

I opened the front door, and as one, the three pistols rotated and aimed at me.

* * *

10:20 AM — *ABOARD THE* HENNINGER-HEITZ ATLANTIC

The bridge intercom rang, and Captain Boeckmann snatched up the handset. "Report!"

"Three minutes to commence a turn to starboard. Two degrees rudder, please," Pilot Green stammered nervously.

"No turn! Not yet!" the captain barked at the pilot. "Say again, First Mate? The cargo on deck five is uncontrolled?" he snarled into the handset.

"Captain, I am in command of the ship's movements within this area. You will not contradict my order," Pilot Green countered, gaining confidence.

The captain ignored the pilot, focusing his attention on the crisis belowdecks. He held the handset away from his ear, the first mate yelling over the sound of crashing metal-on-metal impacts, "Captain, the loadmaster was not exaggerating. Part of the load is broken free. Several of the vehicles appear to be moving on their own. I cannot explain it!"

Boeckmann questioned, "How many vehicles are free?"

"Twenty. Thirty, perhaps!"

"Where are they?"

"Deck five port side, captain. They're mostly clustered to port."

"Stand by."

"Commence turn to starboard. Two degrees rudder," Green ordered.

"Not yet!" the captain bellowed. He had grabbed a pad of paper and was scratching out numbers, muttering under his breath, "Thirty vehicles. Five thousand pounds each. Seventy-five tons."

The captain straightened and commanded, "Engineer. Ballast starboard side to compensate for seventy-five tons improperly positioned on deck five, to port. Pilot, you may commence your turn."

"Four degrees rudder, now," the pilot responded, "we've gone too far."

"Agreed," the captain nodded, adding, "we will compensate with ballast."

✳ ✳ ✳

10:24 AM — ABOARD THE RUSSIAN VESSEL YANTAR

Petrikov wished he had a glass of vodka in hand to toast the carnage visible on decks five and seven. He chuckled, enjoying the show.

On the center screen, the image of the lumbering ro-ro began to change aspect; the ship had begun her right-hand turn into the first leg of the Thimble Shoals channel.

"Perfect," Rodionov commented, examining his tablet chart. "They've overshot the turn and will have to overcompensate. Watch."

As the big ship turned to the right, she leaned to the left, to her port side. And, belowdecks, the mass of piled vehicles exacerbated the list, especially those on deck seven, which her captain had not figured into his orders.

From their secret vantage point, the Russians waited for the ship to resume a straight course, and Rodionov ordered, "Begin pushing cargo to the starboard side. Approximately two miles to green gong 19 and the next right-hand turn. You have at most fifteen minutes. Break them free!"

"The starboard side?" Petrikov asked. "But it is turning to the right again, no? Will that not balance itself?"

"You'll understand shortly," Rodionov responded cryptically.

✳ ✳ ✳

10:30 AM — SALEM, MASSACHUSETTS

I had opened the front door of Jennifer Appleton's home and stared down my squad. And at their pistols. I kept my hands visible, and my body steady.

I had felt like a fool, and like a target.

If I had to pick one, I think I'd take fool.

The standoff had lasted for perhaps fifteen, twenty seconds, until Zimmerman had yelled, "Porter! Put your hands up. Step outside the door!"

Are you fucking kidding me? I had thought. *Put your hands up? Jackass.* Nevertheless, acting on self-preservation instinct, I had complied.

"You want me to cuff him, boss?" Zimmerman had asked Macallister.

Macallister had responded with a snort, "Fuck no. Put your weapons down. Holster 'em. These are our people. Show some respect."

The Acting SAC had turned to the local police and explained, "This is a very unusual situation. No one is in any danger. It's an internal issue. Let me handle it, please. You can secure the perimeter if you are concerned. Okay?"

The Salem police had backed down, the FBI squad had backed down, and I had exhaled.

The hard part was yet to come, though.

It had taken me ten minutes to try and piece together an explanation of what we were seeing on Volkov's screens. To no surprise, Zimmerman thought it was bullshit. Connelly and Jones weren't sure, and Cheng Chen was noncommittal.

Most, unfortunately, though, Macallister was unconvinced. "You're showing me attacks that you say are on Teslas, but that they're in tunnels? Porter, I called Washington after you called me. Before I called you back when we arrived here. Washington has been in contact with Virginia State Police. Not a single accident reported in any of the tunnels. 'Light Sunday morning traffic,' they said. 'Nothing unusual.'"

The problem was with our dots on the Volkov's screens. Every one of them, now five, hovered in the blue-colored part of her map. There was a tunnel nearby, Interstate 64, crossing from Hampton to Virginia Beach, but according to Macallister, it was unscathed.

And, contrary to every reasonable expectation, the dots were moving, very slowly, but moving.

They seemed to be trending eastward. Further into the blue area on the map.

"It's another one of Volkov's diversions!" Zimmerman bellowed, unable to contain himself. "That screen looks like a video game. That isn't real. Arrest her and get her off that computer before she does real harm. We have no idea what she's doing!"

This was a problem. I wanted to say something to counter that argument, but for all I knew, Zimmerman was correct. What was Volkov *really* doing?

Macallister, I knew, had his doubts.

The stalemate was broken for a moment when Cheng Chen sat down next to Volkov. She pointed at something on her screen and murmured. He responded in kind, nodding and whispering, "Hmm. I understand, yes."

"But this isn't ready."

"Yes, I see," the Cyber Division veteran agreed. I didn't see anything, but I got the feeling that with Chen and Volkov side-by-side, the momentum was about to shift in our favor.

✳ ✳ ✳

10:32 AM — ABOARD THE HENNINGER-HEITZ ATLANTIC

"We will begin a slow right turn at gong 19 and accelerate the turn at gong 17. Two degrees rudder at 19, then four degrees at 17. Captain, do you have your ballasting under control?" Harbor Pilot Gordon Green demanded.

"Yes," the captain said definitively. "Our issue on deck five is contained. I will need to report this, of course, but it appears it was caused by a runaway vehicle."

The pilot decided to take a more cooperative approach, "You are comfortable with the rate of turn?"

"Yes, very good. Thank you," replied the captain, politely. "The first mate and loadmaster are checking the other decks, starting at the lowest and working up. They have already reported that deck one is unaffected."

"Strange that a single, unrestrained vehicle can cause so much trouble," the pilot commented.

"According to the mate, it may have been several vehicles improperly secured," elaborated the captain. "Once one or two are in motion, it becomes what is referred to as the free-surface effect. A small change in the balance of the load, especially up high, can cause an exponential change in stability. Now, however, we are prepared with the correct ballast calculation. We will ballast as the ship turns, on the starboard side. When we are in the channel, and on a straight course, we will begin resecuring the cargo."

The pilot nodded his understanding, "Very well. I don't expect any course changes after gong 17. Should be a straight course down the channel, past the Chesapeake Bay Bridge-Tunnel, and out to the marker where I'll depart your vessel."

Verifying the ship's position relative to the green gong #19, the pilot instructed the helmsman, "Commence your course change to the right, two degrees rudder." As the ship began to slowly turn, the pilot checked the various displays; traffic remained clear except for the fishing vessel that had been trailing the ship. Green pointed at the AIS display, commenting, "Our shadow is using the auxiliary channel to pass. Keeping well clear. Good for him."

✳ ✳ ✳

10:36 AM — SALEM, MASSACHUSETTS

The tension in the room was palpable. Now, instead of the previous outdoor standoff with guns drawn, we had a different kind of standoff: Volkov frantically working with Cheng Chen at her shoulder, the pair oblivious to Macallister's second-guessing as Zimmerman stared me down. Again.

My pulse was racing. I had to do something. Anything.

But what?

I had nothing. Cheng Chen did not seem alarmed by Volkov's screens, and if he was calm, we all should be calm. Right?

Taking my cue from him, I, too, peered over Volkov's shoulder. She muttered, "They've got six of them now. I need a break so I can set up a countermeasure. But they're very active. But in the middle of nowhere! They must be spoofing the signal or something. I don't understand."

She stopped typing for a moment, clenching her fists in frustration, and tilted her head back for a moment, stretching the muscles in her neck.

The middle of nowhere.

Without her head leaning in, I took a closer look at the screens. The screen painted all blue showed six dots moving in a herky-jerky pattern, almost at random. Short movements, forward, backward, a bit sideways here and there.

But . . . always trending to the right. In a clump. "It's a swarm," I muttered to myself. No one heard me.

"Porter." Macallister's voice interrupted my analysis. "I think we're done here. I'm not sure what's going on, but let's take a step backward, okay?"

I looked up at him. Then down at the screen. *A swarm. In the middle of nowhere.*

"Can you zoom out that map screen, please," I said, directing my normal volume of voice toward Volkov.

"Porter. We're done. *Okay?*" Macallister repeated.

As he spoke, Volkov manipulated the trackpad, and the image enlarged, the dots clumping together tightly as the scale decreased.

It was obvious. The dots were nowhere near the yellowish-orange lines that indicated the bridges and tunnels, nor near the grayish color spidered with white lines that denoted roads crisscrossing land. The dots were isolated in a sea of blue.

In a sea.

"They're on a ship!" I exclaimed. "That's why they keep moving to the right. The *ship* is moving. And the swarm is moving *inside* the ship."

Volkov gasped. "That's it!" She leaned to the side, bumping into Cheng Chen.

Zimmerman, of course, cried, "That's bullshit!"

Macallister was beginning to put it together, and even as I stabbed a finger at Volkov's screen and snapped, "And that's a potential target," the Acting SAC was yanking his phone from his suit-jacket pocket.

My finger was pointing to a yellow line that crossed the expanse of blue, marked with a little shield logo, indicating a state road, with a number 13 inside the shield outline.

Volkov zoomed in quickly to where I was pointing. Words appeared, overlaying the yellow line: "Chesapeake Bay Bridge-Tunnel."

* * *

10:40 AM — ABOARD YANTAR

"We've seen crewmembers on deck five. None so far on deck seven," reported one of the Unit 29155 technicians seated in the second row of the information warfare suite.

"Focus on deck seven, then," ordered Rodionov. "Any additional vehicles we can use?"

"Yes. Two more."

"Assign them to Alpha. The final turn will commence in moments. Break as many free as possible. Don't worry about moving them. They'll move themselves." Rodionov sat back in the tall-backed, black leather chair.

Petrikov began, "I don't und—" but before he could complete the word, Rodionov shot a look that even the petulant Petrikov understood. He would wait and watch.

But, in his opinion, they had lost their opportunity to capsize the ship. One final turn, and it would maintain a steady course. And that final turn was inconsequential.

Or so he thought.

* * *

10:41 AM — SALEM, MASSACHUSETTS

One of our early big breaks in the Operation E.T. case had been our discovery, one that is obvious to anyone with any maritime interests, that vessel traffic can be monitored on several freely-accessed websites. Arguably the most popular was a site called Marinetraffic.com, which Volkov had quickly pulled up on one of her computers.

Vessel icons in the lower Chesapeake Bay were sparse, and a single contact approached the Chesapeake Bay Bridge-Tunnel from the west: a car carrier named "Henninger-Heitz Atlantic," pictured on the website as a large, drab gray, box-shaped ship, with the ship's name painted on her slab sides in boxy letters.

I took one look at that image, and, in a flash, I understood.

I pulled out my own smartphone, opened a browser app, and googled. I brought up an image of a roll-on/roll-off car carrier ship that had capsized only last month, in September, off Brunswick, Georgia.

The resemblance was uncanny, if only askew. The giant ship lying on its side in the Brunswick channel looked very much like the upright image on Volkov's screen.

"Macallister, Volkov. Look at this." I shoved my phone in front of them. "Same type of ship. We gotta get on it. Or get someone on it. Or stop it!"

"Why?" Zimmerman whined. "I don't get it."

"They've been moving the swarm inside the ship for the last hour. Inside a car carrier. Just like the one in Georgia!" I shot back.

Upon seeing the image on my phone, Macallister, unlike the useless Zimmerman, quickly reached the same conclusion I had, and he had already dialed into the FBI's Washington, DC, Hoover Building, where the Bureau's headquarters were located, and where the Strategic Information and Operations Center (SIOC) maintained a 24/7 presence. Within a minute, SIOC was on the case and preparing to liaise with military and police assets in the Chesapeake Bay area.

"What the fuck?" Zimmerman bleated. "So, what if they got cars moving on a ship?"

"Do you read the news, ever?" I asked, my voice as heavy with sarcasm as I could manage.

"Porter, you got no idea what you're talking about," he whined.

I didn't respond. Instead, I handed him my phone, still displaying the news article on the ship that had rolled off of Georgia, and I stated flatly, "Read that, jackass. And let us get back to work."

✳ ✳ ✳

10:42 AM — ABOARD THE HENNINGER-HEITZ ATLANTIC

"Passing green gong 17," Pilot Gordon Green announced. "Add two degrees rudder. Total four degrees to make your course one-two-zero degrees magnetic."

The 787-foot ro-ro began her slow turn to the right.

Her ballast tanks on the starboard side had been partially filled to compensate for the weight of the vehicles that had been herded to the port side on deck five, but the ballast engineer had been unaware of the reverse situation two decks above, where the Unit 29155 team had been breaking more and more vehicles loose by using their electric battering rams.

And, once the stiff northerly wind exerted its pressure on the high slab-sides of the car carrier, the big vessel began to list to the right, to starboard.

As she passed through one degree of list, the ballast became an accelerator.

Two degrees became five degrees.

On the bridge, the captain realized the ship was beginning to roll. "Ballast port side! Pump out starboard side!" Boeckmann thundered.

Five degrees become ten degrees.

With ballast on her starboard side, with a blustery northerly wind pushing against her high-slabbed port side, and with the increasing free-surface effect of the unsecured vehicles slowly, at first, but then rapidly sliding to the starboard side of deck seven as the ship heeled, the ballast pumps could not keep up with the rapidly-changing center of gravity of the ship.

Pilot Green kept his cool. As the ship tilted, it would start to turn itself without input from the rudder. He ordered neutral rudder, which helped slow the growing list but also kept the ship on course. Straying out of the channel was not an option. However, stopping was not an option either; the wind would blow the massive vessel out of the channel in a matter of moments. He had to keep the ship's momentum on.

But he knew the situation was dire, and he brought the microphone of the bridge-mounted V H F radio to his lips, using the words that signified an emergency just short of a mayday: "Pan pan, pan pan. This is the vessel *Henninger-Heitz Atlantic*, traversing Thimble Shoals channel outbound. We have a ballast emergency on board. All vessels stay clear. Repeat, all vessels stay clear."

Without waiting for a response, Green pulled out his issued cellphone and speed-dialed the harbor pilot main office. He repeated his message as Captain Boeckmann urged his engineer to reballast the ship.

The ship's roll stopped at seventeen degrees.

They could only hope that the retaining straps on the still-secured vehicles held under the enormous pressure that they would be under, straining under the weight of a vehicle pulling its mass sideways against the nylon webbing.

If the webbing failed, the vehicles would slide, the free-surface effect would become uncontrollable, and the ship would capsize.

* * *

10:46 AM — ABOARD YANTAR

Their fishing-boat spy camera offered a new angle, a slightly oblique picture of the bow of the heavily-listing car carrier, now that the fishing boat had passed the lumbering vessel by using the auxiliary channel.

The cameras from inside the vessel, broadcast by their swarm of Teslas, showed a mass of twisted metal and plastic and rubber, as cars had piled up against each other on the starboard side of the vessel on deck seven.

"They'll be ballasting the ship to port, now," Rodionov narrated. "It will take some time, but it should ensure some stability."

"Will they get it upright?" Petrikov blurted, unable to resist a question.

With the immediate urgency gone, Rodionov decided to answer, "No. There is too much weight now concentrated to one side. Their only hope is to right it enough to maintain safety and to clear the channel. I'd imagine they are calling for tugs to assist, but that won't happen fast enough. For them, at least."

"Now what, then?"

"Now, we wait. They cannot slow down, or they'll drift out of the channel due to the wind. They cannot speed up. They will maintain their speed. Five more miles, give or take forty-five minutes, and then we execute our final play. We have them in check. It will soon be time for checkmate."

Petrikov grinned happily at the chess analogy. He understood.

✳ ✳ ✳

11:00 AM — SALEM, MASSACHUSETTS

Even though it was a Sunday, the reaction from Washington and beyond had been swift and decisive.

The Norfolk port authority had placed a stop on all commercial traffic, holding several vessels outside the Bay with others held at the docks. The Coast Guard was scrambling a cutter as well as faster boats to get on the scene, altered by a "pan pan" call from the ship. Further details had quickly emerged from the radio traffic that had been relayed first to SIOC, then to us in Salem: the car carrier was listing between ten and fifteen degrees and was in imminent danger of capsizing.

The United States Naval Station in Virginia Beach had launched a helicopter, equipped with cameras that could transmit in real-time, and they had agreed to share the video feed with us.

The Navy was especially concerned, for pier-side at the Newport News Shipbuilding yard was their newest aircraft carrier, the *USS Gerald Ford*. The $13 billion carrier was scheduled to begin her first sea trial in two weeks, after over a year of delays. A sister carrier, the *USS John F. Kennedy*, was being completed in drydock at Newport News, scheduled to be launched in late October. Nearby, the US Naval Station Norfolk, in Virginia Beach, is the world's largest navy base, serving as the home port for over seventy-five Navy vessels scattered through eleven miles of waterfront piers and wharves.

The Navy, unlike Zimmerman, kept up with the news. The car carrier that had capsized in Brunswick, Georgia, last month had been diverted to a shoal in the nick of time, and that vessel came to a halt on its side outside the main shipping channel to that busy port. As the ship settled and its crew evacuated, the port was closed to all traffic. Over a month after the incident, the Coast Guard announced that the ship could not be removed without cutting it up into small pieces, a process that would take months.

A capsized car carrier blocking the US Navy access to Norfolk, Newport News, and Virginia Beach via the Thimble Shoals Channel would be a priority national security emergency.

While Macallister worked the phones, Jordon and I helped with messages, and my squad sulked, Volkov kept at it, occasionally muttering something unintelligible to Cheng Chen, who had taken an active position in front of one of her computers, his fingers working the keyboard.

The Navy had calculated that the car carrier would cross over the southern tunnel section of the Chesapeake Bay Bridge-Tunnel in less than thirty minutes.

The CBBT was an engineering and construction marvel. First opened as a two-lane road in 1964, then doubled in capacity in 1999, the 17.6-mile crossing of the mouth of the Chesapeake Bay was a combination of low and high trestle bridges that intersected with four man-made islands. One pair of those islands lay toward the north of the mouth of the bay; that pair of islands served as the entry points for a tunnel under the Chesapeake Bay Channel that led north to Baltimore, Annapolis, and Washington, DC, via the Potomac River. The southern pair of islands flanked the tunnel entrances to the Thimble Shoals channel crossing.

In between the two channels at the head of the Chesapeake Bay, the water depths in feet ranged from the teens to the high twenties—an impassable depth for the commercial ships or Naval vessels bound for Norfolk, Newport News, and Virginia Beach.

The sole access to those ports was the Thimble Shoals Channel.

And the bottleneck of that channel was the southern CBBT tunnel crossing.

✳ ✳ ✳

11:20 AM — *ABOARD* HENNINGER-HEITZ ATLANTIC

The bridge on the 787-foot ro-ro had been mostly silent for the past twenty minutes. The VHF radios crackled with messages from the Coast Guard and the port authority.

The ballast engineer had reported that the list was stabilized at fifteen degrees. The port ballast tanks had been filled while the starboard tanks had been drained, and the loadmaster had reported that movement on the car decks below had ceased.

Captain Boeckmann had called the company headquarters, and tugs were enroute to meet the stricken ship in the open waters outside the Chesapeake Bay Bridge-Tunnel crossing area, where the ship would have the space to maneuver in order to return to the safety of the docks.

And Pilot Green had continued his work, ordering tiny rudder adjustments to keep the listing ship in the center of the channel, working against the forces of the wind that continually pushed the ship to the right. In less than an hour, the vessel would be at the pilot transfer zone in open water, and another pilot could take the ship back to the docks. He would be relieved of his work. Relieved in several ways, in fact.

Outside, a helicopter with US Navy markings swooped over the bridge, circled the *Henninger-Heitz Atlantic* once, and then hovered a safe distance above and beyond the port side bow of the ro-ro, pacing the big ship as it lumbered southeast in the Thimble Shoals Channel.

✳ ✳ ✳

11:25 AM — *ABOARD* YANTAR

On the electronic chart displayed on his tablet, Rodionov watched the icon that indicated the position of the *Henninger-Heitz Atlantic* as it closed in on the location of the southern CBBT tunnel crossing. At the front of the information warfare suite, the center big screen had been divided into two horizontal halves. The upper half showed the view from the fishing boat's stern-facing camera, and that image was dominated by the bulk of the plodding, listing car carrier. The lower half of the big screen displayed the fishing boat's forward-facing camera, with the two man-made islands that created the southern tunnel entrances just visible on the left and right sides of the picture. In a moment, the islands would move out of frame as the fishing boat got closer to the crossing.

"Commence deck five operation in ninety seconds. Alpha and Bravo teams," Rodionov commanded. "And, transmit a message to our boat. Increase speed and angle its course toward the center of the channel."

A technician sent a message to the operatives on the fishing boat, and within seconds, the image rotated as the boat turned to her left, the wake of the fishing boat frothing as the car carrier slowly receded in the image.

"Alpha is ready. Two vehicles," came a report from the front of the space.

"Bravo. Only one vehicle. Can you get us another?"

"Not required," Rodionov responded. "All you need to do is get that mass moving. Three cars will accomplish that task. I'll do the rest." The left and right big screens at the front of the space showed a clump of perhaps thirty vehicles that had been pushed to the port side, still remaining there despite the ship's fifteen-degree list to starboard, held in place only by inertia and by the friction under their rubber tires on the roughly-painted steel deck.

"Message the boat. Further to the north side of the channel," Rodionov commanded.

The aspect ratio of the stern-facing camera changed again.

"Stand by for my command. I will review the sequence one last time. At the command, Alpha and Bravo teams, break that load free, so it slides down to the starboard side. At the command, our operative's boat is to cut its engines and call a mayday. Confirm your understanding, please."

"Alpha. Confirmed."

"Bravo. Confirmed."

"Sir, the message is sent to the boat. Awaiting final command."

Rodionov consulted his chart display once more, double-checking location with the visual of the northern man-made island now looming in the lower half of the center big screen. "This has to be perfect," he muttered under his breath. "The ship has to turn to avoid the fishing boat just before crossing the tunnel. She will turn sideways, and she will roll just shy of the crossing. Almost there . . ."

✳ ✳ ✳

SALEM, MASSACHUSETTS

SIOC had linked us to the US Navy's video feed from their chopper that was pacing the ship that we had identified, and SIOC had also sent us a link to the audio feed from the maritime VHF radio distress channel sixteen.

"Holy shit, Porter!" Macallister blurted, as soon as the chopper's video image popped up on our screen in Salem. The trouble on board the car carrier was clearly visible to us, thanks to the Navy video feed.

With one brief glance at the image of the ship that was leaning heavily to its right side, Volkov commented dryly, "The Russians have been busy. Look how much they've gotten it to list. Not much more, and it's gonna roll. Free-surface effect, you know."

Macallister groaned, "What the fuck does that mean?"

"It's like a chain reaction," Volkov explained in between rapid keystrokes.

I took over the explanation; she needed to concentrate. "You get enough mass moving, up high on that ship, and the physics work faster and faster. It's kinda like sloshing sand in a container. At first, you tip the container and a few grains of sand move. But at a certain point, once you tip it enough, a lot of sand moves, very suddenly."

Volkov interrupted my oversimplified science lesson. "They've gone silent. Nothing happening. We're almost ready."

As she had worked, we had learned from SIOC that the ship had sent a "pan pan" call, one level of emergency short of a "mayday" call, and the ship had reported that their vehicle cargo had shifted and caused the ship to list.

We had listened over the channel sixteen audio feed as they reported, minutes ago, that they believed the situation was under control. Their plan was to return the ship to port once they had cleared the constricted zone within the Chesapeake Bay waters, and when they had the space to maneuver a slow U-turn in the open ocean.

"They're not out of the woods yet," I offered, repeating Volkov's warning. "Not going to take much to roll that thing onto its side now, I bet."

"How wide is that channel that they're in?" Macallister asked.

Jordon had been quietly working on his smartphone, one step ahead it appeared, and answered, "One thousand feet. And that ship is just shy of eight hundred feet long. If it capsizes like that car carrier ship did in Georgia, it's going to block a substantial portion of that channel."

"Especially if they can time it at the tunnel crossing area. All they need to do is move a few more cars," I exclaimed.

"Sir, Porter's theory is ridiculous. I insist that this charade end, now!" demanded Special Agent Zimmerman, his right hand resting on his hip holster, very clearly visible outside the hem of his navy-blue windbreaker.

Macallister didn't flinch, "I am the Acting Special Agent in Charge. We will see where this goes. Agent Zimmerman, you're relieved. Connelly, Jones, please escort Agent Zimmerman to your vehicle."

Zimmerman frothed, "I'm not moving. Volkov is in on whatever this is. You're a fool!"

"They're pinging the cars again!" Volkov shouted. "Shut up!"

"I see three. You got any more?" Chen snapped.

"No. Just those three. Prepare to send the package," Volkov barked.

Zimmerman howled, "What package? What is she doing?"

* * *

ABOARD YANTAR

"Three. Two . . ." Rodionov paused, now standing, " . . . one. *Now!*"

"Message sent!" a technician on the floor shouted.

* * *

HENNINGER-HEITZ ATLANTIC

"Captain, our shadow appears to be heading out to sea," Pilot Gordon Green had observed, as he watched through the bridge windows as the small fishing boat overtook and passed the massive vessel.

"Yes," agreed Captain Boeckmann, "but why is it crossing the channel?"

Neither man spoke as the fishing boat trended to the north side of the channel, aiming toward the northern man-made island that allowed vehicles to descend below the seabed inside the CBBT southern tunnel.

However, just shy of the tunnel crossing, the wake that streamed behind the boat dissipated, and the boat floated to a stop on the northern side of the channel.

* * *

SALEM

"Counterattack package sent," Volkov reported, her voice quick and dry. "Status?"

"Confirmed," Chen replied. "Stand by."

I could have heard a pin drop. Or maybe that was the "plop" of the sweat running off my brow, dripping onto Appleton's pristine, white carpet.

* * *

YANTAR

On his feet, Rodionov bellowed, his voice shaking, "Alpha. Bravo. I said, *go!*"

"Alpha! I have no response. The target is not responding!"

"Same with Bravo!"

Rodionov's eyes went wide in panic.

Petrikov lumbered to his feet, his face red with fury.

✳ ✳ ✳

ATLANTIC

The bridge VHF radio crackled, "Mayday! Mayday! This is the fishing vessel *Martha Ann*. We have an engine fire aboard. Mayday, mayday!"

"That fool has stopped in the channel!" Pilot Green exclaimed, pointing at the now-drifting fishing boat, bobbing in the whitecaps. "Helm! Prepare a five-degree rudder to starboard, at my command!"

"No," exclaimed Captain Boeckmann in a bellowing voice, the German's demeanor uncharacteristically shaken. "The ship will roll on its side with that turn!"

A much calmer voice replied over the radio speaker, "This is the United States Coast Guard. Vessel reporting mayday, what is your position and number of persons aboard?"

The panicked voice answered, "Near the Chesapeake Bay Bridge southern tunnel!"

✳ ✳ ✳

SALEM

Listening to the audio feed of the radio channel courtesy of SIOC's wizardry, I protested, "That *cannot* be a coincidence!"

As if on cue, the video feed from the US Navy chopper rotated, and we could see a little, fishing-type boat floating in the waves between the two man-made islands that flanked the tunnel crossing.

There were two men standing in the open cockpit of the boat, waving their arms over their heads.

That's odd, I thought, looking at the screen. Staring, the hairs on the back of my neck tingling, I questioned the room, "Does anyone see any smoke from any engine fire?"

✳ ✳ ✳

YANTAR

"My system is frozen."

"Mine too!"

"Same here!" The complaints barraged Rodionov, his tablet hanging uselessly to his side as he stared at the big screens.

The cars were immobile on the decks within the *Henninger-Heitz Atlantic*.

The Unit 29155 technicians' screens were frozen, and their computers would not accept commands.

On the center screen, the image of the car carrier grew bigger and bigger as it closed the distance to the relatively tiny fishing boat.

"Turn!" Rodionov yelled at the screen. "Turn! They won't dare run down a helpless boat. Turn, dammit!"

✳ ✳ ✳

SALEM

The Navy chopper had repositioned itself and was now hovering over the stricken fishing boat. On-screen, we could see that there was no time to evacuate the passengers, as the bow of the car carrier advanced inexorably closer and closer.

But there was still no smoke from any engine fire. Or, really, there was nothing that looked amiss on the fishing boat.

The thoughts zinged in my head like jolts of electricity.

A single boat. All of a sudden stopped. At the one location where there is a bottleneck in the channel? That is not *a coincidence!*

"That boat's gotta be in on it!" I roared. "The ship has gotta run down the boat! If they turn that ship, it's gonna roll!"

Macallister, who had kept a phone line open to SIOC, repeated my words, though it was unlikely that they hadn't already heard them, given my shouting.

✳ ✳ ✳

ATLANTIC

"This is the United States Navy," a voice from the VHF radio announced. "*Atlantic*, hold your course."

Boeckmann himself grabbed the radio handset, "US Navy, *Atlantic*. There is a vessel in distress on our bow. A collision is imminent!"

"Understood. Our orders are to request that you proceed on your current course. A collision is an acceptable outcome, by order of the United States Naval Command."

Boeckmann hesitated for a moment, as the fishing vessel disappeared from view, hidden from the bridge windows by the towering bow of the ro-ro.

"Sound the collision alarm," Boeckmann ordered, on his bridge. A second later, five long blasts blared from the ship's deafening horn.

✳ ✳ ✳

SALEM

The Navy helicopter pilot clearly had no wish to be part of the imminent collision between the huge ship and the tiny boat.

The chopper had increased its altitude, to the benefit of our video feed. We had no idea what to expect. Would the boat's passengers jump into the water? And then get sucked into the undertow of the massive ship? Would the ship pulverize the little boat? Or would the little boat bang and bounce off the sides of the slow-moving car carrier and escape being crushed?

To our surprise, within seconds of impact, the two men disappeared into the cabin of the boat, and, in a frothy white mess of foam and bubbles, the boat began to accelerate and to attempt to dodge the gigantic bow that loomed overhead.

"They're definitely in on it," Macallister grumbled, before speaking clearly. "And they're fucked."

Their evasive action was too late. The massive ship's bulk sucked water under it, and the late-revving engines on the little boat were no match for the undertow as the propellers churned, cavitating uselessly in the frothing water.

The bulbous bow of the ro-ro smacked into the side of the fishing boat, immediately rolling the tiny vessel onto its side and then upside-down. For a split-second, the black-painted bottom of the fishing boat was visible before it disappeared under the bulk of the ship.

"Well, I would have liked to talk to those two clowns," Macallister commented. "I'd say their last-minute attempt at movement probably incriminates them."

"Yeah," I replied. "I'd say it was a set-up. To make the ship turn, just before the tunnel."

The Acting SAC nodded his agreement, adding, "We'll track them down. You think they'll make it?"

His question was answered by the video feed, as the Navy helicopter camera zoomed into the stern area of the ro-ro. Bits and pieces of fiberglass flotsam had started to surface in the wake of the ship, and then a section of the front of the fishing boat popped out to the side of the ship. And then, what appeared to be a human head surfaced, spinning lazily in the wake of the ship.

The head was not attached to a body.

On the VHF relay, we heard a clipped voice intone, "US Navy, *Atlantic*. Reporting a collision as warned. We believe there are bodies in the water."

"Copy that, *Atlantic*. Carry on. Do not alter your course."

With the Navy chopper still on-site, hovering high overhead, we watched, speechless, as the listing car carrier passed, unscathed and steadily, between the two man-made islands, over the tunnel buried in the sand below and through the bottleneck at the head of the Chesapeake Bay, and out into open water.

THE URGENCY IN THE VOICES heard over the channel sixteen radio feed had changed in tone as they coordinated a search for two bodies from the fishing boat, while the car carrier motored the final few miles of the Thimble Shoals Channel to the pilot rendezvous point off Cape Henry, Virginia.

In Salem, we had been told that the ship would turn around and be escorted with tugboats, and a US Navy presence, back into port, retracing her route under heavy guard. Going the opposite way, we learned, she would list into the wind, which would actually help the ship be more stable.

The Coast Guard, Virginia State Police, and the port authority would reopen the CBBT to vehicle traffic; the route had been closed as the ship approached.

And, the Coast Guard had massed small vessels as the site of the collision, and, indeed, located a drowned body, intact, and a second body, less intact and missing a head.

As the chatter on the radio calmed, it seemed to indicate that the immediate crisis was over.

I wasn't so sure. "Any more activity with the cars onboard the ship?" I asked Volkov.

"No, and there won't be any, for some time or forever," she replied.

Zimmerman growled, "How can you know that for certain? Because you're in on it, right?"

Volkov laughed, a peal that broke the tension in the room. "Because I *was* in on it, correct. And because I used that intimate knowledge to know how to compromise their systems. The data flows both ways, from them to the cars, and from the cars, back to them. When they attempted to take over those final three cars, their systems would be open to receiving data. I sent them a little present."

For the first time, Chen addressed the group. "Miss Volkov is very clever. It was her idea. Based on something Agent Porter said, earlier, apparently." He nodded at me appreciatively.

I didn't hesitate to confirm the confusion that I'm certain my expression showed. "I have no idea what you mean."

Volkov smiled, a real, genuinely kind smile, "Remember you said we didn't need to *be* them, but we needed to *freeze* them? We did just that. We coded a program that would simply freeze their systems, a little packet that created an infinite loop. A sequence of instructions that cannot be answered, which then start over again and again, endlessly. Their systems will dedicate all their resources to resolving an impossible question until those resources are maxed out. And then they'll get a bee ess oh dee."

I looked at Macallister, and together, we chorused, "A . . . what?"

Both Volkov and Chen laughed. Volkov explained, "It's what happens when a system gets a critical error and freezes. Doesn't matter what kind of operating system they are running. In the Apple world, the error message they'll get is referred to as kernel panic. If they're running Windows, which is far more likely, they'll get what you've probably encountered at some point on your own. The dreaded, hated, impossible-to-resolve-without-rebooting Blue Screen of Death."

"That's great," Zimmerman snorted. "Until they reboot their computers. Then we start all over. This is useless."

"Agent Zimmerman," Macallister interjected. "You've been relieved of your duties already today. You're not contributing. I have no more patience for you. Agents Connelly and Jones, escort him out. Now!"

Once the trio had departed, Macallister conceded, "He's right, though. Isn't he?"

Volkov agreed. "Yes, in fact, he is. Chen and I plan to remain right here. We will keep an eye out for any future attempts to hack the cars. I presume you can get me in touch with Tesla, correct? I can explain how they can correct this vulnerability, and they can get a permanent patch out. Which should be very easy to accomplish. In the meantime, if my father tries this stunt again, Chen and I will simply resend our program."

"Your father," I repeated. "Petrikov. Any idea where he was when he triggered this round of attacks?"

"Unfortunately, no." Volkov's head drooped. "We might be able to go back and isolate addresses and back-trace a location. But, no, I could not determine where he was located."

"Well, then," I asserted, "this *isn't* over."

EPILOGUE
NOVEMBER 2019

WEDNESDAY, NOVEMBER 6, 2019 —
PORT OF SPAIN, TRINIDAD AND TOBAGO

THOUGH THE ISLAND-NATION of Trinidad and Tobago is considered the south-ernmost island of the Caribbean archipelago, it is located only seven miles off the northern coast of Venezuela on the South American continent.

And it was here, on the sixth of November, several miles north of Tobago, that the Russian Naval Research vessel *Yantar* switched her AIS transponder back on as she navigated a route into Port of Spain. The ship had last transmitted her position over a month ago, leaving Murmansk.

Vitaly Rodionov stewed, a result of both the Caribbean heat and the frustration he felt as land hove into view. The test, in Vermont, had been a productive proof-of-concept. The first mission, in New York, had to have been considered a success. The bridge had remained closed to traffic for a short time while the engineers confirmed that the structure had not weakened considerably, and while the bridge had been reopened to limited traffic as repairs were made, the economic cost to the New York area had to have been enormous.

The second mission, on the car carrier, did not result in the desired outcome.

The Unit 29155 mastermind was greatly disappointed. The team had rebooted its computers and attempted to regain contact with the vehicles within the car carrier as it maneuvered off Cape Henry, preparing to return to port. The technicians were met with the same challenge; they could not establish a connection with the vehicles, and within moments, their computers froze. They tried again as the vessel passed over the southern tunnel crossing for a second time this day, only this time, headed northwest. Rodionov expected the attempt to be futile;

not only had he lost his external visuals of the ship, but he had also lost communications with his camera boat. Rodionov had no way of knowing if the ro-ro had been reballasted, and he had dim hopes that the connection to the vehicles would succeed after the previous failed effort. To no surprise, they failed again.

Once *Yantar* dropped its cable tap, admitting defeat, and continued her way south toward the Caribbean, Rodionov had questioned Petrikov, "Something has changed. Is it possible your daughter has a hand in this?"

"I have no idea," Petrikov had grumbled. "You have better contacts than I. Find her!"

Despite the best efforts by the Russian intelligence agents and agencies assigned to that task, conducted surreptitiously in the United States over the course of the weeks that had passed while *Yantar* had journeyed from Murmansk to Trinidad and Tobago, finding Petrikov's daughter had proven impractical.

For it was discovered that Anastasia Volkov was dead.

Their sleuthing had procured Volkov's death certificate and had provided one additional clue.

As the ship made port in Tobago, Rodionov addressed his guest, "We will be transported to Caracas, Venezuela. The passport we gave you in Canada will be good enough here."

Petrikov grunted, "And then what?"

"You and I shall make our way back to Moscow. We will discuss the arrangements that we have planned for you. In the meantime, during the search for your daughter—and as you know, you have my condolences, despite the circumstances—one name reappeared time and time again. An FBI agent named Ben Porter. Who is he?"

"I know that name!" Petrikov blurted. "My daughter told me that name two years ago!"

"Hmmm," Rodionov muttered. "We must learn more about him. For he, too, has disappeared. It seems that this Ben Porter was sworn as an agent about a year ago. Yet recently, it appears that he has been placed on administrative leave from the FBI."

* * *

BRISTOL, RHODE ISLAND

"Thanks for dinner, Benbro!"

My sister Grace gave me a light peck on the cheek before she skipped up the steps to her tidy, Cape-style home in Bristol.

"It was on the Bureau," I reminded her, to her back.

She turned at her open door to face me. "Right," she said, her smile drooping slightly. "Your short career with the FBI. But you said that's okay. Right?"

I laughed, "Yep. All good. Thanks for joining me. Good night!"

"Good night!"

She closed her door, and I ambled back to my black Dodge Charger, chuckling to myself, replaying Grace's words in my mind: my "short career with the FBI." It had been November 1st, last year, when I took my oath as a Special Agent. I had been a Special Agent for about a year.

And it hadn't ended as I hoped, or as I expected.

In fact, it hadn't ended.

The team and I had remained at Appleton's house for another day. Volkov and Chen reported that Petrikov had made two more attempts on the cars, several hours after the ro-ro cleared the tunnel area, first as it was turning around to head back into Norfolk and again as it passed through the bottleneck at the southern tunnel. Both attempts were blocked easily with their endless-loop program, and no further attempts had been made.

By that afternoon, Macallister had Volkov on a priority call with Tesla, with engineers and programmers summoned on a Sunday to respond to the demands of the FBI. Within hours of that call, a patch to the tiny, heretofore undiscovered vulnerability in the firmware that Volkov had exploited had been uploaded to every Tesla vehicle.

As night fell in Virginia, FBI agents had tracked down the owner of the boat that had been pulverized by the ship; the fishing boat had been rented out only the previous day. The charterers had paid in cash and had spent the morning of the charter not setting up fishing gear and bait, but cameras. They told the owner that they wanted to video their fishing expedition. Yet, as they cast off their lines, they had no fishing rods. And, according to the owner, they spoke with Russian accents. Circumstantial, to be sure, but certainly suspicious. Dare I say, fishy . . .

The ship had returned safely to the pier, and FBI investigators had begun combing it, interviewing the crew, and documenting a crime scene.

Meanwhile, in the days and weeks that followed, we realized that the implications of this investigation had ramifications well beyond this case. A national bulletin was being drafted. Citizens would be advised to exercise caution with technology, and the FBI would take a far more proactive and public approach to try and anticipate instances where an apparently benign device could be used in inappropriate, illicit, or improper ways not intended by its manufacturer or promoter. For example, the Bureau identified that smart televisions, equipped with cameras for seemingly the innocent but convenient purpose of gesture-recognition control, could be used for nefarious purposes, and therefore the Bureau would issue a warning prior to the holiday season when these devices were purchased in droves.

We would advise citizens to take precautions with the voice-controlled, artificial-intelligence assistants that were becoming ubiquitous in American homes. We would recommend that citizens who, within their homes or offices or businesses, planned to connect multiple devices, colloquially called the "Internet of Things," or IoT, should use a separate, stand-alone network for the IoT.

While, unfortunately, neither of those examples were completely pertinent to the scenario that Volkov exploited, it was more the message than the method that was getting attention. We would seek out these potential security weaknesses and try to prevent them from being exploited. That type of work, for certain, would be ongoing.

For, as long as we have computers, someone is going to try and hack them. And, when a computer, or computer-controlled and connected device, could morph into a weapon, we might consider if any apparent short-term convenience is offset by a future risk.

✳ ✳ ✳

Back in Salem, her part in the discovery and chase over, Volkov finally shut down her computers and got some rest.

Volkov's status, I had been told, was obviously a difficult issue for the Bureau to resolve. She was a murderer and a traitor. Yet, she had been instrumental in stopping a method of attack that could have proved undetectable and unstoppable for quite some time. While the Justice Department and the Bureau debated options, a death certificate was issued for Anastasia Volkov, dated Saturday, August 31, in Brighton Beach, New York. Cause of death: homicide. And, a death certificate that had been held pending an investigation, for a certain Dmitri Tretriaki, had also been released; that certificate was dated as of the same day and place, but with suicide listed as the cause of death.

In late October, a woman named Ann Karin had been admitted to the minimum security Federal Correctional Institution in Danbury, Connecticut. We all had known that she could probably figure out how to escape. She had promised not to. In return, she had been assured a quick review of her unique situation, with a potential outcome of pardon.

Easier to resolve was the case against Jennifer Appleton, which had been discharged within days. Within the month, she would resume her position as the Special Agent in Charge, FBI Boston Division. In typical fashion, she gracefully accepted the Bureau's confidential apology.

As for Zimmerman, a reprimand for insubordination had been noted in his personnel file.

Jordon and Lewis had received commendations in their files for exemplary service.

Upon Appleton's return to duty, Macallister would step down as Acting SAC and would step up into a promotion to Deputy Assistant Director. He'd have to give up fieldwork in Boston, but he'd have national responsibility in Washington.

And as for me?

Well, it had been a complete shock when I had asked for my gun and my badge back, and Macallister had said, simply, "No."

"But, sir," I'd objected, "I was correct. I realize what I did was improper, to give Volkov access to the computer to see if she was legit, and I know it was against orders, but wasn't I vindicated by the outcome?"

Macallister had crossed his arms over his chest and pouted, "Porter, I'm afraid the ends don't justify the means. You cannot be a special agent of the Bureau if you run off on gut instinct all the time. You *must* follow orders. Otherwise, the system breaks down. And, Washington agrees. This was an egregious and unforgivable error on your part."

I had not known what to say.

"I do have some good news for you, though," Macallister had said, ignoring my obvious discomfort and disappointment. "I still owe you and your sister that dinner, I promised."

"Oh. Okay. Thanks, I guess."

"It's my pleasure. Take her somewhere nice. Let me know when and where, and I'll call ahead with my Bureau-issued credit card. Spare no expense. Got it?"

"Uh, yes, sir."

Macallister had grinned, and he had leaned close to my ear, whispering, "And then let's talk. You're too valuable to be restrained as a Special Agent. Once I assume my new position as Deputy Assistant Director, I have a plan for you. A plan not only for you, but also for Volkov—er, Ann Karin."

My eyebrows had shot up. *That* was unexpected.

Macallister had continued, "And as you know, we have some unfinished business to take care of, which may be outside the nationally constricted jurisdiction of the FBI."

I had turned my head to face my former boss, and had looked him in the eye, uttering a single word, "Petrikov!"

"Right. Let's go get him."

REFERENCES

WHILE THIS STORY IS CONSTRUCTED in the real world, including but not limited to referencing actual companies, places, news outlets and articles, events, and things, it is a novel, and it is a work of fiction. However, the following primary source materials are referenced, listed below in the order that they appear within the text:

Greenberg, Andy. "Hackers Remotely Kill a Jeep on the Highway—With Me in It." *Wired.com*. Condé Nast. July 21, 2015.

Shilling, Erik. "It's Possible for a Tesla to Be Hacked and Here's Why Knowing About It Is a Good Thing." *Jalopnik.com*. G/O Media, Inc. April 2, 2019.

Shane, Scott and Mark Mazzetti. "The Plot to Subvert an Election." *Nytimes.com*. The New York Times Company. September 20, 2018.

The Associated Press. "New Nuclear Sub Is Said to Have Special Eavesdropping Ability." *Nytimes.com*. The New York Times Company. February 20, 2005.

While this story may be constructed in the real world, many artistic liberties have been taken, among them the capabilities of Unit 29155 and of the Russian Naval Research vessel *Yantar* (which, indeed, departed Murmansk at the beginning of October, turned off her AIS transmitter, and reappeared on November 6 as she approach the island of Trinidad—an approximately five thousand mile journey that should have taken the research ship just over two weeks).

It is unknown if this story exaggerates or understates the abilities of the Unit, or of the ship.

Schwirtz, Michael. "Top Secret Russian Unit Seeks to Destabilize Europe, Security Officials Say." *Nytimes.com.* The New York Times Company. October 8, 2019.

Sutton, H.I. "Russia's Suspected Internet Cable Spy Ship Appears Off Americas." *Forbes.com.* Forbes Media LLC. November 10, 2019.

THE END

THANK YOU

I HOPE YOU ENJOYED this story!

Would you do me a favor?

Like all authors, I rely on online reviews to encourage future sales. Your opinion is invaluable. Would you take a few moments now to share your assessment of my book on Amazon or any other book review website you prefer? Your opinion will help the book marketplace become more transparent and useful to us all.

If you are new to Ben Porter's world, please check out the prequel to this story, *False Assurances*, available on Amazon, Apple Books, or by order through your local bookstore. And stay tuned for the sequel to *Threat Bias*, as Ben goes on a globe-spanning hunt for Anatoly Petrikov. He's going to be surprised by what he learns, and so will you . . .

Thanks for reading!

ACKNOWLEDGMENTS

WHEN I FINISHED THE FIRST DRAFT of my first novel, *False Assurances*, I had two sequels plotted out, in my head at least. By the time I revised that first draft for about the ninth time, I had even more ideas on where Ben Porter's story could go. I couldn't wait to write this story.

I've learned that a writer's work is very solitary, at first, but then, like many things, once that first draft of a manuscript is completed, it becomes very much a team effort. And I am fortunate to have an amazing team.

My thanks and love to my parents; as with the first book, my father was the first person to read this one. His editorial comments are, of course, incredibly useful. But even more important is his, and my mother's, constant cheerleading. Thanks, mom and dad, for always being there for me.

I am extremely grateful for the continued support of James Patterson. That endorsement means the world to me.

After reading an early draft, my editor, who remains in the shadows, said something like, "you've really grown as a writer since the first book." And then the editor sent back a redline, which was mostly red. I'm lucky to have both the honest critiques and the praise.

Once more, I'm happy to acknowledge my friend Dr. Phillip Dickey. I hijacked the name of his boat for the first book, and when I asked for permission to use it, I also asked for some help with the neuroscience of spinal injuries. Dr. Dickey explained it all but, well, it's really complicated, and any misrepresentation of Anastasia's injuries and recovery is my error, not his.

And, of course, my everlasting appreciation for my amazing family. They've watched, sometimes with bemusement but always with encouragement, as I've written and edited and proofed, and then done it all over again. I simply could not do this without their love and support. Thank you: Maggie, Keilan, Connor, and Meghan.

ABOUT THE AUTHOR

WHEN NOT WRITING, Christopher Rosow works in the design and construction space. And, when not working or writing, or enjoying time with his amazing family, he's probably found out on the water somewhere, sailing. He lives in Connecticut with his family, his dogs, and way too many boats.

www.ChristopherRosow.com

Facebook, Twitter, and Instagram: @RosowBooks

Also by Christopher Rosow:

False Assurances (2020)